We Heard You

A Novel by

Susan Stone

Kathy,
Please
help us wake up
the others!
Susan

To Parker, Stone, Mary Alice, Ian, Mirabel, Amelia, Grace, Felipe`
and Sadie Moon;
I dedicate this book to all the children who will inherit the New
Earth. The future is indeed a bright place, thanks to you.

ACKNOWLEDGEMENTS

So many people contributed to the writing of this book. I will do my best to acknowledge you all.

First, I need to thank my beloved Garvin . . . who has withstood (with a great sense of humor) a complete upheaval of our life.

To my family; Momma (Arlene), Dianne, Beth, David, Cristy, Jessica, Nathan, Parker, Christopher, Michele, Ashley, Anthony, Michael, Amanda and Katie, for lending your names to the colorful characters of the story. And for your love and support.

I must also thank the *Babes in the Woods* for their encouragement and for holding the space of joy twice a year at our campout by the sea.

To Janie Torrence, I thank you for allowing me to publish, *"We are One"*.

For excellent proof reading and editing skills, I must thank Julie King, Alia Manning and Michelle Mancini. I was lost without you.

To Sarah LaRose, you kept me focused, calmed my fears and helped me to remember who I truly am. Thank you from the bottom of my heart.

So many friends deserve to be acknowledged for their love and support; Bree, Laughing Heart, Holly, Bobbie, Tom, Beverley, Elaine, Dee, Wade, Mary, Yellow Horse Man, Teri, Crystal Rain, Heidi, Caris, Linda, Teresa, Thomas, Charlotte, Rekel, Clay, Marcie, Virginia and Shelly. (To all those that I've neglected to mention, my sincerest apologies and appreciation, with hope that you will understand).

And finally, last but certainly not least, I thank you Spirit/God for changing my life and answering my prayer. I am forever yours.

About the Author/Introduction

In the spring of 2004, I said a prayer which launched me on a journey I have not yet returned from. In fact, I hope never to return to the life I had before.

I was living the American Dream. I had a successful career, making a great living. Over the years I was able to build my first house, buy my first new car and had earned the freedom to go where I wished and buy anything I wanted. At first it was great fun. I had never known such a life. This high living came at a great price: the things I owned came to own me. To maintain this lifestyle, I had to work long hours and make myself available even on holidays to be of service to my wealthy clients. As a result, I missed out on a lot of gatherings with family and friends, didn't get the rest I needed, ate on the run (if at all) and in time, my health began to decline.

One of my favorite getaways was, and still is, a camping trip with the greatest group of women on the planet. Twice a year, we gather on a little island on the coast of South Carolina and camp on the beach. For three days we walk the sand, play in the surf, fish on the docks and laugh till we cry. No makeup, no bras, open fire cooking and every night we sit around the campfire and talk about life. Since I am such an early riser, I always put the coffee on and watch the sunrise over the Atlantic. Early morning has always been my time for contemplation. On the beach, twice a year, I had time to really think and nurture my Spirit.

After eight years on the fast track, I was growing steadily unhappy. Nothing was wrong in my world. I was in a healthy relationship, had a wonderful family and a great job, I had no financial struggles and yet I was beginning to hate my life. On that Saturday morning in May, 2004, I sat in my chair on the beach, facing the ever-brightening horizon and just cried. I cried out to God, "What am I doing wrong? I have so much I'm willing to share, but I feel like I'm not doing enough. I'm trying to save the whales, feed the children and help wherever I can. I donate thousands of dollars every year, but nothing seems to be getting better." Nothing I was doing seemed to make a difference in the world. Certainly there was more to life than this. I was haunted by the feeling that I wasn't doing what I came to this life to do. And so I said a prayer.

I don't remember the exact words I used, but I remember pleading for guidance. The American Dream had turned into a nightmare; I had become a slave to my lifestyle, and the world was falling apart at the seams. I asked what I could do to help, and offered myself to the Universe.

Three weeks later, this book started to come right out of my hands. I had never written anything longer than a business proposal. I wasn't a good student in school and really had no creative writing skills that I was aware of. My creative endeavors had always been in the field of fine art and design.

To make a very long story, shorter, the urge to write came every day between 3:09 and 3:11 in the morning. I would write for five hours or so, and then work a ten hour day at the office.

Within nine months I became so sick, I ended up in the Urgent Care. The physician asked me if I had been swimming in sewage, literally. My body was so toxic that he threatened me with hospitalization. Afterward in the parking lot, again I prayed, "I don't understand. You want me to write a book about healing the Earth. I'm doing the best I can. I don't know *how* to heal the Earth. Why did you give this to me? I'm a kitchen designer! I don't have the credentials to write about this! I need some sleep! I need my job! I can't do it all!" I just sat in my car and sobbed. On my way back to the office I called my chiropractor, who was and still is a very dear friend. She knew all about this mysterious urge to write and the turmoil it had brought into my life. She had already suggested that I take some time off work, but I couldn't hear it. I was obligated to my clients and couldn't leave in the middle of thirty-five or so projects. Then suddenly I felt as though I were having a heart attack as I turned in to the office parking lot. I told her it felt like an elephant sitting on my chest. I couldn't breathe. She said, "If you don't quit your job *today,* I am coming over there and quitting for you!"

I had no choice. I had to leave. I was suddenly incapable of doing my job. I had been an award winning designer, creating illusions of grandeur. And I knew it was over. I did go in and resign that very hour. On the thirty minute drive home, I made a full and permanent recovery. God had kicked me out of the nest. Now what? *Just a note*: Don't *ever* ask that question unless you are prepared for great change.

The words that came out of my hands each day blew my mind. I would say out loud, "This can't be true!" And then I would hear, "You have no idea what you are writing. Stop until you do. This is not *a* story. This is *your* story." It has taken me years to understand this message: This is *our* story.

I researched each topic as they appeared on the pages. I've decided not to list my references so that you would find your own. Everything stated is public knowledge. It certainly isn't general knowledge, but it is public domain if you know where to look. The internet has been an invaluable resource. It took a while, but I came to understand that I don't live in the world I thought I did. Some of it was upsetting, to put it mildly. But I also found a great deal of love and magic in the world, which gave me great hope. I have no expectation that you believe. In fact, I think the whole message of the book is to find your own truth.

Michael Harrington wrote a book called *Touched by the Dragon's Breath*. In it, he presents easy to understand information about cosmic cycles, with emphasis on our current day and 2012. His sentiment regarding self-knowledge is so well stated, that I will include it here.

"Many people will dismiss the material presented here anyway, no matter how insightful. It will be at odds with what they've been taught; in other words, it will be contrary to their

~ - 11 - ~

Belief System. This is why any outside information should be viewed simply as seed material for contemplation." He goes on to say, ". . . it is entirely up to us to establish our own self-knowledge. Verification is solely our responsibility. Had I not believed this myself I would never have written this book." I couldn't have said it better myself! Enjoy the ride.

Bright Blessings,
Susan

There are three things that cannot long be hidden

the sun

the moon

and the truth.

Buddha

Prologue

Morning dawns on the Ohio State campus, but it hardly feels like day. Dark, heavy clouds have hung in the skies over the Ohio Valley for weeks and the rain continues to fall.

Claire peeks from under the covers not sure if it is day or night. Looking toward the window, she sees no sign of the sun, only a gray veil with a white frame, like a painting of blurry grays. She pulls the blankets back over her head. "I'm going back to sleep," she mutters to herself.

Unable to drift off, Claire lays wondering what David is doing and if the sun still shines in his part of the world. She peeks out again and looks at her clock. She has another hour before she has to get ready for final exams. Looking across the room, the still made bed reminds her that her roommate Michele has spent the night with her boyfriend so she has the place to herself. She gets up to make a cup of tea, thinking of David as it steeps.

Claire wonders what time it is in Australia. Then she shrugs and whispers to herself. "What difference does it make? He doesn't sleep anyway."

David was Claire's first friend, and through the years had become her best friend in the world. They first met when she was three years old and David, five. Hundreds of miles separated them, but one night, synchronistically they each lay in their beds thinking of faraway things unable to sleep. Just as they began to relax, a silver umbilical cord appeared. Very naturally they followed the cord and found themselves looking back at their bodies lying in the bed. Claire moved slowly at first, floating around her room, then with the speed of thought she found herself in her parents' room. She felt reassured by the sounds of slumber and decided to go outside to explore. The farm was the only place she knew, but from her story books, the ocean was a place she really wanted to see. Very quickly she moved, faster and faster as the landscape sped by. In no time at all she was flying over the ocean. At first it was too dark to see, but gradually she came to the sunrise and stopped, amazed by the beauty.

David shot through the roof the moment he realized he was free. He too loved the ocean he had never seen and began to fly at amazing speeds. When he reached the sunrise, he halted, taking in all the colors which seemed more vibrant than he remembered.

Claire noticed David as he arrived. She instantly flew to his side. Too young to understand the significance of what had just occurred, they stared at each other, knowing that they were not asleep. And without the physical brain as a filter, their telepathic communications were instantaneous. Time disappeared for these two as they flew at great speeds, enjoying their unlimited freedom.

It would be years before they would talk about their first meeting. They had tried to tell their parents about their silver cord and about flying around with a new friend, but imaginary friends are common in small children, so for that reason neither Claire nor David were able to convince them that their experience had been real. To this day, Claire and David have never met in the physical.

Claire was fortunate. Her parents were left-over hippies and more open to metaphysical concepts. Even though they did not understand their young child's fascination with her imaginary friend and other unseen things, they encouraged her and nurtured her with fresh air, fresh food grown from their farm, and lots of love. In time they began to realize how unique their daughter was and that her stories of David and the other children were not the result of an over active imagination.

David on the other hand had some pretty tough years. The son of an Air Force Colonel, harsh discipline coupled with a strict adherence to rules was against everything a budding Indigo Child could tolerate. When David was in the first grade, his parents took him to a variety of doctors and specialists, looking for an explanation for his defiant behavior. Eventually diagnosed with Attention Deficit Disorder, they put him on a variety of medications to keep him subdued. As soon as he graduated high school, he left for Australia. He said he just could not tolerate closed minded people anymore. Today he lives in solitude near an Aboriginal tribe in the Outback.

Claire lies down and takes a couple of deep breaths. "Okay, relax." Beginning with her eyes, she relaxes every part of her body, breathing into each part as she goes. Colors fill her field of vision. No color she has ever seen with her eyes. She focuses on a strand and a direction. She inhales deeply, exhales and *zoom* . . . she's gone. To outsiders she is still lying on her bed, appearing to be asleep.

"There you are! Hello, hello, hello my dear Claire!" says David. "It's really dark where you are. Is it still raining? "

"Yes. I miss the sun. Can I stay here with you for a while?" Claire tells David all about her final exams, her upcoming graduation and her hopes of being selected for an internship in the SETI (Search for Extraterrestrial Intelligence) program.

Then David fills her in on news of the Tribe. For months they have been hosting a Council to discuss the radical change in the weather, and about the plants and animals dying off. "We have not seen rain for over a year now. Some of the landscape was being fed by underground springs, but the water is dwindling away. Many of the animals are not returning to breed. The birds are becoming rare as well. It feels as though they are leaving the Earth."

She could feel his sadness. A pang of guilt ran through her for complaining about the rain. But the rivers were cresting. Flash flooding had caused thousands of people to flee their homes. "Claire, the Aborigine are people who can live on almost nothing. They use so little. When I look to their future, I see only dust."

"Isn't there some kind of rain dance you can do? I thought the native people would do some kind of ceremony to end the drought." Claire inquired.

"This is no ordinary drought Claire. The Earth is becoming increasingly unbalanced. Remember, as within so without. If our minds are not at peace then neither is our world. We have forgotten we are stewards of this beautiful little planet. How do we convince the world to wake up and realize we are doing this to ourselves?

"I don't know David, but I do have the feeling that something is about to change, something big."

"I think you're right Claire. I get that feeling too. But if we're going to change things, we're going to have to move fast."

"Hey, I've got to get going. I don't want to be late. I love you and I'll check in on you later. Peace to you and your Countrymen."

"I love you too Claire, I know you'll do well, I see straight A's. You will also get your internship. In fact you must. We are all counting on it."

Sitting up on her bed she wondered what he meant by *we're all counting on it*. David had a clearer vision of the future than she did. Her insight was limited to events that were only moments away, like a phone that was about to ring.

Chapter 1

"Do you remember when you told us who we were? Honey, you were four years old. Your friends in play group were still sucking their thumbs and putting play-dough up their nose. We were looking through the telescopes that night. Your mother had made hot chocolate and brought it out to us. She said something about how star gazing was a spiritual experience for her. You sat us down and told us that we were very special. Imagine, any other four year old having this conversation with her parents."

Claire lit up. Her huge blue eyes sparkled in memory of that night. "I told you we were not humans having a spiritual experience, that we were spirits having a human experience."

"Yep, you blew us away, and we have never been the same since." Tom Montgomery smiled and slung a towel over his shoulder, then continued to chop spinach. "You helped us wake up. You show everyone to themselves. It's not your fault if some people don't like what they see." Looking down his nose over his glasses, he started to look around for something.

"Garlic," she said as she whizzed past him.

"Thank you."

Claire glided around the kitchen handing her father ingredients he needed for the manicotti before he could think to ask for them. It was not her unique abilities as an Indigo, it was her favorite dish and her father was making it in honor of her graduation and homecoming. Over the years they had made it dozens of times.

"You are here for a reason sweetheart. The world needs you and as many like you as possible. You are the future. Without you and others like you, there may not be a future."

Tom was up to his wrists in ricotta and mozzarella cheese, pointing his finger at himself then at her. "It's our fault that you haven't met any of them, or even left Ohio. We wanted to keep you here for as long as we could. Maybe we were wrong to try to protect you from the world, but we knew you'd see it soon enough. We just wanted you to have the best life . . . the most wonderful life possible."

"I have the best life anyone could ever hope for." Claire trailed off.

Tom could see she had something on her mind, but didn't want to pry. "Your momma made the cobbler this morning and the mushrooms are ready to stuff. The sauce, thank you very much, is the last thing I need." As he took the jar from her, he waved at the stool. "Sit down and tell me what's new? Where do you think they'll send you?"

"I'm not going anywhere yet, Daddy. They won't even make the announcement for two more weeks."

Tom just looked at her and stuck his tongue out. "How could they resist you? You're brilliant!"

Claire looking down said, "I'm strange Daddy, a lot of people are afraid of me. I've tried to pretend like I'm like other people, but I'm not."

Tom lifted her chin with his finger and said. "Thank God for that. Claire, it's time for you to go and do whatever it is you came here for."

"But I don't know what that is," Claire said looking up at her father.

"You will sweetheart, you will."

👀👀👀👀👀👀👀

Beth Montgomery looked like a gate guard sitting in front of her road side stand. She was soaking up the long awaited sun in her high back wicker chair. Her blonde hair was shimmering like the sun itself. You would have thought she was napping, except for the broad grin on her pretty face. Her old road sign read:

Grandmother Bee's Remedies

Herbs-Tinctures-Honey

OPEN MOST DAYS

(If nobody's around leave your money in the jar)

Beth inherited the farm from her grandmother. She learned how to keep bees and how to heal things using herbs and natural remedies. Grandmother Bee, as she was known across the county, was the only doctor the valley had known until the first hospital was built in 1958. Even then, folks came to her for a second opinion and medicinal herbs, just in case.

Under the tutelage of her grandmother, Beth grew up close to the earth. She learned the wisdom of the local Indians. She looked like a child of the sixties. She loved to wear her long golden hair in braids. Sometimes just one down her back, but more often than not, she wore two like a squaw. She almost always wore long skirts. "No place for the bees to sneak in" she would say. From a distance she looked like she was in the wrong century, but make no mistake; she was a modern woman, strong and opinionated.

She smiled at the aroma coming from her house. The smell of garlic meant he was making Claire's favorite dinner.

Tom Montgomery was a fine cook. He loved to experiment in the kitchen. Beth did most of the baking, but Tom was the self-proclaimed chef of the house. In his younger days people remarked that he looked a lot like Gregory Peck. He was tall, dark, lanky, and of course handsome. Tom was working on a survey team for Ross County when he saw the prettiest girl he had ever seen, selling honey at a road side stand. He bought a jar of honey every day for two months. It was Grandma Bee who told Tom he didn't have to buy any more honey, and asked if he would like to take her granddaughter to the county fair. It wasn't really that he was all that shy; he just didn't think he had a chance with such a pretty girl.

Beth jumped at the sudden hand on her shoulder.

"I'm sorry Momma; I thought at least the dogs would have heard me coming. Great sentries *you* are," she said as she bent down to pet Andy. The big black dog just rolled on his back so she could reach his belly. Miss Ellie, their white toy poodle, was still asleep on her mother's lap.

"We were just basking in the rays." She looked up at Claire and took her hand. "Smells wonderful; your father loves having you home. We both do."

"Well I hope you're hungry, cause he made enough for a small army." Taking her mother's hands, Claire raised her from the chair and they walked hand in hand down the lane.

Tom watched as they slowly made their way to the house and he realized, perhaps for the first time, how similar they were. The sun glimmered and danced on their golden hair. Claire had always worn hers short in contrast to her mother's. Although Claire was tall like Grandmother Bee, they walked with the same gate as they threw their heads back in laughter, unaware of their synchronicity. "I am the luckiest guy in the whole world," he said as they walked up on the porch. Then he realized it was their eyes that set them apart. Beth's were a beautiful shade of emerald, but Claire's eyes were dramatic; large and the clearest blue he had ever seen. They had a way of looking through you instead of at you. He smiled and bowed deeply as he opened the screen door for them. "After you Mademoiselles, dinner is served." Then blocking the door, he addressed the dogs. "*Your* dinner is on the *back* porch".

Chapter 2

The Columbus Optical SETI (COSETI)
Observatory:

"Alright everybody let's find our seats! We have a lot of work to do before lunch. We have a record number of candidates this year. C'mon people grab a bagel and sit down! We have eighty-seven students representing twenty-five of the finest schools in America, about to compete for five intern positions." Dr. Graham Sullivan, the human resources director for SETI, heads the selection committee.

"Miss Taylor, you are representing Ohio State University. We would like to thank you again for hosting this year's conference, so you may go first. We noticed that your school has submitted only one name this year. We are accustomed to Ohio State topping our list with many gifted new scientists."

"Yes sir. We are very proud of our alumni. We knew there would be a lot of competition this year for the precious few positions, and decided to present only one young woman who should not be overlooked. The University has never had a student quite like her. May I present her transcripts?"

"Of course Miss Taylor, I'm intrigued." Dr. Sullivan began to read. "How old is this young woman?"

"Twenty, sir," she said with a grin.

Dr. Sullivan, now looking like he just won the lottery said, "What is she . . . a *savant*?"

"No sir, Claire is an Indigo."

His face turned into a frown. "I don't think I am familiar with that term, Indigo. What exactly *is* an Indigo?"

Miss Taylor took a deep breath. "Well sir, it's a little complicated. There are at least three different personality types for lack of a better description. They've been arriving like waves on a shore, in order, but sometimes overlapping. The first group has come to be known as the Indigo Children. The second is known as the Crystal Children and the new one's coming in are referred to as Rainbow Children. Some have even called them The Star Children."

"These are children, for lack of a better explanation, who were born *awake*. For those who can read and see auras, the first group has a band of indigo blue, hence the nickname. The color indigo in the auric field is very rare, or it was until now. It's probably premature to talk about the Scouts."

Dr. Sullivan sat motionless, making no sound or expression, so Miss Taylor continued. "Claire Montgomery has aced every test she has ever taken, without exception as far as we can tell. She speaks five languages fluently, and although she has never physically been outside of Ohio, she has memorized every satellite map she has ever seen. She can give you directions to anywhere you want to go. She has, as far as we can tell, perfect recall. She is the most gifted student I have ever met. Her intuition alone could accelerate scientific research decades ahead of where we could be without her. She is *not* the only one of her kind, but she is the only one who is graduating at the top of her class, in astrophysics from Ohio State."

After a momentary silence, Dr. Sullivan came out of his stupor. "You mean there are more of them?" Other people in the meeting hall began to laugh.

"Well yes sir, hundreds of thousands, maybe millions. We have known about them since the seventies sir."

"Well where the hell have I been? I have spent the better part of my life dedicated to the search of extra-terrestrials. I have been looking up at the stars since I was a little tike, looking for something special and new, and right here . . . under my nose . . ." He started to laugh. He got so tickled that he couldn't stop.

After wiping the tears from his face with his handkerchief he finally said, "Please forgive me. That just struck me so funny. I consider myself to be an informed man. I pride myself on being up on current events and these *Children* have been here for forty years. My Lord, well I don't know about any of you, but I could use a five minute break. But only five, we have a lot to do before lunch. Still laughing to himself, Dr. Sullivan got up from his seat and huddled with the other committee members.

Chapter 3

Claire sat staring at her laptop, intending to return emails but she couldn't concentrate. The mail arrived every day between 3:00 pm and 4:00 pm. It was 3:45 and she was getting agitated. The sun was below the porch roof now and was in her eyes. She was afraid she would miss the mailman in the glare. She stretched up tall in her rocking chair trying to shade her eyes.

"Just go out with your mother to the road stand, you won't miss him from there." Startled, Claire spun around to see her father inside the screened window.

"I'm not, I . . . Oh Daddy I can't stand the suspense!"

The screen door slammed behind him. He shaded his eyes with his hand looking out at the road and then sat in the rocker next to Claire. "Okay, then I'll come out and wait with you."

Claire closed her laptop and hugged it against her chest. "I have never wanted anything so bad in my life. I hate to put all of my energy into one thing. I have set my mind on SETI for so long that I don't know what else I would do." She brought her knees up and started rocking.

"Claire, you are a gifted scientist, and I'm not just saying that because I'm your father. Honey, I've seen the job offers, even from NASA for God's sake. Why SETI? Why is this one thing so important?"

Claire stopped rocking; she put her computer down on the table beside her and turned to face her father. "Do you believe in destiny?" Tom nodded. "I have these dreams. They're out of focus. Not normal dreams where I see people I know and places I've been. This is like a story. It started about five years ago. I don't really see anything but I hear something. I can hear this voice, if you can call it that. It's not even an audible voice. It's like on the grid, I can hear but not hear. See but not see. I don't know who is speaking, but *it* knows *I* am listening. I try to write down what I've heard as soon as I wake up, but it goes away so quickly. I have tried to program my crystals to record my dreams but so far no luck. I know it sounds crazy."

Tom put his hand on her knee and said, "Sweetheart, I got used to that a long time ago." They both laughed.

"Claire! CLAIREE!" Beth was running toward the house. She had hiked up her long skirt with one hand, and in the other was the mail. Tom and Claire froze for a moment. Out of breath Beth collapsed on the third porch step, the other two rushed down to join her.

Claire grabbed all the envelopes from her hand. Throwing the envelopes one by one to the ground until she found the one she had been waiting for. She put it to her chest. "I'm afraid to open it."

"Well if you don't open it this second your mother and I are going to tackle you to the ground!" Tom was on his feet.

Claire held the envelope against the light. She didn't want to tear the letter. Tom groped in his pocket for a knife. "Here use this." He said opening the knife and holding the blade, handed it to Claire.

She took the knife and with surgical skill carefully sliced the letter free.

She started to read it to herself when Beth said, "Aloud! Read it out loud!"

Claire straightened up the letter and cleared her throat. "Dear Miss Montgomery…Oh no it begins with Dear Miss Montgomery!"

"That's your name dear." Beth was trying to be patient with her. "Do you want me to read it to you?" Claire tossed the letter in the general direction of her mother.

Beth picked it up and said after a long pause, "California." She put a pout on her face and said, "My baby is going to California!"

"Berkley?" Claire eyes widened as she snatched the letter away. "I've been accepted to participate in the SERENDIP program at Berkley." Her hand dropped.

Tom looked at her with a puzzled face. "Honey isn't this what you wanted? You told me just two minutes ago that this was the only thing you really wanted to do.

"It is. I'm happy. I just thought they would want me in Columbus, or maybe West Virginia. I never dreamed I would go so far away."

Both Tom and Beth put their arms around her. Tom whispered "It could have been Puerto Rico."

"What time is your flight tomorrow?" Beth was making her famous blueberry pancakes.

"10:45, we'll have to leave for Columbus by 7:00 at the latest." Claire was busy with last minute details. She had gone shopping for clothes in Cincinnati. It was the closest Ohio had to a metropolis. She had convinced herself that everyone in California was 'hip'. Her real concern was not to look like a country bumpkin.

Even though the Montgomery's did not own a television, Claire was able to check the latest fashions on line. The Internet was their connection to staying current with the world. Tom's astronomy work depended on technology. He had his telescopes programmed to specific locations in space. Some months he was comet hunting. At other times, he had one fixed on a far away planet that would be in just the right orbit for viewing, but he always kept one trained on the moon. He was fascinated by the moon.

"Momma, let's star gaze tonight, one last time all together." Claire was sampling the batter. "Mmm, I'm gonna miss these."

Her mother smiled, "All the more reason to come home once in awhile." She felt a big lump in her throat.

As day gave way to night, Tom set up three telescopes and Beth made hot chocolate even though the evening was expected to be warm. Claire could smell the convection up in her room and it reminded her of all the family traditions they had kept over the years. Her favorite one was started by Grandmother Bee. At every evening meal they would begin by blessing the food and then she would ask: "What was the best part of your day?" One by one they would share something that had made them happy that day. Her chin quivered as the tears welled up in her eyes. Quickly coming back to the present, she chided herself. "Knock it off you big baby! You can do this." Looking in her mirror, she dried her eyes and smiled. "You can do this."

Out on the lawn, Tom explained where he had focused each telescope. They took turns looking through each of the lenses. After a long silence Beth said, "What kind of message can you send out there anyhow? I mean what are the chances that they will understand any earth language? And what does SETI stand for again?"

Tom and Claire both chuckled. "Momma, SETI stands for Search for Extraterrestrial Intelligence. SETI does not send out messages, it listens."

"That sounds boring." Claire could see her mother scrunch up her face even in the dark.

"Not when you're trying to develop new ways to listen. When Professor Drake started this experiment in 1960, he could only scan one radio channel at a time. Now there are millions of channels. It's like trying to find a tiny intelligent needle in a vast cosmic haystack. It's not just a question of knowing where to look in the sky, but also choosing the most likely point on the radio dial." She paused. "You guys, I am so excited. I cannot believe I am actually going to California. I am going to miss you both so much." Claire's voice began to quiver. She sipped from her mug and held Miss Ellie close to her chest.

They were quiet for a while, just listening to the night. "Did anybody else see that?" Tom looked up from his lens. "I think my surprise is here."

"What surprise?" The women said in unison.

"There is a meteor shower tonight." Tom said with excitement in his voice.

Putting him on, they both said "ooooooooooooooohhhh wishing stars!" The three of them laughed in delight, savoring their last night together. Wishing stars brought back good memories.

Chapter 4

The sign read, Claire Montgomery. It was the first thing she saw when she walked from the gate. The girl holding the sign was tall and thin, barely out of her teens. Her short hair was spiked in all different directions, and besides the streak of shocking pink, it was jet black. She was dressed all in black. Claire thought everyone in California had a tan, but this poor girl looked as though she hadn't seen daylight in years. It wasn't until she smiled that Claire realized how pretty she was.

"Hi, I'm Claire." She said, fumbling for a free hand to greet her.

"I'm Ashley. I'm your guide to the stars." Ashley broke out into a broad grin. "Right this way."

They made their way through the crowded airport to the baggage claim and took their place amongst the herd to wait for the carousel to begin its rounds. "So, where ya from?" Ashley asked, rocking back and forth as though the short wait had already been too long.

"Chillicothe, Ohio." Claire was trying to think of something to say to fill the time. "Are you in the SETI Program?"

"Me?" Ashley giggled. "No, my mother is one of the big wigs there. I'm just her official chauffeur. I mean I think it's cool and stuff, but mom's the brains in our family."

Just then Claire caught a glimpse of her yellow name tag. It took the skill of an offensive lineman just to get close to the carousel. Ashley helped her with the bags and they were off.

Claire had her fingernails buried in the arm rests with her brake foot pressed against the floor. Ashley was obviously used to the traffic because she talked, checked her hair and teeth in the mirror, and crossed three lanes of traffic all at the same time. She changed for radio stations four or five times before she said, "Do you like *311?*" without waiting for a reply, she searched the console until she found what she was looking for and put the CD in.

Once they were away from the airport, Claire was able to relax and enjoy the ride. Looking out to the bay, she was captivated by the view. There were sailboats, yachts and merchant ships traveling on the bustling waterway. Clare thought, *we're not in Kansas anymore Toto.* From the Bay Bridge, she could see the Golden Gate Bridge. "Wow, pictures don't do it justice." There was no response from the driver's seat.

"It's so crowded out here," Claire said quietly and almost to herself.

"What?" Ashley turned the volume down.

"There are a lot of people here!" Claire said too loud.

"You should see L.A." Ashley bobbed her head to the music and turned the volume back up. Claire didn't say anything else until they got to the Berkley campus.

"I'm supposed to drop you off here. They want all of you Interns to have some kind of orientation before you unpack. Good luck, have fun, nice to meet you." Ashley popped the trunk open but didn't make a move to get out.

Claire thanked her and said she hoped they'd meet again. "God, I sound like Mary Poppins," she muttered to herself.

She wondered if she was supposed to stay on the curb, or go into one of the five buildings in front of her. School was out for the summer so there weren't many people around, no one in fact, nearby to ask. It seemed late to Claire. It was 6:00 back home and dinnertime. Here it was just midafternoon. She was tired and hungry and completely out of her element. There was a circular bench that had been built around an enormous tree standing in the middle of a courtyard. She decided to make her camp there.

It took two trips to get all of her belongings to the bench, but it didn't look like she was going anywhere soon. She had read all of her magazines on the long flight and had even written to her parents during her layover in St. Louis, so she decided to get comfortable and relax awhile.

She woke up with a start. Someone was shaking her shoulder. "Sorry if I scared you. Are you Claire Montgomery?" She nodded, rubbing her face. Standing before her was a young man, tall and fair. He had a kind face with perfect features and a broad smile that revealed his perfect teeth. She looked down at herself, clothes wrinkled and feeling disheveled, and then back at the young man, very neatly dressed with every hair in place.

"I'm Michael. I was sent to look for you. We called Ashley to find out what she had done with you. She said she dropped you off, but couldn't remember if she told you where to go. She was supposed to drop you in front of the Lawrence Hall of Science. This is the Lawrence National Laboratory. Close, but not close enough. Anyway, the others are waiting for us, so let's be on our way. Here, let me get the big one." He huffed as he lifted the heavy duffle bag.

Still a little befuddled, Claire obediently followed with her backpack and computer case. As they drove the short distance he told her about the apartment they had selected for her. He rattled off something about food vouchers and a Laundromat. He told her where she could buy organic groceries, as well as what neighborhoods to avoid and where it was safe to go for a run if she liked.

It reminded her of the drive to the airport earlier in the day. Her mother and father took turns giving instructions about how to behave, what she should do while she was in California and not to trust strangers. She just smiled and nodded as Michael spoke.

Claire was in awe of the beautiful campus. There were towers and fountains, gardens and large grassy areas she imagined were full of sunbathing students during the school year.

It only took a few minutes to get to the right building. Michael had filled her in on all the key people she would be meeting, including the other students who had been chosen. It was quite a line up.

Representing UCLA was a brilliant student named Dove Ling. Descended from a long line of notable scientists from China, her father was currently working as a researcher for NASA.

From MIT came a strange but funny guy named Nathan Mann. He preferred to be called Nateman. A computer genius, he wrote new programs in his sleep. Only fifteen, his lists of accomplishments was already long.

Next was a beautiful red headed girl from Texas Tech, Jessica Leigh. She was as sweet as Texas was big. Known as a star finder, she had logged more than fifteen hundred new stars. She says you can just see more of them in Texas.

The final lucky intern was Christopher Kincaid. He was the oldest of the team at twenty one, but still the youngest graduate from Harvard to be published in the A&A (Astronomy & Astrophysics) Science Journal.

When they arrived, the first to greet Claire was Dr. Arlene Sullivan, who had rushed over to the group when she saw them walk in. "I am so sorry, you must be Claire."

She shook Claire's hand, and then held on to it with both hands. "Ashley is my daughter. We were spread pretty thin today, what with everyone arriving on different flights from different airports. I am so embarrassed that we misplaced you."

Claire smiled warmly at her and told her that she needed the nap. "Good, okay then, let's get started with the dinner. You look famished." Claire just smiled and nodded.

They met in a large conference room with one enormous oval table. It was obviously custom made to fit the oval shape of the room. At one end was a state of the art media center, where the monitors were stacked five high and ten across, following the contour of the room. The monitors were programmable to show fifty different images, or one fiftieth of a single image. They were running a slide show of the radio telescope program, featuring SETI projects and facilities from around the world.

At the opposite end of the room was a beautiful buffet table, again, curved to fit the wall complete with elaborate flower arrangements. Steaming hot food was being set in place by what appeared to be a catering service. No cafeteria food for *this* crowd.

They ate like they had been starved for weeks. No one had been allowed to start until they found Claire. The search had taken about two and a half hours. Apparently Ashley didn't answer her cell phone right away.

The food was fabulous. There were salads, sushi, pastry wrapped vegetables, tender meats in wonderful sauces, and breads of all sorts. Once they had their fill, the main course was taken away and replaced with a coffee station adorned with an elaborate assortment of desserts.

It was almost too much; Almost. There was very little talking during the meal. It wasn't until people started getting full and picking at their plates that the conversations began.

Claire was seated between Dove and Nathan, whose personalities could not have been further apart. Everyone seated in this room was brilliant. There was no doubt about it. Each one of the interns had skipped two grades or more. But Nate was a freaking genius and still just a kid. Everyone found him hilarious, with the exception of Dove.

She found his antics immature and distasteful. She was born and raised in China until she was ten. Her parents were very traditional and had given her little freedom growing up. She had always been tutored and attended private schools for the gifted. Her playmates had even been arranged, like so many Chinese marriages.

Fortunately, Nathan's parents encouraged him to be a kid. He stayed in public schools because it was within the family budget. The schools allowed him to advance at his own pace, and he graduated high school at the age of eleven. Nateman and Christopher were the only two males selected for the internship and it was clear from the beginning that they were going to stick together, in spite of their age difference.

Claire sat back and observed. She could see that alliances had already started to form in her absence.

The chatter in the room was growing steadily, until the lights began to dim. It was then that they noticed Dr. Sullivan had taken her place at a podium to the side of the slide show.

Dr. Arlene Sullivan was of average height for a woman and slim. She was in her early sixties but looked healthy and fit. She had a natural beauty. She could best be described as sensible; from her slightly grey at the temples hair to her Buster Brown shoes. She was no frills, no nonsense but very genuine and warm. "Good evening everyone. I hope that everybody enjoyed their dinner. I think the folks at Heaven's Gate did a marvelous job."

"Welcome to Berkley for those who have not been here before, and welcome back to those who have. I know most of you are exhausted from your travels, so I will make tonight's introduction as brief as possible. Besides Claire, I don't think anyone else had a chance for a nap today." She chuckled and smiled warmly at Claire.

"We're going to get an early start tomorrow, so I want everyone to be rested and ready to get to work. Since we only have five interns this year instead of our usual twenty, we will most likely keep you together here in California. I know some of you were hoping for Hawaii or Puerto Rico. I'm sorry," she said in a genuine tone. Our funding has been drastically cut again. If it weren't for the private and corporate donations, we would be out of business altogether. You were all selected for your unique abilities. We look forward to nurturing your individual skills and hope you will consider a career with SETI. Now without further ado, let me introduce you to Dr. Stewart Griffin. He will be our continuing education coordinator this summer, and will act as your immediate supervisor."

No one applauded. Claire thought, *his reputation must have preceded him.* "Thank you and welcome to boot camp." He laughed alone. "Just kidding! Boy I feel like a tick about to pop. That was a great spread." He said grabbing his belly. No one moved or said a word. Even Dr. Sullivan just stared at him, appalled by his behavior. It was hard to guess Dr. Griffin's age because he was balding but not gray. His face was pinched but not necessarily wrinkled. And he was stout and round looking, but not obese.

Of all the people that the interns were introduced to that night, Dr. Griffin was neither a researcher nor a scientist. He was a shrink and assistant to the director of human resources at SETI. Claire guessed that it made sense to psychologically evaluate people who were *supposed* to be hearing things.

"I would like to thank Dr. Sullivan for inviting me to the summer program this year. This will be a temporary post for me though; I am only standing in for the lovely Dr. Jennifer who is on maternity leave." He said with an air of sarcasm. "We have a lot of work to do in the next twelve weeks. I hope you came prepared for long hours and tedious study. You'll get all the sleep you need when you die." He paused a long time waiting for laughter that never came and so concluded. "Get some rest and we'll see you in the morning."

At first nobody moved, even Dr. Sullivan sat stunned. Dr. Griffin made a motion with both arms as if to shoo everyone away. "Go on now, go go go."

Michael stood on a chair and said "Can I have your attention for just a moment?" Everyone stopped.

"We don't want to lose anyone else today, so please listen up. We have already loaded your gear into the bus. Your apartments have been stocked with a few essentials until you get a chance to get to the store. We will provide transportation to and from the observatory each morning at 7:00 am and a return trip each day at 6:00 pm. For you astronomy students who are used to working at night, we can arrange for you to do some work with the vampire's if you'd like."

Claire perked up. Just the thought of getting out of working with Dr. Griffin would be worth it. "We like to refer to Dr. D as the bride of Dracula and her lab as Dracula's Castle. You'll meet her tomorrow," he said with a shrug and a smile. "Okay let's roll! We still have a bit of a drive in front of us tonight." On that note, the room began to clear. Everyone was murmuring about how weird Dr. Griffin was. Even the members of staff had their heads together, whispering in a huddle.

Stepping outside they couldn't help but notice the bus, it was small, old and bright purple. Someone had painted planets and stars on it. They all joked that they were going to be riding *the short bus* this summer. Dove was the only one who did not see the humor in it. She frowned and huffed and then climbed aboard.

Dr. Sullivan waved and shouted as they were pulling out, "I hope you enjoy your home away from home!"

"Home," thought Claire. She had tried to reach her parents to let them know she had arrived safely, but no one picked up, so she left a message. She thought maybe they'd stayed in town to shop or perhaps went out to eat since they were in Columbus anyway. She closed her eyes and thought of the farm as she bumped along down the road.

Chapter 5

Claire awoke to someone pounding on her door. "Claire! The bus is here, it's time to go! Claire!"

"Shit." She began to fly around the room in circles. Finding her suitcase which had not been unpacked, she tossed her clothes out until she found the jeans and T-shirt she was looking for. "I'm coming! I'll be right out. Hold the bus five minutes!"

It was Jessica on the other side of the door. She put her fingers in her mouth and whistled toward the bus. Everyone turned around at the startling noise. She held up her hand with fingers spread. "She needs five minutes!" She said; louder than she needed to be. The bus was only ten or fifteen yards away. Dove was sneering, but Nate was laughing. He thought Jessica was funny, and gave her thumbs up.

Combing her hair with her fingers, Claire emerged from her apartment. Actually 'apartment' was an overstatement. This was an old roadside motel that had been converted into efficiency apartments, rented by the week. They were clean but with one tiny one room and a bath. Each had a fridge, a stove, and a sink, all miniature in size. No cabinets to speak of, just a shelf above for two plastic plates, two bowls and two coffee mugs, all pink to match.

She was greeted with applause from the bus. Everyone, including the driver, welcomed her to the bus thanking her for being *on time*. Embarrassed, she went to the back of the bus apologizing all the way.

Nateman, who was seated in front of her turned and said; "Don't worry about it. We had to give you a hard time." He gave Claire a big smile. "I wonder what they're planning for breakfast; I didn't have any milk or juice in my refrigerator, did you?"

Claire was still groggy. She yawned saying "I don't know. I fell asleep with my clothes on last night. I was so tired I just sat down on my bed and the next thing I knew Jessica was pounding on my door."

The observatory was only about a fifteen minute drive from the motel. Everyone was glued to the windows as soon as the first radio telescopes came into view. They were much bigger than they had appeared in pictures. Claire's heart pounded wildly at the sight.

Everyone was welcomed inside with a choice of coffee, tea or juice and a tray of pastries and bagels. As much as she needed a cup of coffee, the sight of the observatory had awakened her sufficiently. Eventually she stopped gawking and followed the others to the table for breakfast. They were barely through their first cup of coffee when Dr. Griffin showed up. The look of disappointment on everyone's face was hard not to notice. However, Dr. Griffin walked directly toward a chocolate doughnut without acknowledging anyone's presence in the room. He was not aware, nor did he appear to care how he was received. The look of instant pleasure on his face was amusing. Nateman could not pass up the opportunity to mock him. He rolled his eyes back in his head, rubbed his stomach and made sounds of ecstasy. Dr. Griffin didn't notice. He just went on stuffing the doughnut in his mouth and looking around on the tray to see if it had a twin. Three doughnuts and a slurpy cup of coffee later, Dr. Griffin spun around and addressed the students. "That's better, good morning!" Dr. Griffin was rubbing his stomach just as Nathan had a few minutes before. Even Dove had to laugh at that.

A bit puzzled he hesitated, but then continued; "Today we are going to break up into two groups. Since we have an uneven number of students we will split up by gender. You three *girls* over here and you two *men* . . ." He looked over at Nathan and cleared his throat, but decided not to correct himself.

It was obvious that none of the *girls* appreciated being referred to in that way. They responded with crossed arms and did so as though on cue. However, they did not respond except to sigh, grunt and snarl. You could guess who snarled.

Dove raised her hand. Dr. Griffin nodded in her direction. "Dr. Griffin, when will Dr. Sullivan be joining us?"

"I am here now." Everyone spun around, surprised to see Dr. Sullivan descending a spiral staircase from a room above. The young women were delighted and hoped that she had overheard the previous remarks. Seeing the pleasant look on her face, it appeared that she had not. "Welcome and good morning. I hope everyone is rested from their travels. Please let us know if there is anything you would like to make your stay more comfortable. First Michael is going to give you a tour of the facility and introduce you around. We will meet back here at 10:00 and then we will assign you to your work stations. Since there are so few of you, I don't think it will be necessary to separate you into groups." She smiled. "We will see you back here at 10:00. Dr. Griffin will you join me in my office please?" Still smiling, but now through her teeth, she ushered Dr. Griffin up the staircase.

Along the corridors were large color photos taken by the Hubble Telescope. Of these images which were so familiar, Claire thought the Eagle Nebula was the most beautiful. She wondered how could anyone look at that image and ask 'is there life out there?' It was a life giver itself. The Eagle Nebula is a nursery for stars and planets and it represented intelligent creation to her, so organized and precise. Claire just stood there in wonder. Jessica walked up and stood beside her. "Ain't that the prettiest thing? That's my favorite. If I could go anywhere in space, that would be it."

The two stood side by side. "Me too," said Claire.

The rest of the tour was mostly introducing the Interns to the lab techs. The computers which lined many of the walls were whirring away, spitting out line after line of digital information. There were very few windows in the place, so it really wouldn't matter if you worked day or night. It was almost time to get back.

Back in the main hall they gathered again. This time Dr. Sullivan was in charge and Dr. Griffin stood towards the back. "Well it looks like we have a slight change in plan; we're having some technical difficulties with the orientation presentation. So please bear with us until after lunch. I promise it's worth waiting for." She clapped her hands together and smiled apologetically.

"Michael, can we impose on you for a couple of more hours?" Michael stepped forward. "Will you take Dove and Christopher and let's see . . .um . . . Nateman, to the frequency lab?" The three of them stood next to Michael.

"Jessica and Claire you will be going with Dr. Griffin to the Data laboratory. I will be joining you there in a little while. I have a few things I need to attend to this morning. Lunch is at noon. You probably passed by our little cafeteria on your tour. I'll see you in a little while." She looked back at Claire and Jessica sympathetically as she went up the spiral staircase.

☯☯☯☯☯☯☯

Their work station was less than glamorous. Jessica and Claire were seated in a gray hallway at a folding table. The florescent light above them was flickering and humming. It looked like a supply depot. There were metal shelves with office supplies lining one side of the passage way.

Jessica was incapable of hiding her displeasure. "Y'all want us to do what?" Her arms were crossed against her chest.

"We want you to analyze these documents." Dr. Griffin dropped a huge bundle of computer paper in front of her, shaking the table.

"I can't read this. It's . . . its gobbledygook! How do you expect us to read this?" Jessica's voice was getting louder.

"You don't read it exactly; you will be looking for patterns. You are looking for inconsistencies . . . a blip on the screen so to speak." Dr. Griffin was trying to mime Sherlock Holmes. He bent over the paper as though he had a magnifying glass in his hand, then he left them for a moment.

Jessica whispered loudly across the table; "This is not exactly what I thought we would be doing and I don't think Dr. Sullivan had this in her mind either. When we see her at lunch we're going to straighten this out!"

Claire was about to respond to her when Dr. Griffin came back with an equally large stack of paper. "Here's one for you." He held it high and let it drop on the table with a thud. "Have fun girls, someone will come around to check on you in a little while." Claire and Jessica both huffed, looking at the tall stacks in front of them.

"I'm not sure if mine is upside down or not." Jessica turned the stack one way and then another. "Y'all are crazy if you think we can read this!" She yelled over her shoulder, hoping he was still within earshot.

Griffin *was* still within earshot. He had walked down the hall and then tiptoed back and found a place to hide behind a wall of shelves. There he sat on the edge of a box, edging forward until he was able to glimpse the two women through a small opening. From this vantage point, he could hear everything.

Claire started to flip through the pages and then stopped. Furrowing her brow, she looked up at Jessica who was still turning the paper one way and then another. Then she looked back down, now softening her eyes, slightly out of focus. *This can't be right.* Claire swallowed hard. *"Beloved Ones . . ." "Stand together . . ." "Precious people of the Earth . . ."* She read silently. *Is this possible?* Claire looked up at Jessica. *She doesn't see it.* Now more slowly, she thumbed through page by page. *"We are stardust you and I . . ." ". . . through your fear and greed . . ." "Your collective attitudes affect the wea . . ."*

"What are you doing?" Jessica sounded irritated.

Claire froze. "Ummm . . . nothing."

"You look like you're reading."

Claire smiled a strange smile.

"*Are* you reading?"

"Not exactly." Claire shrugged her shoulders and gave her another awkward smile.

Jessica leaned forward and spoke deliberately. "*Exactly* then, what are you doing?"

Claire's mind was racing. She didn't want to admit what it didn't exactly say. "Take a look at mine." She said as she slid the stack across the table. "Do you see anything different from yours?"

Jessica flipped through the pages. "It looks just like mine. I can't make heads or tails out of it."

Claire pulled Jessica's stack toward her and started to thumb through it, only to discover that is was as plain to her as her own documents. She inhaled deeply and sighed.

"What!" Jessica's voice was raised. "What do you see?"

Claire didn't respond. She lowered her head and continued to flip pages.

Jessica slammed her hand down on the stack and startled Claire. "Hello! Earth to Claire, earth to Claire, do you read me?" Jessica stared at her with her hand unmoved.

Claire looked up and quietly said. "Yes, I think I can read this."

Jessica sat back and said "Holy shit . . . how?"

"I don't know . . . I just can. When I soften my eyes it comes into focus. Remember the opt-art posters? The ones that look like abstract art until you stared at it long enough and then a scene appeared? Claire sat back.

"Yeah I remember those stupid things. I would stare at em' till my eyes watered, but I never saw a picture in any of 'em". Jessica leaned forward across the table and spoke very slowly and deliberately. "Well, what does it say?"

"Well I just scanned it quickly, but this section here talks about hurricanes. They appear to give instructions about how to downgrade them and push them out to sea." Claire turned the stack and pointed.

Jessica squinted and shook her head. "I don't see anything but ink."

Unable to contain himself any longer, Dr. Griffin popped out of his hiding place. "What did you say?"

Both women jumped. Jessica let out a small scream. "You little sneak!" She was on her feet, adrenaline pumping. "What were you doing behind those shelves? Spying on us?" She screwed up her face and said, "You're a creepy little dude."

Unabashed, he repeated himself, glaring at Claire. "What did you say?" He stood over them poking his finger repeatedly at the stack of paper.

Claire shrunk. Memories from school came flooding back. When she would answer a question that hadn't been asked yet, she would get hounded by people wondering how she did it. Unfortunately some people were quite aggressive and made Claire feel like a freak of nature. "It looks to me like instructions for diminishing hurricanes . . . sir" She said quietly, not looking at him.

Griffin walked away mumbling to himself and grabbed a yellow legal pad from a nearby shelf. "If this is some kind of joke . . ." he paused. "We've been listening to space for over forty years and no one; *no one* has ever heard anything! Not one thing . . . well back in '77 there was something back in Columbus..." he trailed off, almost talking to himself.

"The Wow recording;" Jessica said nervously. "Something like seventy-two seconds was recorded, but nobody could figure out what they heard and they haven't recorded anything since."

He put the pad down in front of Claire and gave her a pen. "Write down everything you see! I'll be right back."

Claire wasn't sure if she should write everything or not. What if they thought she was making it up? If no one else could see it, how could they verify it? She wasn't sure what to do. She was lost in thought when Jessica asked her; "Can you really see writing?"

Snapping back to the present Claire said; "It's not written exactly. The computer has translated a sound into a digital format. The word 'sound' is not exactly correct either. It's more like a frequency vibration. As you know, vibrations make what we hear as sound. To someone without ears, it would not be heard as sound.

Jessica tilted her head toward the paper and said "What kinda thing doesn't have ears?"

Claire responded, "What kind of thing doesn't even have a body?"

Jessica's eyes popped wide open and she slapped her hand over her mouth. "They don't have bodies?"

Claire put her hand on the stack of paper and closed her eyes. "I don't think so."

Jessica rolled back in her chair and said "Jesus, Mary and Joseph. . ." and then she whispered "daaaamn."

Knowing now that Dr. Griffin could not be trusted, the women decided not to write anything down until they had a chance to talk to Dr. Sullivan. A decision they would not regret later, for he had stopped to make a phone call along the way.

Huddled together, Jessica and Claire pored over the documents. Claire spoke in soft whispers so as not to be overheard again, while Jessica listened intently. They were so engrossed in the work that they didn't hear Dr. Griffin or Dr. Sullivan approaching.

"Why aren't you writing?" Griffin demanded.

"Oh my heart, y'all scared us!" Jessica put her hand on her heart and sat back. "You gotta stop sneakin' up on folks!"

Dr. Griffin picked up the yellow pad and said, "Why aren't you writing? Were you bullshitting me earlier? Were you trying to make a fool out of me?" His face was getting red and a vein in his neck was beginning to throb. He was fanning the yellow pad in the air.

"No sir, I uh . . . we . . . uh decided it was better to talk to Dr. Sullivan about this first.

"Settle down Stewart." Dr. Sullivan took the pad from his hand and said; "We need to go to my office. This is not the place for this discussion. You should have brought them to me in the first place . . ." then realizing where she was, said, "and what are they doing in the supply hall?

He just shrugged his shoulders and gave the girls a stern look. He picked up the stacks of documents and clutched them to his chest. As they walked in single file toward Dr. Sullivan's office he muttered under his breath. "I *told* them to write it down."

For the first time they got to see what was up the spiral staircase. It opened to a circular room, housing a telescope laboratory. The giant white telescope was located in the center. Surrounding it was a metal rail. Everything in the lab was a shade of white. On the outside of the rail were individual offices, each with a glass wall facing the telescope. Dr. Sullivan's office was the largest, although not really large by any standard. There was enough room for her desk, tall bookcases behind it, and two chairs in front of it. She grabbed an extra chair on her way in. "Have a seat. May I have those?" She made a gesture toward Dr. Griffin. He just stood there with the paper crushed to his chest. "Stewart, may I please have the documents?"

As though distracted by deep thought, he said, "Yes, of course. I'm sorry, I still feel a little woozy."

Smiling, Dr. Sullivan turned to the two girls who were now seated across from her. Griffin remained standing, not taking the offered chair. "Claire, Dr. Griffin tells me you can read this. Is that accurate?"

Trying not to sound crazy or vague she responded, "Yes and No."

Griffin, turning red again said, "I heard her say it said something about HURRICANES!" His voice echoed in the lab vibrating the glass. Everyone outside the office stopped what they were doing and looked in their direction. Then he said in a loud whisper, "Arlene, I heard her reading it to . . . to . . . Tex over there!"

She got up and sat on the edge of her desk. "You need to settle down." She said pointing to Dr. Griffin. "Claire, it's alright. You can tell me what you saw."

Jessica couldn't stand the long pause, waiting for Claire to find the courage to speak. So she blurted it all out sounding like machine gun fire with a southern accent. "They don't have bodies, so they can't talk, so they sent their vibrations, and frequencies and that's what was recorded."

Claire just looked up, grinned and nodded.

"How do you know they don't have bodies?" Dr. Sullivan was speaking very calm.

"I think they did. I just don't think they need them now. They are communicating with us through a frequency. That frequency has been picked up by the radio telescope, and the computer has translated it into a digital format. Somehow I can read it, like you can read a typed page of text. The reason I don't think they have physical bodies any longer is because of the way they sent this communication. It was sent telepathically, not in the form of a language. They did not use a mechanical transmitter of any kind. I think that is why we didn't know that they were talking to us."

Dr. Sullivan crossed her arms, shook her head and said, "I'll be damned. They heard us."

Just then a young woman who appeared to be Dr. Sullivan's assistant waved to her from the door. "Arlene, you have a call on line three." She smiled with a nervous smile.

"Can you take a message? I'm in a conference right now."

Linda waved nervously again and still smiling said, "It's NBC, the network. They would like an interview *today*. What's going on?"

The expression changed immediately on Dr. Sullivan's face. "Stewart, what have you done?" Griffin backed out of the office and ran for the staircase. "Wait here, *all* of you!" she said running after him.

The entire staff gathered in the cafeteria at noon. No one was allowed to leave the building for lunch or for any other purpose. All incoming calls were being monitored and all outgoing calls had been suspended. Everyone was asked to turn off their cell phones until further notice. This was the first lock down the facility had ever experienced. The murmuring was growing with each group arriving in the small room. Without enough chairs, people were starting to line up against the walls. As soon as Dr. Sullivan arrived, the room went silent. In tow were Claire and Jessica.

"Thanks for coming everyone." Then she laughed. "I mean thanks for honoring the mandatory meeting, it means a great deal to me and in a moment you will understand the need for it. Has anyone had any contact with the outside since 11:00 am?"

Linda raised her hand, followed by Dove, two young men at the back of the room and Dr. Vaughn who had just arrived.

"Okay, thank you for your honesty. From this moment on I must insist that you honor a code of silence. We have the potential for media frenzy on our hands." This time Dr. Sullivan was not smiling and her staff seemed to understand that something very important was happening.

Dove stood up. "What is going on? We have a right to know if we are in some kind of danger. I was just trying to call my father at *NASA* when some *ASSHOLE* took my phone away and refused to tell my why!"

More murmuring erupted. "Let's calm down people . . . calm down." Dr. Sullivan was being ignored so Jessica put two fingers in her mouth and whistled loudly. The room went immediately silent. "Thank you Jessica, you'll have to teach me that later. Okay, now everyone settle down and listen. No one is in danger and we are not under attack." Then under her breath she whispered, "Well not yet." She smiled again and said. "Something really incredible was discovered here this morning." She clasped her hands and took a deep breath. "Claire and Jessica were assigned to look over some data that has been recorded over the years. To our surprise a sort of code was discovered. Apparently Claire has the unique ability to read this data." At that moment, every eye turned to Claire. She felt like a spectacle and sunk down in her chair.

"All of these years we thought we were listening to empty space. As it turns out, *they* heard us and have been communicating with us for some time and we just didn't have the ability to see it until now. The reason for the lock down is Dr. Griffin. The little rat called the networks before he even came to me, so I'm afraid this has already hit the news and from what I have gathered, he has already started giving statements to the press. Now we haven't had to a chance to verify this yet and I would like to make sure that we have what we *think* we have before we go public."

She looked around and saw her staff nodding in response. "I for one believe that Claire can see this . . . read this, but it must be verified. We are simply asking for your cooperation to keep this from getting out of hand."

Linda raised her hand and Dr. Sullivan nodded in her direction. "Arlene, there are news crews on the way. We have to prepare a statement. What are we going to do about protecting the Interns? Griffin has probably already told the press everything he knows about them. We need to get them out of here before they are followed everywhere they go." Arlene rubbed her eyes and forehead and began to pace.

Ending a long pause, "I have a suggestion," said Dr. Dianne Vaughn. Known to all as Dr. D., her career had started as a young scientist working on the Hubble Telescope. She had joined the SETI team five years before and had been at Berkley ever since. "I would like to offer an option for the Interns. My folks have a place in the mountains. We use it in the winter for a ski retreat. No one is up there this time of year. I think they would be safe there."

Still rubbing her forehead and pacing two steps one way and then another; "That could work, yes I think that could work." Now looking up and trying to smile convincingly. "Yes, I think that is a good start. Michael, can you get their belongings packed and loaded in the next hour or so? They will need more supplies. We'll send someone to Costco and stock up on essentials. How far is this place?"

Dianne hesitated for a moment, then said, "No offense, but we should discuss that privately. The less everyone knows, the less likely someone is to talk about it."

"Your right," nodded Dr. Sullivan. "Please don't anyone be offended. We have already been betrayed by one of our own. That little rat bastard!" She covered her mouth. "Did I say that out loud?" She giggled, "Oops, that sort of just slipped out. Oh well.

Seriously, we do have a *situation* on our hands. We need to proceed like the professionals we are. We're not trying to hide anything. We just want to present this information as intelligently and responsibly as possible. Right now we don't know *who* sent this, or *where* they come from. We have over forty years' worth of data to look at. All we know for now is that we think we have discovered something wonderful and that our effort has not been in vain. Someone is out there and *they* want to talk to us."

This brought a tear to her eye. "For now, please do not talk about this to anyone on the outside. Not even your families." She said addressing the whole room, but then turned her attention to the Interns. "Before we get you out of here, you may call your families and let them know you are fine. After we move you, there can be no more communication until we can sort this out. Hopefully we can resolve this in a few days. This is for your protection. We've had dealings with the press in the past and they can be more than intrusive. They *will* run you off the road just to get an exclusive. Now may I see my staff up in the sky lab? Interns, try to enjoy your lunch. We're really sorry about all this. I wish I could have caught the little rat." Rubbing her shin bone she leaned toward them and said quietly, "If I was ten years younger I would have caught him."

Jessica waited till everyone had gone, then turned toward her fellow interns and began her story. Claire remained silent. Everyone listened intently until she was done. "Wow," said Christopher, "That is so cool. You mean you just looked down at it and it was right there all along?"

~ - 60 - ~

Jessica was enjoying the attention and continued. "They said all we had to do to downgrade hurricanes was to work together. If we would concentrate our attention on moving it out to sea, or calming the winds, it would die down or move out." Everyone breathed a collective "Wow".

Claire finally spoke up. "But this isn't news. We have known this for a long time. It's a Universal Law. What you put your attention on expands."

Dove piped up in a sarcastic tone. "That's New Age garbage. People have been spouting that crap for years." Now mockingly she was waving her arms and hands around. "Wish it away, ooooh, wish it away."

Then Nathan added, "Actually Dove, it's called Quantum Physics. Experiments have *proven* that the mere viewing of an object changes it. Imagine if the population of a city would put their focus on pushing a big storm out to sea, instead of putting the attention on it coming onto shore, I would love to see the effect of that. What else did you see Claire?"

Quietly, Claire said, "I really didn't get a chance to study it very long. There were some pages about agriculture and instructions about how to increase our crop productions, but again nothing new that I could see. So I don't know what to think. It wasn't like they were imparting any new information that I could tell, or sharing any startling secrets. Honest, ask Jessica we didn't see anything else. I really don't know why it's such a big deal."

Christopher stood up. "You don't? Claire, we have been sending radio signals out into space for about 100 years and we have been listening and waiting for over forty. This is the first proof of intelligent life we have ever had."

Nodding her head Claire said, "You're right. I just thought they would tell us something new. There is a lot more data to look at. Maybe there will be something useful in it after all. You're right, this is ground breaking, I was just hoping for something more."

Christopher rolled his eyes. "God, you make the greatest scientific discovery in the twenty first century and you wanted something *more*! Chicks!"

👀👀👀👀👀👀👀

Each of the five was allowed to make their phone calls under the supervision of a staff member. They were asked to limit their conversations to acknowledging the events of the day, but not to go into detail about what the data said. Nor were they to speculate about who had sent the messages, or from where, and one other stipulation, they were forbidden to mention who had discovered the code, just in case that detail hadn't gotten out yet. They were simply instructed to let their families know they were safe and they would be able to tell them more in a few days. Under no circumstances were they to mention the 'Rat Bastard' (as he would now forever be known) in any way.

Claire had not been able to reach her parents the day before. She had not spoken to them since she last saw them at the airport. It seemed like a week ago, and yet it was only yesterday. So much had happened already. The phone rang six times before a breathless voice answered. "Hello?"

"Momma!" Claire could feel a lump grow in her throat. "Momma, can you hear me?"

"Yes, sweetheart, I just had to catch my breath. I was coming in from the herb shed when I heard the phone. How was your trip? What is California like? Oh God, I miss you so much already! Tell me all about it. Oh, your father is here." Beth covered the mouthpiece with her palm and said, "Tom pick up the other phone. It's Claire!"

With that she heard another click and then the sound of her father's voice. "Clairee honey, its Daddy. How was your trip?"

Now Claire could hardly speak. She was glad that they couldn't see the tears streaming down her face, though they could hear it in her voice.

"Hi . . . uh, the trip was great. I had my face plastered to the window the whole time. This country is really beautiful from the sky. Well they lost me almost as fast as they found me at the airport, but that's a story for later. You guys are going to hear some things on the news tonight. You may want to log on to CNN for the details as they become available." Claire sounded calm. "I really can't say what's going on, except that we have discovered a code in the data collected by SETI. It was leaked to the press but it has not been verified. They want to move us to a secure location until SETI can make an official statement. So I don't want you to worry. They just want to protect us from the press."

"Claire, what did you find?"

"I can't tell you Daddy. I'm sorry. There is someone here with me now who's listening in, so I don't give too much away. I should have told you that we are being monitored."

Beth said, "Are you sure you're alright? Can you tell us when we can talk to you again? I don't like the idea of not knowing where you are."

"I'll be fine Momma, it's only for a few days. Evidently the paparazzi are pretty relentless in California, what with all the celebrities out here. So they just want to err on the side of caution. Honestly you guys, I'm fine. What's happening at the farm? I tried to call you two last night. Did you stay in town?"

Claire was getting the sensation that her parents were keeping something from her. "Uh, yes sweetheart! We decided to stay in Columbus last night. We don't get to the big city that often." Tom was trying too hard to sound light hearted.

"What's wrong?" Claire knew for certain now that something was wrong.

"Nothing Claire, we're fine." Beth tried to sound convincing.

"Alright you two, I only have a few more minutes, don't do this to me." Claire closed her eyes, took a deep breath and concentrated. "Momma! Why didn't you tell me? Is it malignant?"

Beth sighed. "I don't know yet. We went in for the biopsy after we dropped you off." Beth started to choke up. "Clairee don't worry. I'll be fine."

"Why didn't you tell me? Why did you let me go? How long have you known?"

Beth was unable to speak so Tom said; "We didn't want you to miss out on this. We knew you wouldn't go. Your mother found the lump three weeks ago. We have already decided to treat it homeopathically. Your mother will not have chemo, or radiation. We wanted the biopsy so we would know what we are dealing with. We'll get the results in a few days."

Claire was now sobbing. Her heart felt like it was breaking. "I was so busy with myself that I didn't read it. I can't believe I missed it."

Beth recovered and said; "Do you have any idea how difficult it is to keep a secret from a psychic child? We had to mirror you constantly. It was exhausting." Now Beth laughed. "Honey, it's going to be fine. I have the best people around me. I will beat this thing. I have faith."

Sniffling, Claire tried to sound positive. "You will Momma, you can do this. I will contact someone on the Grid to help you. There are healers Mother, good healers who can help you." Claire was getting the signal to wrap it up. "I have to go. They're giving me the evil eye. I'll call you again in a few days. I will pray for you Momma. I always pray for you two. I love you both so much. My heart is broken; I can't stand being away from you right now."

In unison Tom and Beth both said "We love you too Clairee. Good bye sweetheart." As the phones disconnected, all three broke down in grief.

Claire looked up at Michael who was standing near her not knowing what to do and said, "My mother has breast cancer."

Chapter 6

The phones were ringing off the hook at the observatory. CNN, NBC, ABC, CBS, Fox News, The National Inquirer and every other sleazy tabloid rag wanted an exclusive interview with the 'Aliens' who sent the messages.

"This is turning into a circus!" Linda had not stopped since lunch. A press conference had to be arranged to keep the press from mobbing the building. As it was, extra security had to be called in to keep traffic flowing out on the street.

At 2:00 pm the White House called. This was one call Arlene *had* to take. It was the Press Secretary asking for a copy of the statement the Institute intended to make to the public. No statement had been written yet, but she had promised to send them a copy before it was officially released.

"Okay people, what do we know for sure?" Dr. Sullivan was pacing before her staff. "We must stick to the facts. We know that we have been sifting through data for over forty years, when a summer intern, who happens to be an Indigo Child, walks in, sits down, and starts to read letters from space. Do we know how crazy this sounds?" She stopped and looked around the room. "We can't tell them this!" She was pacing again, unable to stand still.

Dr. Vaughn spoke as she entered the room. "Arlene have you seen the news yet? They already know that we have an Indigo and that her name is Claire Montgomery. They are reporting that she is some sort of psychic. Some of the stations have already found their own psychics to appear on camera as experts. We have to be very careful how we handle this. This could really blow up in our face."

Arlene stopped in her tracks and threw her hands up. "We'll tell the truth. I know it sounds crazy, but why don't we just tell the truth? We don't know *how* Claire was able to see the message. It may have nothing to do with her being an Indigo. We need to find out if anyone else can see this code so we can verify what it says. Next, we don't know *who* sent the message, or *where* they are from. For all we know it could be a loop of information that has come from right here. Claire said herself that she didn't see anything out of this world. This *could* be a recorded message that has been playing for decades. Let's downplay this thing for now. Let's tell the public that one of our staff got hysterical at what was thought to be a communication from space and jumped the gun." She looked around to see if anyone else agreed.

"This is why you're the boss." Dianne said. "You have a way with simplicity. Besides I like the idea of making Griffin look like a hysterical school girl."

Everyone smiled in agreement. "I'll get it typed up and send a copy to the White House."

"Thanks Linda. I hope they're not too disappointed. You may want to add that we will be launching a full investigation. They'll like that." Linda saluted and turned on her heel and headed for her office.

Once the staff had been dismissed and she and Arlene were alone, Dianne said, "We need to send a few boxes of data with Claire so she won't get bored in the mountains."

"Do you think she can train someone else to read it? It would take her years to decode everything by herself." Arlene sighed, "Certainly she is not the only one. There must be someone else who has this sight. So do we look for other Indigos or do we look among the psychic community? This could get pretty sticky. The media is already making this look like a bad Hollywood stunt."

Arlene was beginning to rub her head again when Dianne said, "We have dedicated our whole lives to this work. We have paid our dues as scientists. We are not going to let the media and one little Rat Bastard ruin this for us."

"You're right. We have to maintain our integrity; we have to keep our heads."

"I have some friends in the city." Dianne said, "In fact there's a woman in Chinatown who may be able to help us. I think she'll be very discreet. I don't think she would go to the press if I asked her to try to read some of it."

Arlene nodded her head in agreement. "That's a good start. I hope that someone else can read it. I just want to take some of the focus off of Claire. She has been singled out as different her whole life. She doesn't want to be in the spotlight. However, she is a scientist and I don't want to take this discovery away from her either, though I get the feeling that she would really appreciate a diversion. Dianne, be very careful that you're not followed."

"Yes 'Mam." Dianne saluted and then turned around to go. She stopped at the door and said, "Good luck with the press conference. Don't let em' get to you. They can be such jerks." Arlene just saluted back to her and smiled.

☯☯☯☯☯☯☯

It was foggy in the city, but Dianne didn't care. She was born and raised in San Francisco. One of her greatest loves was her vintage Mercedes. She had bought it already restored at auction. In her glove compartment she kept a selection of scarves. Dianne's long auburn hair needed to be restrained as she cruised year round with the top down. She was a petite woman with the body of a fairy. The car allowed her to fly everywhere she went.

She was getting close, she could smell it. Chinatown was another world. Much of the Chinese culture was preserved there. Of course they catered to the American tourist in their store fronts, but it was the back alleys that revealed their true culture. *The Fortune Cookie,* read the neon sign. This was the place.

She took the side stairs up to the second floor. The door was curtained but she could see movement inside. She was in luck, someone was home. She knocked.

A tiny wrinkled man opened the door a crack and peered out, but didn't speak. "My name is Dr. Dianne Vaughn. I am here to see Miss Lee."

"What you want? Miss Lee have long day." The man frowned.

"I'm sorry to bother you. I need her help. Would you please tell her that I am here? I'm sure she knows that I was coming."

Without a word he closed the door. Dianne just stood there hoping he would come back. She was surprised how quickly the door opened again. This time it was a child. She was beautiful, maybe six or seven years old. She didn't speak either, she just smiled with her missing two front teeth and opened the door wide.

Once inside, Dianne realized she had interrupted TV time. She counted seven or eight people crowded in a small side room. The only light was the television flickering on their faces; she could see the old wrinkled one staring back at her. The child led her to the kitchen, smiling all the way. She was told to sit down and that Miss Lee would be right out.

Everything about the place was foreign. Dianne felt as though she had walked into another country. All the furniture was Asian. Everything was simple and clean. Even though it was a small apartment, it was very tidy. Everything seemed to have its place. Having the restaurant downstairs saved them from needing dining accommodations. In fact the kitchen was sparse, with a small square table and two chairs. The kettle was steaming on the stove. She thought perhaps she really was expected. Miss Lee was a gifted fortune teller.

A few moments later she entered the room without a sound. It startled Dianne a little. Miss Lee seemed to float into the room, not walk. She was wearing black silk pajamas. Her hair was silvery white and pinned up in a tight bun. It was difficult to guess her age.

She could have been seventy or a hundred and twenty. Her face was heavily lined, her body thin and frail but her bright eyes revealed a keen mind. She went to the counter and made a pot of tea. She prepared two cups and served it on a tray. Without a word she was seated. She took Dianne's hand and looked at her palm.

"Madam Lee, I am not here for a reading. I would like to pay you to read something else for me."

The woman smiled faintly but did not look up. "Are you sure? This is very interesting."

Dianne put her free hand on top of the old woman's hand and said; "Well maybe later, but first I need to know if you can read this." She pulled a sheet of paper out of her purse and handed it to the old woman.

Miss Lee looked at it and immediately handed it back. "No," she said.

"Please look at it again. Do you recognize any pattern or see a code in the numbers? She tried to hand it back to the old woman but she wouldn't look at it. Instead she got up and took a bowl from the cabinet. She poured the tea grounds into the bowl. She swirled the contents, went to the sink and poured off most of the liquid. Continuing to swirl the tea leaves, she came back to the table and sat down. Looking into the bowl she said. "Sadie Moon."

Dianne looked at her and said; "I don't understand. What does Sadie Moon mean?"

Just then the little girl who had answered the door appeared in the kitchen. "Sadie Moon will read for you." The old woman handed the paper to the child.

Sadie looked at it for just a moment, broke into a big smile and said, "They heard usth."

Before Dianne had finished her tea, Sadie had disappeared and returned with a little red suitcase. Dianne looked at both of them, unsure of why.

"You will need her. She is ready to help you. She will stay with lady who has yellow hair. They are the same."

Dianne could not disguise the look of shock of her face. "Do you mean Claire? You are the same as Claire?" Sadie Moon smiled so proud of the void in her teeth that she stuck her tongue in the gap and shook her head yes.

Miss Lee got up and hugged Sadie Moon and said something to her in Chinese. She patted her on the head and started to glide back out of the room. "Wait a minute . . . please," Dianne said stopping her with a touch on the arm. "Are you coming with us?"

"You don't need me, you need Sadie Moon." The woman said casually. "My Sadie will help you. She is good girl, she be no trouble."

A little dumbfounded, Dianne continued. "But you don't know me."

Miss Lee squared herself in front of Dianne and took her by both shoulders. "I do know you. I know your heart." She turned and left Dianne standing slack jawed.

Sadie stood ready to go. Dianne picked up her purse and Sadie's little red suitcase and together they walked out into the night.

As they approached the car Dianne said. "It's getting late. You will need to stay at my place tonight. I will take you to see Claire tomorrow."

A little voice said; "Okay." Dianne grinned to herself. She could tell that things were just beginning to get strange.

She took her mobile phone out of her pocket and dialed Arlene. When she reached her voice mail, she left a message that just said; "You will not believe what just happened to me."

The next call she made was to Ryan. She thought it only fair to warn him that she was bringing home company. "Hi sweetheart, I'm on my way home."

Ryan sounded happy to hear from her. "Well hey there yourself. I hear you've had an interesting day. You're all over the news."

Dianne laughed. "You don't know the half of it. I thought I would give you a heads up. I am bringing home an unexpected guest. She says she would like pepperoni pizza for dinner tonight. Could you arrange that for me? We should be there in about forty-five minutes." Dianne looked over at Sadie Moon who was smiling as usual, this time enjoying the convertible.

"I'll call Ha Ha's pizza. They deliver. Be careful, I'll see you soon. By the way who's your guest?"

"It would take too long to explain. I'll fill you in on all the details when I get there. See you soon."

As Dianne pulled up to the house she passed the delivery driver going in the opposite direction. "Good timing. The pizza should be hot." The girls put the top up on the old Mercedes and headed to the house. Dianne had been sharing the old brown stone with Ryan for three and a half years. Marriage had not been in the cards yet, but Ryan was hopeful. They were weekend remodelers, so they lived in a construction zone most of the time. The current project was a new front porch. The path to the house was lined with new timber and pallets of brick.

"Be careful Sadie. Watch your step." Ryan must have seen her head lights because he met them at the door.

"I couldn't wait to see your surprise." He looked down at the sweet little girl, with her full smile and missing teeth. He could not help but smile back. "This is quite a surprise. Are we adopting?"

Dianne rolled her eyes and brushed past Ryan, grazing him with a kiss. "You can set your things down there sweetie. I'll make your bed up after we eat. Are you hungry?"

Sadie nodded. Ryan and Dianne started to talk about their day when they realized that Sadie had not followed them into the kitchen. "Okay Houdini, where'd you go?" She wasn't in the front hall where they had left her. Ryan went to the living room and Dianne went upstairs. Together they called out for her. "Sadie where are you?"

When Dianne got to the master bedroom she noticed the door was open and the closet light was on. "Sadie? Are you in here?" She was getting the creeps now. The whole day had been something right out of an old science fiction movie. "Sadie?" Dianne slowly pushed the closet door open and there she was, petting the cat. Apparently Caris the cat decided to have her kittens in the closet and was still in the process of it. "What did you find?" She said more gently, "Is the momma kitty having her babies?"

Sadie nodded but didn't look up. She just kept stroking the cats head and telling Caris that she was doing a good job. Just then Ryan walked in, "Did you find her?" Dianne put her finger to her lips and pointed to the closet floor. "How did she know she was having her kittens? I've been here all day and I didn't know."

"Men." Dianne said with a smirk on her face. Sadie looked up and grinned. "Let's wash our hands Sadie and eat our pizza and then we can come back and check on them later, okay?"

"Can I have Ginger Ale?" Dianne laughed "Of course you can have Ginger Ale. I hope I have some."

"You do." said the little voice.

Dianne shook her head and smiled. *This child is amazing. Where do these kids come from? How did I live all these years and not know they were here?* Once settled, they sat down for dinner and Dianne told Ryan about their day.

Chapter 7

On their way to the mountains Dianne told Sadie all about Claire and why she was going to see her, when she realized that Sadie probably knew better than she did why she was going. "Sadie, can I ask you some questions?"

Sadie rolled her eyes and leaned toward Dianne looking up at her. Dianne took the gesture as a yes and continued. "Have you seen Claire before? Do you know who she is?"

Sadie shook her head no, and then yes.

"How do you know who she is?"

Sadie sighed and shrugged her shoulders. "We can juthst tell." Then she turned away and watched the landscape speed by.

After an hour or so, Sadie got tired and laid down falling fast asleep. Dianne decided to check in with Arlene. She attached her ear piece and pressed a key. After checking her caller I.D., Arlene answered; "Thank goodness it's you Dianne, where are you? How did it go last night?"

Dianne smiled and said, "I think we really have something here. The code . . . *is* . . . there. We have confirmation."

Arlene was delighted. "Did Miss Lee see it right away like Claire?"

Dianne took a deep breath and said, "Well, yes she saw it instantly, but it wasn't the *she* I thought it would be. Miss Lee has a great granddaughter. Her name is Sadie Moon Lee. She is the most adorable six year old I have ever seen. She is pretty amazing. I'm on my way to my folks place. I have Miss Sadie with me. I'm taking her to Claire."

"Is Sadie an Indigo?"

Dianne looked over at the sleeping child; "I would bet on it. Arlene, I was thinking earlier; How could I *not* have known these kids have been here for thirty some odd years? I consider myself to be pretty well informed and up on current events. You know I'm not religious, I'm a scientist, but these kids make you feel like you're in the presence of something Divine."

Arlene answered, "I first heard of Indigo Children back in the eighties. At that time they were thought to only be living in Europe and Asia. As it turns out they were here in America all along, but most were diagnosed with a variety of disorders, like A.D.D., and drugged into submission. Many people still do not know that they exist. At least the media has overlooked them until *now*." Her voice trailed off. "I look forward to meeting her. I'll be there as soon as I can get away. I need to take care of a few things before I come up. The press conference didn't go well. Apparently Griffin spilled everything and more. The University is holding him liable and pressing charges for giving up privileged information and violating privacy agreements. It serves him right. Anyway, I'll smuggle out some more data and bring it with me. Need anything else?"

"Not that I can think of, but give us a call when you're on your way. We'll see you later. Bye for now."

It was a beautiful drive. The old Mercedes seemed to remember all the curves in the road. She was feeling carefree with the top down and the wind blowing through her hair.

Just then Sadie sat straight up and yelled; "Thtop! Thtop wight now!"

Dianne was so startled that she slammed on the brakes and swerved to the shoulder off the road. Just as they rolled to a stop, she could see up ahead, just beyond the next curve, a rock slide had recently occurred, in fact there were still small rocks bouncing down the mountain and the dust had not yet settled. Dianne was speechless for a moment, and then she looked at Sadie Moon, who was straining to see over the dash.

She wasn't tall enough to get a good look. "A big truck ith coming."

Without hesitation Dianne got out, opened her trunk and took out a road flare. She ignited it and set it on the road a ways back from where they had stopped. When she got back to the car, Sadie had gotten out and stood in front of the car looking at the broken rocks.

"You are handy to have around young lady. You saved us. I was going too fast and would never have been able to stop." Dianne knelt down and put her arms around the child who didn't seem disturbed in the least. Dianne's heart was still beating out of her chest. Only now did she hear the sound of the truck Sadie had just mentioned. Its brakes squealed to a stop and a young man got out.

"What seems to be the trouble?" As he walked a few more yards he said; "Oh, rock slide. Have you called anyone yet?"

Dianne shook her head. "No, we just got here and put out a flare right away. It looks like it just happened a few minutes ago."

He looked back at the truck and signaled to someone. A young woman stuck her head out of the passenger window. He yelled, "Charlotte! Call my dad. Tell him where we are and that there's been a rock slide near mile marker one seventy. Tell him it's pretty bad. He needs to get the County out here right away to set up road blocks on both sides. He turned back to Dianne and Sadie and said, "I'm Thomas, that's my wife Charlotte. My dad is the County Sheriff. Are you two okay?"

"Yes we're fine. We were on our way up to my parents' cabin. If I turn around here, I'm not sure how to get up to Eagle's Pass by any other road."

Thomas thought about it for a moment, and then gave her directions to get there from the other side of the mountain. He estimated it would take at least another hour to detour. She thanked him and started to walk toward the car when she realized that Houdini had disappeared again. Looking frantically from side to side, "Sadie . . . please don't disappear now! Sadie!"

From the truck, Sadie and Charlotte came walking up hand in hand. "You have a little angel here," said Charlotte. "I don't know how she knew, but I've had terrible migraine headaches for the last few months and without a word Sadie just put her hands on my head and my neck and the pain went away. I don't know who she is or where she came from, but thank you. That was amazing!"

Thomas went over to his wife. He put his hands on either side of her head and looked at her saying, "Is it really gone?" She just nodded and Thomas turned to Sadie and said;"How did you do that?"

Sadie just shrugged her shoulders and took Dianne's hand, ready to leave. "We'd better get going. We have a long drive in front of us. Thanks for the directions."

"Anytime. Hey, be careful out there. Sometimes one slide can trigger another."

"Don't worry. I have my own little angel with me." They waved as they drove away. Thomas and Charlotte stood in the road with their arms around each other and watched them as they drove out of site.

☀☀☀☀☀☀☀

Dianne could see the cabin just ahead on the left as it sat on the side of a rocky cliff. The drive twisted and turned up and up. It was more suited for jeeps and goats than for vintage sport cars. They bumped along in the dust until they reached the front of the house. No other vehicle was there and she wondered where Michael had gone with the van. On the porch sat Nateman, Christopher and Jessica. The boys were playing guitars and rocking in the old redwood rockers her father had made. Jessica was singing and playing a portable keyboard.

Dianne and Sadie applauded as they came up to the porch. The musicians stood and bowed.

"Wow, you guys sound tight, like you've played together for years!"

Just then Dove came out the front door letting the screen slam behind her. "They've had plenty of time to practice." She said with a sour expression on her face. "Who's this?" She said pointing at Sadie who was stepping on to the porch with her red suitcase.

"I am Thadie Moon Lee;" and she smiled her toothless smile stopping in front of Dove. "Don't worry. You won't be here much longer." As Sadie strode past Dove and went into the house, everyone followed her with their eyes.

"I guess she's gone to find Claire." Dianne shrugged her shoulders. "She can see the code too. I found her by accident but she seemed to know I was looking for someone to help us and she volunteered."

Dove was still standing there looking a little stunned said; "How old is she?"

"Six going on sixteen," answered Dianne.

Dove stood tall and straight and said. "Dr. Vaughn, how long do you plan to keep us prisoners here?" The others froze and looked in her direction.

"First of all you are *not* prisoners. You are here for your own protection. We have security issues to consider. The whole SETI program is at stake. Of all people Dove, you should understand this. Your father works for NASA. If someone had breached *their* security and stolen *this* type of information, you can be sure that no one would have left until it was resolved or secured again. For us, that could happen today. Dr. Sullivan is working on it. She will be here later this afternoon. In the meantime you may make brief phone calls home or to loved ones when Michael comes back. By the way where is Michael?"

Nate stepped forward and said; "We heard something about an hour ago. It sounded like rumbling so Michael went to check it out."

"It was a rock slide. That's why it took us so long to get here. We had to detour back and come by another road. I need to call Dr. Sullivan and give her directions around the slide. Does anybody need anything special? I can have her pick it up on her way."

"I just want to go home." Dove said as she spun around and went inside with a bang. Everyone cringed as the door slammed *again*.

"Y'all, *that*'s getting really old, I may have to teach that girl some manners." Jessica said clenching her fist.

Then Christopher spoke up. "Someone thought we were all health nuts or something. There's no cookies or chips or anything like that. We've been feeding rice cakes to the birds and squirrels for entertainment. Can we have some good old fashion junk food?" The others nodded their heads wildly.

"Of course. I'm sorry. Michael did the shopping. I'll tell Dr. Sullivan to stop at the grocery on her way."

In the house Claire was sitting on a window seat writing in her journal. The radio was playing softly on a jazz station. Suddenly she stopped writing and looked up. Sadie Moon was standing in the doorway. "Hi." Claire said and smiled. Sadie ran to her, jumped on her lap and flung her arms around Claire's neck, like she hadn't seen her in ages. "Well hey there little one, who are you?" Sadie sat back smiling up at Claire.

"I am Thadie Moon Lee; I am here to help you." Claire instantly fell in love with the slant of her eyes and her toothless grin. She was a precious sight.

"Can you see the code? Is that what you mean?" Sadie nodded. "Did Dr. Vaughn bring you here?" Sadie nodded again. "Let's go down and see her okay?" Nodding again, Sadie took Claire by the hand and pulled her along.

Dove met them at the bedroom door with her arms folded tight against her chest. "I see you've met the *other* one." She said crinkling her nose as if there was a bad odor in the room. Sadie let go of Claire's hand and went to Dove.

She flung her little arms around Dove's hips and said "I love you." Then she took Claire's hand again and pulled her down the hallway. Dove was dumbstruck and had gone rigid. She wasn't used to being hugged. She couldn't move, she just stood there replaying the moment in her mind.

Dr. Vaughn was in the kitchen. She had just hung up from talking to Arlene. "Hi girls, I see you've met. Dr. Sullivan has good news. I think we'll be able to get out of here tomorrow. Anyway, she's on her way up and will be here for dinner. She said she'd fill us in when she gets here.

"Where did you find Sadie Moon?" Claire asked as she sat at the kitchen table. Sadie jumped up on her lap.

"Chinatown," she began. "A couple of years ago I had my fortune told by an old Chinese woman named Miss Lee. She was amazing. She knew things about me that she could not have known. She told me that I would inherit a house and so many other things that came true. So when we needed to confirm what you had discovered, I thought of her. She could not see the code, but her great granddaughter can." Dianne walked over and kissed the top of Sadie's head. "We are going to need more help though. There's over forty years of data to read and the White House is getting very anxious to know what they've been saying to us. Not to mention all the researchers who have dedicated their lives to this effort. The question is, where do we find more help?"

"I talked to my friend David in Australia and he says that SETI has a center at The University of Western Sydney. He's going to be recruiting from there. Then I went online and left messages on as many Indigo sites as I could. Later, Sadie and I can surf the Grid together and see what we come up with," she said giving Sadie a squeeze.

"I've heard you refer to The Grid several times. I'm sort of new to this, can you illuminate me?" Dr. Vaughn asked.

Claire looked at Sadie and then back to Dr. Vaughn. "Well, I'm not sure exactly how to describe it. We see it as an electromagnetic field that weaves itself in a grid-like pattern above the earth. But I've read many accounts of astral travel, remote viewing and bi-location that sound exactly like what we experience. We are physically in one place and yet can travel to or view another location. If we are on the same wave length or strand, we can actually communicate in real time with that other person."

"Will everyone be able to see what you see in the data?" Dianne asked.

"I seriously doubt it." Claire said shaking her head. "But of those who can, how will we get everyone together? Will they come here or will we have to find a SETI location near them?"

"That will be a good question for Dr. Sullivan. She may have already worked that out. She said she had good news for us."

Michael pulled up in the van, creating a cloud of dust in front of the cabin. "Jeez, we've got instruments up here man!" Nathan was very protective of his guitar. He had to save for a year to buy it. Jerking it up to his chest, he went in the front door.

"Sorry Nateman!" Michael yelled from the drive.

Dianne came out on the porch and said, "Where have you been? We were starting to get worried about you."

Michael came up on the porch put his hand on Dianne's shoulder and said, "Can we talk about this somewhere else?" He looked serious so Dianne followed him inside. No one was in the kitchen so they settled there.

"What is it? You're making me nervous Michael."

Michael looked around to make sure they were alone and then said, "I was just talking to the Sheriff and we were talking about the rock slide. He said that his son had reported it first. *Then* he told me something *weird*. His son told him that when he came to the rock slide, he met a woman and little Asian child who were already stopped. While he was talking to the woman, this kid went over to the truck where his daughter-in-law was. I guess she had been really sick with headaches. The little girl just got in the truck and told his daughter-in-law that she was going to be fine. She put her hands on her head and neck and the woman was healed, instantly . . . but get this, the lady with the kid was driving an old Mercedes convertible and he's looking for them."

Dianne was shocked and didn't know what to say. "Uh . . . well it was me alright."

"Who's the kid?"

Dianne got up and went to the window. "Her name is Sadie Moon Lee. She is an Indigo child who is here to help us. I didn't think . . . *shit* . . . what do we do? What did you tell him?" She spun around.

"Nothing! Dr. Vaughn, I was pretty sure he was talking about your car, but I didn't know anything about this little girl and besides we're kind of hiding out up here, so I didn't say anything. I just listened and nodded politely and left as quickly as I could."

Now Dianne was pacing across the kitchen back and forth. "The last thing we need is for *this* to end up on the news. Maybe I should call him before he talks to anyone else."

Michael just shrugged his shoulders. Dianne went to the phone. She hesitated and then picked up the receiver. The number was on the wall by the phone, but Dianne just stood there and stared at it.

Michael had left the kitchen for a moment and then came back, "Don't bother, he's here and he's not alone. There's a woman with him."

Dianne raked her fingers through her hair and said, "Great!"

All of the interns were on the front porch except for Dove. As Dianne came out, the Sheriff was coming up the steps followed by the woman. He took off his hat and said; "'Mam, who does that car belong to?"

Dianne stepped forward, "It's mine Sheriff. Won't you come in? I was just about to call you." She gestured to the rest of them to stay on the porch. "I'll explain later."

They were still standing when Michael walked in. The Sheriff looked at him and signaled with his hat to sit down. Without a word every one sat. "I see you know why I'm here. Can you tell me who you are, why you're here with all of these young people and where is that little girl?"

Dianne sat forward in her chair. "Of course Sheriff, my name is Dr. Dianne Vaughn. This house belongs to my parents. I am an Astrophysicist at the University of California Berkley. The young people here are summer interns in the SETI program. Before I answer any more questions may I ask who this is?"

"Oh yes, of course I've forgotten my manners. This is my wife Beverly. I'm Tom Lawford and I believe you met my son Thomas and his wife Charlotte this afternoon. My wife owns the Diner down in the valley. This time of year we don't get many folks from out of town, but the last few days we've had a lot of people stoppin' in and askin' questions about some students who are supposed to be hidin' up here in the mountains. And, now this unbelievable story about a little girl who heals people. I wouldn't normally believe things of that nature but it happened to one of my own, so I am very curious as to what is going on around here."

Dianne got up and walked over to the window. It made her uncomfortable to think that they were being sought after. "This is hard to explain." She turned around. "One of the interns found a code in some data that we've been collecting. The nature of this data is astounding. An employee of the University alerted the press to this finding before we had a chance to document its authenticity. We were being hounded by the media so we decided to bring them up here until we could research it more fully and then make a public statement about our findings." Dianne took a very deep breath. "The young woman who made this discovery . . . is an Indigo."

Beverly spoke up for the first time and said, "The Indians call them Star Children."

Dianne's eyes brightened. "That's right! They are one in the same. Anyway, we need to verify our findings, and the little girl your son met has come to help us."

Beverly and Tom looked at each other. "We wanted to thank her," Beverly said. "Charlotte has been so sick. Thomas has taken her to so many specialists and none of them have been able to help her. They just knock her out with drugs so she can have some relief, but *that's* no way to live. She said that this little girl just put her hands on her and the pain went away. We're so grateful."

"She's taking a nap right now. Michael, will you go check on Sadie? Maybe she's awake." Michael went up the stairs.

"You could do us a huge favor though. Would you be willing to keep this a secret? We need a few days to read this data and get a statement prepared. The White House is waiting for our report."

Tom got up and said. "I'll do my best. The main road being out should help. I'll instruct my officers not to give anyone directions up here."

"Neither will I, your secret's safe with us. We will call the kids and tell them to keep this under their hats for a few days. I know Charlotte wants to shout from the roof tops, but we'll hold er' back." Beverly said with a soft smile.

Then Michael came down the stairs carrying a sleepy bundle. Sadie was awake but unwilling to walk.

Michael put her down next to Dianne. "Come here sweetie." Dianne said softly. "This is Miss Beverly and Sheriff Tom. They wanted to thank you for helping their daughter-in-law. Remember that nice lady in the truck this afternoon?"

Sadie nodded her head. With hat in hand, Tom got down on one knee and looked Sadie in the eye. "Thank you darlin', that was a very nice thing you did today."

Sadie looked straight at him and said; "You want me to fix your ear?" He cocked his head in disbelief. She vigorously rubbed her little hands together and then placed her tiny hand over his left ear.

He hadn't mentioned to anyone, not even his wife that he had woken up with an earache that morning. With a tear in his eye he stood up. "Holy Mary Mother of God," he said. "My ear just popped . . . and feels fine now." He stood up with his hand covering his ear. Beverly smiled at him.

"We will do everything in our power to keep you all safe. If you need anything at all you just call. I can be reached at the Diner and Tom here can be reached anytime day or night just tell the dispatch who you are. We will leave instructions that you are special guests and that you are not to be disturbed."

"Thank you," Dianne said. They all walked out on the front porch and waved as the Sheriff and his wife drove away.

Chapter 8

It was still early afternoon when Jessica said "I'm gonna make some chili. I was chilled to the bone last night. I need somethin' to warm me up. Anybody wanna help?"

Claire stood up out of her rocker. "I'll give you a hand. I'd like to know what's so special about 'Texas' chili. Besides, we do need something to warm us up tonight. Maybe we can have a *fire*." She threw a look to the boys who were still playing around on their guitars.

"I'm going to check on Sadie, I'll be there in a minute," said Dianne.

There was plenty of food in the house. If they got stranded they could survive comfortably for a month. Claire was under orders to chop the onions and peppers while Jessica seasoned the meat. Michael bought only ground turkey, but they figured with all the spices nobody could tell. When Dianne came down she asked what she could do. Jessica put her to work grating three types of cheese.

Then Jessica asked "Are you going to tell us what the Sheriff was doing here today?" Both girls looked in her direction.

"*Alllll will be reveeeealed at dinner tonight.*" She said in her best Dracula voice, and then with a chuckle she continued. "When Dr. Sullivan gets here. She'll have news for us as well and then we'll tell you everything we know. I promise."

Claire stopped what she was doing and said; "Can you at least tell us if Sadie is okay? She's been sleeping a lot since she got here."

"I just checked on her. She is awake and she's with Dove. It looked like maybe Dove was sleeping. Sadie was stroking her hair. I didn't want to intrude so I left them alone. That is a very special little girl. Claire, what were you like when you were that age? Did you know how special you were?"

"I knew how special we *all* were. I could always see the potential in others, but I could also see the fear that kept *them* from seeing it. I realized when I was very young to keep things to myself. It frightened people when I told them what was coming. There were a lot of religious people in our little town who thought I was a witch and wouldn't let their children play with me. It was the Indians who lived nearby who understood me. In their culture it is a gift to see beyond the now." Then she sighed and became sad. "I wish I had the gift of healing like Sadie does. Maybe she can help my mom. When I called home last night, I found out my mother has breast cancer." Claire's eyes were already tearing from cutting the onions. She went to the sink and washed her hands. Looking out the window she said. "I didn't see it. When I left, I didn't know she was sick. What kind of clairvoyant am I anyway?" She left the kitchen on that note.

Dr. Sullivan arrived with more groceries just in time for dinner. The interns greeted her on the drive and cheered over potato chips and soda. They were so happy to see something with real sugar in it!

"Candy! We love you!" Nate yelled as he ran up the steps waving a big yellow bag over his head.

"My goodness, what a welcome." Dr. Sullivan said as she was handing out bags to waiting arms.

"You would have thought we were starving them," said Dianne as they walked up the steps. "How was your drive?"

Arlene sighed, "Pleasant. It's so beautiful up here. You can really breathe." She inhaled deeply and exhaled smiling. "I've got some good news and some not so good news. It will hold til we get everyone together. Let's eat first, I'm starving."

The big table in the dining room was the only space they could all gather for a meal. The noise level rose as each one came in to find their place, but a hush came over the room as Dove entered carrying Sadie. Dove's entire appearance had changed. Her face was relaxed, revealing her flawless Asian features. There was a softness that had not been present before and the look of distain was gone from her expression. She placed Sadie in an empty chair before slowly seating herself. Looking up with a soft smile she said, "Ummm, smells good." No one dared break the spell.

They laughed and talked and teased each other. Everyone complimented Jessica on her chili, but teased that they would be regretting it later. With their bellies full, the talking subsided.

Finally Dr. Sullivan sat forward, "I know everyone is anxious for news. I have good news and what you may think is not so good news. I understand there has been some excitement here as well and I am very curious to hear from Dr. Vaughn. So, the good news is that Washington is willing to allocate funds to get the data processed as soon as possible. They are very anxious to know the content of these messages. The not so good news is that we have one month. That's thirty days to decode four decades worth of data." She looked around the table. "They want guarantees that there will be no more leaks to the media. I have assured them that we can handle our own security and that we have already taken measures to make sure that nothing further gets out before we release it. This has become a matter of national security."

Unexpectedly Dove said, "We can do it." Jaws dropped open. The others sat frozen, eyes wide, wondering who this strange new creature was. Dove looked around at all of them smiling. "We can! Claire, you said there were others who were willing to help. Sadie can help you find more!"

Then Dr. Sullivan spoke up. "Now you have to get me up to speed. I want to hear all about how this little angel ended up with this motley crew." She nodded and smiled at Sadie.

For the next half hour Dr. Vaughn told the story of how she had found Sadie in Chinatown. She recounted how she had saved them from the falling rocks and about her healing Charlotte and the Sheriff. "Thanks to Sadie, I really believe they can be trusted to keep our secret and I feel sure the Sheriff will help us out in any way he can."

With dinner out of the way and the kitchen cleaned up, the whole crew made their way to the front porch. The stars were spectacular so high in the mountains. Christopher and Nathan picked quietly on their guitars.

They were all gazing at the sky when Sadie said in her tiny voice. "They heard uth and they want to help."

Dove put her arms around Sadie's shoulders. What do they want to help us do?"

Sadie looked up at her and said, "They want to help uth thurvive."

☯☯☯☯☯☯☯

It took a few days to gather the needed equipment and get everyone in place, but now they were ready to get down to business. Jessica and Dove went to wake up Claire. "C'mon sleepy head get up, we've got work to do!"

When they got downstairs the boys had already transformed the dining room into an office. There were four laptop computers set up, two with wireless internet access. A printer was set on top of an end table that had been moved from the living room. Lamps were placed to give plenty of light where needed, and boxes of data were placed at one end of the room on a long table so it could be organized by date.

Claire cocked her head when she saw the copper wire grid lining the room. "What in the world is this for?"

Jessica ran her fingers along the smooth wire. "Security."

Nathan popped his head up from under a make shift desk. "By now, they've figured out that all of our cell phones are still back in Berkley. I've made it virtually impossible for their hackers to trace us by computer, so now we just have to guard ourselves against spy satellites." Even though he was certain he had taken every precaution, he also knew without question that someone, most likely from the NSA, was working just a hard to find them. He smiled. "This copper wire acts like an invisibility cloak."

"Oh . . . is that really necessary? Why would we have to protect ourselves from our own government?"

Everyone froze in amazement at her naivety. Jessica giggled. "Did you just fall off the pumpkin wagon? I know y'all don't have TV's back in Ohio, but surely you've heard of Roswell." Claire didn't respond. "Chemtrails? The Illuminati? The Bohemian Grove?"

At that moment Sadie burst into the room giggling. She was running around with a miniature tape recorder in her hand. "Lithen to thith!" She pressed a button and her tiny voice was heard singing 'Itsthy bitsthy sthpider', she squealed with delight.

"Good morning," Arlene said as she gracefully descended the stairs. "My goodness we are organized. Has anyone made coffee yet?"

Jessica pointed to her cup and said, "Help yourself."

The front door opened. Dianne and Michael had been out running. "Is everybody up? Gosh you guys did a great job. Nateman, are we online?"

Nateman saluted Dr. Vaughn and said; "Mission accomplished `mam."

Dianne smiled back; "Good job sir! It looks like we're in business. We'll get started after breakfast."

Michael said; "We need brain food! I'll make protein shakes!" Everyone froze. His offer was met with dead silence.

"Can I have chocolate syrup in mine?" Nateman said, as he popped his head up from under the table.

"I'll fix my own breakfast." Michael muttered to himself. "Get your sugar fix, see if I care."

Claire put her hand on Jessica's arm. "I want to talk more about this conspiracy stuff later, okay?"

"Yeah, we'll talk later. Sorry about the pumpkin reference." Jessica said apologetically.

The teams were established. Christopher and Nathan were in charge of security as well as sending data and receiving translations from the satellite SETI offices around the world.

Claire and Jessica were Team Two. As Claire read the data into a voice activated tape recorder, Jessica transcribed the information onto one of the off line computers.

Dove and Sadie made up the last team. The two were now inseparable. They settled into the corner of the room. Sadie was quietly speaking into her recorder as Dove typed away.

By noon they had already discovered that many of the messages had been repeated over and over through the years. By late afternoon, it became apparent that the Beings sending the messages had been trying to make contact as early as the 1930's.

At dinner that evening, they gathered to share information of interest. Arlene, Dianne and Michael were very anxious for their news.

The first to give their report was Christopher and Nathan. They had received confirmation that volunteers were already beginning their work at the following locations:

Arizona Radio Observatory, University of Arizona

Park Wild Observatory, Narrabri Australia

Caltech Sub Millimetre Observatory, Mauna Kea Hawaii

Dominion Radio Astrophysical Observatory, Canada

Green Bank Observatory, West Virginia

Hartebeesthoek Observatory, South Africa

Hat Creek, California

Nuffield Radio Astronomy Lab., Cheshire UK

Max-Planck-Institute fur Radioastronomie, Bonn Germany

Molonglo Observatory, Canberra Australia

Mount Pleasant Radio Observatory, Tasmania

Westerbork, Holland

When they were finished with their presentation, everyone applauded. The boy's got up and took their bows. After everybody settled down again Christopher said, "Claire, I don't know how you got everyone to respond so fast. I mean some of them *had* to travel great distances and not all of them are adults. Some of them *must* have had to get permission from their parents. How did you do it?"

Claire thought carefully for a moment before she responded. "First of all not everyone did respond or could. The opportunity to use your *gift* comes at least once in a lifetime, but usually many times. The ones who came forward have been waiting for just this opportunity to bring more light to the planet and to be of service. Fortunately, many who are still underage have parents who are probably Scouts."

"No offense Claire, but I'm not sure I'm really buying in to the whole *Indigo* thing. And is *Scout* just another word for Hippie?" Christopher said playfully, trying not to hurt her feelings.

Claire smiled at him. "No offense taken. Its okay, in fact it's more than okay. I don't like all the labeling myself. I think everyone is special and has come to this life with a purpose."

Humbly, Christopher asked; "Then what's mine? I mean how can we really know?"

"Just ask . . . set your ego and all your expectations aside, ask the question with a humble heart and then pay attention. The answer may come in the next song you hear, or it may be in the next article you read. Pay attention to everything. You will know when it is meant for you. Be careful not to judge the package it comes in. That's why people think their prayers are not being heard. Because the answers usually don't come in a form they expect."

Next Dove made her report. "First of all I would like to say that Sadie Moon is amazing. This is hardly first grade reading material. The data that we worked on were instructions for cleaning the planet . . . literally, cleaning it up. It talks about our ability to bless water to make it clean again."

Dr. Sullivan spoke up. "That's what Dr. Emoto's research is all about. Several years ago he discovered that when you bless water, play beautiful music near it, or just thank it, the molecular structure changes. When frozen, the water turns into beautiful crystalline snowflakes. Likewise when you curse it or ignore it, the frozen image becomes distorted and ugly. His research is really fascinating. He's proving that water is intelligent."

Dove nodding her head said. "Yes, he's mentioned by name. We are instructed to use this wisdom to clean up our waterways and also to make our bodies healthier. They tell us that we can literally drink to our health." Sadie then raised her hand like she was in school.

"Yes Sadie," Dr. Sullivan said.

"We are thupposed to thank our food too. It makth it good for uth."

"Do you mean thank God for our food?"

Sadie shook her head no. "The Guardianth thaid, *thank the food*."

There was silence, then a collective, "Who?"

Claire cleared her throat. "That was going to be part of *my* report. They call themselves The Guardians."

Dr. Vaughn said, "Wow, you've got to be kidding. They have a name?"

Claire took a deep breath. "Well, it looks to us that they are a collective unit of consciousness who . . . may have survived the death of their planet. I think they're quite ancient. It appears that they have mastered dimensional travel, using the astral body, thereby referring to themselves as *travelers*. Naturally, along with the advancement of travel without physical bodies, they also communicate telepathically." She looked around and saws disbelief in their eyes. "Really, if you think about it, we are only using 10% of our brains. What do you think the other 90% is for . . . a paper weight? Seriously, I think they simply dropped their bodies and left. I don't think they are disembodied spirits lost in the cosmos. The Guardians seem absolutely alive and perfectly happy." Claire smiled and drew a deep breath. "They first heard us when we started sending radio signals out over a hundred years ago. It's not clear yet when the Guardians began their communication with us. In fact they haven't given us much information about themselves at all. The Guardians say that we have all the knowledge and resources we need to have peace and live abundantly, we just aren't using them wisely."

Sadie couldn't contain herself another minute. "They heard uth cry for help. That'th why they're here."

Dr. Vaughn said, "These *Beings* are here?"

Sadie nodded her head. "They're everywhere, they're like Angelth."

Dr. Sullivan put her hand to her heart. "We can't say that." She shot a look at Dr. Vaughn. "Dianne, we're scientists! We *cannot* tell the President of the United States that we've been contacted by *traveling, Guardian Angels!*" Sadie just giggled and pretended to fly around the room.

There was a knock on the door . . . everyone jumped. Michael was the closest to the door and went over to open it. "Hi there!" he said with a tone of familiarity. He opened the door wide and stood aside. It was Beverly. She was carrying a heavy box.

"I hope I'm not interrupting anything. I thought you all might like some home cooked food."

Nathan was the first out of his chair and took the box from her hands. "Let me help you with that!"

Beverly laughed. "I've raised boys; I know how they like to eat."

Dianne and Arlene got up, temporarily forgetting their manners. "Please come in. Thank you for thinking of us." Arlene said and waved to her empty chair. "Won't you sit and visit awhile?"

Beverly noticed that she was breaking up some kind of meeting. "I didn't mean to intrude, can I see you two in the kitchen for a moment?" Everyone looked around at each other. Arlene and Dianne led the way to the kitchen.

As the women seated themselves around the kitchen table, Beverly looked back to make sure the others were out of earshot. Then leaning forward she began, "I thought you should know what's been happening around here. Tom would have stopped by himself but I asked if I could come instead." The two other women edged forward in their seats as well. "You all have stirred up the hornet's nest, that's for sure. We've had a lot of out-of-towners coming in to the Diner looking for you, reporters mostly. A few crack pots, UFO seekers and the like, but mostly reporters. The news has been thick with it. That Dr. Griffin is on every station you turn to. He doesn't seem to know much but is promising more information soon. It's been great for business but we're worried about you up here. Tom is afraid to put patrols out here because his deputies are being followed, so he's sending them to the other side of the county to throw them off the scent. I'm not sure how long we can keep you safe. Are you getting close to whatever it is you're working on?" She glanced toward the dining room, but decided not to ask about the copper wire.

Arlene and Dianne sat back and sighed in unison. Arlene was the first to speak, rubbing her forehead. "We have to make a report to Washington in three weeks." Then she looked at Dianne.

"We're making progress. I think it's safe to tell you that much." Dianne continued; "We are really grateful that you and Tom are doing what you can to help us. We had no idea that anyone would bother you. We're really sorry for all the trouble."

"Sorry! Oh heavens don't be sorry! This is the most excitement we've had around here in a long time! I'm havin' a ball! We both feel like we're in a spy novel." Beverly laughed. "Don't you worry about us. We love having the drama, especially in the off-season. Gosh, I usually have to hear about all the local gossip, which by the way is no more than who didn't speak to whom at the grocery and debates about the best cure for athlete's foot. You all have made my summer! We'll have something to talk about for years to come! Well I don't want to overstay my welcome. I can see you were in the middle of something." She said as she was getting up. "There are fresh pies just made this morning, and two loaves of honey bread. If there is anything you need, just give a yell. Oh, I almost forgot . . . we think the phones are bugged." She said with such delight. "If you need us, just call and identify yourself as Aunt Emily, you know Auntie Em from the Wizard of Oz." She threw her head back laughing. "This is so much fun!" The two doctors walked her out to her Jeep, thanking her for her kindness. The interns were all on the porch waving and saying "Thank you".

"I think we should tell them." Arlene whispered.

"I agree. I wonder if the Sheriff would be willing to temporarily close our section of the road with a few *rock slide* signs. I don't think anyone is staying above us."

"Good thinking Dianne."

Chapter 9

Dianne and Michael ran at least five miles every morning. Considering the terrain, five miles was adventurous even for seasoned runners. Mornings were chilly in the mountains even in June. This particular morning was really cold. They could see their breath. They were coming up over a ridge when they thought they heard someone call for help. The sound echoed around the rocks so it was difficult to determine which direction the call came from or from how far. They both stopped, panting. Dianne said she thought she heard something down below and Michael said it sounded like it was coming from above them so they tried to still themselves long enough to hear it again. Very faintly they heard; "Please help us." Now, they were sure of the direction and bounded down off the side of the road. That's when they saw the car.

Dangling from a broken Aspen tree was a yellow sports car. The tail lights were dim, but still visible. It was perched precariously above a deep ravine. The dense vegetation prevented them from seeing the bottom. Just below them was a rock ledge with two girls huddled together. When they saw Michael and Dianne peek over the edge they started to cry with relief.

"Oh God, Amanda you *did* hear someone! Help us, please help us." Then the girl broke into sobs. She was being held by the other who was trying to calm her down.

"Are you injured?" Michael yelled. The girl who was holding the other replied; "I don't think so. I think we're just bruised." The other girl was still crying tears of relief.

Michael turned to Dianne and said. "I think I can get down there and bring them up . . . look." Michael pointed to a place the girls couldn't see from their position. The remnants of an old rock slide cascaded down to the back side of the huge boulder.

"Be careful," she said quietly to him. "Girls? We think we see a way to get you up here. Just hang on a minute, Michael is going to try something." And with that Michael started toward the stone staircase. The girl who was crying had settled down but was still clutching the other one, probably for warmth as well as security.

Taking small steps, Michael bounced on each rock, making sure it was stable. He slowly made his way to the other side of the boulder, where the girls were huddled. From Dianne's vantage point she could see how close they were. Michael waved up to her.

"Okay girls, Michael is on the other side of the boulder. Can you climb over it? Shakily the girls stood up still holding on to each other. There wasn't much maneuvering room on the narrow ledge. They were fortunate that the upright boulder had a jagged surface, making easier footing for them.

"One at a time, try to climb up." Dianne called to them. The girl who had been crying went first at her companions' insistence. "There you go, good, just a little higher. Can you see him?" A very weak "Yes" waifed up to her. Michael was on the other side with arms outstretched.

"C'mon you can do it" He encouraged her. One leg over the top and then she fell into his arms.

"Good girl! Okay, one more to go." Dianne said, and with that the other girl started to climb. She climbed much faster than the first, anxious to get to safety. With both of them clinging to Michael they made their way to the top where Dianne stood blowing into her hands. She smiled at the two girls and said, "Twins."

They were identical. As dirty and scratched up as they were, it was still easy to tell they were twins. They all looked over the edge where the car still hung on the tree. Both of the girls were shivering with cold, but trembled harder at the sight of their car.

By the time they reached the cabin, Michael and Dianne had discovered that their names were Amanda and Katie McKee, and that the twins were from Los Angeles. Dianne thought it wise to get them warm and inside before any more questions were asked. The early crew was up, coffee was already brewing and breakfast was started.

The cabin smelled of a wood fire, coffee and bacon. The twins were brought in front of the fire, briefly introduced, and then the girls were instructed to get blankets and hot coffee for them. Sadie was the only one who ignored the order. She was fascinated by them. She kept looking back and forth between them, touching their faces. Dianne had gone upstairs to wake Dr. Sullivan. As they came down the stairs they could see Jessica and Dove firing off question after question. The twins did not *appear* to be in shock, but the doctors thought it prudent to give them some air.

"Thank you ladies, we can take it from here." Arlene had already been briefed so she wasn't surprised by the identical faces following her to the rocker. "Good morning, I am Dr. Arlene Sullivan. I'm not a medical doctor so we have called the Sheriff for you. Just in case you have injuries you are not aware of."

Both of the girls grinned at her over the rim of their cups. In unison they took a sip. Dianne cocked her head as though she was seeing double. Then she shook her head slightly with a grin. "How long were you on the ledge? Do you know?"

Amanda who seemed to be feeling better spoke up. "It was just getting dark. We were singing to a new CD, not paying close enough attention I guess. Before we knew it we were sliding off the edge of the road. It was sort of slow motion." The other twin retreated further into her blanket. "From the tree we landed in, we could see that rock ledge just outside Katie's door. It took us *hours* to get the courage to even *try* leaving the car. But the tree was creaking really badly so we knew we had to get out. We didn't think to take our jackets and then we were too afraid to go back for them. So we sat together on the ledge all night . . . freezing. It was almost light when we thought we heard someone coming. We had called out a few times during the night, but then we were scared that wolves or mountain lions would hear us, so then we just sat there, too chicken to move or make a sound."

"If you are from Los Angeles, may I ask what you were doing up here? It's pretty remote this time of year." Dianne was suspicious. The girls looked at each other and suddenly neither one of them felt like talking. "Do you have any friends for family up here that we can contact for you?" There was no response.

"What is it; some kind of secret mission?" Arlene said with her usual warmth.

Now Katie spoke. "We're . . . um . . . reporters and I think *you* are the ones we were looking for." This dazed both the doctors.

Michael had overheard the last comment and gulped audibly. "I just got off the phone with the Sheriff. He found the car and he's on his way." No more words were exchanged until he arrived. Everyone sat quietly sipping coffee . . . pondering their next move.

Sheriff Lawford finished his report and was being escorted back to his patrol car. "What are you going to do now?" He asked.

"We haven't had much time to think about it yet." Arlene said looking at Dianne. "I think we will offer them the story if they agree to stay here with us until we can make our report to the President. We can't keep them *captive*," she said with a grin eyeing the officer.

"No, of course not, but we have gone to a lot of trouble to keep you out of the public eye until you're ready to come out on your own. I know my wife was here yesterday to let you know how many people are trying to find you."

"That reminds me." Dianne had an idea. "We were wondering if you would consider closing off our section with a few *rock slide* signs."

The Sheriff scratched his head making his hat bob up and down. "Sounds reasonable enough. Nobody's stayin' up at the Summit House. That should take care of anyone just passin' by or . . . He smiled, "landing in one of your trees."

Dianne laughed. "Well they don't have a vehicle anymore and we took their cell phones, not that they would work up here anyway. I think we can trust them not to hike out. Besides, this story is worth waiting a few more days for. They will get an exclusive story in exchange for their cooperation."

"I just don't trust strangers, especially reporters. If you have any trouble, you just call us, here? Oh, I almost forgot. Some wild fires have flared up about twenty miles west, I'll keep you informed if they look like they're heading our way. Nothing to worry about, I just thought you should know."

They thanked the Sheriff and then he drove off in a cloud of dust.

Inside, the young women had warmed up and the shock of the accident had all but worn off. They were sitting with Claire and Jessica in the kitchen. The two doctors halted outside the kitchen, satisfied that the girls were only making small talk, they entered the room. Claire and Jessica looked up expecting to be asked to leave, but Dr. Sullivan gestured for them to stay put. Dianne sat up on the counter and Dr. Sullivan took her place at the head of the table.

~ - 111 - ~

Dr. Sullivan began. "First of all, we are very relieved that you two were not seriously injured. I'm sure you have family who would like to know that you are okay." The twins both nodded twice. "No doubt you would like to make a few calls." Again both nodded twice. "Do you have any idea what we are doing here?" Once again two nods, but this time they both started to grin. She got up and stood next to Dr. Vaughn. "We have dedicated our entire professional careers to space exploration. Dr. Vaughn was one of the scientists who helped develop the guidance system for the Hubble Space Telescope. Her credentials are impeccable. I joined SETI as a volunteer after I graduated from college in 1960. I went back to school for my Doctorate when my daughter Ashley was born and I've been working for them ever since. My point is that we are not tabloid UFO hunters." She folded her arms and continued. "As you already know we have discovered a code. In fact it was Claire who discovered it. The rest of us cannot see it. None of us can . . . except for Sadie Moon. We have enlisted the help of other gifted young people around the world to help us answer the questions we have been asking since the time of Galileo. Are we alone? Is anybody out there?" Her smile was warm and sincere. "And the answer is no and yes. They have heard us, and fortunately for us they are intelligent, and loving beyond our expectations."

Katie spoke up "Who are they? Where do they come from?"

"Not so fast." Dr. Vaughn said sliding down off the counter. "We know that this is the story of the century and that you two risked your lives for it. We are fairly certain that Washington will not want it to become public knowledge. In fact, unless things have drastically changed in Washington in the last few minutes, they will want to pretend that this is some kind of hoax.

"Well is it?" Amanda asked.

"We will let you decide that for yourselves. This story *wants* to be told and I honestly think you two were sent here to us." Dr. Vaughn crossed her arms and leaned back.

Claire nodded her head. "I knew when I woke up this morning, that someone was coming. Sadie came into my room and told me to make room for company." And then leaning forward she said, "She's kind of spooky that way."

"Can we call our Editor? He expects a call from us every day. We had to *beg* for this assignment. We've only been at the paper for six months and celebrity news is all they've let us cover so far. Katie really wants to be a meteorologist and a story like this would give both of us the credibility we need to advance."

Dianne responded; "After you break this story you should be able to get a job anywhere, doing whatever you want."

Getting back to business, Dr. Sullivan said, "We've been allowing the interns to make periodic phone calls to home, but we monitor the calls. We cannot take a chance of giving up information about our location or our progress. Not to sound dramatic, but it *is* a matter of national security. So you may make your call, but one of us will be with you. None of us, including me, has had a private conversation since we've been here. It is too tempting to let something slip. No email. No contact with the outside world. Do we have your word on this?" Now she was looking stern.

"Yes 'mam." They said together. They seemed like sweet girls and everyone in the room wanted to trust them.

"Claire and Jessica, will you show them where they will be staying? I'm sure they would like to get cleaned up."

As Claire and Jessica ascended the stairs Claire asked; "Can we go for a walk after we get the twins settled? I would really like to finish our conversation about your conspiracy theory."

"It's not *my* theory, but sure, let's get out of here for a while."

☯☯☯☯☯☯☯

Not wanting to stray too far from the cabin, Jessica and Claire walked a short distance down a trail and decided to settle in a small clearing of small boulders. "Tell me about the Chemtrails." Claire said, breaking the silence.

Jessica took a deep breath. "Well let's see, where do I begin? From my own investigations, I've found that our government has been conducting biological experiments on the civilian population without its knowledge as far back as the 1940's. They called 'em Vulnerability Tests. Back when they started, the scientists would fill light bulbs with pathogens and bacteria and then break 'em in busy subway stations. According to declassified military documents, they would calculate the effects, by the number of people reporting sudden illness in area hospitals." Jessica noticed the look of shock on Claire's face. "I know. I felt the same way. Unbelievable isn't it?" Claire just nodded. "That was just the beginning, it gets worse." She continued. "During the late forty's, they began above ground nuclear testing out in the western deserts. The fallout of those blasts made its way across the food belt, contaminating everything in its path. No one was safe from the effects from the testing. So in the last thirty years or so, the cancer rates of those poor souls has sky rocketed." Claire still sat silent. "So the Chemtrails began in earnest around the early to mid-1990's. We might be too young to remember what the sky used to look like, but we're not stupid enough to believe that they're natural. A contrail is a natural condensation trail that forms when moisture from hot jet engine exhaust momentarily condenses to ice crystals . . . usually above thirty-five thousand feet. They look like a comet tail behind a jet. But Chemtrails are sprayed at about twenty-two thousand feet and don't dissipate within the usual sixty seconds. They are laid, line after line, sometimes crossing to make giant X's. They hang in the sky for hours and when they join, they create artificial cloud cover."

"But why? What are they spraying?" Claire asked.

"The *why* I cannot answer. I have my theories, but I'll keep those to myself for now. *What* they're spraying, according to biologists are heavy metals like barium oxide, aluminum oxide, some pathogens have been found as well. What we *do* know is the effect. Acres and acres of Douglas firs are standing dead in the Appalachians and biologists are blaming it on heavy metals in the soil, delivered of course by way of rain. They're contaminating not just vegetation and soil, but sample tests on deer antlers are showing that the heavy metals are building up in the animal kingdom as well."

"What about us? We're animals too. Is it making people sick?" Claire said quietly.

"Asthma is up over 700% and lung cancer 1000%. The overall health of our nation is declining. But it's not just happening here. They're spraying all over the world! But nobody is looking up. Everyone is pretending that nothing is happening. No one will admit that anything is going on. Even though the planes have been identified as modified C-135 refueling jets, even though you can go to public military sites and view them, the official response of the government is: *We see nothing, those lines in the sky are natural, so ya'all go back to your TV's and drink some more fluoride water.*"

"Did you say fluoride?" Claire was confused. "I thought you said fluoride."

"Yep . . . I did say fluoride. I thought you were gettin' used to my accent. Am I sayin' it funny?" Jessica was trying very hard to speak slower.

"No, no, no, I just don't understand what you mean. The toothpaste stuff? What does fluoride have to do with anything?"

"Sodium Fluoride is a toxic waste by-product. Didn't you know that? Look it up in the dictionary. Its rat poison! We got the idea from the Germans and the Russians. The Nazi's used it in the concentration camps to keep folks from risin' up and fightin' back.

It makes people docile and stupid. You don't think they were concerned about their prisoners getting' cavities do you? Sodium Fluoride has been proven to cause bone cancer, kidney disease, hyperactivity and it changes our brain function. Why do think people are so upset about it being put into our drinkin' water? It's like a mass experiment."

Claire thought for a moment; "I've always lived on spring water from our well. I've never had to think about drinking contaminated water. And I've never used commercial toothpaste. My mother makes all of our soaps."

"That's probably why you're so smart. Darlin', you have lived a life that we thought died out decades ago. You are so lucky. That's what most of us are tryin' to get back to . . . a simpler life . . . ya know?" Jessica gave her a big smile.

"Is this part of the shadow government that the Guardians talk about?" Claire said looking into the sky.

"I think so. The Guardians want us to start thinking for ourselves again. They want us to stop sleepwalking through life. They point out that what we have been putting into our bodies is making us basically stupid and sick. And I don't think it's unintentional. People are easy to control when they're poor, sick and dumb."

"I'm finding this really hard to believe. Maybe I just don't *want* to believe it. It's too horrible and sadistic." Claire shook her head.

"Don't believe it! Don't believe anything you hear, unless you test it against your own truth first. What I told you is what *I* have discovered and researched. And these are *my* conclusions. The time has come for all of this to come out. I think that's what Washington is so worried about. They don't really want transparency. No matter what the talking heads say. They don't want people thinking for themselves. They want us to continue being distracted . . . by money, cell phones, video games, war, terrorists, unemployment, junk food, television and wanting more . . . oh . . . the pursuit of *more*."

Sadly, Claire said; "but I've always been such a patriot. I love this country. This is our home."

"Stars-n-stripes forever Darlin'! No one is more patriotic than me. As a Texan, we were so proud to have one of our own in the White House. But G.W. proved to be a real disappointment. Don't get me wrong, after 9/11 we needed a cowboy in charge to kick some ass. But when the evidence started to surface about the miraculous fall of buildin' seven, the absence of a plane at the crash site in Pennsylvania and at the Pentagon, the witnesses who saw little explosions moving down the towers like a controlled demolition. I had to admit, the official story was looking pretty fishy. Even amongst the theorists, I don't think the real truth has come out yet."

Claire shifted on her boulder. "I'm really happy that the Guardians addressed this. I feel better knowing that there really aren't any diabolical characters and that everyone on a soul level has agreed to play their part in creating the new Earth. Brother Bush & company were simply preparing us for the shift."

"Darlin' you might have a hard time sellin' that one to the people who've lost their loved ones, or the ones who lost their life savings in the stock market. I love this country too. I just think it's time we take it back. It's time for another revolution." Jessica smiled and stood. "C'mon we better get back before they send a posse after us."

Chapter 10

Claire couldn't sleep. She had been thinking of her mother. She thought that some hot chocolate would make her feel closer to home and went down to the kitchen. When she got downstairs she noticed she wasn't the only one with insomnia. The kitchen light was already on. Dr. Sullivan was deep in thought over a cup of tea. Her eyes were closed in contemplation.

"I hope I'm not disturbing you." Claire said quietly.

Startled, Dr. Sullivan jumped. "Oh my, what are you doing up at this hour? Couldn't sleep?"

"No. I thought some hot chocolate would help. Do you want some?

Dreamily, Dr. Sullivan answered. "That sounds wonderful. I haven't had hot chocolate in years." So Claire went about her preparations without further comment. "Claire? Did everything go okay today? Were the twins in the way?"

Without looking up from her task she said. "No. They were actually helpful. I just . . . um . . . I can't stop thinking about my mother. The data that we processed today was about physical healing. The Guardians told us that we have the ability to heal ourselves and that we've had this ability all along. He says that we have just forgotten this wisdom." Claire was stirring the milk.

"We do have the ability Claire. There are people here on earth right now who can heal in miraculous ways. Every culture has its healers and medicine people, but I am most familiar with energy medicine. I must have missed something. Is your mother ill?" Claire continued to stir in a trance like manner. The lump in her throat prevented her from answering right away. Dr. Sullivan got up and went to Claire. "Honey, I have been so preoccupied with our project . . . is there anything I can do?"

The tears were freely running down Claire's cheeks. She wiped her face and said. "My mother waited till I was in California to tell me that she has breast cancer. She knew I wouldn't leave her. I feel so helpless. I don't know what to do." She could no longer hold back the grief she had been trying to hide. She turned and went into the arms that were waiting for her. Dr. Sullivan held her tight and patted her head while she sobbed. Feeling a little better, she looked up at Dr. Sullivan and said, "Thanks" and then went back to stirring. Dr. Sullivan took two mugs down from the cupboard. Without a word they both sat at the table blowing on their hot chocolate.

"What exactly is energy healing? I've heard the term thrown around a lot."

Dr. Sullivan looked up and grinned. "Well, there are many techniques. The theory is to bring all the bodies . . . spiritual, mental, emotional and physical into balance. Acupuncture, Reiki, Chi Kung and Kriya Shakti are *ancient* practices. Dance therapy, music therapy, Tai Chi and even Fen shui are forms of energy healing. I'm certified as a Reconnection healer.

Claire looked at her in surprise. "You, a Healer?"

Dr. Sullivan nodded with a satisfied grin on her face. "I know, it sounds funny coming from a scientist. This was a tough concept for me. I had judged the mystic arts as airy, fairy drivel. However, that being said, I still had an open mind and was willing to look at the possibility that this beautiful universe had an intelligent design. I was in L.A. about ten years ago, visiting one of my friends from college. Long story short, she was attending a seminar that weekend with Dr. Eric Pearl. I had never heard of him so she filled me in on the details of how he had come to discover this frequency of 333 coming out of the healer's palms. Do you know what the Meridian lines are?" Claire nodded in recognition. "We have lost our connection with the power grid on the earth. We can use this frequency to connect with others. It's a hands off technique, where the healer acts as a conduit between the person and the energy source. What I discovered from practicing this technique were signals and sometimes symbols coming from the body, like a communication, giving me pictures of what was causing the problem. Our physical body is directly related to our emotional body." Claire sat forward at this. "Whenever we experience something physical, an illness or an accident, we need to understand the underlying issues around the manifestation. Nothing is accidental, nothing. There is a reason that the right foot is injured, opposed to the left or that it's the foot instead of the head! We have an intelligent body that is designed to tell us what's wrong in a metaphorical way, so that we can correct our thinking or our actions to restore balance to our body. As within, so without. Nothing happens *to* us, everything happens *through* us."

She could see confusion on Claire's face. "Let me put it another way. Everything in your life is an out-picturing of your thoughts. So the healing process must begin there. By taking drugs, you are only masking the symptoms. Eventually the same problem will out-picture again in another form. You cannot skip steps. Let me give you a quick example. I met a woman once at the observatory. She was visiting with one of the other scientists. She had a bad limp. I had an opportunity to speak to her and told her I thought I might be able to help her, and we set up a time to meet. Later, at the end of her session, I asked her if she had any issues with authority. She laughed and asked me why. I told her that when I had come to her feet, that the word *authority* kept flashing at me. She said that in her business she had to fight for the rights of her clients. She had to deal with political red tape on a daily basis and it frustrated her and kept her up at night. Then I asked her to close her eyes again and to dialogue with her feet asking them what she had done to make them manifest this condition. Then she began to laugh really hard. "I'm digging my heals in!" She exclaimed. "Wow, do you mean that I have this problem because I'm stubborn?"

Claire had hung on every word. "Metaphorically, what does breast cancer mean in the body?"

Dr. Sullivan knew she would ask this question. "It doesn't mean the same thing for everyone Claire. In general the breasts represent nurturing. Sometimes disease manifests over issues concerning a woman's relationship with their mother or their children. There are women who try to control or women who neglect or women who make themselves sick with worry. Many times the woman cannot nurture *herself*. The parts of the body affected by dis-ease or injury, give us clues not definitive answers in every situation."

Claire was feverishly thinking if her mother had ever mentioned losing a child and then she said. "What if you have a very *unusual* child and you constantly worry that she might be too different for the world?"

Dr. Sullivan frowned "Oh Claire, sweetie, this is not your fault. Life lessons are very personal. You are not powerful enough to give someone an illness. However it would go a long way to help her get well if you could let her know that you are happy. She just wants to know that you are happy and well. It's what every mother wants for her children."

Claire did not seem relieved by this. "But my name is being splashed all over the news! She must be worried sick about me." She slapped her hand over her mouth and then she whispered, "worried sick about me." Claire got up and refilled her mug. She offered more to Dr. Sullivan, who just shook her head no.

"So why are *you* up at three o'clock in the morning?" She said raising an eyebrow.

"Oh me, uh . . . well I've been thinking about our project. Over the last week, I've spoken to many of the SETI directors. They are very excited and cannot wait to find out whom and what has been sending us messages. But Washington is a horse of a different color. They may not want us to release this information to the public. Over the years, our government as well as many others has classified reliable reports of UFO activity and they have been openly hostile toward those who want to disclose this information. We have struggled to keep this work alive. Budget cuts have not only hampered efforts, but have crippled many programs that were making progress. The obstacles and difficulties that space research present have advanced our technologies in so many ways. If it weren't for the space program we probably wouldn't have cordless tools yet, but I'm afraid that Washington may not see our project as an advance."

Claire was indignant. "How could they *not* see this as advancement? We are documenting information that could lead us to become energy independent. This knowledge could lead to lasting peace among all the people of the world, and what about self-healing?" Even as she spoke, she realized how much the governments around the world have to gain from selling oil and medicine and war. She looked pleadingly across the table. "But Dr. Sullivan, we have to get this out! *We* are causing our weather to change. *We* are devastating our environment. The Aids epidemic is wiping out the continent of Africa! We're running out of accessible oil and we are losing plants and animals to extinction faster than we can count them." Claire gasped for breath.

"You're singing to the choir Little Sister," Dr. Sullivan said with a grin. "I know the future looks dim at times, but don't despair. The Guardians talk about the human race with such optimism. We are capable of doing great things. Truly, I think we needed to get to this point in order to turn it around. As long as things aren't too bad, people will continue to be complacent. Look how quickly green technologies bloomed after the movie *The Inconvenient Truth*. Al Gore got people thinking. Even if the scientific community is conflicted about the evidence, the message is clear. *We the people are affecting the health of our planet.* That's a pretty powerful insight. Now if we can just get the special interest groups and lobbyists in Washington to stop sabotaging out efforts . . ."

"So what can we do about Washington?" Claire said with a yawn.

"We can work on that tomorrow. Why don't you try and get some sleep?"

Claire got up, washed her cup and asked, "Are you going to bed?"

Dr. Sullivan was back to the thoughts that woke her up to begin with. "Not yet. I want to go over the data from yesterday. All of you have worked so hard and have gotten so much done. I am really proud of you. Thank you, Claire. This information wanted to be found . . . before it was too late to use it. There is a loving energy in it. Don't worry, we will find a way. And Claire, we will call your mother tomorrow."

Chapter 11

The early crew was busy in their routine. The coffee was brewing and the girls had decided to make blueberry muffins and a fruit salad for a change of pace. Michael had come in from his run, followed by his new companions, Amanda and Katie. They were in high spirits.

"Can we help with anything?" said Amanda still a little out of breath.

"Oh, strawberries!" Katie exclaimed and snatched a freshly washed strawberry from Sadie's bowl. Sadie growled like a dog protecting its food bowl. Katie pulled both of her hands back to her chest like she was afraid of being bitten. Sadie giggled and tried to look ferocious. With the two front teeth missing, she looked rather silly.

Everyone was in such a good mood. Michael sat on the counter and started to sort and clean the blueberries. "Are these organic?"

"I don't know, how can you tell?" Jessica questioned.

"Well, organics are labeled. Where's the package?" Michael picked up the cellophane. "*Certified Organic, No GMO's*; good. What about the strawberries?" He inspected the label on the basket. "Damn . . . see this is the problem. No labeling. There's no requirement to label genetically modified organisms or GMO's, so the consumer has no idea what they're eating. If I wanted to be a guinea pig . . ." Then he said under his breath. "This pisses me off!"

Michael what are you getting so angry about?" Jessica took the basket from him. "It *has* a label."

"Yes it tells us that the strawberries came from a farm in California, but it doesn't tell us if they're GMO's or not. Look at the size of them. They're huge! I doubt very much that their size is due to superior soil conditions" Michael made a face. "I don't want to eat a strawberry that has been crossed with a pig or anything else! I try to avoid pesticides and other toxins, no matter what the acceptable levels are. I do not like the idea of being a test subject!"

"What are you talking about?" I thought the Bio-tech companies were helping to feed the hungry. I thought that they were trying to find a way to stop the spraying of pesticides." Jessica crossed her arms in defense.

"By definition, every species is a closed gene pool. When you start splicing genes and cross plants with animals, you cannot predict the long range effect. They're playing genetic roulette. People are protesting all over Europe, burning genetically modified food crops and threatening to hold grocers accountable for the health threats they pose. We have all become test subjects without our consent. We have no idea what the ramifications will be to nature or to us. Worldwide, over fifty percent of the soybeans and a third of the corn has already been spliced with other life forms." Michael pulled up a chair and sat down. "Do you really want to know what's in your food?"

All eyes were on Michael. He had everyone's undivided attention. "Bread, popcorn, strawberries, potatoes, tomatoes, macaroni, tofu, chocolate, peanut butter, hard candy, butter, milk, ice cream . . ."

"Oh God, not ice cream!" Jessica said in jest. Smiling she said, "Sorry Michael, continue."

"Pancakes, pizza, cheese and the lists go on." Michael looked around at everyone. "The problem is that so many products contain chemicals and GMO's, or genetically modified organisms that it's nearly impossible to avoid them."

Claire went to the pantry and pulled out a bag of corn chips, a can of soup and a box of cookies. "Even though you're freaking me out and I may never eat again, show me what to look for."

Michael read the labels starting with the cookies. "Perfect, this is a good example. Monosodium glutamate . . . MSG is a proven addictive substance. It's sort of like nicotine for food. It is the stuff that enhances flavor so you eat more of it than you actually want. It's making America obese."

"But these are low calorie, fat free cookies. I buy them so I won't get fat! Jessica sucked in her stomach and stood up straight.

Michael looked at the label again and said, "You think you're making a healthy choice by cutting back on calories and fat, but you actually double your health risk. Aspartame is a nasty little neurotoxin, which can cause blindness, headaches and even convulsions. MSG and aspartame can cause brain lesions and the FDA is making it easier for food manufacturers to hide these ingredients. MSG is known by at least twelve different names, including *natural flavors*."

Jessica took the box of cookies from Michael and dropped them in the trash. "How can this happen in America? The FDA is supposed to protect us!"

"Don't get me started on the FDA . . . look, I'm sorry I brought this up." Michael got up and went back to sorting blueberries.

Sadie looked concerned. She held out her arms to Jessica, who obliged her with a hug. Michael knew he had rained on their happy morning. Trying to make up for it, he started to clown around with Sadie. "Oh, this one won't do." He popped the berry in his mouth. "No, this one is too small." He tossed the blueberry in the air and caught it on his tongue. "This one is too large." He said as he offered it to Sadie.

Jessica rounded on him and grabbed the basket. "Out!" She said pointing to the door.

He pretended to be completely wounded by this and sulked away sniffling. As he got to the back door he slowly turned around and gave them his best sad puppy look.

"Out!" She said again, barely able to keep a straight face.

Amanda and Katie both got to their feet intending to follow him.

"Stay!" Jessica said pointing to the seats they had just left, and both of the girls sat back down.

"Sorry we're late." Dr. Vaughn and Dove came into the kitchen. Dove walked over to Sadie and said "What are you making?"

"Fwoot salad!" She said pushing the air through the hole where her teeth used to be.

"Mmmmm I love fwoot salad." Dove answered playfully.

Dr. Vaughn seemed pleased that breakfast was underway. "You girls seem to have everything under control. Oooh, are we having muffins this morning?"

Sadie nodded her head exaggeratingly. Amanda and Katie were being quiet, not sure of why they had been *ordered* to stay.

"Girls, we need to have a family meeting this morning. Will you go and wake the rest? I'll take the muffins out when they're ready." She placed a hand on both of the twin's shoulders as to say 'you stay' and smiled as the other girls filed past them.

Dr. Vaughn made herself a cup of coffee and sat down across from the twins. "Before we meet with the others, I need for you to be *honest* with me." She looked each one of them straight in the eye. "Are you willing to help us?" Both of them nodded. "This story could make both of you very famous. It could also make both of you look like cheap tabloid reporters. I mean we aren't talking about three headed cats, but we are talking about admitting that we are not alone in the universe. This is going to turn religions from every corner of the world on their ear. Governments . . . and not just our own will wage war against us. Are you prepared for that?" This time they looked at each other.

Katie was the first speak. "When we left L.A. we were determined to find you and get this story. We agreed we would do *anything* to get it. We have been covering the celebrity news for Months now and we hate it. We want to prove that we were capable of covering serious news."

Then Amanda continued. "We had a feeling that this was not your usual UFO story. We thought *this time* it's for real. We decided on our way up here that *if* we found you and *if* it was on the level that we were going to write this story in a way that could open people's minds. We think it's wonderful that someone out there *cares* whether we survive or not."

Katie spoke again. "Do you remember the old black and white Twilight Zone show?" Dianne nodded. "There was one episode where aliens had landed on earth. They were solving the earth's hunger problem and started to feed everyone. They had a book and the scientists were busy trying to translate the alien alphabet. Well they started to shuttle people to their distant planet proclaiming it was some kind of paradise. The scientists had managed to translate the title of the book to read *How to Serve Man* and everybody thought they were wonderful to help mankind. So now more and more people are being shuttled off and finally one scientist decodes the alphabet. Just as all his friends are boarding the ship he comes running across the tarmac screaming, "It's a cookbook!"

Dr. Vaughn said, "I remember that one. Oh God, I haven't thought about that in years. Well, we'd better be on our toes, hmm?" She smiled at them. "Actually, this is exactly what I'm talking about. Ever since Roswell, the government has covered up all the evidence that could explain the nature of their existence. Secretly we've been reverse engineering extraterrestrial technology, building our own crafts and weapons systems. The saddest part is that we as Americans have portrayed them as hostile and something to be feared. Sightings, especially in South America are a common occurrence and for the most part, people have accepted them into their culture. While we were watching the tragic death of Anna Nicole Smith for the *third* week, *they* were watching a fleet of several hundred ships fly over Lima on live TV! Even in Europe, sightings are televised. We have an uphill battle ahead of us. Girls, I just don't want you to get hurt. The media is a powerful tool, controlled by powerful people. You know as well as I do that we're treading dangerous waters."

Amanda said, "We admit we had no idea *exactly* what we were getting into. Yesterday, when we were helping with the data . . . we were amazed, but some of this is not new."

"None of this is new! We already know this stuff. Well, not everyone and not all of it. That's the point. There are people on this earth right now who know this, or know part of it and then there are others who live it. I think the Guardians or whoever they are, just want us to share what we already know. Make it general knowledge. Knowledge is power. They want us to take back our personal power. I think that's why they don't tell us anything about themselves, because it's not about *them*. We need to figure out a way to keep the focus on the message, not the messengers. Of course we need to reveal what we have learned, but at the same time we want to avoid looking crazy."

With everyone assembled, the meeting began. Dr. Vaughn took the lead. "Good morning everyone, I understand some of you were up to all hours of the night." Claire looked over to Dr. Sullivan who was heavy lidded and letting the steam of her coffee rise over her face. "We only have fourteen days left before we have to present our report to the White House. I want to make sure that our partners across the country and around the world understand our position perfectly clear. We realize that all of the data cannot be analyzed in time, but we are getting a very clear picture of the Guardian's intent."

Sadie was sitting on Dove's lap, anxious to speak. "They don't want uth to do it." She said. All eyes shot to Sadie.

Claire said, "Are you getting this message too?" She already knew the answer to her question, but felt the need to say it out loud for the benefit of the others in the room.

Sadie nodded her head. The eyes were now on Claire. She looked around at everyone and said. "This is hard to explain. Sadie and I are feeling a *resistance.*" Sadie was nodding harder. "Yesterday when we were translating, Sadie and I both were feeling rather than hearing; *don't tell THEM.* I disregarded it for a while until Sadie confirmed that she was getting the same message. I know I should have said something but I didn't think we had a choice in the matter."

Jessica screwed up her face and sat at the edge of the couch. "I'm not following ya'all. Who is *THEM?*"

"The White House," Claire said in a low voice. "This message is for *us*, it's for all of us. It includes the small them, but not the big THEM. I think the Guardians know that if we give this report to *any* government, they will try to keep it from the big *us*. They have too much to lose, and oddly enough everything to gain."

Dr. Sullivan spoke for the first time since coming downstairs. Not fully awake yet, her voice croaked, "Well said." Then she cleared her throat and continued. "We all have a great deal to gain from this message. But how many organizations, not just governments, would dissolve if these new ideas actually caught on? Think about it for a moment. What would happen to Greenpeace if we actually respected our environment? What would happen to the Red Cross, Feed the Children, The Aids Foundation or Save the Whales if we actually heeded this message? Back in the sixties we used to say; *what if we had a war and nobody came?*' Then what? The ramifications of this message are far reaching and we want to be responsible about how we go about releasing it. But release it we must. It's too late to put the lid back on *this* can of worms."

Dove rocked forward with Sadie still wiggling on her lap. "I never even gave that a thought. Wow, I mean there are people who have worked so hard to help the less fortunate. What would they do if nobody needed them?"

Dr. Sullivan sighed and said, "That's not to say that if you asked these same people, *would you put an end to their suffering,* they would *all* say yes without hesitation, but if there was actually a sudden end to suffering, many of them would be lost. Helping the needy has given them purpose in life."

Claire went to the kitchen and brought out a fresh pot of coffee and proceeded to refill the empty mugs around the room. The room was quiet with everyone in deep thought.

"We need a plan, we need to think of a way to bring this valuable message to all the people it was intended to help . . . thank you." Katie said as Claire refilled her mug. "I wasn't kidding in the kitchen. We need someone who is taken seriously in the media or entertainment business. We have no guarantees that our paper will even run the story or give it to our television affiliates."

Dr. Vaughn agreed. "We need to get this into hands that won't be daunted by public opinion or a media blitz. The key is to do it without getting in trouble."

"We could arrange for someone to steal it from us." Nateman who had been quiet all morning was getting into the spirit of the conversation. "I mean really, what *could* Washington do if it *leaked* out?" He said naively. Shivers ran down the spines of those who knew that the consequences would be severe.

Chapter 12

Dr. Sullivan got up and went to the window. "Looks pretty hazy this morning." The smell of smoke was so heavy that they were becoming concerned. They had contacted the Sheriff's Office and were told that the winds had just shifted, blowing the smoke in their direction. They were assured that they were still at a safe distance and that someone would contact them if they needed to evacuate. They had gotten used to fresh mountain air coming in through the open windows, but now the cabin had to be closed up in an attempt to keep the smoke out. Central air had never been installed in the old cabin, so without air circulating, *everything* smelled of charred forest.

The dining room was buzzing with activity. Nateman and Christopher were busy updating and downloading information from around the world. Sadie and Dove worked quietly at the card table. Claire and Jessica had decided the floor was more comfortable, and the twins were sorting the documents by date and topic on top of the big table.

The two doctors walked in and looked pleased. Dr. Vaughn was the first to speak. "You guys are really amazing! You look so organized." She walked around the table with an approving nod at the neat stacks of paper.

Dr. Sullivan said "How would you like an opportunity to demonstrate what we've learned so far?"

Claire popped her head up. "What did you have in mind?"

"Well there's a town meeting tonight down at the Diner. They are going to be discussing the wild fires and make evacuation plans," she said, looking around at everyone.

Jessica popped up next to Claire, "I thought we were hiding. How can we go?"

Dr. Vaughn answered. "It seems the smoke has chased *most* of the reporters away." She shot a look at Amanda and Katie, who both shrugged their shoulders and smiled. "Miss Beverly deserves the Academy Award for her acting skills. She has managed to tell tales of strangers passing through giving bogus directions to fictional places with such conviction that most have tipped her generously and been on their way. We really owe her one."

"That's why we decided we should get involved. The people of Eagles Ridge stand to lose everything if the fire makes it this far. So we thought that it was time to see if these directions from the Guardians are worth their salt." Dr. Sullivan folded her arms. "Besides you've earned your shore leave. You've worked so diligently."

Nathan and Christopher chimed in. "Is Miss Beverly cooking?"

Dr. Vaughn laughed. "She's already started." The boys high-fived each other.

Everyone was showered and dressed. Michael was taking as many people as he could in the van. Dr. Sullivan had her car as well, so they loaded up and headed down the mountain.

When they arrived at the diner, they were surprised by the number of cars in the parking lot. Granted, they had not had the opportunity to tour the mountain or the beautiful valleys that surrounded it, so they had no idea how many families lived there full time.

As they walked through the door, they were immediately greeted by Charlotte. "I'm so glad you made it! Miss Beverly has been cooking all day! She said the boys would be hungry so she's been making cobblers, casseroles and enough BBQ for a small army!"

She wrinkled her nose at the smoke that followed them in the door "Whew, I hate that smell. It scares me that it's so close."

Just then her husband Thomas came up and introduced himself to the ones he hadn't met yet. It was obvious he was trying to make his way to Sadie who was being carried by Dove. "Hi Sweetheart, do you remember me?" He said hopefully.

Charlotte glided to his side. "Hi Sadie," she said adoringly.

Sadie just said, "How'th your head?"

"Just fine, I haven't had a headache since you helped me." Charlotte stroked her hair. "Is this your mommy?"

Sadie giggled, and said, "no, not yet." Dove looked a little shocked. She had never asked Sadie about her parents and now that she thought about it, she couldn't remember anyone talking about them either.

Beverly was waving at them from the other end of the room. All of the tables had been rearranged with extras brought in to accommodate the crowd. Sheriff Tom had made his way to greet them. "You had better get a plate before she has a fit. She thinks you all are starving to death up there in that cabin."

So the whole crew made their way through the food line and found a table at the front of the room that had been reserved just for them. It was marked with a handwritten sign that said SETI TEAM. Dr. Sullivan frowned at this. The Sheriff saw her concern. "You said you needed *all of us* to make this work. So we might as well trust them. I've got patrols set up to keep unwanted visitors from showing up unannounced."

Dr. Sullivan wasn't sure exactly how they were going to conduct this experiment without the participant's knowledge and now it was no longer going to be an issue.

The food was superb. Beverly and her staff had really out done themselves. When everyone was getting their coffee and cruising the desert table, Sheriff Tom got up on a crate and softly blew his police whistle. When that didn't work Jessica got up, put two fingers in her mouth and gave it a blow! Dr. Vaughn leaned into Dr. Sullivan and said, "I really need to learn how to do that." Both of them laughed.

Sheriff Tom nodded his thanks to Jessica and raised his arms to quiet the crowd. "Folks! Let's get this started. Everyone find a seat!" The room started to quiet down. "Thanks for coming tonight.

We really appreciate everyone coming out to support our community."

Someone in the back shouted, "We just came for the BBQ!" Everyone laughed.

"Well now that you're here, we could use your help. As I explained to you all when I asked you to come, we have some guests who have been staying up on the ridge. They are a team of scientists who have been working on a special project. Part of that project involves protecting us from the wild fires." There was murmuring in the crowd. Dr. Sullivan was shifting in her seat. She was nervous that the sheriff would forget the agreement they had made earlier in the day to share as little as possible with the public in order to maintain their anonymity. It was risky to come out in public but the fires were advancing on them fast. "Without further ado I want to introduce you to Dr. Arlene Sullivan and Dr. Dianne Vaughn." Applause and whistles hailed from the crowd.

Dr. Vaughn stood up, "Thank you, we are really glad to be here. As the Sheriff said, we are working on some experiments that could alter the way we experience future disasters. It occurred to us that this fire would be a perfect opportunity to try it on a large scale, but we need your help. Dr. Sullivan is going to explain how this works."

"Hello everyone, and thank you for having us. I also wanted to thank everyone who contributed to this fabulous feast. The food was divine." The room erupted in applause once again. "This experiment is quite simple really. It requires us to picture an alternate reality. We know that the fire service has predicted that thousands and possibly hundreds of thousands of acres will burn. And the weather service has given us no hope for rain or a change in wind direction. You can continue to talk about the fire, which, *if we are correct*, only serves to feed the fire and keep it going. *Or,* we can picture an alternate reality if you will, the rain which puts the fire out. We have evidence that this technique has already worked on the coast to push hurricanes back out to sea or to downgrade their severity. A few years ago, an experiment was conducted in our nation's capital. A group of people meditated on *peace,* and the result was a significant decrease in crime. It made national headlines."

Voices were heard saying, "That's crazy. That won't work."

She looked over the crowd and said, "It does sound crazy, but it's possible. Are you willing to risk your homes? Are you willing to lose everything you've worked for?" People were quieting down again. "It won't cost you anything. It is an experiment. We want to see if people can work together to create change. Can you work together to save your homes? Can you set aside a few minutes, the amount of time it took to eat your dinner, to preserve the beauty of this community? We aren't asking anyone to go out into the forest, or in anyway way delay your evacuation plans, if that becomes necessary. You can do this from the chair you sit in right now and you could potentially bring the soaking rain that will save Eagles Ridge. People were beginning to nod their heads. "We're going to ask little Sadie to come up here and lead this meditation. Are you ready sweetheart? Here is a child who believes in miracles. She doesn't know the meaning of the word *can't*. We must all remain *childlike* in our hearts and know that no-thing is *too good* to be true.

The crowd went dead silent as Sadie Moon was raised up on a table. She smiled her toothless smile and won the heart of every person in the room. "Now closthe your eyth and don't peek. Take a deep breath and blow thoftly out of your mouth. Jutht let go." She said, and everyone complied. Charlotte squeezed Thomas' hand. "Now picture in your mind, where you love to be when it rainth...thmell it. You know how it thmells when it first thtarts to rain. Lithen to it. Hear the thound it makth on the roof. In your mind watch the rain thtart to come down. Let it thprinkle at firth, then rain harder. You can have a little funder if you want. I'm not scared of funder." There was snickering in the crowd. Sadie continued. "Think about what you like to do when it rainth. I like to take a nap. I like to bundle up with a cool blanket and I like the thound it makth on the windowth...lithen. Just thtay there for a few minutes and enjoy the rain." For fifteen minutes, the only sound was that of distant crickets. "Okay, open your eyth!"

"Thank you Sadie." The room erupted with applause. Dr. Sullivan allowed the hoopla to die down before she spoke. "You see? It's a very simple process. There are three things you must do if this is going to work. One: don't talk about the fire getting closer. Avoid the word altogether if you can. Try replacing the word fire with the word rain. You can say, *the rain is getting closer*. There is a Universal Law that states: *what you put your attention on expands.* Two: do not fear the fire. There is another Universal Law that states: *you attract what you fear.* And three: do this rain meditation several times a day, if you can. Just close your eyes and remember Sadie's sweet little voice and picture the rain. Every time you catch yourself thinking about the fire, change your thought by putting on a movie such as *Singing in the Rain.* You can just let the movie run, even if no one sits to watch it. For now, avoid the temptation of wanting to keep abreast of the latest news. Our local stations are covering the fire news continuously. Inviting the news into your living room is just like inviting the *fire* into your living room." The fire department will not of course be discouraged from their duties. It is *their* job to watch the progress and keep the public informed. Trust them to keep you safe."

Dr. Vaughn stepped up on the crate next to Dr. Sullivan. "Our only wish is to be helpful. If prayer is more comfortable than meditation do that, but *know* that your prayer has been heard. A prayer of thanks for the rain that is coming is more powerful than asking for the rain you don't expect to get. Let me repeat that one more time . . . a prayer of thanks for the rain that is coming is more powerful than *begging* for the rain you don't expect to get. Gratitude is very powerful. So please, before you go to bed tonight, visualize the rain, soft at first, then steadier. Don't try to picture the *fire* going out. Let's not give the fire any more of our energy. I just want to say one more thing. Just so you know for *sure* that I'm completely crazy. I wouldn't want anyone to have any doubts in their mind when they go home tonight." The crowd laughed.

"Sometimes disasters happen because people long for that sense of community. There is nothing like a good ol' tornado or earthquake to bring people out of their own little world to help their neighbor. It has a way of bringing people together. Community is something most towns have lost. I am pleased to observe that it doesn't seem to be the case here. I am really impressed with the turnout. You all seem to care deeply about your community. I believe we *can* bring the rain and squelch *the thing we will not speak of.*" She caught herself before she said *fire.* People were looking around at each other and smiling and nodding their heads.

"I think that went pretty well don't you?" The sheriff said leaning into Dr. Sullivan.

Beverly had made her way from the back of the room and stepped up on the crate. "We've got plenty more coffee and Teresa is putting out more deserts. Help yourselves! She got a standing ovation and brushed it off like it was nothing. "Oh go on," she said waving a hand like she was shooing flies.

Charlotte and Thomas approached the table. Charlotte was looking around at everyone smiling. "I think they'll do it. That was brilliant to use Sadie Moon."

Dr. Sullivan was sitting back with a hot cup of coffee in her hand eyeing a piece of cake that had been placed in front of her. "We didn't plan that."

Dr. Vaughn said, "She's right. We had asked Claire to do it, but at the last moment we looked at each other and the next thing out of my mouth was . . . *we're going to ask Sadie to come up here* . . . so

I just went with it." She shrugged her shoulders and took a sip of her coffee.

The room was buzzing with talk of the idea of putting the fire out with rain. They could overhear various conversations speculating whether the same idea would work for other problems.

Dove was sitting with Sadie Moon on her lap. "Listen to everyone. They are really excited about this. A few people are over in the corner practicing their meditation. I heard one woman say that she had a sound machine she uses to sleep and it has a thunderstorm recording. She intends to use it to help her concentrate."

Then Christopher spoke up and said; "Yeah, but I heard this other guy say it was a load of crap. But, then he said he'd do it anyway, what the hell it couldn't hurt."

Sadie was rubbing her eyes. "He'll do it. They all will. They will think about it and jutht the thought will help. Dove, I'm thleepy can we go home now?"

Michael stood up "Me too Sadie. Who wants to ride with me?" The excitement of the evening was enough to keep them all up for a while, but the heavy food was winning and everyone was winding down.

"You all go back to the cabin. Dianne and I are going to stay for a while, just in case anyone has any questions." Dr. Sullivan was fighting back a yawn.

The rest of them got up, but Amanda and Katie looked at Dr. Sullivan and asked if they could stay. They wanted to talk to some of the locals, knowing that in a few days or so there would be a big story here.

❀❀❀❀❀❀❀

The smoke was too thick to go for a run, so Dianne and Michael put the coffee on and puttered around the kitchen. It was still dark.

"I dreamt about rain last night." Dianne said as she stared at the coffee maker willing it to brew faster.

"Me too." Michael said, "I was on a dive trip down in the Bahamas sitting on the beach watching a storm come in off the ocean. It was surreal and beautiful."

"After you left last night, a few of the neighbors sat down with me and Arlene. They are really nice folks up here. There was a woman named Teresa. She works at the Diner. Her husband is in Iraq with the National Guard. His tour of duty is almost over and she is worried sick that he won't make it back home. They have a young son named Miles and she wants him to grow up with a father. Her father was killed in Vietnam." She sighed and took two mugs from the cupboard.

"What do the Guardians have to say about war?" Michael sat down at the table and took a deep sip of the fresh brew.

"You know, surprisingly they do not judge our violent ways at all. They have said that if we value peace we can have it, and if we value harmony, it is within our power to have that too. They make the observation that we have abolished human sacrifice in most of our modern societies and yet we send our young men and women to their deaths by the thousands and call it war. We have just changed our words around. Instead of saying that *we* are sacrificing *them*, we say *they* are sacrificing for *us*."

"Wow, that gives me chills," Michael said before he took another long sip of coffee.

"The interesting thing about these Guardians is that they simply report their observation of us. They heard us cry for help and help is what they offer. I read a few pages that put it into perspective. "*If your intention is to live in a world of peace and abundance, then you're going the wrong way. You may want to travel north, but you are headed west. The paths will never cross. You cannot reach your destination by the current path you're on. You must change direction.*" Dianne took a sip of coffee and continued. "And then it ended on a cryptic note when they said; *if you insist upon the path of destruction you have chosen, you will get to where you are going. Veer only a degree and the destination will change.*" Dianne sat back and thought about it for a moment.

Michael responded. "It's true if you think about time as a vast ocean. Imagine setting a course for a long voyage and then a storm throws you off course by just a degree, it would be barely noticeable . . . until you missed the continent you were aiming for."

"This also ties neatly into their message of critical mass. Today people feel insignificant in the world. They don't believe they can make a difference. They don't realize how few it takes to tip the scales and change the course of history. In truth it takes only one . . . just one more person . . ." Dianne trailed off.

Claire came into the kitchen, sat down and yawned wide. "I had this dream that it was raining." Both Dianne and Michael laughed and then told her they did too. They sat and talked about organizing The Report and discussed how they were going to present it. It had already been decided that they would deliver it in person. Dr. Vaughn, Dr. Sullivan and Claire would be going to Washington. Meanwhile, Michael and some of the other SETI directors would organize the press release. No one had *officially* told them not to. They had decided to play ignorant with Washington. This was too important to be filed away with all the other National Treasures. The twins had been promised an exclusive interview for The Times, and it would all play out in the next seven days.

Chapter 13

"We leave at 9 am on Friday," Dr. Sullivan said as she unplugged the phone and put it back under lock and key in the file cabinet. "We can stop living like fugitives and join the world again." She sat back from the desk and looked at Claire.

"After all of this attention, will we ever be able to *just join the world* again?" Claire said with a look of sadness. "We both know that releasing this report is not the end, but only the beginning. I for one do not relish the idea of defending the message, or debating it. In truth, I'm afraid to. I'm already being portrayed as some kind of nut case. Why did this come to me? Why did this come to *us*?"

"I believe that on some level, this is what we came here to do Claire." Dr. Sullivan got up and sat next to Claire on the small sofa. "I don't think we came into this world to be spectators. It takes a great deal of courage to challenge long held beliefs." She paused. "They used to call us *heretics*."

"Dr. Sullivan, aren't you just a little scared?"

"Of course I am." She said patting Claire's leg. "By definition, to have "courage" does not mean that you are not afraid. To have courage means to do what you must in the face of fear." Dr. Sullivan got up and turned back to Claire. "What do you hope to accomplish by sharing this message. What would make this all worth it to you?"

Claire thought for a moment. "Well . . . I think that if people knew for a fact that we were not alone in the universe and that someone or something out there cares about us, that we might see ourselves for what we really are; the Brotherhood of Man. Just maybe we would realize that we are all in this together . . . and that we need each other. But I also think that if people wake up to the fact that we don't live in the world we think we do, it might piss some people off. I mean, I felt shocked by some of this stuff. It hurts to know how selfish and greedy our leaders have behaved."

"Well maybe they'll get pissed off enough to do something about it." Dr. Sullivan smiled.

Sadie came running in to the small room. "C'mon everybody's up! Let'th do it now."

"Okay Sweetheart, we're coming." Dr. Sullivan said as she was rising off of the sofa. She extended a hand to Claire. "Be brave. You are not alone in this, not by a long shot."

They all had agreed to do a group meditation. Pillows had been set in a circle on the floor. Candles had been placed in the middle of the circle and were lit. Claire and Sadie sat next to each other. Everyone else had found their place and was getting into a comfortable position. Dove was the only one who chose to lie on her back. The others had chosen to sit.

Dr. Sullivan, who was very limber, sat in the full lotus position and quietly said, "Claire will you lead us?"

Claire cleared her throat and began. "Take a deep breath. Concentrate on your breath as it fills your lungs. Breathe out through your nose and release the tension in your body. Begin with your head, then your neck. Feel the tension releasing. Now breathe

~ - 151 - ~

into your shoulders and relax them. Continue down your body, one part at a time." The only sound was that of synchronized breathing and Claire's soft voice guiding them through a rainy day. The candles wavered to and fro.

For thirty minutes they sat quietly. Sadie was gently moving as though she was in her favorite rocker. The others sat motionless. Claire picked up a tiny bell and rang it once. "The sky is clearing now. Look down in the valley and see that the sun is beginning to break through the clouds. A rainbow appears. Welcome back."

Slowly every one came back in to the present moment. Stretching and quietly moving from their positions. A dreamy pleasant look was on everyone's face.

"Wow that was cool." Yawned Nateman. "I've never meditated before. That felt really great."

Jessica was stretching and said "What a wonderful feeling. I could really hear the rain. I was so comfortable. I could have stayed there all day."

"Meditation is a wonderful gift to give yourself. Prayer is when you speak to the Divine. Meditation is when you listen. Neal Donald Walsh in his first book said, *if you don't go within, you go without.*" Claire spoke in the same quiet voice, not wanting to break the serenity of the moment.

No one seemed in a hurry to move. Christopher broke the silence. "Dr. Sullivan" How were we chosen?

She opened her eyes, but didn't speak right away.

Christopher sat forward. "I mean, we were all told that our chances would be slim and that budget cuts had nearly ended the Intern Program completely."

"Well Christopher, the truth is . . . my was-husband heads the selection committee, so I requested the crème de la crème. You are all brilliant in your own rights and you all have the potential for greatness in this field of research."

"Except for me," Dove said quietly.

Dr. Sullivan patted the floor, summoning Dove to come and sit next to her. "Don't say that, you are brilliant. You will find your path and your place in this world, even if it takes you in another direction."

Dove sat down next to her and relented to a hug. "I've never made my own choices. I don't know what I want or where I belong." Dove started to tear up. "You have protected me and kept my secret and I thank you, but I think it's time they know." Dove wiped a few tears away and cleared her throat. "I wasn't chosen for this Internship; my seat was bought and paid for." Sadie sat down next to Dove. "My father arranged it." She looked down and paused. "I've already apologized to Dr. Sullivan and Dr. Vaughn." Looking up she tried to continue, whispering "Sadie has me under her spell." And then the tears flowed unstoppable. Sadie stood and wrapped her little arms around Dove's neck.

Dr. Sullivan would never have divulged Dove's secret, but with only part of the confession out, she felt she had to clear the air. "Listen to me all of you." She said, as she addressed everyone in the room. "Not many people are aware that NASA and SETI have been at odds for years. The argument over disclosure has been a fierce one. NASA cannot continue its commitment to space exploration without the government's money. So in order to keep the space program in business, they have been forced to keep many of their discoveries a secret. On the other hand, SETI has only one purpose . . . to listen and to record the sound of life beyond our own.

"So this isn't the first time we've heard something?" Christopher asked.

"Oh no, far from it, we hear things all the time. Half the shooting stars you see at night are ships coming into our atmosphere." She took a deep breath. "I could get in a lot of trouble by telling you this. But, we already know that we are not alone. We've known for decades. But until we know who they are, where they come from, why they're here, or what they're saying, we are forbidden to disclose. This is the first time we've had the answer to all of those questions, and I think the world deserves to know it."

The room fell silent for a moment. "So . . . this is why SETI was cut off." Christopher said.

"Exactly. And why they want someone on the inside to keep an eye on us. NASA doesn't trust us. They want to be the first to disclose, *if* and when the government decides the time is right." Dr. Sullivan said with a sigh.

Nateman was excited by this revelation. "Then is it true that there are humanoid looking aliens already living here? What about underground and undersea bases? Is it true that they come here for water and other minerals?"

"Whoa Nathan, slow down!" She laughed. "There are some pretty interesting theories floating around out there. I'll admit some of the stories are very plausible. But I think it's wise to err on the side of caution. People claim to know a lot more than they can prove. The Guardians talk about our celestial family several times, but they don't give us any details about who they are or where they're from. Hopefully there's more information in the unprocessed data. And speaking of which, we really need to get back to work"

Chapter 14

With luggage loaded, Christopher and Nathan were bringing the final load, *The Report*. It was contained in two locked storage file boxes. "How are you guys going to get through the airport with these? They weigh a ton!" Nathan said as he huffed and strained to put his box in the trunk.

"You're going to have to check these." Christopher said heaving his box in the air. "They won't fit in the overhead." Then he coughed. "The smoke is getting worse. I hope you can find your way down the mountain."

Dr. Sullivan wrinkled her nose. "It is really bad this morning. Maybe our escorts will get lost in it." After a brief moment, they heard the sounds of cars moving in their direction from the gravel road below. "No such luck." She said with a grin and a shrug.

At the insistence of the Homeland Security Secretary, Dr. Sullivan finally gave up the location of the cabin so that the Secret Service could follow them to San Francisco. However she would not budge on the issue of a private plane. Dr. Sullivan insisted on a commercial flight.

Four black sedans pulled up to the front of the cabin adding a cloud of dust to the already smoky air. Nathan covered his face and wondered why they call themselves *secret*.

Everyone, except Sadie and the twins came out to say goodbye. No one could take their eyes off of the men in black who had gotten out of their cars and stood in position.

"I feel like I'm in a movie," said Jessica.

Sadie stood behind a curtain, peeking out. "They look like wobots." She said quietly.

Amanda and Katie nodded and smiled from the other side of the window. "We think they look like *wobots* too." Katie whispered.

Michael started the goodbyes. He hugged Dr. Vaughn. "Be careful. I don't like the looks of those guys. They give me the creeps." He hugged Claire as well and told her he wanted to hear all about The White House when she returned.

He started to approach Dr. Sullivan but stopped short. They had worked together for nearly six years and had always had a good relationship, but a professional one. She sensed his hesitation and stepped forward putting her arms around him. She whispered in his ear. "Remember what I told you. They know where you are now. Leave as soon as you can. Sheriff Tom will make sure you get to Hat Creek safely. We will contact you when it's okay to come out. Take care of everyone and thank you."

"God speed." Michael said as she turned away to hug the others.

They were still waving from the cabin porch as the caravan descended out of view, when they noticed something. No one said a word, they just listened and watched.

"Does anyone hear that?" Dove said as she took a step down. "Is that a rumble of thunder?"

"Probably another rock slide." Michael said slowly.

One by one, they stepped down and stood on the dirt drive. When the first drop hit, they looked at each other in disbelief.

"Rain?" said Jessica, "Oh my God it's rain!" The drops were big and made little dirt explosions when they hit the ground. The smoke had been so thick that they didn't notice the rain approaching. Now the smoke was sinking to the ground and disappearing in reverence to the power of the rain. No one cared that they were getting wet. They began to dance. They whooped and yelled and laughed and sang.

Michael dropped to his knees with his hands folded in prayer. "Thank you" he said as he started to cry.

The screen door flew open and Sadie jumped from the porch , right on of top of Michael, throwing her arms around his neck. "Wain!" She kissed his cheek and then shouted to the sky. "Thank you!"

"Oh my God, it worked." Amanda said in disbelief. She looked at her sister and began to laugh. "It worked!"

They all laughed and splashed as the rain fell harder. Yelling their thanks into the air and twirling around with joy.

Dr. Vaughn was nervous driving with two cars behind and two cars in front of her. "I thought I would feel like a diplomat being escorted by the Secret Service, but I have this creepy feeling that we're being led to the gallows."

Dr. Sullivan looked over at her and said, "I know what you mean. They wouldn't even look at us. What do they think we have here, a new weapon?"

"That's exactly what they think we have, a strategic weapon that will give them an advantage over the rest of the world." Claire said looking out the back window.

"I wish you were kidding," said Dr. Sullivan. "Did you see that . . . and that?" There was amazement in her voice. "There's another one!"

"Is *that* what I think it is?" Dr. Vaughn said, straining over the steering wheel. "Is it rain?"

Claire turned around and sat back with a smile on her face. She knew the answer had come. She knew now with certainty that the messages were intended for them.

☯☯☯☯☯☯☯

Thomas and Charlotte were bumping along the road with wipers on full blast. The rain was getting heavier. Rivers were being formed on the sides of the mountain roads. It was a gusher. They could barely make out the cabin as they pulled up. They were so happy they didn't care if they got wet. They both got out of the truck and strode to the front porch like it was a sunny day in spring. "Oh you're soaked! Let me get you some towels." Dove said, as she went inside." Sadie stayed on the porch. She had not gone inside since the rain began. All the others were packing and getting ready to move out.

"Nice weather we're havin'." Thomas said as he shook his head like a dog. "You look like a drowned rat yourself, little one." It was true. Sadie was soaked clear through. She was darting in and out of the rain, jumping off the steps into puddles, laughing and singing. Dove, who had become her self-appointed guardian, saw no harm in letting her have some fun in the water.

Charlotte was beginning to shiver when Dove came back out with the towels. "Thank you Dove," she said, wrapping herself in its warmth. "Do you need any help packing things up?"

"I think we're almost ready to go. Dr. Vaughn made arrangements for someone to come in and clean everything once we're gone. She wants us out of here as soon as possible."

Thomas was wrapping a towel around Sadie's shoulders. "My dad has arranged check points on the roads from here to our rendezvous point on highway 44. That's where you'll meet the SETI team from Hat Creek. They will take you to the Observatory from there. Charlotte and I would like to go that far with you at least."

Charlotte was drying Sadie's hair. "We are going to miss you so much. Thank you Sadie for everything." Sadie just grinned.

All of the computers had been backed up and packed. Copies of The Report had been divided for travel in two different vehicles just in case. They all felt like they were on an espionage mission. They had been given specific instructions on how to pack, who was to ride in which vehicles and what route they would need to take to insure they were not being followed. In spite of the joy from the rain, the team was now feeling the pressure of the move.

Christopher was finished with his part and had gone to see if Jessica needed any help.

"I hope they make it to the airport okay. Those dudes in black gave me the willies." Jessica said, as she was closing her suitcase.

Michael was on his rounds to make sure that everyone was on schedule. "We're pulling out in ten minutes." He announced as he went down the hallway popping his head in to each room.

With vehicles loaded, Jessica and Dove made one last check through the cabin that had become their home. "Well I guess that's it." Dove said with a tone of regret.

"I just can't believe we were here such a short time. So much has happened." Jessica said as she was straightening the couch pillows for the fourth time.

Out on the porch they watched as the rain poured off of the roof. "This is really something." Thomas said. "The folks in town are so grateful to you all. The next time we face a fire, we'll know what to do." Sadie walked over to Thomas and tugged on his shirt. "What is it sweetheart?" He said as he reached to pick her up.

"It'ths not justht for firesth." Sadie said putting her little hands on Thomas' face. "It can work for blithardsth and hurricanesth too. Thometimesth Mother Nature ith justht cleaning housthe and we get in the way. Stho don't be disthcouraged if you don't get the resultsth you want every time. Remember to usthe it when you thsee people in trouble too. When you thsee people hurting each other, picture them being happy. When you thsee someone who is homelesth, picture them in a big fluffy bed all clean and happy.

There is magic in this wisthdom. Thisth ith what is true for all of usth. Teach othersth to uthe thisth magic, sthpread thisth truth to everyone." Thomas was speechless. He felt as though he had just been spoken to by a wise old sage.

Chapter 15

As the convoy reached the airport entrance, the black sedans turned on their blue flashing lights and surrounded Dr. Sullivan's car. Once parked at the curb, agents poured from their vehicles encircling the women as they got out of the car.

Dr. Sullivan looked at the man approaching her and said. "We need to check in." Ignoring her words, they took her by each arm and began to walk toward the building. "Hey! Wait a minute!" She said in a frightened voice. As she looked back, Dianne and Claire were being pulled from the car. Another agent was loading the luggage onto a flatbed cart, while onlookers stared and whispered at the sight.

"No one would have even noticed us!" Arlene whispered to Dianne as they were hurried along. "Why did I agree to this?"

Dr. Vaughn was no happier. "I didn't think they gave you much choice."

"Well I could have thought of something, anything to avoid this sort of drama." She said glaring at the man walking close to her side.

They were approaching the security checkpoint. Six metal detectors and a large security force loomed ahead of them. As they approached the checkpoint the men in black moved in closer.

"What are you doing?" Dr. Sullivan said, as she tried in vain to release herself from their grip. The men were absolutely silent. They moved together as though rehearsed and escorted the women through the side of the checkpoint without stopping and without going through the metal detector. The women were beginning to look worried.

"This is not the way to our gate!" Dr. Vaughn said, sounding frightened.

Claire was trying very hard to focus. She was trying to see the truth of the situation, but it was difficult with all the noise and the crowds. "They're taking us on a chartered jet." Claire said when she was finally able to feel the truth. "We are in custody."

"We're what?" Both doctor's yelled at once.

"Are we in custody? There is no need for this. We *want* to go to Washington! We called *them*! Will one of you sons of bitches please answer me?" Dr. Sullivan was getting pissed, but no one would answer her; they only squeezed her arms tighter and moved more swiftly.

They were led through a door marked '*No Admittance- Authorized Personnel Only*'. "I had always wanted to see what was behind these doors, but now I think I'd rather not know." Dr. Vaughn said in a shaky voice.

They were led down four flights of stairs. As they approached the bottom, they could feel fresh air and hear the sounds coming from the tarmac. It was there at the bottom of the stairs that they finally came to a halt. The lead man spoke quietly into his cuff, turning his back so the women could not hear.

They stood there waiting, for what exactly, the women were not sure. A ground transport vehicle pulled up and stopped. The driver was no airport employee; behind the wheel was another man in black. This was making the women very nervous, especially when they were pushed inside the transport, forced to sit with a man on either side of them in separate rows. Even though no one could have helped them in the airport, there was some comfort in having witnesses around.

They drove away from the terminal, toward private hangers, where corporations and the very rich kept their jets. The doors to one of the larger hangers began to open and in they went, without hesitation. The women turned to look at each other with fear in their eyes.

It was dark inside and took a few moments for their eyes to adjust. The transport doors opened and the women were pulled from their seats. As Dr. Sullivan stepped out and onto the concrete floor, she exploded.

"What in the hell is going on around here! I demand to know why we have been treated like criminals! We have an appointment with the Defense Secretary, not the electric chair!" She was wildly looking around for someone in charge, but they all looked alike. "Who is responsible here?"

Only one of the men moved. He turned and spoke into his cuff again, then turned back around with arms to his sides. The other men stood completely silent.

For a moment the sound of silence was deafening, then the distant sound of a door opening. Footsteps echoed from an unseen passageway. Someone was approaching. At the far end of the hanger emerged the last person the women expected to see.

"Stewart; Oh my God, what are you doing here?" Dr. Sullivan was stunned.

"Dr. Griffin?" Claire shook her head in disbelief.

"You son of a bitch." Dr. Vaughn said through her teeth.

He was not being escorted, but was simply being followed by two more secret service personnel, one of them a woman.

"Good afternoon ladies, what a precious picture you all are. Confused?" He chuckled and smiled. "Let me enlighten you." He said with a sneer.

"What are you up to?" Dr. Sullivan was in no mood for games. "Stewart, what have you done?"

"Done? What have *I* done?" He chuckled, and then put his hand over his heart. "I've been a good citizen, loyal to my country. I've told the President himself that we must be very cautious with *any* information that we cannot verify the source of *and* that it would be irresponsible for any *serious* scientist to allow a group of children to interpret valuable data that could threaten national security." He was so smug that Dr. Sullivan came unglued.

"Why you sorry son of a pig!" She said as she lunged for him. He did not move a muscle as the security force seized her and forced her to the ground.

"Smile, you're on Candid Camera!" He said smiling at the video cameras pointing straight at them. "The President will be very impressed."

With her hands zip tied behind her back, Dr. Sullivan was pulled to her feet. Claire and Dr. Vaughn struggled to get to her side. "This is completely unnecessary." Dianne said pleadingly. "Please . . . please release her."

Claire summoned all the light she could before she spoke. "We will peacefully come to Washington with you to deliver The Report. We promise that we will not be any further trouble to you. We were not told of the change in plans, so we have been understandably confused and upset."

A strange calm came over the hanger. Just a moment before, there had been chaos. The head agent spoke into his cuff again and they started preparations for departure. Dr. Sullivan was released from her binds and led away from Dr. Griffin. All agreed that it was best if they did not have any further contact with each other for the remainder of the trip.

☯☯☯☯☯☯☯

As they drove along Eagle Lake, they could see the rain letting up. It had poured down rain for nearly six hours. For the first time they could see where the fire line had been. On the far side of the lake they could see the devastation. Sticks poked up from the mountain where stands of Aspens and majestic pines once stood tall, while steam rolled off the charred remains of the forest.

Michael and the boys were leading the way in the van. They looked out the windows toward the lake at what could have been truly disastrous for them. "You know the forests *need* fires." Michael said. "We used to think we knew better than Mother Nature so we began a hundred year campaign to put them out. As many as we could, we put them out. It was during the sixties that forest conservationists became aware that there were very few young lodge pole pines, which cover close to fifteen million acres in the west. In fact, the only seedlings they could find were in the re-growth areas where fires had occurred. What they discovered about the species is that they needed fire to propagate, and because we were putting out all the fires, we almost wiped them out. The other thing they didn't think about was the fuel left on the forest floors. When there are no fires, the underbrush is allowed to flourish choking out new trees and the old wood on the forest floor is allowed to build up. The result of *our* wisdom has been mega fires. There is so much fuel to burn that the fires get out of control, burning millions of acres instead of hundreds."

"We are brilliant, aren't we?" Christopher said looking out the window. "Did you know about Yellowstone? What they did to the wolves?"

"Tell us Grasshopper, what did they do to the wolves?" Nathan said in jest.

Christopher smiled at Nathan and continued. "Well apparently the ranchers around Yellowstone didn't get along very well with the local wolves, so they hunted them into extinction. They didn't just reduce their numbers, they wiped them out. Well, about fifty years go by and the herds of elk are topping over ten thousand head.

There are so many elk that they're starving, right? Meanwhile another group, probably biologists, is noticing that there are no elm trees less than fifty years old, right? They're looking for all kinds of reasons why they stopped propagating. Okay, back to the wolves. They realized that they *needed* the wolves to keep the elk herds in check, so they go to Canada and get wolves from two different provinces so they don't inbreed, and they reintroduce them to Yellowstone. The wolves do their job getting the elk under control and everybody is happy because they're *so* smart. What they didn't realize yet was that with the elk herd in check, the elm saplings had a chance to mature and so they solved two problems with one stroke. Luckily we sometimes get a chance to correct our mistakes."

"And sometimes not," Michael said. "We've got to get smarter about a lot of things, guys. I'm afraid we are making some mistakes that we may not have the chance to correct."

"Is it time for lunch?" Nateman said, eyeing the 'thank you' baskets of food from the townspeople that Miss Beverly had sent with them.

The girls' car was much less serious. The music was loud and the spirits were high.

☯☯☯☯☯☯☯

Once in the air, Claire tried to relax. The two doctors were huddled in conversation, no doubt worried about being in the hands of Dr. Griffin. The only way she could get word to anyone was telepathically. She pretended to sleep. It was difficult to concentrate because they were experiencing some turbulence. Bouncing around made her nervous. She needed to relax. Unlike a commercial plane there was plenty of room to stretch out. "David, please be there." She thought. Claire deepened her concentration and breathed deep. The lights…the strands…zoom… she was gone. Light rushed past her. Whispers passed too. She focused on David and only David.

"Aho mate!" She could see David's smile. "Where are you? I hear something odd. Are you flying?"

"Thank God it's you!" Claire sighed in relief. "David we're in trouble. We need your help." Claire explained what had happened after they left the cabin and asked him to call the Hat Creek facility to let the others know about Griffin and his plan to undermine the project.

David could sense the fear in her. "Claire, it's okay. Nothing has gone wrong. I know you didn't expect to see Dr. Griffin again so soon, but you are exactly where you belong. Who knows what fate awaited you on your scheduled flight. You know that if this story wants to be told that none of us are powerful enough to stop it. Mankind's desire to survive brought about this discovery and it will play out exactly as it needs to. *All* of us are just playing our parts, even Griffin."

Claire smiled knowing that David was right. "Thank you. I forget how it works sometimes. And before I forget, thank you again for all the long hours you must have put in to transcribe so much information for us."

"I had plenty of help."

"I thought you could only find two Indigos." Claire said.

"Yes, I only found two like *us*, but I was keeping a surprise for you. I can see you could use some good news right now so I'll let you in on a little secret. The Aborigine can see it too." David smiled.

"What? They can?" This news was so good it almost ran Claire off The Grid. "Tell me more!"

"Well I was getting depressed because I really wanted to help you out. I had gone to Sidney in search of *others* and found only two who could see the code. The amount of data that we had was overwhelming. After getting them settled in at the observatory, I went back home. The only reason I can give is that I heard my name and went back."

When David arrived back home he found some of his Aborigine friends waiting for him. A bit puzzled, he asked if they had called him. "You called for us mate," said Jacko. Jacko was David's best friend in Australia. They met in the wilderness in search of water about a year before. Jacko showed David how to use a dowsing rod to find water and the two became fast friends.

David smiled to himself knowing now what he had suspected all along; the Aborigine people were Indigo too. Knowing that they were shy people who don't like being in public places, he wondered how he was going to get them to the observatory. His mind raced. Should he try to set up a satellite lab in the Outback, or a field lab outside of the facility? He wasn't saying anything, just pacing back and forth inside his tiny abode when Jacko said, "We'll go with you, mate." David stopped in his tracks. The two men looked at each other and smiled. "We will go with you. We held Council last night and decided that we want to help your friends. We are packed and ready to go when you are."

David related this story to Claire along with their accounts at the Observatory. "People are just full of surprises, aren't they David?" Claire was smiling.

"Hey, why are you smiling?" said a distant, quiet voice.

Claire jumped! "Holy crap!" Claire sat up with a start.

"I'm sorry honey. I didn't mean to disturb you. Go back to sleep." Dr. Sullivan was going back to her seat when Claire finally regained her composure. It took a few minutes to clear her head when she snapped back from The Grid too quickly. She looked out the window and thought about what David had told her.

Claire had always suspected that Indigo's were much older than the experts thought. She could not imagine that she and the others were the first of their kind. Even in her parents, she could see that some humans are just more evolved than others. She leaned toward the window as the plane began its descent. She had never been to Washington. They were coming down through the clouds when the captain spoke. "Folks we're beginning our descent. We'll be landing in just a few minutes. Please make sure your seatbelts are fastened." Claire had never loosened hers. The turbulence had kept her glued to her seat through the whole flight.

Dr. Griffin was seated several rows behind them. Breaking his silence he said. "Ladies, I would really like to trust you. Do you think you can behave yourselves or will restraints be necessary?"

"Stewart you really are an asshole." Dr. Sullivan said, unwilling to contain herself. "Do you really think we would compromise the integrity of this material just to make you look bad, tempting as that is?" She just sat back and smiled to herself. She had no idea what was ahead, but she was certain Stewart Griffin would make a fool of himself and that thought alone gave her immense satisfaction.

Once on the ground the plane was escorted away from the terminal to a hanger at the far end of the small airport. The Presidential Seal split in two as the huge doors magically opened before them. Inside the hanger, arranged in a semi-circle, were six armored Hummers, and in front of the vehicles stood armed, uniformed servicemen.

"We must be pretty damn important." Dr. Vaughn mused. "Or they're scared shitless of us."

"What has he told them?" Claire murmured under her breath.

Stewart Griffin was standing in the aisle with his arms stretched forth as though he was gathering sheep. "Ladies, after you." The nuance of this gesture was not lost on the women. They all had the feeling that they were being let to slaughter.

Armed soldiers stood at the base of the stairs and as each woman reached the last step she was seized and ushered to one the vehicles.

"Hey! We want to stay together!" Dr. Sullivan protested, but to no avail. The women were placed in separate vehicles. Dr. Griffin was not without a huge grin as he stepped lightly into a Hummer of his own.

The trip to the capital was no longer than thirty minutes, but to the women, it seemed a very long way.

ΘΘΘΘΘΘΘ

The drive to the rendezvous point was beautiful, but uneventful. The deputies who had been placed at the check points followed in unmarked cars once the caravan had safely passed. The meeting point was a motel parking lot on the outskirts of Hat Creek.

Led by Thomas and Charlotte, the vehicles pulled to the rear of the building one by one. At the back entrance to the motel stood Dr. Cristy Merrill, ATA Project Leader and Director of the Center for SETI Research at Hat Creek. As the caravan came to a stop, Dr. Merrill stepped off the curb with a big grin. She clapped her hands in welcome.

The deputies were the first to get out of their cars. The others were instructed to stay where they were until the deputies had made sure the area was secure. After thoroughly checking I.D. badges, the deputies were convinced that Dr. Merrill was legit, and that they were now in safe hands. The officers gave them the 'all clear' signal to leave their vehicles.

"We are so excited and honored to have all of you at Hat Creek." Dr. Merrill began. "We want to get you to the facility as soon as possible, so once you've had a chance to use the restroom, or get something to drink, we would like to be on our way. The Sheriff has asked us to do what we could to insure that no one would know your location, so we've enlisted the help of some friends." Dr. Merrill pointed out a semi with a trailer at the end of the lot. "Your car and van will be loaded onto this trailer so that no one will see you pull up to the facility. I'm afraid the press has been hanging around, hoping that you would come to us. Then we will transport you in this." Now she was pointing to an old delivery truck. The logo had long faded out, too faint to be legible. "I assure you that your trip will be comfortable. We have modified the interior to accommodate passengers."

The group was ready in no time. The semi was loaded and already pulling out when they got their first look inside the delivery truck. On the outside it looked old and rusty. But the inside was renovated just for them. It was freshly painted. Bench car seats had been bolted to the floor. A monitor was set high on the wall behind the driver so the occupants of the cargo area could see not only where they were going but where they had been. It wasn't fancy but it was comfortable and functional.

Sadie Moon was the first inside. "I love what you've done with the plathe!" she said giggling. Dove was right behind her, ushering her to a seat that had a good view of the monitor. The others boarded and found their seats. All buckled in, Thomas and Charlotte stood at the back before the door was pulled shut.

"Take good care, we're really going to miss you," Charlotte said.

"Thanks for everything" said Thomas. "We will be anxiously waiting for news from you, so don't forget about us."

As the door lowered and locked, a light inside the compartment came on. A deputy rode up front with the driver who was head of security at Hat Creek. No chances were being taken with this precious cargo. Dr. Merrill and two staff members drove in her car back to the observatory.

With eyes fixed on the monitor, they passed the time with little conversation. Sadie had fallen asleep against Dove, when out of the blue Sadie sat straight up and said, "Uh oh".

"What is it?" Dove said brushing the hair out of her eyes. "What's wrong Sweetie, did you have a dream?"

"Not a dream. Claire and the Doctors are in twouble." Sadie was wide awake. She held up one finger as though she was listening to something. All eyes were on her. Everyone held their breath as moments passed.

"What is it?" Jessica couldn't wait. "Sadie, what did you see?"

"The fat guy, Griffin. He took `em and they're thcared."

"Griffin? Are you sure?" Jessica sounded panicked.

Sadie cocked her head and looked at her like, *me, sure? Of course I'm sure. Do you think I make this stuff up?*

Jessica looked at Michael and said, "What does he want Michael? What is he doing?" She knew that Michael was the only one who had worked with him and had any idea what he might be up to.

Chapter 16

Claire was trying not to look like a tourist, but she couldn't help herself. Her face was pressed against the tinted windows, trying to absorb as much of the capital as she could. What impressed her most so far was the change in the energy field. The mountains were serene. The energy felt like gentle music. Washington was at the opposite end of the scale. She was buzzing, and uncomfortable, aside from the fact she was being treated as a criminal.

The Pentagon was bigger than she had imagined. Pictures could do it no justice. She was intimidated by its sheer size. The Humvies aligned themselves in front of the south entrance. Armed military personnel greeted the convoy. One by one the drivers were given instructions to unlock and release their passengers. The three women remained separated by escorts. In a single file they entered the building. Once through security check points the women were taken to separate holding areas.

The rooms were obviously set up for interrogation. A two-way mirror that flanked one wall was the only break in the otherwise sterile grey windowless room. A single table in the center of the room was adorned only with a microphone and tape recorder. There was one chair on one side of a large rectangle table and two chairs directly opposite. The sides were beginning to look uneven already; obviously there was no place set for legal counsel to even out the sides. Two video cameras were set up on tripods in addition to the four security cameras set near the ceiling in each corner of the room. There was no way to even scratch your nose without six angles of the event being caught on tape.

The women were told to sit in the single chair at the table and wait for further instructions. At this point their escorts left them to their thoughts. Of course it did not go unnoticed by any of the women that all the cameras were already rolling.

Dr. Sullivan was the first to be interviewed. She sat up straight in her chair trying not to appear nervous, stoic in her posture. She felt intimidated by the cameras, but did not want her discomfort to be construed as guilt in any way. She was the picture of confidence.

Two women entered the room. The first was dressed in military uniform and from the metals on her breast, a decorated officer. She was tall, of medium build and appeared to be in her thirties. She had dark, short, spiked hair and wore red lipstick. She was good looking, but very serious. The doctor thought to herself, how pretty she would be if she cracked a smile on that serious face. The second appeared to be her aide, wearing a conservative navy suit; she was carrying a thick file and came prepared with pad and pencil. Next to the officer she appeared very small.

After they were seated, the first woman offered Dr. Sullivan something to drink and gestured for the file to be handed to her. The doctor requested some water. The officer just glanced back at the two-way mirror and gave a three finger wave and a moment later, the door opened to a young man in uniform with three bottles of water. The first woman never looked up from the file or even thanked the young man. He returned to his invisible post without a word.

A few minutes passed before she looked up and said; "I should probably introduce myself. My name is Captain Parker James. I've been assigned by the NSA to investigate your claim of a code you think you have discovered. We believe that this is a matter of national security and you will be remanded to our custody until we have had a chance to check all the facts and determine if this document has any merit. Do you understand?"

"No, I don't understand. Have I been arrested?" Dr. Sullivan asked as calmly as she was capable of, trying desperately not let her voice crack.

"No 'mam, you are being held for questioning. In light of the security threat that this information could pose, we must insist on the containment of you and your colleagues. We are also requesting a list of all persons involved, directly and indirectly. It is of national importance that we act swiftly on this matter."

"*This matter,*" she said with a note of defiance, "is a matter of *global* importance, Captain Parker . . . I'm sorry, Captain James." She said as she was trying to remain composed. "This *matter* is the most significant scientific discovery of the 21st century! We have been contacted by the most loving and gentle beings who have probably ever existed. They are trying to *help* us not *harm* us."

"Dr. Sullivan, with all due respect, it is still unclear to us the exact content or the intention of your findings. We have not determined if this report of yours is even real. For all we know it is a hoax. And, if it is not a hoax, we have a responsibility to the nation and to the world to ensure the safety of its people by examining the evidence and getting the top people in our division to advise us on how to manage this information *and* how to act upon it." With a deep breath the Captain continued. "Now we have a few questions that we need to ask to determine where we are and where we need to go from here. Are you willing to cooperate with us?"

"Of course Captain. I apologize for my outburst." She said as she sat forward leaning on the table. "I want you to understand that my colleagues and I were on our way here to meet with the Homeland Security Secretary when we were kidnapped without explanation. We have been through a frightening ordeal and we would appreciate some credit for volunteering this information and making it *and* ourselves available to you. Our team has worked endless hours to make this report as concise and accurate as possible. Believe me when I tell you that *nothing* is being withheld from you. No plot has been uncovered. No threat of any kind has even been *alluded* to in this communication thus far. That is to say, as far as we have been able to determine. There are years of documents still untouched and it is our opinion that the theme of the entire communication is that of love. They have come to help mankind and to aid us in lessening the threat that *we pose to ourselves*." With a sigh, she sat back and assumed her stoic pose.

"I have a few questions about your team. It says here that the young woman who allegedly discovered this code is an Indigo.

Could you explain to me exactly what that means?" Captain James sat back and folded her arms across her metals.

Dr. Sullivan began, "As I understand this phenomenon, Claire is one of many, maybe millions, born to this planet in the last thirty or so years with special gifts. All of the Indigo Children are gifted in some way. Some are musical prodigies, some are artists and healers, some have the ability to read minds and predict future events. Most of them have heightened sensitivities that translate into allergies and feelings that they do not belong here. The world we've created seems foreign to them, even alien at times."

After giving Dr. Sullivan a puzzled look, Captain James continued. "We have done our homework on Miss Montgomery and nothing in her records would indicate that she is anything more than a genius. We have spoken to her professors at Ohio State and they don't recall any special abilities beyond intelligence. In fact, other than her roommate in college, Claire had very few friends. She had never been outside the state of Ohio until she came to California to join the SETI team. Isn't it possible that this lonely little farm girl from Chillicothe has a great imagination? Is it possible Dr. Sullivan that this very bright young woman has conjured up this story in her mind and sucked all of you in, just to draw attention to herself?"

Dr. Sullivan smiled. All of the tension drained from her body as she relaxed into her chair. Now composed she said; "She isn't the only one who can see this. *This,* Captain is much bigger than you have imagined."

Now it was Captain James who was trying to compose herself. She looked at her aide and said "Michelle, I think we're going to be here for a while, would you arrange for some lunch to be sent down here?" She looked at Dr. Sullivan and said; "Would a deli tray be okay?"

"Sure," she said with a smile.

Chapter 17

Dr. Merrill didn't want everyone to pull through the gate at the same time, so she called the other drivers to wait at a rest stop. She wanted to enter first to get a look at who was watching the place. Reporters had been hounding them ever since the story broke over a month ago. Black sedans sat ominously parked in neighboring businesses.

Satisfied that it was the usual surveillance teams, she called the delivery truck first. "It's as clear as it's going to get, bring em' in." Then she called the semi. "You will be clear in thirty minutes, thanks again for your help."

She was nervous. She felt like she had stepped into a bad spy novel. Once inside the facility she paced. She couldn't remember the last time she said a prayer, but today she felt she needed some extra help, Divine help. "God, if you can hear me, please help these kids get here safely. And one more thing, I don't know what to do next, would you please send us some help? Thanks…uh…I mean, Amen." It had been a long time since she had left the church and had gotten out of the habit of prayer. It wasn't that she didn't believe in God, it just seemed to her that God stopped caring. It was hard for her to understand how the world could be so corrupt and vile when something benevolent and loving was supposed to be in charge.

When the delivery truck arrived, the driver who was the security chief at the facility made sure he didn't get through the gate too quickly. He knew he was being watched not only by reporters and the FBI, but by satellite as well. He pretended to hand over documents which were dry cleaning receipts and waited for the guard to make a scripted phone call. They knew their phones were bugged so everything needed to look and sound legit. After a few moments they were cleared to enter the gate. Once inside they backed up to a loading dock that had an awning over top. The door to the building was already open and ready to receive its precious cargo.

A warehouse meeting had been arranged for this hour so that no one would be near the dock when they arrived. The driver and the deputy, dressed in old green jumpsuits, got out and unlocked the door. Dr. Merrill was the only one from the Observatory staff to greet them. When the door opened, it was Sadie who jumped out first.

"Welcome to Hat Creek, I hope your ride wasn't too uncomfortable."

The others filed out of the cargo hold, one by one. "It was a little bumpy back there, but I think we're all in one piece." Michael said stretching his arms over his head.

"Good. Our warehouse staff is in a meeting for now but I don't want to take any chances of your arrival being discovered, so if you'll follow me, I'll take you to the Data Center where we will get some dinner and figure out what our next move should be." Dr. Merrill led them to a staircase and then through a maze of corridors. Finally they entered the Data Center. She asked everyone to join her at the conference table. "I called a few of my colleagues to a meeting when we found out you were coming here. We still aren't quite sure how to handle this, and would like your input as well. Our situation is this: we have a lot of people coming and going throughout the day, mostly volunteers who come in part-time. Even though we actually staff a small number of people, we aren't sure how secure it would be for them to know about you. As you found out in Berkley, it only takes one person to go to the press, *and* it is vital that we keep your whereabouts a secret until the all clear is given. Do you understand my problem?"

Michael spoke up. "I think we do. Is there any place for us to sleep here? I mean how set up are you for guests?"

"We do spend many nights here because of the nature of our work, and much of the year the roads are closed due to deep snow, so there is a residential room of sorts with futons, a TV and a foosball table, but I don't have separate living quarters for all of you. What we did come up with is a system where you three young men could basically live here. Dove, Sadie and Jessica can come home with me. And Amanda and Katie can stay at my brother's house. This could be rotated if it takes longer than a few days. And of course after the main staff goes home for the day, you would be free to roam around. What do you think?"

"I need food to think." Nateman just couldn't function without a steady stream of food.

"How many choices do we really have?" said Jessica.

"Sadie and I can always bunk together." Dove said as she scooped up the young girl onto her lap. Sadie just sat there looking sleepy.

The twins looked at each other, both uncomfortable about leaving Michael. "We need a place to write." Amanda said.

"We would rather stay here." Katie said looking at Michael, pleading with her eyes not to be separated from him. "We can sleep anywhere, on the floor is fine with us. It's just a few days right?"

"That poses a real problem girls, just having you in the building could blow the whole cover. Please take this in the spirit that it is intended. You're blonde, beautiful, very tall and identical. You would hardly go unnoticed. There is no way I can see to explain who you are and besides you're right; you need to be writing your story. My brother is on his way here with dinner. We live just a short distance away and he has agreed to help us out."

Amanda and Katie went to each side of Michael and hugged him.

"Okay then it's settled for now. We have a short range plan. I hope this business in Washington goes well and . . ."

"Dr. Merrill, I'm sorry to interrupt, but Sadie had a vision that things were not exactly going according to plan." Dove stroked her hair. "Sadie? Can you tell us exactly what you saw? Do you remember honey?

Sadie sat up and pushed her hair from her forehead. "I thaw the fat guy and I felt Claire being thcared. They didn't fly on the plane they wanted to go on. And thosth wobot guyth were there. I can call Claire if you want me to."

"You can?" Dr. Merrill was amazed. She had heard of people with this ability. She had read of telepaths and heard myths of old masters, but she had no idea that people still existed that could do this.

"I can twy." So Sadie got down from Dove's lap and went to sit in a chair by herself and closed her eyes.

It was at that moment that Dr. Merrill's cell phone rang. "Oh!" She almost jumped out of her skin. "I'm sorry I have to take this." She got up and walked to the far corner of the room. "Really! Oh this is so strange. Yes, yes of course, give him this number. Okay, yeh, uhuh, thanks, we'll see you soon."

She returned to the group with a strange look on her face. "Well that was my brother. He said I had a call from Australia today. Someone by the name of David has been in contact with Claire." She still had a strange grin on her face and went over to Sadie. "Sweetie, do you know who David is?"

"Yep; David ith going to marry Claire thomeday." Sadie said, smiling her toothless smile. "He talkth to Claire all the time. Do you thtill want me to find her?"

"If you can darling. I mean all the information we can get would be great. I would like to know what happened to their flight. Can you also find out where they are *and* what is going on in Washington, if it isn't too much for you?"

So Sadie closed her eyes again and searched for Claire. She sat quietly looking as if she had fallen asleep sitting up. Her eyes rolled around under her lids and her head began to roll back and forth. Her little feet were dangling off the floor. Then she began to smile and she held her pose.

All eyes were on Sadie. The only sound came from the computers on their endless rounds collecting and storing data. It was as if everyone stopped breathing. Sadie opened her eyes and sighs were heard all around the room.

"What did you see Sadie?" Dove walked over to her and picked her up "Did you see Claire?" Sadie always needed a few minutes to come back after she returned from The Grid. "Take your time Sweetie. It's okay, we can wait." Everyone else in the room was restless for the news and paced around until Sadie was ready to talk.

"She'th by herthelf." Sadie said finally. "She'th in a grey room but she'th not thcared anymore. She'th mad."

"Can you see where she is?" Jessica asked.

"No, it kind of got blurry after that." Sadie shrugged her shoulders.

"Well maybe her friend David will know more. Thank you Sadie." Dr. Merrill patted her on the head.

"No problem." Sadie smiled.

Claire was getting really mad by now. She had been in the interrogation room for six hours. No one had even checked on her in two hours. The last time was a restroom break. She had nothing to read, nothing to look at except her own reflection in the two way mirror. She was having some fun with the mirror a few hours before, but she was even bored with making faces at the people she assumed to be watching her. She could only imagine how boring the videos of her would be. In a fit of frustration she turned to the mirror and yelled. "Will somebody please come and talk to me? This is crazy! I'm going mad!" and she pretended to faint back in her chair. After a few minutes she began to get uncomfortable so she sat up with a huff and wondered if anyone was really watching her at all.

The door opened and in walked Captain James. She was alone. She didn't look at Claire as she took her seat with her back to the mirror. She was still looking at the file when Claire spoke.

"Yoo-hoo! Am I really invisible? Does anyone know that I am here?" Claire had a tone of sarcasm in her voice.

"I'm sorry to have kept you waiting. Would you like something to drink?" The Captain said without looking up.

Claire looked at her and wondered if the woman in front of her was some sort of a drone. The Captain looked stiff and mechanical. "I would like lemonade please."

For some reason this request took the Captain off guard. Finally lifting her head, she looked at Claire in an odd way, then nodded to the mirror and looked back at the file.

"Miss Montgomery, I was sincere in my apology for the delay. I didn't expect it to take so long to hear your story. I have spoken to Dr. Vaughn and Dr. Sullivan. Both of them are very convincing. They have a lot of confidence in your ability to read this code. And I have gathered from their depositions that you are not the only one with this ability. When did you become aware of this unique talent?"

At this point an aide brought in a tray with canned soda's and cups of ice. There were also small vending machine cakes on the tray. "I'm sorry this was all I could find Captain. It's late and the cafeteria is closed.

"That will be all for now, thank you Sam." Captain James poured the soft drinks into the cups and sat one down in front of Claire. "Are you hungry?"

"Yes, thanks." Claire helped herself to a cupcake. "To answer your question I discovered the code quite by accident. We were taken . . . Jessica and I were taken to the data lab as part of our intern program. Dr. Griffin gave us stacks of paper and told us to study them. I just looked at it and understood what it said, like I can read my own handwriting. Nothing like this has ever happened to me before. I didn't know that it was a code. I didn't know that no one else could see it. I felt like a freak."

"Well, we have had our own analysts take a look at the same material and they haven't been able to make heads or tails out of it. We just find it curious that it doesn't match any type of code in existence."

"Why would it? Why would you expect it to match some human creation? I mean if it is from where it *states* to be from, it *would* be foreign to us right? I mean if they really are a Guardian race and not from around here, why would you expect us to be able to recognize the code?" This seemed like a logical question to Claire.

"The question is Claire, why indeed? What were the chances of us finding it at all? If they knew we couldn't read it why did they send it in this form? They obviously have a grasp of the English language. They have communicated it so well. The code was intended to be a secret and that is what has caused us to be alarmed." Captain James sat back and took a long drink from her cup.

"I hadn't really thought about it that way. I've been pretty busy just translating it. It never really occurred to me that it was a secret." Claire was thoughtful for a moment and took another bite of cupcake. "I don't think I can answer that with any certainty Captain. But I can tell you this; not one word of this message has been menacing in any way. We have taken random years and looked for more off the topic messages. We haven't found any yet. Everything so far has been helpful. I'll admit that a lot of people won't like being called selfish, greedy and arrogant, but that is the truth of it. We are selfish. We do behave greedily, and it is arrogant of us to think that we are all that and a bag of chips!"

"Excuse me? A bag of chips?" The Captain furled her brow.

"Yeah it means 'and then some'." Claire stuffed the last of the cupcake in her mouth and sipped her drink.

"Miss Montgomery, tell me about your father. We understand that he is an astronomer. What is his interest in all of this? Does he believe in UFOs?"

The question shocked her. "I think you need to leave my parents out of this." She said with more anger than she meant to. "They don't know what's going on and they're worried sick about me. I haven't been able to even talk to them since this whole thing started." Claire had a lump in her throat the size of an orange. With tears beginning to brim her eyes she said, "You really need to leave them out of this."

"Isn't it true that you spoke to them only last week?"

Claire shot a look across the table and sat straight up in her chair. "Do you know about my mother's breast cancer too? Damn you people!"

Captain James decided it was better to leave this subject alone for now and continued. "Miss Montgomery we are interested in others who can read this code, and more importantly who else knows about it. Can you make a list of names for us?" Captain James pulled out a legal pad and pushed it across the table to Claire. Then she took a pen from her breast pocket and clicked it before handing it over to Claire.

"Did the doctors give you a list?" Claire said knowing that she could see the truth in whatever response she got.

"Yes, they did." The Captain did not look at Claire when she answered.

"No they didn't," Claire said looking straight at her. "I can tell when you're lying to me Captain. But it doesn't take a clairvoyant to know that. If you want the truth from me then you must show me that you can be trusted. This message is a special gift to mankind and it deserves to be shared with everyone. Our survival as a species may depend on it. Do you get that? Do you have any idea how much trouble we're in?" Claire was angry, tired, and hungry for a real meal. Her patience with the whole affair had run thin. "I need a shower and a hot meal. I need to see my friends, and *nothing* you want is important to me right now. I've been here all day in this cell and I'm ready for some fresh air. Okay?"

"Okay, I'll see what I can do. I guess we're done for today." With that the Captain rose up from the table, drained her cup and left the room. She still could not look Claire in the eye.

Claire was escorted under guard to what she assumed was a holding area. There were a number of doors with tiny windows on them. She knew the doctors were close by. She was led into one of the tiny rooms with a single bed, a sink-toilet combination and a chair. Her luggage was in the corner. It *was* a prison cell. She was told that a hot meal would be delivered to her shortly. Obviously a shower was not in the cards for her tonight, but at least she had her toothbrush.

She was exhausted. Her eyes welled up again at the thought of her parents and the farm. She wondered why she had been so anxious to see the world. It was not what she had expected . . . so far.

Chapter 18

Katie and Amanda had been pouting since they found out they would be leaving the others. They found it especially hard to be separated from Michael. Well they did . . . until Teddy came through the door.

Cristy's brother arrived with buckets of chicken and the works to go with it. He was a very handsome young man, obviously Cristy's *younger* brother, appearing to be in his late twenties. Tall, with a slender build, his skin was bronze and smooth. His long black hair was pulled back in a ponytail down his back. The twins stopped talking mid-sentence when he walked in.

"Hi everybody, dinner is served." He glided over to the conference table and unloaded the food with a sigh. "Whew, that should feed a small army." Teddy's eyes were drawn to the beautiful twins.

Cristy came up behind him and gave him a hug. "You're the best. Thank you. Hey everybody this is my brother Teddy. Teddy this is Michael, Christopher, Jessica, Dove and Sadie. Over there is Nathan and the twins are Amanda and Katie. Ladies, I'm sorry I can't tell you apart." She had pointed at each person individually until she got to the twins, and then her hand just waved in the air.

"No problem, we're used to it." Katie said smiling as she stepped forward. "I'm Katie. My sister Amanda . . ." Katie pushed back Amanda's hair. ". . . has a small crescent scar above her eyebrow. That's how you can tell us apart." Both girls gazed at him and smiled.

Teddy became aware that he was starting to blush and so broke away quickly before anyone else noticed. "Who wants a drumstick?" he said quickly, grateful that he hadn't slipped and said *breast*.

"Michael who?" Nathan whispered to Jessica.

She elbowed him in the ribs and giggled. "You're bad Nateman, you're really, really bad."

They were making the best of the situation, as they had done from the beginning. Nathan was making everyone laugh. Sadie especially, thought he was funny. If bubbles had a sound, Sadie's laugh would be it.

In the middle of the entire hubbub, Cristy's cell phone rang. "I think this is it. Will you excuse me? I get better reception away from the computers." And with that, she left the room.

The ring tone was like a switch that had turned off the laughter. Everyone sat silent for a moment.

"Do any of you know David?" Teddy asked, looking around at the team.

"No, none of us have met him. In fact Claire has never met him," Michael said and then continued. "We know he's an American who lives in the outback of Australia. Claire met him on the Grid when she was little. They've been best friends ever since. He's put together a team of his own and has been sending us parts of the message. We would never have met our deadline without him."

"What's The Grid? Teddy asked, "This is all pretty new to me. The Indigo's who came here were busy twenty four-seven. I never got a chance to talk to them." Teddy leaned forward in his chair.

"From what Sadie and Claire tell us, it's some kind of energy grid that covers the earth. The Indigo children use it as a communication tool to visit each other. Is that right Sadie?" Michael turned to Sadie and she nodded.

"I think it's like remote viewing." Nateman said as he tossed his plate in the trash. "In 1995, President Clinton signed the Freedom of Information Act, which declassified some CIA documents, admitting that we've been experimenting with remote viewing since 1972. They started simply by asking people to see objects hidden in boxes. Even though they had good results, they still had concerns about using psychics as spies . . . *until* . . . NASA sent a probe to Jupiter. The CIA asked the subjects to view the planet and asked for details before the probe returned any data. One of the remote viewers saw rings around the planet and NASA officials thought he was mistaken and had viewed Saturn instead. Well, when the probe sent back the new images of Jupiter, it did indeed have rings."

Christopher chimed in. "It's pretty fascinating really, but a little scary all the same. I've read reports where remote viewers were given coordinates and then described physical objects like cranes and airstrips with amazing details. Satellite images later confirmed their findings."

"It's gone way beyond the military though. Wall Street is using remote viewing to predict optimal investments." Nathan added. "It's based on quantum mechanics. Anyone can be trained to do it."

"Wow." Teddy sighed. "Anyone?"

Sadie was licking her fingers. Dove took a napkin and started to clean up her little hands. "It'th fun. How are Janie and John doing anyway?" Sadie smiled.

"Uh . . . fine." Teddy didn't recall saying their names at any point.

Jessica got up to clean the table and throw away piles of bones. "I wonder if he talked to Claire. Y'all, I can't stand this. My stomach is in a knot again. I'd like to get through one meal . . ."

Cristy stepped back into the room and silence fell once again. "Well he talked to Claire briefly this morning. They were diverted to a private military flight. I guess this guy Griffin is working directly with Washington. He had them taken into custody by the FBI and for now they're at the Pentagon. David just spoke to Claire again about an hour ago and apparently they spent the day giving depositions to the NSA. She was pretty upset because they have been investigating her family and suggested that this whole thing might be a hoax. Claire has refused to give them a list of people involved and as far as he knows, the doctors have refused to name names as well." With that, she sighed.

It took a few moments for everyone to digest the news, but then Amanda spoke up first. "What should we do? Katie and I are supposed to prepare a news break."

"We are fortunate not to be entirely in the dark. Without Sadie and David, we'd be flying blind. I think we keep moving on our plan and wait for word from them. In the meantime we have to trust the other teams around the world to sit tight and wait for our signal as well. I mean if anyone jumps the gun this could blow up in our face." Dr. Merrill continued, "It's been a long dramatic day, let's get everyone settled here and then we'll take off. Guys, will you come with me? I want to introduce you to my colleagues on the night shift and get you set up in the residential room. Then we'll meet you in the morning. When I get back I want everyone ready to go. Are we all on the same page?" No one had any questions, so Christopher, Nathan and Michael followed Dr. Merrill. The twins helped Jessica clean up and were feeling much better about their luck of the draw.

Chapter 19

Dianne lay in her cell unable to sleep. She replayed the day over and over in her head. She took out the note again that she had discovered on her dinner tray; *We have nothing to hide. Tell the truth or we'll be up a creek without a moon.* It was simply signed *A.S.* She knew that the note had been seen by the authorities, but was allowed to be passed to her because of its innocuous message. She wished she had paid more attention to Arlene's hand writing to be sure it actually came from her. But the message was pretty clear. Feel free to disclose anything except Hat Creek and Sadie Moon. She was sure this had been Arlene's intention. She laid there and wondered what fun and games tomorrow would bring.

Arlene laid awake as well, wondering if her notes would be delivered. She was sure that Claire and Dianne were smart enough to understand that Sadie and the location of the team were the only secrets they need keep. She wondered how long they would be held and what Stewart had told them. She knew it was far from over and the only way to speed things up was to cooperate as fully as possible.

Claire could sense that she was not alone in her insomnia. She understood the message perfectly and wondered if David had gotten through to Hat Creek without being traced. Then she turned her thoughts to the farm. She missed her parents. She ached for her mother. She soaked her pillow with tears of sorrow. When she awakened to the sound of her door being unlocked, she realized that she must have dozed off after all.

As she was led to the shower, she noticed it too had a small window on the door, making it indistinguishable from the other doors. Claire was given one scratchy towel, and a small hotel sized bar of soap. She was allowed to take her own shampoo and a change of clothes, but nothing else. The female guards who escorted her never looked her in the eye. They commanded her to strip in front of them and leave her clothes outside the door. She knew cameras were on her at all times and she had never hated a shower so much in her life. She found gratitude only in the water that hid her tears.

As Captain James sat at her desk, she read the previous day's testimony while having her morning coffee. These women were not what she had expected. They appeared to be sane and intelligent. Instead of getting a few hours of sleep, she read The Report again and again and again. She tried reading between the lines looking for anything that could have been interpreted as a threat. She had been told about the note Dr. Sullivan had written for her accomplices. *We have nothing to hide. Tell the truth.* She just couldn't find anything covert in these statements. She had thought about the rest of the note, but decided it was an idiom of some kind, like *up a creek without a paddle.* The women appeared to be willing to cooperate. "I guess we'll find out." She said to herself out loud.

Parker heard a soft knock on the door, "'Mam? The detainees are ready." "Thank you, Corporal." The Captain went to the small mirror behind her door and made one last check of her appearance. Satisfied, she made her way to the interrogation rooms for day two.

☯☯☯☯☯☯☯

Stewart Griffin had managed to gain the trust of some high officials in Washington and was preparing his statement for a Congressional Hearing set to take place early the next week. He sat before the mirror in his hotel room practicing facial expressions and hand gestures. He even practiced pounding his fist on the table. He thought it made a wonderful dramatic effect.

Stewart was so pleased with the chain of events so far. His plan to undermine the SETI discovery was working beautifully. He had been treated like a national hero. His suite in the Watergate Hotel was superb. He looked around his room and grinned at the half eaten breakfast on the room service cart. There was so much food that even the glutton he was could not finish all of it. And even though he was stuffed to the gills, he began to wonder what he would order for lunch.

"Thank you Uncle Sam," he mused in the mirror. He was wearing the fluffy white robe that had come with his lavish room. He pulled the collar up around his ears and said, "I could really use a massage," then broke into a laugh.

❂❂❂❂❂❂❂

With no warning the door swung open and scared Claire half to death. "Good Morning Miss Montgomery." Captain James came in with her aide and took their seats across the table from Claire. "I would like to get right to it if you don't mind." Claire did not object so the Captain pulled out her notes and began to thumb through them. She looked around to make sure the cameras were rolling and began.

Claire got to go first in the second round of interrogation. A small thing to be grateful for, but she was grateful nonetheless. It was difficult to sit in that dingy room all day with not so much as a magazine to look at.

"Miss Montgomery, I have been pouring over your report and I must admit these Guardian characters are well informed. Who do *you* believe it is really behind this?"

"Please call me Claire. And please look at me; it makes me nervous when people refuse to look at me. How do you know if someone is being sincere if you can't see her eyes?"

Captain James looked up from her notes and looked Claire straight in the eye and said, "Miss Montgomery your comfort is of little concern to me. What *does* concern me is any shred of evidence that could lead us to better protect the safety and well being of our country. And furthermore, I have sat at this very table across from murderous animals who would look me in the eye and beg me *sincerely* to believe in their innocence. So you see Miss

~ - 202 - ~

Montgomery, sincerity is not necessarily a conveyer of truth. Now would you like to hear the question again?" She said as she looked back down to her notes.

Claire understood too well what she meant and she also understood that the woman in front of her was only doing her job. She knew the cameras were rolling and any diversion from protocol would be recorded and scrutinized. "No Captain, I remember the question."

The interview lasted three hours. The last point of contention was the list that had been asked for the day before. Claire told her that it had already been prepared for them and was contained in the locked file box that they had brought with them. They had come prepared to share that information and she apologized for being obstinate the day before. "As you will see for yourselves, we never had any intention of keeping that information from you. We came to share this beautiful communication. We came in hopes that you would see the value in its message and share it with the world so that mankind would not destroy itself. That's all. That's all we wanted." Claire sounded so tired. "Thank you Claire. I think we're done for the day. I'll send someone to escort you back to your room." The Captain sighed and gave Claire a soft grin. She closed the file and stood up. Her aide stood as well and opened the door for her. "Thank you Michelle." Claire was left alone with the feeling that something had changed.

Back in her office Captain James decided to break for lunch so she could replay the tapes of Claire's interview. She called the security chief and told him to send the women back to their rooms for lunch and that she would let him know when she was ready to continue the depositions. After a moment she picked up the phone and called the best criminal psychologist she knew.

Dr. Heidi White was known around the world for her skill as a criminal profiler. She was invited to join a White House committee to profile terrorists after 9-11. Her celebrity status began when she was called to duty during the famous murder investigations of the Washington, DC Sniper. Even though her career had given her status and fame, you would be unlikely to see her hobnobbing with the elite of the world, unless of course they invited her to play golf. It was her passion and it was on the golf course that Parker and Heidi met and became good friends.

She needed a friend right now, someone she could trust. The psychological profiles she had been given on these women by Stewart Griffin were not squaring up.

Parker was impatient waiting for Heidi to answer. After five rings she answered. "Hey buddy what's up?" Heidi saw the caller I.D. and was glad to take the call.

"Hey are you in town this week by any chance?" Parker sounded hopeful.

"Yeah, I'm in L.A. right now, but I've got a flight back tonight. What's up?" Heidi sounded chipper as always. She was one person you could count on to lift your spirits.

"Got time for nine tomorrow?" Parker asked hopefully.

"Always! When and where? Why only nine? Do you have to work this weekend?" The only time they ever played less than eighteen was when they were trying to squeeze in a few holes before dark.

"Yeah, I've got a new case." Parker did not elaborate.

"I'm on vacation this week so I've got all day open. You want to meet at the club after work?"

"No, not the club. Let me check a few other options and I'll call you in the morning. What time does your flight get in?"

"I should be in Dulles by seven or so. You sound a little agitated Park, is everything okay?" Heidi was beginning to understand her friend didn't just miss her golf buddy.

"Everything's great. I just need to get out there and chase a little white ball around. I'll talk to you tomorrow. Have a good flight."

After they hung up, Heidi realized that she probably called from her cell phone so their conversation wouldn't be recorded. The thought of this made her curious and now anxious to get back to Washington.

Chapter 20

Teddy owned a charming Bed and Breakfast in historic Old Station, a tiny little town at the base of Mount Lassen. The little Inn was busy now, but in a few months it would be time to close for the season. Heavy snow fall made roads impassable for months at a time in the Cascades. Teddy was also a successful novelist. He wrote historical dramas, portraying the lives of the early North and South American Indians, so the annual seclusion created a perfect environment for his writing.

Although his private living quarters were in the main house, he kept the carriage house vacant so he could retreat from the rest of the visitors when he needed some quiet time.

"Wow, this is beautiful!" Katie said as she climbed out of the Jeep. She didn't only mean the old house, but the view as well.

"Yeah, I came up here to visit my sister a few years ago and never left. Phoebe and I were on our way to Alaska. I had some extra cash from one of my books and decided that I wanted to see the country. We stopped in Old Station to see Cristy and fell in love with the place. I bought the very Bed and Breakfast we stayed in."

"How romantic." Amanda said more than a little disappointed that Teddy had a girlfriend or a wife. "Does Phoebe help you run the place?"

Teddy started laughing. "Well she did, sort of. Phoebe was my dog." And then his face saddened. "She died a few months ago. She was the love of my life."

"I'm sorry Teddy." Amanda said with some relief.

"You two can have the carriage house. It's my own little retreat. I do most of my writing up there. You'll find everything you need to write your story. We have wireless internet, but a pretty old PC. I do have a laptop, but it's seen better days too. I've been meaning to order some new equipment before the snow flies this year." Then he muttered to himself. "You better get on that Teddy." The twins made a move to unload the Jeep. "Here, let me help you with that." He took the biggest bags from the back of the Jeep and headed for the little house.

๑๑๑๑๑๑๑

Cristy's house was only a few minutes away from Teddy's. It was a historic cabin style home. Several of the previous owners had added rooms to the original home in no apparent order. It had a quirky, nonsensical layout. Rooms jetted off here and there with no rhyme or reason. It was as though a room was added each time a child was born. Sometimes a room connected through a closet, and another, like the one off of the kitchen was clearly a porch at one time.

"There are plenty of rooms to sleep, but only one bath, so we'll have to share." Cristy opened the front door and led the way.

"What a weird house!" Jessica said as she went room to room, trying to decide where to put her things. "Look there's another one in here!" She had found the room behind the closet. "This is cool. Ya'll gotta come in here and see this!"

Cristy had had some fun decorating the place. It was such an odd house that traditional furniture would have looked out of place. When the others entered the room, you could hear a collective "OOOOOH!" Teddy had helped Cristy make a bed out of tree trunks. Beautiful redwood posts looked as though they grew through the tall ceiling. In fact the two had made all of the furniture for the room.

"Cool. I love the fountain," said Dove. "You feel like you're outside."

"Can I climb the tree?" asked Sadie, already half way up the post when she remembered her manners.

"Of course you can Sweetheart. We made it strong enough for *us* to climb it. C'mon let me show you the other *weird* rooms." She winked at Jessica.

The house was decorated with a lot of antiques. An old wagon wheel chandelier in the dining room had old hurricane oil lamps instead of electric lamps on it. "We lose power up here frequently, so most people just light their homes the old fashion way. I don't mind if you light the candles or lamps. Just please remember to put them out when you're not using the room. House fires up here are all too common." As she continued the tour, the surprises kept coming. She was especially proud of the bath so she made a drum roll sound with her tongue and opened the door. "What do think?"

There was a collective "Wow." She stood back and let the girls get a full view from the door. A claw foot tub sat in the middle of an alcove of glass. It appeared to be sitting outside. Mount Lassen was in the middle of the view.

"How beautiful! Oh my God, what a drop! I guess you don't have to worry about peeping Toms." Dove stood as close to the glass as she dared to, as the bath was built over the side of a deep ravine.

"This was *my* room addition to the house. The old bath was tiny and dark. Teddy helped me rebuild this room last year. He's been a huge help around here." She was proud of her baby brother. "Why don't you girls choose your rooms and we'll get everything in from the car."

❧❧❧❧❧❧❧

Amanda and Katie were getting settled in too. The carriage house was charming. The girls were especially impressed with the vintage teddy bear collection. "They're so cute." Katie said "He must collect them because of his name. Awwwe, Amanda, look at this one." She held up a little bear in a sailor suit. It was missing one eye and looked like it had the stuffing hugged out of it.

"That was my first bear." Teddy was standing in the doorway.

"Oh!" The girls said together.

"We're sorry, we just couldn't help ourselves. They're adorable!" Katie said holding up the tattered sailor bear.

"It's okay, teddy bears are meant to be held. I'm afraid these are all getting dusty in here, but I still like to look at them. My folks split up when I was really young and I guess they made me feel like I still had a family." He walked over and gently took the bear and placed it back on the shelf with the others. "Breakfast starts at seven. It's the only meal I still make myself. It's nothing fancy. I make muffins and have fruit and cereal during the week and on the weekends, I make waffles and sausage. I really like to cook breakfast. I always have. My housekeeper prepares the evening meal and takes care of the rooms. Everyone's on their own for lunch. When you get unpacked come on up to the house and I'll show you around. I just came by to make sure you have everything you need."

"Thanks. We'll be up there soon," Amanda said as she grabbed her suitcase. After Teddy was out of earshot she continued. "What a sweet guy. I wish *he* had a twin."

"Really?" Katie cocked her head. "He's not my type. I mean he's cute but I couldn't live up here. I'd go crazy with no one around for months at a time. I don't know how he does it." She made a face at Amanda. "Could you really live in this tiny little town?"

"I think it would be nice to live this way. It's simple. Los Angeles kind of gets to me sometimes," Amanda said as she started to unpack.

Chapter 21

It was Sunday, and much quieter around the Pentagon. Parker had decided that after two days of interviewing the women separately that she would like a tape of all three of them together for Heidi to view. She knew she would not be able to get Heidi involved *officially* because she had already suggested it. Her boss was satisfied that Dr. Griffin's assessment of the women was accurate. Parker was not so convinced.

After making sure the cameras were readjusted to record every possible angle, she sent for her detainees.

The women were overjoyed to see each other. They had not been permitted to have any bodily contact with each other or to speak to one another until they were safely in the holding room. But once inside they embraced. They maintained contact by holding hands until Captain James arrived.

"Good morning ladies." The Captain's change in demeanor was apparent from the first moment she walked through the door. Her attitude appeared to be changed as well. "This morning I would like to ask you to speculate on the meaning of what you have discovered. We have been primarily concerned with the facts up until now. But I'm curious. I would like to understand how you think this information will impact the public, and if you think it should be released."

"*Should* it be released?" Arlene asked defiantly. "It wasn't discovered so that it could be buried again. Have you *read* this report Captain?"

"Yes, of course I have. But it's not up to me. My job is to collect the facts and to verify as precisely as I can, their source. So far, our experts have been unable break this code. They have yet to be able to *see* what Claire claims to see. We have contacted the SETI offices that participated in the construction of this report. Our people are in the process of gathering the individuals who also claim to have the ability to decode this message. After a complete physical evaluation, we will then try to isolate the area of the brain being stimulated so that we can better understand this phenomenon."

"You want to make us lab rats?" Claire was enraged. "What you are talking about could take years!" She looked at the two doctors in horror. "I don't *want* to be a lab rat. I won't agree to it!" She was shaking.

"What you are proposing makes absolutely no sense! We understand the need for mental evaluations. No doubt you want to make sure that the mental health of a person making such a claim is stable. But to try to isolate a gene or neurological stimuli would take decades and then of course the findings would have to be debated by *more* experts. In the meantime we are blowing ourselves off the planet! Do you not grasp the urgency of this message?" Dianne was out of breath.

"I am just carrying out my orders. My superiors believe that either you have created this code yourself or that you are the victims of hoax. A plot, if you will, to convince the United States to soften its defenses and therefore become vulnerable to hostiles. You have been unable to convince us that this message came from any further than a satellite orbiting the earth." The Captain was scrutinizing their response to her accusation.

"You think that there is an Indigo conspiracy?" Arlene rolled her eyes and laughed. "That's funny." Smiling, she continued. "You have no idea what a treasure you have discovered. You have no idea the pearls of wisdom that are spoken by the youngest of these precious children. They are the light of our world and we keep trying to snuff them out. We have been so arrogant and ignorant, thinking that we know what is best for the world. And what have we accomplished? We are the most hated nation in the world! We have become the big bullies of democracy, invading countries for their resources. We are gluttons for natural resources. We leave a trail of destruction everywhere we go! Take everything and give nothing back. And don't even give me any crap about foreign aid. The scale is so far out of balance now it would take a millennium to correct the effect of our greed. We owe an apology to the earth and to the world. And I can think of nothing more important or appropriate than sharing this message of hope." She was seething. "Fuck your superiors! Don't YOU have a conscience? Isn't it time we start thinking for ourselves? As long as we *follow orders* we don't think we can be held responsible for our actions." Arlene began to cry.

Dianne patted Arlene on the back and just looked at the Captain. "Captain James, contrary to much of the publicized information about them, Indigo children are not smarter, happier, more creative, or *better* in any way than children who do not carry the Indigo signature. In fact, the only trait that can be consistently found in every Indigo child, that which sets him or her apart from others, is a heightened sensitivity to surrounding energies. The Indigo's body is very much like a chemistry experiment. If too much or too little of one ingredient or another is added, the experiment will fail. Practically, this means that when a child or adult who carries the Indigo signature comes into contact with environmental energies that are not matching and supportive, he or she can easily fall out of balance. Imbalance usually takes the form of physical or emotional illness."

"There is no checklist of attributes which can be universally applied to test whether or not a child carries the Indigo resonance. The name "Indigo" is derived from observations of biofields. Each of us has an electromagnetic field which surrounds and supports the physical body. Within this field, otherwise known as the aura, are the various life colors we carry. Before 1965, the color indigo was not a life color in the human biofield. And very few people carried a strand of indigo. These few became the parents of the first Indigo Children. So, these children are fairly new. However, despite this new indigo color identified in the auras of these new children, it would be a mistake to spiritually elevate the Indigo Children above other children or adults. Yes, the Indigos have some very important work to do in this life, but so does everyone else. In fact, placing Indigos on a pedestal would, paradoxically, contradict the purpose for which they came to Earth and would most likely result in imbalance.

So you see, their purpose is very much a transitional generation, placed here as a bridge during this amazing chapter in our collective human experience. Their purpose is to bridge the gap between the old and the new. They are a unique blend of third dimensional old energy existence, and the imminent shift into the new energy's higher dimensional ways of being. They stand as a beacon of hope for the future, ushering in a time of love, strength, and peace. They will force us to re-evaluate our values. They will force changes on a mass scale, away from competition, toward cooperation. And when they're finished, something really exciting will begin to happen. And please, when I say *force,* do not think in terms of how we have forced ourselves upon the world. Maybe *compelled* would be a better word. We will feel compelled to act better." Dianne sat with her arm around Arlene.

"Thank you for that Dianne, really, thanks." Claire turned to the Captain. "I think it's really important that people understand that we're not some race of freaks. Very few of us in fact have unusual gifts. Art and musical prodigies have always graced the earth. Prophets and healers have too. We are not here to take over the earth; if it were possible to take it . . . we would clean it up and give it back to you." Claire smiled gently.

After talking for a little while longer, Captain James said it was time to wrap it up. She had been given a lot to think about. Maybe Heidi could help her sort this out. She turned to the mirror and gave the signal that they were done for the day and then a young soldier entered the room to escort the women back to their rooms. "We'll see you tomorrow ladies. Ensign, will you make sure the ladies get some time in the common room tonight? I'll sign the order before I leave." She smiled at them as they were escorted out.

She walked into the observation room behind the mirror. "Thanks for coming in on a Sunday. Why don't you head out, I'll take care of the tapes. I want to review them before I go home. That was quite a session today, wasn't it?"

"Uh . . . I'm sorry Captain, I set it on auto pilot and went down to get some lunch." The young man looked worried that he had left his post.

"Steve, it's okay. I won't tell. Go on home now and spend a few hours with your family."

"Thanks Captain, I'll see you in the morning." On that note, he left the control room.

"Okay." Parker was talking to herself. "You could get court-martialed for this." She took the tapes out of the cameras and put them in her briefcase. She looked around to make sure no other recording device had been used. When she was satisfied she had collected all of the evidence, she left the Pentagon and headed out to meet Heidi.

Parker was anxious to meet her friend. She kept replaying the session over and over in her head. They had decided to play their round at the Burning Tree Club in Bethesda. Heidi was so well connected that only one call was needed to get a reservation on the exclusive course. She had hoped for the last tee time of the day so they wouldn't be rushed.

Heidi was already on the driving range when Parker arrived. She pulled out her Big Bertha and set down the bag. "How long have you been here?"

"A bucket and a half" Heidi measured time by the number of balls she hit. "Well you've piqued my curiosity. I could hardly sleep on the plane. You're obviously *not* supposed to tell me about this new case, so spill it." Then she whacked a ball into space.

Parker was taking aim at the 200 yard marker. *Whack.* "I tried to bring you in through the right channels, but as I may have mentioned, they brought a new guy in to do the profiles. And this is what bugs me. I think this guy is way off base. I also think he is too close to the situation to be objective. But I also think being *objective* is exactly what they're trying to avoid."

"Who is this guy, maybe I've heard of him?" Heidi set up another tee.

"His name is Dr. Stewart Griffin. He works for the SETI program in Berkley California. Well *did* work for them, I should say. They're suing him for breach of contract and for disclosing sensitive material."

"Never heard of him . . . oh snap! Yes I have, he's the guy who's been all over the news spouting off about discovering some kind of code from aliens, right?" Heidi froze mid-swing.

"Yep. But actually he didn't discover anything, someone else did." *Whack.*

"You mean this is for real? Shit Parker, is this your new case?" Heidi was delighted. She loved juicy, high profile cases. "Oh yeah, that guy is nuts. He's got crazy eyes. They let *that* guy do the profiles?" She bent over and put the tee in her pocket. "Why don't we continue this conversation out there, we don't have that much daylight left." And with that, she kicked her remaining balls into a pile and picked up her bag.

Parker sighed and followed suit. She wondered how much to tell her friend. She knew she could trust Heidi, but she was having second thoughts about making her an accomplice.

Chapter 22

"What would you like for breakfast?" Cristy was delighted to have guests to cook for. They all had such a good time last night playing games and telling stories. Sadie was the hit of the party. Dove had taught her how to toss popcorn and catch it in her mouth. They had rolled on the floor, laughing at her trying to perfect her technique. "I could make pancakes . . . or waffles. Let's see we have . . ." Cristy was looking in the refrigerator. "Sausage . . . and I have some eggs. What do you girls feel like eating?"

"Mickey cakes!" Sadie said jumping on one foot. She giggled and hopped around seeing how long she could go without putting her other foot down.

"I don't know what Mickey cakes are." Cristy said as she straightened up and looked over the refrigerator door.

"We made them at the cabin." Jessica said. "They're regular pancakes that you pour in three puddles. One big one, and two little ones connected at the top. It looks like a silhouette of Mickey Mouse."

"Oh . . . Mickey cakes . . . got it. How about some sausage to go with them?" She handed the milk and eggs to Jessica, grabbed the sausage and orange juice and then shut the door with her foot. "The pancake mix is up there and you'll find a mixing bowl under there." She was giving the directions to Dove by nodding with her head. "I was thinking we might take a picnic lunch up to Mount Lassen today. Teddy and the twins might want to go too."

"Do you have the day off?" Dove asked.

"Yeah, it's Sunday. I always take Sundays off." She reached up for a frying pan that hung from the pot rack over the kitchen island.

"I didn't even know what day it was," Jessica said, trying to think of the last time she did. "So much has happened over the last few weeks, time has sort of lost its meaning."

Sadie hopped over to Jessica and breathlessly said, "We made up time. It isthn't real. If God could give you a watch, it would thay NOW." Then she hopped away.

Cristy turned around to look at her. "She does that all the time." Dove said with pride.

"She's like a baby Confucius. She is amazing. The pearls of wisdom just continue to spill from her mouth. Where did you find her? Cristy still had a look of amazement on her face.

Dove held out her arms for Sadie and she hopped over and fell in to her arms panting with her tongue hanging out. Dove scooped her up and kissed her cheek. "Dr. Vaughn found her in China Town back in San Francisco. It was kind of a fluke really."

Sadie interrupted, "Not really."

Dove smiled at her and continued. "We needed to find someone who could confirm what Claire had found in the data. Dianne remembered a woman who had told her fortune some years before. She was convinced that this woman was the real deal, so she went and asked her if she could see anything besides symbols and numbers and she said no, but that Sadie Moon would read it for her, and the rest is history."

Still curious, Cristy asked, "Why didn't her mother come with her? I mean she didn't really *know* Dianne or what she would really need this child to do."

"Sadie's mother wasn't married and from what we know . . . sort of dropped her off and disappeared. Miss Lee is Sadie's great-grandmother and from what Dianne told us, she was expecting her to show up and knew that Sadie would be able to help us."

"Wow, this is just amazing. The two young people who came to Hat Creek were from Portland. They showed up one day and announced that they were called to help."

Sadie interrupted again, "Janie and John." She said with a toothless smile.

"Yes . . . Janie and John. They were brother and sister and I would say that John was maybe seventeen and Janie was about twelve. They're family resemblance was so striking. Janie looked just like a younger version of her brother. They looked like twins born on different years." Cristy shook her head and smiled. "Where was I? Oh yeah…they showed up one day and got right to work. One would read the data while the other one typed at breakneck speed on the keyboard. It was a fascinating thing to watch. After a few hours, they would switch places. It was astonishing, the amount of work they did each day. I had them stay here with me, but it was kind of weird the way they didn't need to speak out loud to one another. You could tell they were engaged in conversation by the expressions on their faces, but no words would be exchanged. I felt like an intruder in their space, but I'm not sure they even knew I was there. Can Sadie communicate that way?"

Dove looked down at Sadie. "She's the one who called them." Then she looked back at Cristy and said, "and she didn't use a phone."

Chills ran down Cristy's spine. She flipped the sausage patties and then turned around and faced Sadie. "How do you do that exactly? How do you zero in on someone specifically? This is all new to me. I mean, do you hear all of our thoughts at once?"

Sadie rolled her eyes. "Okay . . . you know when there'th a bunch of people in a room and you thee thomeone you know? You focuth on that perthon. You can thtill thee thee the other people, but they get kind of blurry. I hear thort of a buzzing thound and then when thomeone callth me or I call them, they come into focuth." She snapped her fingers like it was as simple as that.

"They also have a grid. It's kind of like the Internet. They can surf the Grid until they find who they are looking for. Their energies join and they feel like they are literally in the same place for a while. It's really cool. I've seen Claire and Sadie both go to the Grid and make contact with the others. They look as though they're having a pleasant dream. And when they get back, they need to rest for a moment and collect themselves so to speak. It's really fascinating to watch. Maybe after breakfast, Sadie would like to try to contact Claire. Besides entertaining us, I would really like to know what's going on at the Pentagon." Dove looked down at Sadie who nodded her head in agreement.

❧❧❧❧❧❧❧

Amanda and Katie were enjoying the breakfast Teddy had made. The dining room could accommodate thirty guests at a time. It was a long room with windows along one wall. The mountain view from the table was spectacular. The room was full of antiques. The long mahogany table was once used in a library that had been torn down in Sacramento. The chairs were an eclectic mix of woods and styles. It was impossible to find thirty antique chairs to match the table, so he bought unique antique chairs, two at a time. He had done the same thing with the china. The mix of styles and colors only added to the charm of the historic home.

"More coffee anyone?" Teddy was making his rounds through the dining room as he did every fifteen minutes or so to make sure his guests had everything they needed. He was perfect for the place and looked the part in his chef's apron he wore all through breakfast. He stopped where the twins were seated and bent down to tell them his sister had called and they had been invited for a picnic on the mountain. They grinned with mouths full and nodded their approval.

Chapter 23

The women were on the first putting green before the subject of the new case was mentioned again. Parker was putting for birdie . . . *tap* . . . *clunk.* "Not so fast Rookie, you're not going to get up on me on the first hole. Heidi had made a wild tee shot, but had recovered on her second drive. She was only eight feet from the hole. She was taking her time looking at every angle. She was fiercely competitive on the golf course. "So have you decided to let me in on this?" She stood over her putter and took a practice swing. Parker decided not to answer until she had made her shot . . . *tap* . . . *clunk.* "I was worried for a moment there," Heidi said, wiping her brow. "C'mon spill it. I can't concentrate."

"Okay first, what I'm about to tell you is Top Secret. Second, I could be court-marshaled for what I did today, and telling you makes you an accessory, capiche?" The two women put their putters back in their bags and drove to the second tee box.

"This is going to be good isn't it?" Heidi gave Parker an evil grin. "I can keep a secret, you know me. Besides, you know I'm the best. Who else could you turn to?"

"I shouldn't be turning to anyone! I have my orders! But something just stinks about this Griffin guy. He is one slimy character. Besides I hate the thought of this discovery becoming another national treasure. These women I want you to profile are really sweet. I am convinced that they are not a part of any kind of conspiracy to undermine our government or any other government for that matter. This message they brought to us is a message of hope for the world. It describes in detail how we can clean up our waterways and clean up our cities. It gives detailed instructions on how to heal the sick and downgrade storms. It's fascinating reading. They tell us they are not here to condemn us but to hold up a mirror so that we can see ourselves *and* that we have everything we need to save our world."

"The million dollar question is...who sent this message?" Heidi set up her tee and ball.

Parker hesitated before she answered the question. She knew that this indeed was the million dollar question and that the answer was a hard one to hear. "They are The Guardians," she said with such conviction that she surprised herself. She had not spoken about this to anyone outside of the interrogation rooms. In fact, she just realized that none of her superiors had even asked her how the interviews were going. She, of course, had been asked to write a report. But the fact that no one had asked had just sunken in. She knew they had already formulated their opinion and had no intention of releasing this beautiful message of peace. They were only going through the motions so they could honestly say they had investigated the matter and found it false. Parker was so deep in this thought she didn't hear Heidi's response.

"Earth to Parker, come in Parker." Heidi had already taken her shot. "Are you still with me? It's your shot."

Parker came out of her trance and apologized. She set up her tee and hit the ball so hard that it landed on the green in one stroke. "Whose head did you just knock off?" Heidi laughed.

"I just realized I've been set up. They don't really care what these women have to say. They aren't going to let them publish their findings . . . and if they do, they're going to discredit them and play it off as a hoax. And *damn it*, they're using me to do it!"

"Okay, back up. You just played a whole scenario in your head and I wasn't there. Would you please fill me in?" The women got in their cart and took off down the fairway.

👁👁👁👁👁👁👁

Claire and the Doctors were happy to be together that evening. Parker had arranged for them to have the evening together in the common room. They were still under lock and key, but the surroundings were much improved. They were able to have dinner together and talk openly. Of course the room had security cameras, but it was better than passing notes. When a young officer came in to tell them it was time for lights out, they were amazed at how fast the time had gone. A stark contrast to the long evenings they had spent alone in their cells. They hugged each other and bid each other pleasant dreams. One by one they were locked up in their little rooms.

Sadly, Claire looked around the four walls, she was beginning to hate. They seemed to close in on her and she longed for sleep so she could be free. She thought about going to 'see' David, but decided instead to concentrate on home. She desperately wanted to know how her mother was. Just the thought of her parents brought tears to her eyes. She thought if she ever got to go home she might never leave again.

Claire lay on her back, concentrated on her breath and thought of her mother. She called to her mother's spirit. She pictured her mother throwing her head back in a big laugh. She imagined how she had looked, the day she came home from college, sitting in her wicker chair by the road, soaking up the healing rays of the sun.

After a few moments, she saw her mother and father both. They were in the presence of their longtime friend, Grandfather Yellow Moon. He was standing in front of her mother, holding a large abalone shell in front of him, fanning smoke with the wing of a large bird onto her body. This was an ancient custom. The burning of white sage brush was a form of purification. The impurities would rise with the smoke and be carried away to Great Spirit Creator. Her mother's eyes were closed. She stood with her arms outstretched to the sides. Grandfather stroked the fan head to toe and then gently tapped her shoulder. She turned around and he repeated the process on her back. As he smudged her, he said a prayer of thanks for their safe arrival and welcomed her to his home. When he had finished, her mother stepped aside. Her father stepped forward and the ceremony was repeated. Her father then handed a small bundle to Grandfather. It was a gift of tobacco wrapped in a red cloth. An offering is tradition, much like bringing a bouquet of flowers to the hostess of a party.

After changing into their bathing suits, they joined the others who were gathered around a fire. Grandfather began by explaining to some who had just arrived that the ceremony had actually begun earlier in the day. The sacred stones were placed on the wood platform and the seven directions were called in before the fire was lit. He welcomed each person as family. He talked for some time about events taking place around the world. With an even tone, he spoke of how man had forgotten his original instructions. He said Creator had not left us without teachers to remind us who we really are, and how we are to care for our brothers and sisters around the world, and our Mother, the Earth. "We are all one family. We have forgotten this."

He looked at each and every person sitting around the fire and continued. "Our prophecies have foretold of this time…a time of unrest and upheaval. These events, dear family, mark a time of great change. Those who fear this change do not understand. Do not be afraid, the dark days will soon be over. There is much speculation about the year 2012. As you know the Mayan calendar ends on the winter solstice of that year. The I-Ching ends also on that same day. Even the Christian Bible tells a story of the end of days, followed by a thousand years of peace. I believe that this is the next step in our human evolution. Our prophecies tell us that this is a time of transition. I believe it will take decades for the transition to be complete. The Earth Mother will also be clearing away the old energy, so be prepared. Brother Bush played his part perfectly, creating a desire for change." At this he paused and laughed to himself. "Don't get me started." He paused again. "And our new president, Brother Obama, has come to bring the great change. I will not speculate on the nature of this change, as many events are yet to unfold. There will be many unwilling or unable to make the shift to a higher vibration. Others will be needed to assist from the other side and so will be called home to Spirit. Millions, but probably billions of souls will leave the earth plane." He looked at Beth and then lowered his head; "Great Spirit, may their journey be joyful and swift and their suffering brief. Aho."

A woman wrapped in a bright beach towel raised her hand. "Grandfather, is this our judgment?"

Yellow Moon paused before he answered. "Family," He stood and addressed the circle. "Please hear me. Throughout history religions have used fear as a tool to control the people. And many have misunderstood the events of the past. It is not a judgment upon man to suffer the effects of a hurricane. It is a consequence of living by the sea. It is not a judgment upon man to suffer illness. It is a consequence of an imbalanced life. And so it is in these times. We are not the first advanced civilization to occupy the earth. What we are experiencing is an imbalance between our intellect and our spirit. We created products to be thrown away before we solved the problem of where to put them. So now our oceans are garbage dumps. We created nuclear energy before we thought of how to safely store the used plutonium. So now we have three legged owls and fish that glow in the dark. Are you getting the picture?" Grandfather looked around and saw that everyone was nodding in agreement. "Technology is not evil. Technology can be beautiful and very helpful, but we must consider the consequence of our actions and not be led by greed. The meek will inherit the earth. Not the weak, but the wise and gentle ones."

Next he spoke of the sacredness of the Sweat Lodge they were about to enter. He explained the importance of entering the womb of Grandmother Earth to purify the body, mind and soul to receive valuable insight and information from the Spirit Realm. He then entered the lodge and began to sing an ancient song of gratitude. After he made his prayers he invited each person to enter the lodge; one by one he again welcomed all of his relations.

As the stones for the first round were brought into the lodge, Grandfather Yellow Moon led the group in another song. When the first seven stones were within the lodge, the door was closed and the sweat began. Water was splashed on the stones with a pine bough, as Grandfather called in the sacred energies desired for the intent of the sweat. In the darkness, each person then offered a personal prayer for self, for others, and for the releasing of pain and suffering. Between rounds, more spirits were called in and more hot stones were brought in as the group sang and chanted.

Claire narrowed her view to her mother alone. She felt the sweat begin to trickle from her brow. She sensed the panic that her mother felt and the rapid heartbeat of fear. But she also felt the comfort of being in the womb of *grandmother*. It was warm and wet and strangely familiar.

In the previous months since the cancer was discovered, Beth had set her thoughts on being whole and well. She knew that concentrating on the cancer would only give it more energy to grow. But inside the safety of Grandmother's womb she allowed herself to experience the fear. It was a sacred place to face her demons. In the dark it was safe for her to cry. She could finally let go of the happy face she had put on for others. She grieved for herself for the first time as she reviewed the beautiful life she had lived. By the fourth round, a sense of peace replaced the fear she had felt earlier. Taking deep breaths of the steamy air filled her with assurance that her journey had not been in vain.

On the other side of the lodge, Tom was grieving as well. His life with Beth had been full of blessings and the thought of losing her was too much to bear. She was more than he ever expected or thought he deserved. He prayed with all his might. He begged God not to take her, not yet.

At the conclusion of the ceremony, each person left the lodge in the same sacred manner as he or she entered; honored as family.

Claire could see her parents smiling at each other. They wrapped themselves in their towels and went back to the fire to sit with the others. Then she saw them laughing and talking around the fire. It warmed her heart to see them. She said a prayer of gratitude for their healing and drifted off to sleep.

Beth and Tom felt wonderful, weak but wonderful. They would share a meal with their new family and regain their strength before heading home. A potluck dinner was tradition at lodge ceremonies. Everyone brought something to share. After recovering some strength, Beth went to the house to offer her help. Grandfather's wife was much younger than he. Eva was not his first wife, not by a long shot. After their marriage, Grandfather and Eva both had dreamed of a special child that would come to them. They did not have to wait long before Eva knew she was pregnant with this child. Four years ago she came into the world as Gentle Rain. Named of course, for the weather on the morning she was born. She began to speak at six months of age. Her first words were "love you." By the time she was a year old she was speaking in full sentences and she spoke publicly for the first time at eighteen months. During a talk her father was giving, she got up on stage, tugged on his pants and asked if she could address the crowd. Even though he was stunned, he gave the microphone to her. She said "Life is about choices and that's all there is." Yellow Moon laughed and said that she had said more in one sentence than he had said in two hours! He was proud of all of his twelve children. He told many stories of their accomplishments, but to him, Gentle Rain was unique, and he felt she had come to this world with a message.

Beth's offer to help was refused. It was considered wise to sit quietly after a lodge ceremony, so she returned to the fire and snuggled next to her husband. Unaware that she had been followed, Gentle Rain appeared before them, taking Tom's hand and placing it around her hand, Gentle Rain squeezed their hands together and closed her eyes. After a brief moment, she opened them and said "Good." And with that she bounded away to go play with the other children. They looked at each other, unsure of what she meant.

Later as they bumped down the road in the old blue truck, they talked of happy times and how they shared the feeling that Claire had been with them all evening.

Chapter 24

Heidi and Parker were finishing their dinner in the beautiful clubhouse dining room. The sunset view from their table was spectacular. They sat back and waited for their plates to be cleared before they continued their conversation. "Well that was quite a story Capitan." Heidi said in jest. "I'll take a look at the tapes tonight. But tell me, what is your plan? How are you going to introduce my findings without telling them you shared top secret information?"

"I *don't* have a plan. I'd be in shackles if they knew I told you. I just don't want to be a party to this. Griffin is going in front of a Congressional hearing this week and my hope is that he will expose himself as the fool he is. It seems obvious to me this message poses no threat to national security. I don't *plan* to mention you at all! I just need a friend to tell me if I'm being suckered in by these women or if I'm being played as a pawn by my own government."

"You got it. You know you can count on me. As long as you keep letting me win out there, you know I'll be your best friend." Heidi winked at her friend.

❦❦❦❦❦❦❦

The day was beautiful on Mount Lassen. Everyone relaxed and enjoyed themselves immensely. It seemed a long time since any of them had taken a day off. Most of the day was spent hiking, but during lunch they did discuss their next move. Everyone agreed that no matter what happened in Washington, a press release was critical. They had decided that a prominent news program should get the first interview with the twins. Which news program was still a matter of debate. They just wanted a chance to tell their side of the story before the media circus began. Katie and Amanda were given permission to call their editor when they got back to town. It was time to prepare him for the story of the century. Since no one but Griffin was talking, the news naturally drifted to current events. But the tabloid rags were still headlining all kinds of claims, from total destruction to salvation. They had fun making up their own headlines and stories. They laughed until their sides ached.

Cristy and Teddy were amazed by the story of the wildfire and how the people of Eagles Ridge called the rain. They talked about the Guardian's powerful message of family. Jessica paraphrased the message by saying, "They tell us that we don't understand what we are a part of, and we have no idea how big our family really is. They thought it was so important, that they repeated it over four thousand times."

Teddy sat up on the blanket. "Cristy and I are descended from the Lakota Souix on our mother's side and so I write from the perspective of the Native American. But from my travels around the world, I've found that all cultures share similar values. Through my stories I try to communicate the wisdom of the old ways, where family and community is sacred. There are Old Ones who still pass on the stories, who remember the way. They tell us that family is not limited to human relationships and stress the importance of respect; not only for each other, but for Mother. There was a time when native people respected nature so much that they traveled on animal trails to avoid scarring the earth. They knew that every species was a teacher and they looked to them for guidance. For instance, animals know what plants are medicinal and how to find water. They also look to nature to tell them when the weather is about to change. They go so far as to ask a tree's permission before cutting it down. They call them the Tree People and the rocks, Stone People. They see the trees and stones as alive, and know that within them, our history is recorded. Today we foolishly damn our rivers so they cannot return to the sea. We hunt animals to extinction so that people can feel rich in their furs. We cut open the heart of Mother and level whole mountains to more easily get to her treasure inside. Mother is begging us to stop, and I think the Guardians are begging us to look at ourselves."

Changing the subject, Dove asked, "Cristy, I was looking through your library and saw a book series called, *The Ringing Cedars*. Is that the Anastasia I've heard about from Russia?"

Cristy smiled broadly. "You've heard of her?"

"A few years ago everyone on campus was talking about her. I thought it was fiction." Dove said, putting emphasis on the word *fiction*.

"I read it as fiction at first, but now I believe this woman actually exists." Cristy leaned forward. "It's fascinating isn't it? To think that someone could actually live this way?"

"I haven't heard of her. Who's Anastasia?" Jessica asked.

Cristy took a deep breath. "Well...to make a very long story short, a merchant ship captain Vladimir Megre` discovered this woman in 1995 living as a recluse in the taiga of Siberia. Her parents were killed when she was a baby and so she was raised in the wilderness by her grandfather and great-grandfather. She lives in harmony with nature, being fed and protected from the elements by wild animals. She is considered to be a surviving descendent of an ancient Vedic civilization, with extraordinary powers, knowledge and wisdom. Her story is *almost* unbelievable, but her message is very clear. We are more than we appear to be. We humans have unlimited creative power and all knowledge is available to us. For a woman who has never been to school or even lived in a house, her knowledge of the Universe is astounding."

"May we borrow the books?" Dove asked. Jessica nodded as well.

"Of course, help yourselves. It will give you something positive to think about while we wait for news from Washington." Cristy noticed how late it was getting. "We should probably think about going pretty soon."

Sadie and Christopher were off in the distance chasing butterflies. Nateman was lying flat on his back gazing at the clouds.

Reluctantly, Cristy called everyone back to pack up for the long descent back to the vehicles.

Chapter 25

Captain James was nervous as she sat outside the Commander's office. She had expected someone to check on her progress with the detainees. No one did, so she made an appointment to go over the details of the interviews. She just realized that the magazine she had been holding for ten minutes was upside-down, and quickly made the adjustment. The only other person in the room was the commander's secretary, Bobbie. Busy typing and answering the phone, she didn't appear to notice.

"Yes Sir," was Bobbie's response to one caller. Then she looked up at Parker and said; "Captain, I'm sorry the Commander cannot see you today. There's been a change in his schedule." She did not smile or give Parker more than a slight glance.

"Well can I reschedule my appointment?" Parker was on her feet, with her hat in her trembling hands.

"The Commander will call *you*." She said in a tone that indicated that she was being blown off.

"Thank you, `Mam." Parker spun on her heel and headed for the door. She stopped short and spun back around. She needed to settle this in her mind before she left. "Miss Bobbie? The commander is not going to call me, is he?"

The woman looked up but did not say a word. She just gave the slightest shake of her head and then returned to her work.

Parker got the answer she needed and left. As she was walking down the hall, she passed Stewart Griffin. He was talking loudly about his debut on the floor of the Senate. He wanted to make sure EVERYONE knew how important he was. She stopped to get a drink from the water fountain and noticed Griffin had stepped into the Commander's office.

She was seething as she walked back to her office. She needed to talk to Heidi, but not from the Pentagon. No phone calls at her level were secure.

She needed to get outside and use her cell phone. She was sitting at her desk thinking of a good reason to leave early when Michelle buzzed her office and said that Dr. White was on line two.

You read my mind. She thought as she picked up the receiver. "Hello Dr. White, so good to hear from you. We haven't seen you around the Pentagon lately."

"Hello Captain. How are you? Forgive me for calling out of the blue, but you introduced me to a forensic specialist last year at little place named The Market Street Grill, do you recall that?"

"Ah…yes Doctor, I remember." Parker was having fun with this.

"Yes, well I was wondering if you recalled his name. I need his help on a case I'm working on." Heidi was having fun too.

"I'll have to get back to you on that Dr. White. You caught me just as I was leaving for lunch. I'll have my assistant give you a call back when I locate that number…yes, you too, you're welcome." Parker sat back and smiled. It looked like she was having lunch at the Market Street Grill.

Captain James gave the order to allow the detainee's to spend the day in the common room. She took the commanders refusal to see her to mean that the interviews were over, so she saw no reason to keep the women separated or isolated.

They were confused but delighted to have a day with no more questions. They knew that their movements and conversations were still being monitored by security cameras, so they were careful not to let their guard down and speak too freely.

It was actually refreshing to talk of other things. Dianne missed Ryan and wondered how Caris was doing with her new kittens. She told them about the house renovation and how much fun they had working on it together. She mused at Ryan's hopes of marriage and told the women that if they ever got out of this that she might just be willing to give it a try and let that poor man off the hook.

Arlene talked a lot about her daughter Ashley, and how she had come so far in her personal journey battling drugs and alcohol. She was proud of the young woman she had become. Ashley was in love with a young man named Anthony. He made her smile and loved her with all of his heart. He had a huge family and wanted nothing more than to marry her and add more children to the family line.

Claire sat and drank up their stories of love and family. They asked her about David and did they have plans to finally meet each other. She sat with the question and wondered after all these years if they were destined to *ever* meet. She shared with them the vision of her parents and the sweat lodge. She asked Arlene if she thought it was possible that her mother received a healing from the experience. If they ever got out of Washington, Ohio would be their next stop. She told the women about their farm in Chillicothe and about the family dogs. Tears rolled down Claire's cheeks as she told the story of how her parents met and her love for Grandma Bee. She was proud of her mother's ability to grow beautiful flowers. She said it was as though they sprung up out of her footsteps.

The women were having such a good time. They thought it was time for lunch when they heard the key turn in the door. "Well, hello ladies." Stewart Griffin entered the room with two armed officers. "Isn't this cozy?" He smirked at them. "I really hate to break up this little hen party, but would you mind coming with us?" He gestured to the open door.

It was like a car crash. One minute they were talking and enjoying the ride and the next minute a big cow jumped out in front of them.

Griffin led the women to one of the interrogation rooms, followed by the armed men. Once inside, he instructed one of the guards to stay in the room with them and the other to wait outside by the door. He made a comment about Arlene having a violent temper and not to hesitate to shoot her if she attacked him again. Arlene rolled her eyes but held her tongue.

He commanded everyone to sit, relishing in his imagined power over the women. He told them of his security clearance and the trust he had been placed in. His chest swelled when he told them about being invited to appear at a Congressional hearing. They were clearing other items off the agenda to make time to hear him tomorrow.

Arlene secretly wished for a hat pin to pop his gigantic head with. She wondered how much of this was true and how much of it was a figment of his inflated ego.

He revealed that he had been watching them and listening to their conversations, not only in the interrogation rooms but in their cells as well. He had managed to convince the National Security Advisor that the plot to undermine the United States was bigger than he had originally thought. Griffin made the women sound like brainwashed victims of a conspiracy.

It did not escape the notice of the women that the cameras were not recording. No red lights were visible on any of the equipment in the room.

Arlene smiled to herself knowing that not only were there hidden cameras but hidden microphones *everywhere* in the Pentagon. She used this knowledge to prod more information out of Stewart, pitting his ego against him. She had no idea how this could help, but it was their only hope.

When he was finished having his fun with them, he instructed the soldiers to take them back to their cells. He warned them not to let the prisoners spend too much time together. He referred to them as psychotic masterminds.

Arlene thanked the soldiers for the escort, and then turned and looked Stewart straight in the eye. "I want to be there when they put *you* behind bars, you little weasel. And oh, by the way, when you meet with Congress tomorrow, zip up your fly." She just grinned as she turned away.

Griffin's eyes narrowed as he grabbed his crotch. The soldiers were powerless to hold a straight face.

☯☯☯☯☯☯☯

When Parker entered the café, she cracked up when she saw her friend. Heidi was sitting at a table in the corner with a baseball cap on. She had dark sunglasses and a newspaper up in front of her face. "You just ain't right in the head. Do you know that?"

"Yeah, I know. I'm a drama queen." Heidi said and took off her glasses with a big smile on her face. "Great cover huh? I even had the waitress fooled."

"Yeah, yeah, yeah, you're a regular master of disguise Holmes." Parker picked up her menu. "What's the special today?"

"Special? Do you really want to discuss the special, or is that code for *what did you think about the tapes*?"

Parker sighed, "Heidi, I'm *really* on my lunch break and I *really* want to know what the special is. Sometimes we spies do come into a restaurant to eat." And she picked up her menu again, but now she whispered, "*And* I want to know what you thought of the tapes while I'm waiting on my food."

The waitress came and took their order. Heidi waited until she was out of earshot before she started. Then she looked around to make sure no one at a neighboring table was listening. She whispered. "Honestly? You're being taken for a chump. There's nothing wrong with those women. They are no more part of an evil conspiracy than we are. Of course, we are here having a *secret* lunch . . . " and she winked at Parker.

"Knock in off a minute will ya?" Parker was trying very hard to be serious, but it was difficult with Heidi. She didn't take a lot of things seriously. Her job as a criminal profiler had put her at some gruesome murder scenes. She spent a great deal of time sorting out the details of brutal crimes, then probe into the minds of deeply disturbed and violent people. Humor was her best defense against cracking up and caving in to the sadness surrounding her job.

"I'm sorry. You know how I am. I may be a goof, but I'm really good at my job. Listen; is there any chance I can get near these women? I would really like to meet them personally."

"Afraid not, we've got them locked up and you know, no one gets in or out of the building without having their picture taken everywhere they go. What else can I do?"

Heidi thought for a moment. "You know maybe it's not them I need to meet. Maybe I should be profiling that doufuss Griffin. He's a free man. I'm sure we can find him hobnobbing around town..." Heidi had an idea. "You know . . . we are *both* Doctors of Psychology and we are *both* pretty famous, maybe he would like to tell his story to me. He's not very smart, so I could just flatter him into thinking I was *very* interested in him, professionally speaking; besides everybody else is probably trying to avoid him by now. I'll bet he's free for dinner!" Heidi was delighted with herself. You could see the wheels turning in her pretty little head.

Parker didn't like the idea of Heidi getting that openly involved, but she also knew that the best place to hide was out in the open. He would never suspect her. He was so self-absorbed, he would probably tell her everything she wanted to know. The more she thought about it, the more she liked it. Now the question was; how to set up a chance meeting.

Heidi told Parker not to worry, she already had a plan. All she had to do was get him to The Club after work. She would do the rest. Getting him to the Officer's Club would be simple. All Parker had to do was mention to him that it was a favorite 'after five' hang out with *free* appetizers and he'd be there.

They toasted with their iced tea glasses and finished their lunch. In the back of Parker's mind she was still grappling with the comment Heidi had made earlier. She didn't like being made a chump. She was still undecided about what to do about *that*. She had served her country as a combat pilot in the Gulf War. She was career Air Force and she had always loved her job...until now.

When Parker arrived back at the Pentagon, she soon realized that her authority had been trumped by Dr.Griffin. She was angry but quickly realized that it afforded her a perfect opportunity to pay him a visit.

He had been given a temporary office of sorts. The area was used for traveling Diplomats. They were provided a secretarial pool and all of the other amenities required to do business away from home. She called the scheduling secretary to find out if Dr. Griffin was in and her response made Parker laugh. Apparently he wasn't making many friends in his new surroundings.

She headed to his office and composed herself along the way. She needed to appear cooperative and friendly toward him even though she wanted to wrap her hands around his chubby little neck.

She stopped at the reception desk and announced herself, then took a seat in the waiting area. It was a busy place. She loved to see Foreign Dignitaries in their native dress. It was customary at the Pentagon to make all foreign officials feel comfortable, so there were various teas and coffees from all over the world at the coffee bar. A buffet of various snacks was available throughout the day. Having just finished her lunch, Parker just sat down and observed with interest.

A lovely round woman wearing a colorful Hawaiian dress came over and told Parker that Dr. Griffin could see her now. She followed the woman down a hall and was then ushered into another interior office. She was instructed to have a seat and was assured it would only be a few more minutes. This interior office had a central room and private offices opening off of it. It was a small version of the Pentagon itself. She sat quietly listening for any sign of life behind the doors. The offices were either empty or sound proof. She could hear nothing but the pounding of her own heart. Then she jumped at the sound of one the doors opening.

Stewart Griffin waved her in. He did not speak to her. He just motioned for her to take a seat. He barely even looked at her. Parker entered the beautiful office, "Thank you for seeing me on such short notice." He looked up at her, realizing for the first time how tall she was.

"Have a seat Captain. I'm very busy. What do you want?" He went behind the huge executive desk and sat down. He didn't fit the room at all. There was a regal air to the furnishings, as it was meant to be occupied by kings.

"Sir, I would like to thank you for taking precautions with the prisoners, sir." Captain James almost choked on her words.

Stewart looked up at her in surprise. He had expected her to be hostile. "Uh…well yes, you're welcome. It is vital that we keep a tight reign on these women. Remember I *know* them and I know what they're *capable* of."

"Yes Sir, that's why I'm here, I need your advice and counsel on this matter. As you know, I've been conducting interviews with the subjects over the last few weeks. From what I have been able to gather, knowledge of this report has spread all over the world. We are in the process of identifying individuals who have contributed to its content, but we believe it will still be difficult to contain. Do you take my meaning sir?"

Griffin cleared his throat and made facial expressions of concern. "Yes, yes, I get your meaning. Well young lady, then it is up to *us* to counter the effort and *expose* this ridiculous document! I mean it is obvious even to the dim witted that its *real meaning* is encoded *inside* the code itself." He cleared his throat again. "This is very complicated. I plan to make my suggestions to Congress tomorrow. Until then I really shouldn't tell you any more than I already have." He cleared his throat for a third time.

"Oh, yes sir, I understand. Um . . . Dr. Griffin may I talk to you on a personal level?" Parker was making her move.

"I don't know young lady, what do you have in mind?" Griffin was intrigued.

"Oh, I don't mean *really* personal sir, it's just that you probably don't know a lot of people in Washington yet, and I just wanted you to know that if you're interested...the Officers Club is a good place to meet people. A bunch of us go there after work. They have free appetizers and drink specials and stuff...and I just thought I'd let you know . . . sir. You know, being new in town and all." She smiled at him and caught him off guard. It was the first invitation anyone had extended to him.

"Uh . . . well . . . thank you Captain. I have so many other engagements to consider... but that was very nice of you to think of me." He said as he nodded in her direction. His mind was already conjuring up images of cocktail weenies and Swedish meatballs.

"Well sir, thank you again for seeing me on such short notice." She smiled at him again as she was putting on her cap, and with that, she left the office. "Putty in my hands" she mused.

Chapter 26

With years of documents still to decode, it was back to work for the SETI team. Dr. Merrill decided that they should probably call John and Janie back to the lab. Sadie was the only one they had now to translate for them. She gave Sadie the choice of *calling* them telepathically or actually using the phone. "*You* should call them Dr. Crithty, their mother ith worried about them."

Cristy sometimes forgot that these wonderful people were still somebody's children. Of course she needed to call their mother. "What was I thinking?" Getting them back to the Observatory was not a problem because the delivery truck was still on site, and her security chief loved to play the game of espionage.

Cristy made the call. She was stunned to find out from the mother that the children had been taken from their home in the middle of the night. A knock at their door late on Saturday revealed armed service personnel with orders to take her son and daughter into custody for questioning. She was devastated and didn't know who to turn to. She was furious at Cristy for getting their family involved.

After she hung up the phone, Cristy had to sit for a moment to collect her thoughts before she told the others what had happened. She confided in Michael first. "I didn't see this coming Michael. I feel terrible about it. Those kids are so young and they were just helping us out."

Michael had to drink it in as well. He knew they were being hunted, but he hadn't expected them to go after the other Indigos. "What do you think they'll do to them? I mean do you think they'll try to send all of them to Washington?"

"I don't know Michael. I have a feeling that this is getting out of hand. We need to get Sadie to contact them and make sure they're okay. Their mother deserves to have some peace of mind. That's the first thing we *can* do. Next, we need to get a hold of Teddy. No calls from here. Use the cell phone. Amanda and Katie need to get this story ready to go. I will contact the network and get an interview set up. We need to blow the lid off this thing soon, before somebody gets hurt trying to protect their child." Michael nodded in agreement.

☯☯☯☯☯☯☯

All over the globe, children and young adults were being taken into 'custody' under the guise of world security. Australia was another story. The Outback can be an unfriendly place for strangers.

David knew intuitively he was about to have company and contacted Jacko. The men devised a plan of defense. It was not necessary to run. The Aborigines were masters of illusion. They were delighted to have such a challenge and they relished the opportunity to teach a lesson to the unsuspecting officials.

After a Ceremony in the wild, they were ready to set their trap. David's home was little more than a hut. There was only one room.

The Elders of the tribe could not remember a time in recent history when they had needed to use the magic of *the mirror*, so they begged to be a part of it, for the sake of honing their skills, if nothing else. The plan was set.

David knew there would be six men. He saw that they were armed, and hoped his plan would not backfire on them. The people who were his family in the wild were precious to him. They had been through some pretty tough times together, but it was the times of joy and camaraderie that sealed their bonds.

Dawn was still an hour away when David started to light the lamps. Light was an essential element in their plan. You must 'see' what you are afraid of. It is not enough to fear the dark. He also lit the torches surrounding his home. A ring of fire is what they would see first. Jacko and David remained inside the hut while the elders were posted outside. One of them had his ear to the ground. He began to smile, as their prey was not far now. They assumed their positions.

The truck stopped a short distance away and two men got out and went to the back of the truck. One of them held back the canvas as four more men jumped down from the back. Five men slowly approached the hut with rifles drawn while one man was left behind to guard the vehicle.

Without a word, the lead man signaled for three of the men to remain outside and indicated that one should follow him. They had no intention of knocking. They hung back for a moment as though they were counting to three and then stormed in.

One scream was heard, and then another. The men outside the hut darted looks back and forth between them, trying to decide what to do. As each of them went to move toward the door they were faced with their greatest fears. Each man saw what he most feared . . . the monstrous dark side of himself. The man left guarding the truck was unsure what to do. He started for the hut and stopped dead in his tracks. He couldn't register the fact that his *mother* was standing in his way. He was dumbfounded and terrified all at once. He was unable to scream. He was frozen with terror. The other men were running for their lives. Jacko was having so much fun that he chased one of the men around the truck a few times. The frightened man was so panicked that he shot wildly over his shoulder. They fought each other to climb into the back of the truck. Only one had the presence of mind to get in the cab, so they could make their escape. In a cloud of dust, they sped away.

Laughter could be heard bellowing from all around the hut. The elders slapped each other on the back in congratulations for a job well done. David thanked the men for their performance as he fanned the dust out of his face. He started to look around for Jacko; he wanted to thank him as well. Then his stomach sank. David knew before he saw the body face down in the dirt that Jacko was dead. The stray bullet had found its target. David rolled him over on his back. The Elders began to wale in sorrow. He brushed Jacko's hair from his face, laid a tender hand on his friend's forehead and said a prayer. His tears hit the dry earth in little puffs. When he had finished the prayer, he took Jacko in his arms and held him.

One of the elders had gone back to the hut and when he returned he had with him a sled made from a table and a bundle of blankets. With heavy hearts they wrapped Jacko's body in the blankets and put him on the sled. David was left alone to watch the sunrise as his countrymen disappeared into the distance.

Chapter 27

There was a crowd for happy hour. The Officer's Club was a buzz of activity. The three televisions over the bar were silenced by the noise of the patrons. The only voice that could be heard over everyone else belonged to Bree, the best bartender in Washington. A tiny little thing, she weighed in at only ninety-five pounds (twenty of it in her chest). But her laugh was as big as Tennessee, the state where she was born and raised. She entertained her clients with stories of Nashville, and it seemed she knew every joke ever told. Her long, blonde hair followed her like a veil, and her thick southern accent was music to the ear. It rolled off her tongue like sweet molasses. "Hey Darlin!" She would yell when she saw a familiar face. She had a way of making everyone feel special. She would make up pet names for people and say things like, "c'mere you hunk-o-burnin' love and give me a hug!" She was exuberant and she was loved by men and women alike. Clients who knew her best called her Breezy, as she *was* a like a fresh breeze after a long, hard day.

Heidi was seated strategically at the corner of the bar where she could see the door. Parker walked in and tucked her cap under her arm. She ran her hand through her short hair to give it a lift and spotted Heidi almost immediately. She nodded in her direction and headed for the opposite side.

"Parker poo poo butt," Bree said sweetly, with a huge smile on her face, "Ya ready for a cold one?" Breezy never forgot what you drank. It was never necessary to ask, *what'll you have?* Parker smiled and nodded, knowing that she couldn't be heard over the roar of the crowd. Heidi was making faces at her from across the bar. *Goofball.* Parker thought. She wondered if Griffin would show up, but she didn't have wonder for long. She gave Heidi the look that said *he's here,* and took a long draw from her beer.

Stewart Griffin hesitated at the door, unprepared for the number of people who crowded the happy hour scene. He stood on his tiptoes in search . . . and found what he was looking for, the buffet. Like a cat following its prey, he kept his eye on his target as he maneuvered through the sea of people. Heidi slunk off of her bar stool and headed for the food line too.

Bree put out a wonderful spread. It took all day to prepare the meatballs and cheese balls. She cut vegetables and arranged them in artistic ways. The cold cuts and cheese trays were always fanned out perfectly. Bree took a lot of pride in her presentation of food and it showed. During happy hour though, she would put someone else in charge of restocking the tables so she could pursue her passion, meeting people. For Bree, alcohol was just the nectar that brought her worker bee's home to her. There was no doubt in anyone's mind that *she* was the Queen Bee.

Heidi maneuvered herself next to Griffin. Parker was watching but didn't want to get caught watching, so she would strategically dip behind other patrons whenever he glanced around in her direction. Heidi was making faces behind Griffin's back. Apparently he was wearing too much cologne, because she was making gagging gestures. Parker signed her to knock it off and then hid behind someone as Griffin turned her way again.

As the line progressed, Heidi began to make conversation, first to the woman behind her and then to Griffin himself. "I've never been here before, is it always this crowded?" He looked at her and just shrugged his shoulders. She squinted her eyes and tried again. "You look familiar; do I know you from somewhere?" *That* got his attention. He knew he had a few moments before he got to the front of the line, so he indulged her.

"You've probably seen me on TV." He said, pretending to look appreciative.

"Oh yeah, you're that famous psychologist! I think you're brilliant! I would love to pick your brain sometime. I'm a psychologist too! Gosh what are the chances of running into you in *this* city?" Heidi could taste the bile in the back of her throat, as she tried not to gag.

"Well, I'm here alone. Would you like to join me?" Stewart said eagerly.

Heidi's stomach lurched as she said, "Thank you, I'd love to."

They proceeded through the buffet line. Griffin piled wings on top of meat and cheese, which were on top of meatballs. He stuffed food in his mouth as he went and at the end had an enormous mound on his plate. Heidi put a few vegetables on her plate and left it at that. There was an outside patio with few people on it, so Heidi directed him to a table and told him to start without her; she was going to get drinks. The thought of watching him eat while smelling that awful cologne was too much to bear. She smiled and said she'd be right back. He was already stuffing his face and barely noticed her departure.

"Howdy Stranger!" Bree greeted her new guest. "What'll it be?"

Heidi was looking to see what she had on draft. She pointed and said, "Sam Adams." While she was waiting on her beer she scanned the crowd in search of her friend.

"Parker . . . you ready for another one Hun?" Heidi spun around to see her friend standing right beside her.

"How's it going?" Parker said nervously.

"I'll do just fine if I don't puke on him first. God, he wears a lot of cologne!" Heidi said as she screwed up her face. "I may have to get good and drunk tonight," she said as she slugged down the beer. She held up her empty mug and asked, "Can I get two more of those?" She turned to Parker, belched, smiled, and then said, "Okay, I'm goin' back in, wish me luck."

Heidi was relieved that Stewart was a fast eater. He was almost through the mound of food when she returned. "I hope you like Samuel Adams," she said as she set down the frosty mugs.

"I love any beer that's free." He burped. Heidi was appalled. "So you call yourself a psychologist. Are you in private practice?" He sat back picking his teeth.

"You could say that. I sort of do consultant work. But I'm really curious about you. I think it's fascinating that you chose the SETI program instead of the traditional route of practice. What attracted you to SETI? I don't know much about what they do." Heidi had opened up a can of worms. Griffin talked about himself for the next two and a half hours, halting only to return to the buffet or when Heidi hailed a waitress for more beer. She put round after round on her tab. Griffin never offered to buy once. He managed to eat all he wanted and drink premium beer all night without ever spending a single dime.

Heidi asked, "Are you alright to get back to your hotel?" Griffin's eyes were starting to cross.

"Yeah, I'll just get a cab." He slurred and then he tried to stand up. He staggered to one side and then another. Then he checked to make sure he still had his wallet, which he hadn't used all evening. "It was nice to meet you . . . thank you for a lovely evening . . . burp." He gestured to tip a hat he wasn't wearing and staggered out the door.

Parker was still at the bar, engaged in conversation with Bree. Heidi overheard the tail end of it as Bree was saying "Honey, trust me . . . I wouldn't steer ya wrong . . . I love ya as hard as brick." Then she erupted in laughter and walked away.

Parker turned to Heidi and asked how it went. "Man, you owe me . . . big time! I'd rather go Christmas fishin' with Scott Peterson than do *that* again. A guy like that could make a woman switch teams."

Chapter 28

Cristy was concerned about the interns safety and so decided to get everyone out of the Hat Creek facility. If someone showed up with a warrant, she would be powerless to stop them. Michael went to the Security Chief and prepared the delivery truck for departure.

The boys were packing again . . . moving again. Christopher was getting grumpy about all of the drama and was ready to go home. "Nateman, how can you stay so happy being moved around like this? You're really getting on my nerves with the whistling!"

Nathan seemed to roll with the punches easily. During the summer he used to travel a lot with his family. They had converted an old school bus into a camper and painted it blue. It was their home for three months out of the year. He found his happiness everywhere he went. He just shrugged his shoulders at Christopher and went about putting dirty clothes in a plastic bag.

To be sure they wouldn't be followed to Old Station, the driver initially headed in the opposite direction for Redding.

Cristy had left her car at Hat Creek, deciding to travel with the group. She didn't want them out of her sight. They traveled quietly with only the highway humming under their feet. "Thsing me a thsong Jethica," Sadie said, as she snuggled next to Dove.

Nathan reached for his guitar. "Yeah Jess, sing us a song." He quietly tuned it as she was thinking.

"How 'bout this one?" She closed her eyes and felt the rhythm of the road. "I am a poor wayfaring stranger . . . while traveling through this world of woe . . . yet there's no sickness, toil or danger . . . in that bright world to which I go." She took a deep breath and sweetly sang; "I'm going there to see my father . . . I'm going there no more to roam . . . I'm only going over Jordan . . . I'm only going over home." Then Nathan played a beautiful bridge of music. She continued. "I know dark clouds . . . will gather round me . . . I know my way is rough and steep . . . yet beauteous fields lie just before me . . . where God's redeemed their vigils keep." Again she took a deep breath and bellowed; "I'm going there to see my mother . . . she said she'd meet me when I come . . . I'm only going over Jordan . . ." Her voice began to crack with emotion, "I'm only going over home."

Nateman continued to play and when he realized she couldn't finish, he softly sang, "Goin' home now . . . oh somebody show me the way home." After a long silence he said, "My grandma used to sing that to me. Thanks Jess, that was really beautiful."

Jessica could only respond with a nod and a grin. The tears she was choking back had taken her voice.

Without warning, the driver suddenly jerked the steering wheel right. Everyone and everything in the cargo hold lurched to the left. "Is everything okay up there?" Michael said through a small peephole.

"Yeah, sorry about that, I almost missed my exit. No one else got off so I think we're in the clear," said the driver.

Christopher was nearly jostled out of his seat, but got trapped by his seatbelt. The pressure on the latch made it impossible for him to free himself. "Fu*^#@+_)(*&^^%%$#$#@@!!!!" The stream of profanity that came out of his mouth was shocking.

"Christopher! Please!" Michael was referring to the women and children in his presence. "Get a hold of yourself man. Here, I'll help you." Michael unlatched himself and went to Christopher's aid.

"I'm sorry, but I'm starting to lose it. I have had enough of this espionage shit. I want to sleep in my own bed. I want to talk on the phone and email my friends. I miss my girlfriend and I'm ready to go home." Christopher adjusted himself back in the seat and refastened his seatbelt.

"We all want to go home, Darlin'," Jessica said in a sweet quiet voice. "It's almost over." She turned to Cristy. "When we get to your place, can we find out if the twins have finished the story? I think its time to move on this. It's getting weird for everybody."

"Yeah, absolutely, I couldn't agree more." Cristy sighed. The rest of the trip was uneventful. Once they got to Old Station, they pulled around the back of the mercantile and unloaded. From there it was a short walk to the house. Still, they were being cautious, and sent only two at a time.

Once they were safely in the house, Christopher and Nathan took their bags into their room. "I need to lie down for a while," Christopher said. "This whole thing has gotten on my nerves." Nathan left the unpacking for later. He picked up his guitar and quietly left the room.

Michael was in the kitchen with Cristy. "I'm getting worried. I feel like our hard work is unraveling. Our friends were kidnapped

~ - 262 - ~

by the Secret Service, we're hiding like fugitives and innocent children are being abducted from their homes in the middle of the night! I'm with Christopher; I'm ready to go home."

"And Jacko got killed." Sadie's tiny little voice came from the doorway.

Michael scooped her up and set her on the island. "Who's Jacko, sweetheart?"

"David'th friend." So Sadie proceeded to tell them about the raid in the Outback. "I went to thee Claire," she told them. "They are ready to go home too. They're worried about uth. Claire told me they had to give them a litht, but *my name* ith not on it and neither ith Amanda and Katie. Nobody know'th about uth. She thaid we are the only theecret left and that we *muthst* protect the *theecret weapon*." She smiled, "That'th me and Katie and Amanda. We're the *theecret weapon*. That'th what Claire callth uth." She giggled.

"Okay, well I think we can consider that message a launch." Cristy nodded her head in contemplation. "Teddy said they had been working hard all day. If the government still doesn't know about the twins then they can freely move about. We still want to be cautious, but at least their pictures won't be hanging in the airports."

"That's good news. That's really good news. Should they take Sadie with them? Would it be safer for her in L.A.? I mean she is the only *free* person left who can read the code. David and his Tribesmen have probably gone even deeper into the Outback."

"We won't be able to maintain contact with any of them without Sadie. We need her." Cristy said, but almost immediately changed her mind. "But we can't *use* her. She is valuable to all of us right now. We have to do our best to protect her. If they find out about her, she'll be hunted down, like the others."

"I'm thtill here," Sadie said. "Can't you thee me? I'm thitting right in front of you." The two just looked at her. "You're talking about me like I'm not thitting here. Don't you want to know what *I* think?"

"Yes, of course Sadie, we want to know what you think." Michael was careful not to sound condescending.

"I have to go to Loth Angelesth. They won't believe Katie and Amanda. Her bosth is going to want proof and I'm the proof! They won't put it in the paper without me," Sadie said matter-of-factly.

Cristy and Michael looked at each other and said in unison, "Okay." Sadie just smiled and kicked her feet like a happy little girl without a care in the world.

Chapter 29

Stewart awoke abruptly. The ringing phone seared through his brain. The poor woman who made the wakeup call took the full brunt of his wrath. He was so rude, she hung up on him.

After slamming down the receiver he stumbled to the bathroom to relieve himself, but stopped short when he saw his reflection in the mirror. What hair he had left was skewed in all directions. His eyes were swollen into slits. His attempt to open them wider was painful. They were so red that he expected tears of blood at any moment. "You fool!" He spouted to himself. "You stupid fool!" He turned from the mirror cursing to himself and clutching his head.

He was appearing before Congress in two hours; not enough time to recover from one of the worst hangover of his life. He reached in and turned on the shower. His head was throbbing with the beat of his heart. He stood in the steam and tried to remember what had led up to…he answered himself before he finished the thought. "Draft beer and that FU*%^&#@* woman," he cursed! He tried to smile when he remembered that he had eaten and drank the whole evening for free, but the explosive pain in his head wiped the grin clean from his face.

❧❧❧❧❧❧❧

The short trip to Capitol Hill was excruciating. Every time he burped he was reminded of chicken wings and chili. He was having trouble focusing and kept closing one eye to test if it improved his vision. His head felt like it was about to blow off of his shoulders.

After waiting for what seemed like an eternity, he was informed that the hearing had been rescheduled. Even though he vocalized his resentment for his inconvenience, he was ready to go back to bed and was truly grateful for the opportunity.

Just as he was heading for the exit, he heard his name being called. He made a split second decision to ignore it and move as quickly as he could to the taxi lane. "Doctor Griffin! Please wait!" Parker was running to catch up to him. "Doctor Griffin, I'm so glad I caught you!" She could see from the look on his face that he was not pleased to see her. In fact, he looked as though he could kill. "Dr. Griffin?" Parker stopped short of approaching him. He hailed the next cab and got in without even a look back.

Parker reached into her pocket and pulled out her phone. She punched in the number and waited. "They bumped him."

Heidi was still in bed. She too was a little worse for wear after last night. She had Stewart pegged in the first few minutes. Why then, she wondered, did she keep the charade going the whole evening? She lay there pondering the question. She replayed portions of the evening and smiled remembering how easy it was to manipulate him. Every time he would turn his head or go back to the buffet, she would refill his mug. He would act so amazed at this magical mug that never seemed to empty. She mused at how much fun it was to screw with his head. She was even more pleased with the thought of him testifying before Congress with a banger headache. "What? What do you mean they bumped him?"

Parker looked around to make sure no one was near. "The Speaker of the House got a note just before Griffin was scheduled to appear and gave the order to recess. Griffin was informed that his testimony would be rescheduled. What do you make of that?"

Heidi sat up. "Hmmm, zee plot thickenz." She was mentally clearing out the cobwebs and trying to think what could they be so afraid of that they wouldn't want him to testify in a public hearing? "Did you try to ask him about it?"

"Yeah, I chased him outside, but he got into a cab and took off. He gave me the creepiest look, like he would have shot me if he'd had a gun." She shook off again, the chills she felt when he looked at her. "Now what?" Parker was at a loss. She was more convinced than ever that this whole event was a set up and that someone behind the scenes did not want Stewart Griffin to tell his story to Congress. "I need my Uncle Pete."

"Who? I didn't think you had any family left." Heidi was puzzled.

"We're not actually related. He was my father's mentor and commanding officer. His real name is Colonel Samuel Brunsen. After my folks were killed, Uncle Pete saw to it that I was accepted into the academy and come to think of it, I don't know why I call him Uncle Pete…" Parker trailed off. "Anyway, he's gotten up there in years and I don't even know if he'll recognize me. He's at Glenview…" Parker trailed off again.

"Do you want to meet me later for lunch? I might be brilliant again by then." Heidi said, holding her head. "I don't know what else I can do, but maybe we can put our heads together and come up with something that won't land us in the brig."

"Yeah maybe a quick bite, then I think I'll drive up and see Uncle Pete." Parker needed someone experienced in these matters. But she wondered if he was even capable of helping. The last time she saw him, she was unable to wake him from his nap and just sat for hours reading a book she found next to his bed. "The Bistro at noon," she said before she hung up.

Chapter 30

Cristy folded the phone in her palm and turned to Michael. "Teddy and the girls will be here in a few minutes. They just stopped for some snacks and drinks. He is really excited about this movie. I guess he just got it in the mail today."

"Didn't Teddy say it has something to do with our project?" Michael moved over to the window. He was worried after getting the news of all the other children being taken. "*The Secret*, didn't that come out a long time ago? I never got a chance to see it." Michael moved the curtain back to get a wider view and scanned the countryside for any unusual movement.

"Michael I think we're safe here. No one knows that the kids even came to Hat Creek. For all they know you're still up on Eagle Ridge somewhere." There was no conviction in her voice. She too was afraid ...very afraid. "Do you want to go check on Christopher? I think maybe he'd like to freshen up before everyone gets here." She moved in closer and patted Michael on the shoulder.

As Michael moved through the house, he was proud of how well they had all held up, under the circumstances. Dove and Sadie were busy putting a puzzle together. Nathan and Jessica were hashing out a new song. Christopher had just been the first to vocalize it. Everyone wanted to go home.

Michael softly knocked on the door but got no answer. He knocked again a little louder, still no answer. His face flushed with fear as he tried the door. It was unlocked. Michael slowly turned the knob, suddenly afraid to open the door. He paused. His knuckles turned white under the pressure of his grip.

"Excuthe me!" Sadie said in her *big* voice as she brushed past Michael, pushing into the small room. "Kwisthtofer" she sang. "Kwisthtofer you sthleepy head, get up, get up, get up! The girlth are coming over!" She jumped on the bed and giggled and then she pounced and giggled some more.

"Alright I hear you! C'mere you little monster! I'll teach you to wake up a grumpy old bear." Christopher had thrown back the covers and proceeded to chase her around the bed roaring and growling like an angry bear to Sadie's great delight.

Michael stood in the doorway, smiling in relief. After the events of the last few weeks, he was getting a little jumpy, and didn't relish the thought of any more unpleasant surprises.

After a light knock, a key turned in the front door latch, and opened. Even though they had just spent the weekend together, all were happy to be in one place again. Cristy felt a sense of peace just knowing everyone was together. Teddy already had an armful of Sadie to balance with the grocery bags in the other. The Twins were equally happy to be reunited. They had been working diligently and wanted some feedback on their story. Jessica and Nathan grabbed bags and headed for the kitchen.

Nathan's face lit up the moment he peeked into the first bag. "I love this guy!" He pulled out a jumbo box of microwave popcorn, a big can of cashews, a variety bag of chocolate bars, and a bag of suckers. "My hero." He mocked by wiping away non-existent tears.

Jessica was busy putting away the soda in the refrigerator. "Nate, have you heard of this movie? I remember a bunch of people on campus talking about it a couple of years ago, but I never went to see it."

"Can't say as I have, I don't watch much TV and I don't date so I don't go to the movies much…" Jessica shot him a look. "What! First of all, I'm only fifteen which makes dating college girls somewhat awkward. Second, I like my guitar better than *any* girl I have *ever* met and third…" Jessica broke into a smile. "And third…" Nathan was now turning red. "And third is…SHUT UP! That's what third is!" Nathan put a purple sucker in his mouth and stomped out of the kitchen.

The steaming popcorn was being poured into large bowls and pillows were scattered all over the living room floor. They were so happy to be together. They had decided to watch the movie before going over the story Katie and Amanda were writing. Everyone needed the break from reality. After getting settled, the lights were turned down, and the movie began.

Ninety minutes later, the credits rolled. "Thith ith *our* mesthage." Sadie sat forward from Dove's lap. "Thith ith why we're in trouble."

"How could this message get us in trouble? I mean it's been told over and over again, by master after master. There is nothing new here, granted most people have never heard it put quite that way, but the message is *ancient*." Christopher was heading for the kitchen. "Anybody want anything?" When he came back he popped open a can of soda and sat down. "I don't get it, could someone please connect the dots for me?"

After a moment of silence, Teddy cleared his throat. "The problem isn't really that people have never heard of the law of attraction before, the problem is that they have never believed it. Someone, a long time ago coined the phrase, *if it's too good to be true, then it probably is*. I think NO-THING is too good to be true. Our truth becomes our reality. And the sad truth about humanity is that we're basically lazy. Disciplining ourselves to be conscious of our thoughts, words and actions takes a lot of effort. Criticism requires none."

"But if you could be, do, or have anything you want, wouldn't it be worth it?" Christopher was still struggling.

"Ahh . . . that's just it! You see, if you concede that it's possible to create wealth and health and happiness, then you have to concede that you've been creating your life all along and have attracted all the trouble you've ever experienced. The fact that you have created your own life and all of its contents is beyond what most people can accept responsibility for. They want to blame someone else for their troubles. Being a victim is the only way they can explain their unfortunate circumstances. But I think the larger issue here is the idea that someone or something else answers our prayers. If we accept this *Secret,* and admit that we are answering our own prayers, where does that leave God? This is really huge. The idea that we are in control of our own destiny individually and collectively is just . . . *HUGE*." Teddy sat back and reflected on his own words. The word '*huge*' hung silently on his lips.

Dove sat up and wrapped her arms around Sadie's shoulders. "I think what has everyone so nervous is that *this* time the message came from somewhere beyond the planet. It's one thing to pass down a story through the ages, it is quite another to have the same story revealed by unseen, self-proclaimed Guardians of the Universe."

Katie had been deep in thought. She was trying to remember why *'The Secret'* sounded so familiar. She looked at Sadie. "Didn't the Guardians mention that our original instructions were also our biggest *secret*?" Sadie nodded her head.

Christopher said, thinking out loud, "Okay, so if people actually wake up to the fact that they are creating everything anyway, then they would begin to create wealth for themselves, and they would develop clean fuel, and they would stop fighting over oil, they never really needed in the first place." He hesitated and then continued, speaking more slowly. "This would put the oil giants out of business as well as the coal industry. And just think what would happen to the pharmaceutical industry if people figured out they could heal actually themselves!" He paused again. "Oh shit, no wonder we're in trouble! There are a lot of very rich, very powerful people who already know this secret and would probably kill to keep it from becoming general knowledge. I mean as long as they keep poking holes in it or even ridiculing the people who suggest it as a possibility, they stay in business. Now I get it. But I'm kind of having a problem with this whole . . . *we answer our own prayers* thing. I was raised in a Christian Church. I went to Sunday school and everything. This isn't adding up. I understand the concept of Universal Laws. It's logical and it makes sense, but I was taught to pray to God and leave it to God to decide how it would be answered. You know, *Thy will be done*, not mine."

Everyone looked at each other, but no one wanted to interject. Teddy looked at Chris and said. "That's a really good point and we are treading some dangerous waters when it comes to religion. Every religion thinks that theirs is the true one. Some go as far as to say that if you don't agree with *their* doctrine . . . well, then you're screwed." Teddy started to look around the room for some help, but none came. "A few minutes ago, you were talking about all the wealthy powerhouses that have been running things? Let me just suggest to you for now that you do some research into Christian history and the political environment of the time. Start with Constantine and the Counsel of Nicaea. You might also check out the account of Roman officials burning the Library of Scrolls, which contained dozens of additional gospels. I think it's interesting that only four of them made the cut in to the Christian Bible. I'm not saying that you should change your beliefs; I would never say that to anyone. The only reason to change anything in your life is because it no longer serves you. I wouldn't change anything that made me happy. If you have questions, educate yourself . . . trust yourself and your own inner guidance. Everything we've been taught is a collection of someone else's ideas or truths.

This is really important to understand." Teddy sat straight up. Speaking very deliberately he said again. "EVERYTHING WE'VE BEEN TAUGHT IS A COLLECTION OF SOMEONE ELSE'S IDEAS OR TRUTHS." And then he said in a normal tone. "Remember, the Guardians talk about Jesus too . . . and in the most beautiful way."

Christopher nodded and quietly said, "Thanks."

Cristy got up and started to collect popcorn bowls. "We need to talk about tomorrow." She paused and took a deep breath. "Katie, Amanda and Sadie are leaving for L.A. first thing in the morning."

"No!" Dove yelled in horror. "No Sadie, you can't go! I won't let you! It's too dangerous!" She looked around for support, but there was none.

Sadie climbed up on her lap and brushed her hair with her little hand. "It'th okay Dove, I have to go. They need me." Dove began to cry. She couldn't control herself. She wrapped her arms around Sadie and sobbed. It was difficult for the others to witness such heartfelt grief, so they quietly left the room.

"I feel kinda sorry for her," Jessica said, fighting back her own tears. Katie and Amanda were tearing up too. Just the thought of being away from the safety of the group, going into the unknown was daunting for them.

"It's up to us now," Amanda said to Katie. "We have to get this out, so the madness can stop."

Katie sniffed and straightened up. "I'm just scared. Miller was such a jerk on the phone. How do we convince him that this is all for real and that no matter what, it has to be published? How are we going to pull it off? *Everyone* is depending on us."

Chapter 31

In the old kitchen, the smell of hot biscuits sent Tom's mind to far off places and long ago times. He thought of Claire as a small child helping her mother bake batch after batch of her famous cheddar biscuits, to sell at the local restaurants. The two of them would sing songs and laugh the day away. "Oh Clairee;" he whispered to himself, "Please come home soon, your Momma needs you." The tears streamed down his face as he stood at the sink rinsing spinach leaves. He wondered how he would tell Claire that the cancer had spread. How was he going to tell her that her mother was going to die? He wiped his face with the sleeve of his shirt and steadied himself.

He looked out from the porch and saw his beautiful Elizabeth sitting by the road in her high back chair. Even from such a distance he could see her face lit from the sun. He swallowed hard to choke back the emotion that was welling up inside of him. "This can't be happening," He said as he shook his head in grief. He cleared his throat, straightened himself up and stepped off the porch.

The dogs were lying at her feet. The smile on her face showed the contentment of her spirit. He hated to disturb her rest. "Sweetheart? Beth Honey, are you awake?" Her smile broadened. "Honey, I made us a spinach salad for lunch, just the way you like it, with Grandma Bee's hot bacon dressing."

"Mmmm, that sounds good. I thought I smelled biscuits baking a little while ago...must have been a dream." She stretched without opening her eyes, making sounds of contentment. "What time is it? Have I been out here all morning?"

"It's only 11:30, but you got up so early, I thought you might be hungry. The biscuits were going to be a surprise. I stole your cheddar recipe, I hope you don't mind." Tom was massaging her shoulders.

"No Sweetheart, I don't mind. It's time I start passing down my secret recipes. In fact, it's time that I show you a few other things as well." With that, Beth rose from her chair and blinked her unwilling eyes into focus. She wrapped her arms around Tom's waist and pulled him to her. He couldn't breathe. It wasn't that her grip was too tight, it was the thought of losing her that look his breath away. He felt so helpless and so heartbroken. Twenty-five years is too short a time with a woman like Elizabeth Clara Montgomery.

As they walked toward the house, Beth hesitated. Looking down toward their home and land, the fields were full color and the fruit trees were ripening. She felt a sense of accomplishment and completion. With a sigh, she look Tom's hand and started walking again, dogs in tow.

Chapter 32

Claire was getting frustrated. After nearly two months, the little box of a room was closing in on her. She lay on her bed wishing for relief from the boredom and the uncertainty. Captain James had not been by in two days. Dr. Griffin had also not returned. She was sure they were not on the same side. She had seen such a change in the Captain's attitude; she just couldn't imagine that Griffin had convinced her too.

She decided to try The Grid again. David was nowhere to be found when she tried last night. This was the first time in many years he wasn't right there waiting for her. She also tried to reach the other Indigos working on the project, but no luck there either. Maybe Sadie would be available . . . relax . . . deep breath . . . lights . . . strands . . . ZOOM, she was gone. A few moments later she was back. No David, no Sadie . . . nobody she knew. She sat up confused and worried. "What does *this* mean?"

In the next room, Arlene was getting worried as well. She too was convinced that Captain James had had a change of heart. She was very concerned about the show of power that Stuart was so anxious to demonstrate to them. How did he gain their confidence so quickly and what would he do to them next? Her thoughts were not only for their own safety, but for all of those they left behind up on the mountain.

ଐଐଐଐଐଐଐ

"Sadie? Do you want anything from the beverage cart?" Katie looked over at the little one whose face was pressed against the window of the jet.

"Juithe," she said without looking away.

"Juice it is then." Katie handed the juice box and a bag of pretzels to Amanda, who was busy typing on her laptop. Amanda passed them along, never looking up.

"I've got to finish this before we land. I'm so glad we showed this to them last night. The changes are perfect. I told you it was too long. Short and sweet, that's the key to keeping people from turning the page or turning the channel." Amanda never turned her head, she just kept typing.

"Have you forgotten about Mr. Miller? How are we going to convince him to run this story? We've already seen how big stories get censored or canned completely. It doesn't matter if they're true or not." Katie put her hand on her sister's. "This isn't going to be easy. Whoever is behind the kidnappings has already managed to keep this from hitting the papers around the world. Amanda . . . Amanda! Are you listening to me?"

Amanda stopped . . . and looking straight ahead said, "The Guardians will find a way. *This* cannot be stopped . . . not now." With that, she resumed her work.

Parker arrived at The Bistro first. As much as she wanted a glass of wine, she declined her first impulse and ordered an iced tea instead. The waitress didn't get a chance to leave before Heidi arrived and ordered the same. "Hey Captain, you look like someone ran over your puppy, what's up?"

"I don't know what to do. I am at a complete loss. The bogus hearing, my boss won't see me, Griffin has the run of my department and three innocent women waiting who knows what fate. I'm actually scared for them."

"Is there any way to get them out? I mean since you're probably already facing a court martial." Heidi was being comical, but the humor was lost on Parker.

"I don't see how. Griffin trumped my order to allow the women to see each other and doubled their guard. The man I saw this morning frightened me. I mean, he really gave me the creeps. I don't think he's stable." At that, Heidi laughed out loud. "Knock it off Heidi! This isn't funny! I feel responsible for those women. I know I didn't get them into this mess, but I feel like I should help them get out of it." She looked over at her friend who was looking now at the menu. "All they're trying to do is save the world...no big deal. Are you listening to me? How can you be so cavalier?"

"I'm not being cavalier, I'm hungry! Parker, I don't know what else you can do. We don't have the clout to get them out and we don't have any knights at our disposal to storm the castle. I suggest you keep your eyes open and wait for the perfect opportunity as it presents itself." Heidi looked up from her menu and said, "I think

I'll have the veggie calzone." Parker got up and left the Bistro without another word or even a look back.

Chapter 33

Teddy arrived back in Old Station shortly after lunch. The drive to and from the airport had taken all morning. Cristy had gone to work, but had left all of the others behind to spend the day at their leisure. So he thought he'd do a quick drive-by before heading back to the Inn. The departure of Sadie had left them all feeling vulnerable and sad. Dove of course had taken it the hardest of all. She hadn't been allowed to go to the airport, it was too great a risk. If they got careless now they would threaten the success of the entire mission.

Dove and Jessica had gotten up very early to see them off. For the first time since they met, the two of them found themselves alone at the kitchen table talking over coffee. "Sadie's mother was a crack addict." Dove said to the steam rising off of her cup. "No one has seen her in four years."

Quietly, Jessica said; "What about her Dad?"

Dove looked up from her cup, "No one even knows who he is."

"Are you thinkin' of adoptin' Sadie?"

The tears welled up in Dove's dark eyes and spilled over. "If God will give me the chance." She said as she bowed her head deeply.

Jessica touched Dove's hand gently and got up to rinse her cup. Standing at the sink she said "Oh shit! This can't be good."

The look of horror on Jessica's face frightened Dove. "What is it?"

"We've got company." Jessica said, as she ran from the window." Michael!!! Chris . . . Nateman! Get up!" Just as she was crossing the living room, the front door flew into splinters . . . BAM! She kept going even though she heard the glass door shatter in the kitchen. "MICHAEL!!!" She screamed.

Teddy was just about to arrive at Cristy's house when he saw two black Suburban's pulling up. He made a quick decision to turn on the next street and park behind the Mercantile. From there he had a good view of the cabin. "Oh God, what now?" He said to himself as he watched the front door shatter into pieces. Men wearing gas masks tossed in smoking canisters, then charged inside. In no time at all, limp bodies were carried out and unceremoniously tossed into the vehicles.

As the initial shock was starting to wear off, his first thought was of his sister. "Oh shit Cristy, what do I do?" He knew he couldn't return home. Mrs. Beal, his housekeeper, would just have handle to things there.

Teddy watched helplessly as the SUV's peeled out onto the roadway and sped out of town. He fumbled for his phone. With hands trembling he started to dial Cristy's number. So many thoughts were racing through his head. The twins . . . Sadie Moon . . . the kidnapped children . . . KABOOM! Teddy was nearly knocked off his feet by the blast. Cristy's old cabin erupted into a giant fireball. The ground shook as the fire cloud mushroomed high in the sky.

People poured out of the Mercantile and began to scream and run toward the fire. "Oh my God, her fuel tank exploded!" He heard one person yell. No one else had seen the black SUV's come in to town or leave. He was the only witness. With his head still swimming, Teddy managed to climb into his Jeep. Tears were blinding him, he almost couldn't breath, but he was grateful, grateful at least that they didn't blow up the house with everyone still inside, but mostly grateful that Sadie Moon was with Amanda and Katie. The *secret weapon* was safe . . . for now.

๑๑๑๑๑๑๑

As Cristy passed through the gate, she immediately realized Charlie wasn't at his post. In his place was a man wearing a black suit who spoke into his cuff the moment he saw her. He motioned for her to continue forward. Chills ran up her spine as she passed him. "Uh oh," she said to herself, "I'm trapped." She parked her car and took a deep breath. "Okay, what do I do . . . what do I do." She muttered to herself. She sat in her car for what seemed like years. She knew now that she hadn't been paranoid and that getting the girls to L.A. immediately had been the right thing to do. "It's all up to you now." She said to herself as she got out of her car.

Her office was a disaster. She gasped when she first turned the corner and saw all of her files strewn in every direction. Apparently they were finished there and had moved on to other offices. No one was around. She moved slowly, wading through her life's work.

"Dr. Merrill." An unfamiliar voice called out. Cristy stopped but did not turn around. She was still in shock and trying desperately to think. "Dr. Merrill, will you come with me?" A woman wearing a black suit took her arm and let her to the laboratory. No words were exchanged along the route. Cristy didn't put up any resistance. She knew better. Instead she found herself just trying to muster up the strength and courage to speak.

Once in the laboratory, she again was thrown into shock to see TV camera's set up and lights being adjusted. "What is going on?" she heard herself say out loud, but no one answered her. Now, more composed, she asked again in a more forceful tone. "What exactly is going on here?"

"You are about to deliver a statement to the public Dr. Merrill." Out of the shadows stepped a man who Cristy had never seen before. He glided toward her silently, his shoes made no sound on the hard floor. "Your friends are safe for now, but I cannot be responsible for their fate should you refuse to cooperate with us."

"What exactly am I going to inform the public of? Mister . . . I didn't get your name." Cristy looked at him fully expecting to get a response. She stood staring at his blank expression, unsure of what to do as he turned and walked away as silently as he appeared. She wondered, *what in the world is wrong with these people? They won't look at you or god forbid give you a straight answer!* As he glided back to her, he handed her some note cards and with only a nod he left her again. She began thumbing through them and felt the heat of her anger rise to her cheeks. "Who is in charge here? I demand to know what is going on! This is bullshit, and I'm not going to say this!"

"Yes, my dear you will," said a soft voice. "Dr. Stevens?" Christy was dumbfounded. It was her boss Dr. Cedric Stevens. He was semi-retired and had been with the SETI project from the beginning. "Listen to me Cristy, it's over. We've been ordered by our President to put this matter to rest."

"But it's not over! It's just the beginning! This is what we've been working for!" Tears began to fill her eyes.

"This is beyond my authority. The world isn't ready for this yet…we don't have a choice here." He looked down at the floor, defeated.

Cristy swallowed hard, determined not to let the tears fall from her eyes. Her mind was racing. She knew she had to do it for the safety of the others involved. To refuse would endanger their lives, not to mention hers. She took a deep breath and looked straight at the man with the silent shoes and said, "Let's get on with it." She straightened her shoulders and took a deep breath. A faint smile crossed her lips when she remembered her ace in the hole, *Sadie*.

☯☯☯☯☯☯☯

Teddy lucked out with a stand by flight to Los Angeles leaving in an hour, which was just enough time to buy a carry-on bag and a few essentials he would need for a few days.

After placing his bag on the conveyer belt to be screened, he bent over to take off his shoes. His eyes locked on five familiar faces. There they were. Michael, Jessica, Nateman, Christopher and Dove, on the FBI's ten most wanted poster. As he straightened up and walked through the metal detector, he wondered how long before *his* face would appear next to theirs. If they knew about Cristy, then they weren't far behind him. He hoped Mrs. Beal was safe and that his Inn wouldn't suffer the same end as his sister's cabin. He bought a hat and a magazine on his way to the gate.

Chapter 34

Parker made the drive to Glennville in less than an hour. Along the way she prayed that her uncle would be awake and remember who she was. "I need your help old man," she whispered softly to herself.

As she pulled up to the gate to present her I.D., she questioned, *are they worried someone will wander off, or that someone could wander in?* Granted, she hadn't been to a lot of nursing homes, but it just struck her that it had more the feel of a military base than a nursing facility. After checking in at the front desk, she was directed to the duck pond. She was told that Colonel Brunsen could be found down by the water.

Several slumped figures were lined up in their wheelchairs along the shady bank. None appeared to be awake. "I shouldn't have waited so long to come." She whispered. Quietly she walked among them, bending to peer at each figure, looking for a familiar face. Finally she spotted him, a lone figure, small and frail, sitting away from the others, next to a concrete bench. She sat down silently. It had been nearly a year since she had seen him. She always came on his birthday, but now that she saw how much he had changed, she vowed to come more often. It hurt her to see how the years had ravaged him.

"Uncle Pete?" Parker spoke softly not wanting to startle him. Uncle Pete . . . it's me Parker." She laid her hand on his bony arm. "Please wake up Uncle Pete . . . I need your help."

Without lifting his head or moving a muscle, he said, "Hello Peanut."

"You're awake . . . good . . . what's wrong . . . can't you move?" Parker bent down to see that his eyes were still closed.

"I'm awake . . . but if I lift my head, *they'll* see, so just pat my arm and don't give me away."

Parker cocked her head in confusion, but did as she was told. "I don't understand. Why don't you want them to see you awake?"

"Well if they see me awake, they may suspect that I didn't take my meds this morning . . . which I didn't. And if they find out that I didn't take my meds, then they'll knock me out by injection . . . and that my dear is what I'm trying to avoid."

"Why would they do that?" She said in a condescending tone. Parker was beginning to wonder if her uncle was delusional and not playing with a full deck anymore.

As though reading her mind he responded. "Because those are the orders and no, I am not senile . . . yet. Unfortunately I'm as sharp as I've ever been. I only *wish* dementia would rescue me from my hell."

Parker's heart sank. "I had no idea. Why didn't you tell me this before? You can come live with me. I'd love to have you."

"I'm glad you're here. It's been a long time. I've missed you. Thank you for the invitation. You have a generous heart . . . just like your mother. But they will never let me leave." Parker started to say something, but her uncle stopped her with a squeeze of her hand. "Now listen to me Peanut, it's time you knew a few things.

First of all I didn't choose to be here. After my retirement, they kept me on the payroll as a consultant. But when I had my stroke a few years ago, they made me sign a power of attorney and stuck me in here. Because of my security level, they can't risk the chance that I'll become loose lipped in my old age and spill Top Secret information. So here I am, sitting by a duck pond . . . pretending to sleep. See those guys over there?" She turned and looked at the small figures lined up along the shady bank. "Top level men . . . all of them. I'm surprised they don't just kill us all and be done with it." Changing his tone, he continued. "So please understand I would much prefer to sit up and look at your pretty face."

Parker smiled. "Uncle Pete, I'm so sorry. I didn't know. That's sort of why I'm here. I need some advice." And so Parker related her story to her uncle. She spoke low and even, looking out over the pond, as though she was talking to herself.

When she finished her story, there was a long pause. She was afraid that he had fallen asleep after all. She was startled when he broke his silence with a forceful whisper. "God damn them! I warned you about the NSA. Can't trust `em." He snorted and then became quiet again. "The Guardians . . . I don't recall them being on the list. Do they hail from our part of the galaxy?"

Shocked by his response she said; "What list?"

The Colonel continued without answering her question. "They sound like Andromedan's. They're definitely not Reptilians." He continued to mumble to himself. "You mentioned three women. Who else is involved?"

"I'm not sure. They gave us a few names. They call themselves the Indigo Children. And so far they're the only ones who can see the code. Our people have had no luck at all. We can't make heads or tails out of it. Two days ago, we started collecting other Indigo's into custody. You haven't answered my question yet . . . what list?"

"Parker, some of what I'm about to tell you is still classified, but most of it is a matter of public records, if you know where to look. I'm not worried about myself. Shit, my life is over, but you're still young. Use only what you have to. Don't get yourself killed over these women."

"Killed?" Parker thought she was being dramatic with the thought that she might be court- marshaled.

"Honey, Presidents have been killed for less." He said with little emotion. "Okay, get comfortable, this could take a while . . . I hardly know where to begin." The Colonel kept his head bent to his chest and took a deep breath.

"So many have lost their lives . . . trying to bring this out in to the light" He said softly.
"I don't have time to fill you in on the back story of the Illuminati; you'll have to research that on your own. Begin with Galileo. Believe me when I tell you that the plot for a one world order goes back to the 1760's, and every war since then been financed and orchestrated to reach such an end."

"The Council of Foreign Relations, commonly referred to as CFR, is the Illuminati in the United States. England's branch is called the British Institute of International Affairs. France, Germany and other nations operating under different names and all these organizations, including the United Nations, continuously set up numerous subsidiary or front organizations that are infiltrated into every phase of the various nations' affairs. But at all times, the operations of these organizations were and are masterminded and controlled by the International Bankers; they in turn were, and are still controlled by the branches of the Rockefeller and the Rothschild families."

"What do the Illuminati have to do with this *list*?" Parker asked, still anxious to have her original question answered.

"My dear, the Illuminati owns, operates and controls everything from the price of bread to the leaders of the world. Do not underestimate their power. I've had up close and personal experiences and have watched my friends die at their hands. And now I'm too old to care who knows." With a short pause he continued. "I attended one of the annual meetings of the Bohemian Grove when I worked for the Nixon administration. I was invited to join the President along with several cabinet members. I had heard of this *boy's club* by rumor, including demonic rituals and other equally disturbing things, but nothing prepared me for what I saw. Powerful men, including the President, dressed in robes worshiping a huge owl. The images of burning human sacrifices in effigy and the haunting sounds they made chanting is something I still fear in the darkness of night." A chill went down his spine. "This was the year that Kissinger announced his plan for global depopulation. After his speech, he met with Nixon and other top world leaders. I knew that night that I was *in* for life. I had been allowed to see them for who they truly were. It was a privilege I immediately regretted." His voice fell. "I mention this because I want you to have a clear picture of who you are dealing with. This club is exclusive to the elite male figures of the world. Many women in high office have desperately sought an invitation, but someday when all of this comes to light, they will thank their lucky stars they were excluded." He risked a stray glance at his companion and then resumed his position. "There are a few celebrities, but most of the members are high ranking political, military and corporate CEO's. This is where politicians are selected, not elected. And it's where they gather to make alliances and plans for our future. It's scary stuff."

"Okay, I'll look it up;" sighed Parker.

"I'm telling you this because the media in every form, including Hollywood, is owned and controlled by those who wish to brainwash and control the population. You do not live in the country you think you do. Individual rights . . . freedom of speech? What a crock of shit. They are skilled masters of manipulation. What an opportunity the events of 9/11 became. The Patriot Act stripped the country of our right to privacy. Those days are gone. We can now storm in to any home or business without a warrant or consent. All financial transitions are now open books to Homeland security. Every email you send, every call you make is recorded. The GPS system in your car and the microchip in your passport make you traceable everywhere you go. Already they're selling the public the idea of putting microchips into pets and children . . . just in case they get lost. Your entire medical history can now be put on a chip and injected into your arm so you can be scanned for personal information. The media is selling *protection* by bombarding the population with *danger*. It's frightening . . . just frightening to see how easily manipulated people are." He paused only to change the tone of his voice to mock a typical commercial. "If you have these symptoms, call your doctor."

Parker looked at her watch. "How long will they let you stay out here?"

Ignoring her question he said, "Sorry, I got off track. Please believe me when I tell you that I had no part in this. They had already phased me out of day to day operations when this plan was hatched." His fists clenched. "I still can't believe they did it on live TV. I was in Dulles waiting for a friend to arrive when the news broke. We all watched in horror as the second plane flew into the tower. People were jumping to their deaths to the escape the flames. I knew as the first tower fell, that it had been brought down. No building of that size collapses into its own footprint after being on fire for only ninety minutes. Then moments later, the second tower fell in exactly the same way. No one has *ever* been able to explain why Building Seven collapsed at all! That one wasn't even hit by a plane! Tons of thermite was found in the aftermath. It's a nano compound used in building demolition, very volatile. It turns steel into puddles of molten iron, exactly like what was found at Ground Zero. No jet fuel or office fire can burn at those temperatures. Since no independent investigators were allowed on the site, they collected samples from the streets of New York. This shit is very high tech, Defense Department stuff. We're not talking about the stuff at the end of a Fourth of July sparkler. No fucking way did that shit come from a cave in Afghanistan." He sighed. "In the days that followed, I watched as they laid the groundwork for the invasion of Iraq." Again he glanced at her. "Iran will be next. Mark my words."

"You can't be suggesting . . . no, Uncle Pete. Those are high security buildings. Tons of material can't be smuggled in a backpack. Not to mention the time it would take to set up the charges." Parker felt ill.

"About nine months." He said. "They started to modernize the elevator system in January. They had direct access to the hoist way. Think for *yourself* Parker! Use your own guidance system. Don't even believe what *I* tell you as the gospel truth."

Parker's voice quivered. "But Uncle Pete, I was *at* the Pentagon on September 11th. Remember? It was horrible! We were all gathered watching what was happening in New York, when we heard the explosion. It sent a shockwave through the entire building, everything went black, people panicked . . . there was total chaos." She trembled at the memory.

"On September 10th, the Army confessed to misplacing three trillion dollars then coincidently the Pentagon took a direct hit . . . right into the Army's treasury office. Didn't you ever wonder what happened to the plane? C'mon Peanut, think! None of it squares up. Do your homework and draw your own conclusions."

She could barely speak. "How could we . . ." she trailed off.

"In 1999 we secretly contracted with Halliburton and KBR to build citizen containment camps. Since the attacks of 9/11, we've collected the names of over a million people, mostly U.S. citizens, adding about twenty five thousand a month to a list of terror suspects. These facilities can also be used as quarantines."

"Hold on, wait one minute. Who is on these lists? Parker was struggling to maintain her composure. "Quarantines . . . you mean in case of some kind of pandemic? How could they know ahead of time?"

"To answer your first question: peace demonstrators, anti-war protesters, a few six year olds with the same names as anti-war protesters and anyone who brings up 9/11 or speaks out against the government. You are about to put your own name on that list, I hope you know."

Parker's head was swimming. *More lists*, she thought. "And the quarantines?"

"I'm guessing they will be for anyone who refuses to be vaccinated against the viruses they're cooking up in their labs," he said as he patted her hand. "I've done some terrible things for my country, Peanut. I believed in duty and honor and I was a good soldier. The truth is that we as a nation are guilty of war crimes and crimes against humanity that make Hitler look like a school yard bully." He paused.

"Keep an eye on the World Health Organization; if they're successful in spreading one of their viruses, the laws, as they stand on the books right now, gives them authority to declare Marshall Law. This will dissolve the chain of authority of every U.N. member country. Crisis committees will step in to govern the affairs of these nations; answerable only to W.H.O. They would emerge as the global health department, insuring that the United Nations will become the global government."

Parker was having difficulty swallowing. She reached into her bag for a bottle of water. Uncapping it, she took a long pull from the bottle. "You know, a couple of years ago I would have called you a traitor and a liar, but I suspect what you're telling me is true. Even though my clearance is not at the highest level, I hear things. Most of it I chalk up to speculation, but today I'm beginning to understand that I don't work for the government I thought I did."

Quietly he continued. "During Vietnam, I sentenced thousands of our boys to certain death by ordering the use of Agent Orange. In 1973, we learned of a new weapon from the Israeli's . . . depleted uranium. In the first Gulf War we took three hundred and fifty tons of solid radioactive material and dispersed it across Saudi Arabia, Kuwait and Iraq. We didn't tell our troops that the exploding ammunition would put tiny particles of radioactive material into the air they would breathe, the water they drank, or the food they ate. We called it the Gulf War Syndrome and pretended we didn't know what was making them sick. Hundreds of thousands of our own soldiers suffered illnesses from skin irritations and headaches to cancer, and finally, when they got home, horrible birth defects. We also knew the radioactive material could never be cleaned up and will never go away. The substance moves in the drifting sands of the Middle East and is directly responsible for the deaths of countless children. In Iraq alone, over 300 children die each day. Haven't seen *that* on the news have you?"

"You're blowing my mind. I need a minute to process all of this." She paused. "I never left the ship during my whole tour . . . did you have anything to do with that?" He didn't respond. "Did you?" She asked one more time.

Again he ignored her question. He was deep in thought. "Let's get back to your original question before we run out of time." He squeezed her hand. "First of all, we know of about sixty- two species of non-human beings. The Grey's, as we call them, are just one of the species that live subterranean, in underground cities. There are undersea bases as well. Most of the reports are centered around the *triangles*. Bermuda and the one off the coast of Japan are the most active today, but the North Sea was a hot spot during the Cold War. Credible naval reports from various countries recorded flying ships diving into the sea and bursting back out from the depths."

He was becoming animated. "Many hybrid races exist as well. You would *never* suspect they weren't human. No doubt you've seen some of them walking the halls of the Pentagon. We've been borrowing their technologies since the time of ancient Egypt. As you know, I spent most of my career at Wright Patterson. After the crash at Roswell, the debris was sent to us. We managed over the years to reverse engineer much of the technology, including their propulsion systems. We did try the easy way first . . . we asked. But our cosmic brothers didn't trust us for some reason. They thought we might use this knowledge to make a weapon . . . imagine that." He said with an air of sarcasm.

"You mean we've been making contact all along? So if they're walking the halls of the Pentagon, why the big drama over this message from the Guardians?" She hesitated. "Underground cities?"

"Underground cities, underground bases and highways . . . shit, you can go from New Mexico to Ohio without ever coming to the surface! Most of our underground facilities were constructed during the Cold War, but once we had a treaty in place, we were able to use their existing complexes. The big drama, I'm sure, has to do with the treaty."

"We have a treaty?"

"Oh yeah." He said in a deep tone. "Neither side has any idea who they're dealing with. It's interesting though, that like humans, they have so much diversity within a species. I mean these Guardians, as you describe them, seem to be a benevolent group, capable of high intelligence. Many of them exist more like a colony of insects. They receive information telepathically and act as a unit, each doing his job in the hierarchy, much like ants or bees. You don't want to fuck with these guys. They have *no* sense of humor." He paused for a moment. "We were given fifty years to complete

~ - 300 - ~

our genetic experiments . . . time was up as of January 1, 2000. I was being phased out the program by then, so I don't really know how they've managed to delay the disclosure all these years."

"Okay, so if we have the technology to duplicate their space crafts, have we used them to go anywhere? Is this what people are reporting as UFO's?" She questioned.

He couldn't resist turning his head to look at her. "Our pilots aren't use to flying at those speeds." He chuckled. "In the last few years, commercial pilots have been reporting near collisions with unidentified aircrafts. Our guys are like little boys flying really fast toys. So yes, we fly them, but apparently not very well. As for reported sightings, it's hard to tell now which UFO's are us and which are the real deal. To orchestrate a mass sighting, let's say a fleet of ships, we can bounce images off the sodium layer about sixty miles above the earth, producing a hologram. But we're limited to daylight hours. The Phoenix lights? Oh yeah, that was the real McCoy. You should watch the live coverage of the Space Station sometime. It's sort of like watching paint dry, but once in a while you get to see a ship or two go by."

Parker thought she was beginning to connect the dots. "Are the Indigos some kind of hybrid race?" Is that what they're so worried about?"

"No darling, I think the Indigos are the next link in the human chain of evolution. Research began on them about thirty-five years ago, and even though we thought that their effect on the world would be negligible, a new program was developed to deal with the issue just in case . . . psycho-stimulants. We convinced the AMA to push speed on them. It completely fucks up their systems and makes them easier to control. Without it, they think too fast . . . and we can't have that."

"You have to be fucking kidding me!" She said louder than she intended.

The Colonel started to open his mouth in response, but put his head back down instead. A large shadow loomed from behind Parker and momentarily blocked the sunlight. "Oh, you startled me!" She said as she spun around.

"Sorry for that `mam," said a slow booming voice. The man was enormous, and his dark skin was in stark contrast to his white uniform. "It's suppertime for the Colonel. I have to take him back to his room now."

Parker composed herself as she rose from the bench. She smiled at the orderly and then she bent down to kiss her uncle's cheek. "I'll be back for your birthday." She said in a normal tone of voice, but then whispered. "What do I do now?" She put her arms around his neck and placed her ear next to his lips.

"Franklin has a lover. *His* name is Lieutenant Brice Daniels. They've been involved for years. Use it if you have to."

She almost fell over, but managed to conceal her shock. *Franklin's aide;* She mused to herself. She smiled and thanked the large man for taking good care of her uncle. Once in her car, she began to rifle through her console for a pad of paper and a pen.

Chapter 35

When Captain James arrived back at the Pentagon, she bypassed her office and went straight to see her Commander. As soon as she opened the door, she realized she had walked in on something important. The outer office was full of top brass. Bobbie saw her in the doorway and waved her in. Her Commander saw her as well and with a grin said, "Captain James, *you'll* want to see *this.*" There was a small flat screen TV mounted high on the wall where CNN ran all day long.

She arrived just in time to see the anchorwoman set up the clip they were about to see. "Well, it looks like we can all sleep a little better tonight. After months of investigation into the allegation of alien contact, the truth has finally surfaced. Live from SETI headquarters in Berkley, California is Dr. Cristy Merrill, the ATA project leader and director of the center for SETI research."

Dr. Merrill did not look directly in to the camera. She appeared to be looking at someone or something just off to the side. "We were so hopeful that at last we had made real contact with beings from another planet. But after months of investigation and with the help of the FBI and the NSA, we have discovered that instead of coming from half way around the Milky Way, this message was coming to us from halfway around our own Earth. The source of the transmission was pinpointed to a secret military base in Iran. For obvious reasons we can't go into much detail except to say it has long been suspected that Iranians were experimenting with anti-gravity technology and were planning to stage an attack on the U.S. under the guise of an alien nation. Although we are disappointed to know we are still, so far, alone in the universe, we are relieved to know that the threat was only human." At this point Dr. Merrill took a deep breath and looked straight in to the camera. "I would like to add one more thing . . ." The screen went blank.

"We must have lost our satellite link;" The anchor woman adjusted her ear piece and cocked her head. "Yes, it looks like we've lost them. Well, there you have it. If you're just joining us, let me re-cap . . ."

Applause and laughter erupted in the room. The men were slapping each other on the back, congratulating each other for a job well done. Parker stood in silence. When the commotion began to settle Parker approached her Commander. "Sir?" He ignored her first attempt to get his attention. With more force, she said; "Commander Franklin…*Sir*, what happens now…with the detainee's? Are they to be released?"

The smile drained from his face. He stood silent for a moment and then said. "It's a little premature for that Captain. In the game of chess, you have to know who all the players are and you must be able to predict your opponent's next move. How do we know that these women aren't enemy agents? You are hardly an interrogation specialist. Maybe we need to bring up some of our people from Guantanamo. *You* will tell them *nothing* of this…do you understand Captain?"

Parker saluted and said, "Yes Sir." And then she spun on her heal and left for her office.

She collapsed into her chair and sat for the longest time with no expression on her face. "He was right." She whispered to herself. "Oh God, Uncle Pete, what do I do?" The tears welled up in her eyes at the thought of those innocent women in the hands of men who were capable of such cruelty. She felt devastated that the message from the Guardians would be lost. The madness would continue and the people of the Earth would never know how much they were loved and supported. Images of ice berg's melting and wolves being shot . . . hurricanes and hungry children crying, played before her eyes. With her face in her hands she sobbed.

☯☯☯☯☯☯☯

A housekeeper at the Watergate was running her vacuum in the hallway on the fourteenth floor, when she heard a man scream, "NOOOOOOOOOOOOOOOOOOOOOOOOOOOOOOOOO!!!!" She made the sign of the cross, left her vacuum and ran down the hall.

☯☯☯☯☯☯☯

A crowd had gathered around the newsroom monitors. All the networks had shown the same broadcast from SETI. In Washington, the political annalists were being interviewed and commenting on the implications of the message. Military strategies to strike Iran

were already being considered. "They don't waste any time."
Garvin sat on the edge of a desk with his arms folded. "Amanda,
Katie can I see you in my office?"

Garvin was standing at a huge picture window looking out at the
city. "Close the door," he said without moving a muscle.

"Mr. Miller, what do you want us to do?" Katie asked quietly.
He didn't answer right away. The question just hung in the air for a
few moments.

"I was just thinking about how much I like Aruba." He turned
around with a smile. But immediately his expression changed. "I'm
not playing this time. I'm just not doing it anymore. They've been
telling us what to say and how we can say it for too long. News
people are supposed to report the *truth*. We're supposed to inform
our public about what's *really* happening in the world, but every
time a worthy news story comes along, they pull the celebrity card."
He was heating up. "While South American television was
broadcasting *live* footage of hundreds of UFO's flying over Lima,
we were reporting on the *unfortunate* death of Anna Nicole Smith
for the *third week*! God! I am so bored with celebrities! Who got
arrested . . . who's back in rehab...Paris Hootihoo, Lindsey what's
her name...who killed Michael Jackson? WHO FUCKING
CARES!!!" Gritting his teeth, he said, "I can't take one more
fucking minute of it!"

"Mr. Miller, I know we don't have a lot of experience, but is this
the way it works? Is freedom of speech just an illusion? Are we
really mandated to lie to the public?" Katie said pleadingly.

Garvin looked at the young women with wide eyes. "Didn't they teach you about Neuro-Linquistic Programming in journalism school? In case you don't remember, that's short for; *manipulate public opinion to see the world you want them to see*. It's the old shell game."

Amanda sat forward in her chair. "If I remember correctly, NLP helps to define your outlook on the world through changing your perception based on words, actions and ways of thinking, depending on the model you choose. Basically through propaganda, you can make people believe anything if you repeat it often enough."

Then Katie added, "They've been able to map the brain to determine the neurological pathways of pleasure, fear, desire and so forth."

Garvin looked pleased. "I can see you two were excellent students. Distract them over here with nonsense . . ." He said dangling his fingers to one side. "And then they won't notice what is happening over here." He slammed his other hand down on the desk. Making the twins jump in their seats. "God damn it, I'm tired of it." He returned to the window and was silent for a moment. "Those crazy mother fuckers are trying to start World War III. The *talking heads* have been preparing us at every newsbreak, telling us we don't have enough troops because we're still fighting the last war. And *I*...I've been tossing out all the reports that question the wisdom of this move into nuclear war." Then he muttered to himself, barely audible to the twins. "I don't think I can sit back and let this happen." He was still talking to himself. Then he turned around. "I can't believe I'm about to involve myself in this. I have a strict policy never to get involved in *anything*. Why do you think I'm not married? Jesus Christ, I'm two years away from retirement." He said through his teeth. Pacing back and forth across the window, he shook his head and took a deep breath. "Before I do anything, I need to talk to Sadie one more time. Meet me at the Venice Fishing Peer at 6:30." He paused, looking straight at them. "Now get out! You're bothering me!"

Chapter 36

The World Trade Center towers fell night after night on the evening news to remind the American public that they would never be safe from terrorists. Every network and cable news channel had their analysts preparing the country for a possible nuclear war. The Iranian government refused to admit they had any part of a plot to attack the U.S. For weeks the tension built, and the people prayed.

Parker visited the women every day. So far, no one had arrived to interrogate them or otherwise coerce them into changing their story. She had no answers for their questions. Commander Franklin was completely avoiding all contact with her, and had not reassigned her to new duties.

Alone in her office she thought of her uncle. She felt regret for not being closer to him over the years. Today was his birthday and she planned to go visit him after work. She picked up the phone and dialed the nursing home. "Yes, I'll hold." She said to the receptionist. After a few moments, the receptionist returned. "Yes, this is Captain James, I'd like to see Colonel Samuel Brunsen this afternoon." There was a pause.

"We'll have to call you back Captain." The woman said.

"I'm his niece. I'm on the list." Parker said with an air of irritation.

"I'll have to have his nurse call you back `mam. At what number can you be reached?" The woman said in a flat tone.

"You can call my office at the *Pentagon*. Do you have that number?" She said trying to sound important.

"Yes 'mam we have that number. The nurse will call you as soon as she can," she said again flatly.

"And how long do think that will be?" Parker was agitated.

"As soon as she can." The receptionist repeated and then disconnected the call.

What the hell? Parker thought to herself. *Why would they stop me from seeing him?* She wondered if the orderly had overheard anything. Maybe someone saw him talking to her after all. In her mind she replayed her visit. She was lost in thought when her phone rang.

"Captain, you have a call on line one. It's someone from Glennville; she wouldn't give me her name," Michelle said apologetically.

"Thanks Michelle," She said and picked up the receiver. A few minutes later she replaced the handset on the cradle in a daze. "Dead." She said sadly. "Died peacefully in his sleep my ass!" She shouted at the phone. *They probably smothered him with a pillow.* She thought as the tears spilled from her eyes. *I should have gotten you out of there . . . I shouldn't have left you . . . oh Uncle Pete, I'm so sorry.* She could see in her mind's eye, his frail body fighting as the orderly held a pillow over his face. She shook with grief replaying the scene over and over.

She felt like such a failure. She had failed her uncle and the women still sitting in their cells. She felt like she had failed the world. With her head on her desk she cried her heart out. Finally she was settling down and she quietly said, "What do I do? Uncle Pete, help me, I don't know what to do." After a few moments she sat straight up. The expression on her face changed to a grin. "That's it." She said quietly at first. "That's it! Uncle Pete, you're a genius. Thank you!" She grabbed several tissues from the box on her desk and blew her nose. She took a long drink of water and cleared her throat. "Okay Uncle Pete, this is for you." She said softly to herself.

Parker took out a piece of paper and composed herself. She began her letter with *Dear Commander Franklin*. She laughed to herself a few times as she relished in her work. When she was satisfied with the content of the letter, she ended it with one word, *checkmate*. She knew her uncle would have been proud of her. With a deep breath she sealed the letter in its envelope and left her office.

Chapter 37

Teddy insisted on going to the meeting. He didn't trust anyone at this point and was not willing to let Sadie out of his sight. They arrived fifteen minutes early. It was a long peer and Garvin hadn't specified where exactly to meet, so they walked to the end and then back to a spot where only a few people were gathered.

Right on time, Garvin arrived with his fishing pole and tackle box. And without acknowledging anyone, he stopped beside them and began to set up his rig. "This must be Teddy," he said without looking at them.

After Garvin sent his lure flying into the Pacific, he finally said, "It took some doing, but I think I have all the right people on our side. Sadie . . . I need you to do something for me." He paused. "If I give you a person's name and picture them in my mind, can you view them? Can you tell me if they can be trusted?"

Sadie frowned a little. "I think tho. But I need to move clother to you. Can I?"

"Sure," he said without looking away from the horizon.

So Sadie stood right next to him as he gave her name after name. Teddy and the twins just looked out over the ocean, patiently listening to Sadie giving her answers. Satisfied that all of them were telling the truth, he thanked her.

But Sadie warned him. "Remember thome of them could thtill change their mindth. I can only feel how they feel right now."

"I know Sadie. I just have to trust that they will be brave."
Garvin sighed.

"Are you going to tell us what you're up to?" Katie asked.

"Nope." He said curtly, slowly reeling in his line.

"See you at work tomorrow," Katie said quietly as they prepared
to leave.

Teddy picked up Sadie and put her on his shoulders. He patted
her leg and said. "Good job Sadie. You're as handy as a pocket on a
shirt." She just giggled.

Amanda was nervous. She sped up her stride to match Teddy's.
"Sadie, is everything going to be alright?"

"No matter what happenth, it will be alright," she said looking
down from Teddy's shoulders.

Amanda dropped back to walk with Katie. She took her sister's
hand and squeezed. "It's gonna be all right." They both said in
unison.

Chapter 38

Commander Franklin strode into his office after lunch, stopping at Bobbie's desk, only to be handed his mail without a word or having his secretary look up. She had worked for him for so many years that speaking was rarely necessary. They had their routine. Every morning she preceded him to the office, set his newspapers on his desk and prepared his coffee. She knew his schedule better than he did and was always one step ahead of him.

He sat at his desk thumbing through the envelopes, memos and phone messages. Initially the hand written envelope had not piqued his curiosity. He was on the phone returning a call when he realized whose handwriting he was looking at. Quickly finishing his call, he opened the envelope and began to read the letter. His heart sank into his shoes. After a long silence he whispered, "You *bitch*." He sat back in his chair. He could feel the blood rising in his head and his face heating up. When he read her final words . . . *"checkmate"*, he came unglued. "You fucking bitch!"

Bobbie heard his cry and jumped. The shrill pitch to his voice sent chills down her spine. She quickly ran to his door and knocked. "Is every thing okay Commander?" She said through the door.

Just as she did, the door flew open. "Where's Brice?"

Nervously, she said; "Sir, you sent him to sit in on that committee meeting."

"Well get him in here NOW!" He screamed.

"But Sir, it's a . . ." Bobbie didn't get a chance to finish her sentence before Franklin cut her off.

"I don't give a shit how you do it, I want him in my office now . . . right now." And with that he slammed the door in her face.

She stood there for a brief second in disbelief, then ran back to her desk and picked up the phone.

☯☯☯☯☯☯☯

"Your travel arrangements have all been made. I think you'll find everything in order, first class of course. We would hate for you to think we were bad hosts." Parker laughed. "I wish things had turned out differently, but I'm glad you're going home." She looked up at the camera in the corner of the room and then back at the women and said, "I really am sorry this took so long. Just sign next to the arrow and we'll get you out of here."

Dr. Sullivan was the first to sign. She'd had plenty of time to think about it in her cell. She knew it was the only way they'd ever see the light of day again. With a sigh, she stepped aside and made room for Dr. Vaughn. Last was Claire. She didn't hesitate a second. She stepped up, made a scribble, and headed for the door. "Are we free to go now?"

"Your car is waiting. Right this way." Parker was solemn. The day she signed her own Security Contract, she also turned in her request for transfer. Her career with the NSA was over.

It had been over two months since the women had breathed fresh air or seen the sunshine. They stood on the curb, faces turned up as the driver loaded their luggage. "I had forgotten how noisy it is out here. I don't think I'll ever complain about it again." Dr. Sullivan chuckled to herself.

Once they were checked in at the airport, they immediately headed for the phones to let their loved ones know they were finally headed home.

"Ryan? Oh god Ryan, it's so good to hear your voice. Yes, Sweetie I'm fine. I'm coming home. I'll be arriving on Delta flight 825. With the time change, I should be home for dinner." Tears were streaming down Dianne's face. "Honey, would you do me a favor? Would you call Father Joe and ask him if he's busy Sunday afternoon? Yes, that was a proposal. I'll see you soon. I love you Ryan . . . yes, I'll fill you in when I get there, bye bye."

☯☯☯☯☯☯☯

The taxi bumped down the old road. The Montgomery farm was just up ahead. Claire could feel her stomach clench in anticipation. Arlene patted her hand. "Are you okay?"

"I'm ready to jump out the window and sprint the rest of the way, but yes I'm okay." Claire blew out a sigh.

The roadside stand was coming into view, but something was missing…the high-back wicker chair. Claire's throat started to close. She couldn't swallow. The taxi made its last turn onto the gravel drive. There it was . . . Home. The trees were ablaze with color. Fall was such a beautiful time on the farm.

The old blue truck was pulled up to the barn door. As usual, the hood was up and her father was bent over the engine. What a familiar sight. It took all her strength to stay in the taxi till it came to a stop. The dogs were the first to greet Claire. Miss Ellie jumped straight up into her arms. Tom was close behind. He captured Claire in his arms and cried for joy. "You're home. Thank God you're home."

Arlene paid the driver and instructed him to put the bags on the porch. She kept her distance and waited to be introduced.

"Oh Daddy, I'm so happy to be home. Where's Momma?"

Tom's face dropped. "Down by the pond." They both looked in the direction of the pond and Claire saw her mother's chair. "She's taking a little nap Sweetie, she wanted to be rested when you got here." Claire buried her face in her father's chest and wrapped her arms tight around his waist.

Tom wiped her tears and said, "Why don't you introduce me to your friend so we can invite her in the house?" Claire composed herself and walked with her father to the porch.

Arlene had already made herself at home and made a new friend as well. Andy was getting a generous rub down. "You must be Tom. I'm Arlene Sullivan. It's a real pleasure to finally meet you. She got up and extended her hand.

Tom took her hand and pulled her into a hug. "Thank you for keeping her safe." He stepped back and smiled at both of them, "let me show you to your room so you can get freshened up. I'll start dinner in a little while, but there is plenty of stuff to eat if you need a snack before dinner. Claire, I'll be right back."

Claire was anxious to see her mother. Her father would just have to catch up to her. She stepped off the porch and headed for the pond, but before she got ten steps, she noticed someone coming out of the barn. Wiping grease from his hands was a handsome young man. As she got closer, she began to smile. She set Ellie on the ground. "David! Is that really you?" He smiled at her and opened his arms. She flew into them, almost knocking him off his feet. "What are you doing here?"

Putting her down, he stood back, checking her out. "You're beautiful." He said quietly and almost to himself. "You're absolutely beautiful." He hugged her again. "It's a long story that I'll save for a little later. I know you want to see your mom first."

The look suddenly changed on her face. "Yes . . . uh . . . I'm just so surprised to see you here. Do you want to walk down with me? I have so many questions." David put his arm around her as they walked down to the pond.

The old wicker chair was facing the water. Beth was asleep with her feet on a stool and a quilt on her lap. Claire froze when she saw her mother. She was unprepared for the change she saw before her. "She's so thin . . . oh, Momma," she whispered. Claire looked up and waved her hands before her eyes trying to keep the tears at bay. In a stronger voice she said, "Momma! I'm home!" and knelt down beside her.

Beth opened her eyes slowly and grinned. "Sweet Baby Girl of the Stars . . . there you are . . . where have you been? I've missed you." Claire laid her head on her mother's lap and quietly gave in to her grief. David was already on his way back up the hill.

Chapter 39

Nate, Jessica, Christopher, Dove and Michael were released without explanation, but not without conditions. After the debriefing, they eagerly agreed to sign the non-disclosure documents. Their ordeal had been frightening. Days before, when the effects of the tranquilizers had worn off, they found themselves alone in a cell. None of them had any idea where the others were being kept, or even if they were still alive. They had little to eat and were denied sleep as they were questioned day and night. They heard the same questions over and over. *Who are you working for? What is the name of your contact? How long have you been working for the Iranian government?*

Dove went to Los Angeles to get Sadie Moon and returned her to San Francisco. Miss Lee was thrilled at the prospect of adoption.

All of the Indigos from around the world were released. When the Interns returned home, Dr. Sullivan contacted each of them and told them what she could. She admitted to them that she really didn't know why they had all been released. But that she was confident their questions would be answered in time. Because of the security agreement, she couldn't give them any details of their captivity in Washington. She could only tell them how grateful she was for their safety and that she would be in contact with any news.

Just days after coming home, Dianne was up on a ladder plastering a wall, when she heard the warning tone on the TV with an announcement of a breaking story. "Ryan, turn that up." She descended the ladder and sat next to him on the couch.

BEEP BEEP BEEP . . . then a deep long tone, followed by three more beeps. The *National Broadcasting System has been activated . . . Please stay tuned to this local station for the following important message.*

The television screen went red with the words; *STAY* **TUNED** . . . in bold black letters. "We interrupt this program with a special announcement," said a female voice.

After a brief moment, the screen changed to a newsroom setting with a well-dressed, well groomed, but unfamiliar anchorman. "In recent weeks the escalating tensions between the Iranian government and the U.S. have been building to a show of force. Based on intelligence information gathered by the C.I.A., the Iranian government was accused of planning a terrorist attack on U.S. soil by using advanced anti-gravity technologies, stolen from the U.S. Defense Department back in 1990.

We were also told that a group of summer interns from the SETI program at Berkley in California were responsible for discovering the transmission.

I have before me now, direct from the White House, a statement citing that the original C.I.A. intelligence report was provided by an independent source. Since the N.S.A. was unable to break the code found by SETI, they sought help from an independent code analyst. This individual was a trusted sub-contractor who had worked for many years with the Defense Department. The C.I.A. now believes this man intentionally falsified his findings to provoke the United States into initiating a war with Iran. The investigation continues."

The anchorman cleared his throat, and silently reread his material before continuing. "As it turns out, SETI did indeed discover a message not of this world." At this, the anchorman paused to maintain his composure. "This message is not believed to be of human origin or even from our solar system. And the transmission itself is reported to be over sixty years in length. The group, who call themselves the Guardians, state that they have come to help humanity. Topics of interest from this transmission include available free and clean energy, global communities, healthcare, weather, healthier food crops and much more.

The SETI team who discovered this message has reported that only a small portion of the transmission has been translated so far and that much more is to come. They are recruiting experts from all over the world to speed up the process. Public access to this information will be available as soon as it can be translated and categorized.

Top cabinet officials have also announced that the President will first privately speak to Iran's President Mahmoud Ahmadinejad and then publicly apologize to the Iranian people. He is quoted as saying; *"In these times of uncertainty, when suicide bombers and other terrorist activities are a daily occurrence in our world, it is the policy of this administration to take all possible threats very seriously."* The President will address the nation on this issue tomorrow night at 8:00 eastern standard time. This is indeed good news for our nation and for the world."

Then the female voice announced, "We will now return you to your regularly scheduled programming."

Chapter 40

It was a Saturday and Garvin Miller had called to ask if he could stop by. Knowing that he would arrive in time for the broadcast, he instructed Katie and Amanda to turn on their television.

After it was over, Garvin reached for the remote and turned down the volume. "I wish I was a fly on the wall of the Oval Office right now."

"Oh my God . . . how did you do that?" Katie was still in shock.

"You did a good thing, boss." Amanda grabbed her sister's hand. "The next few days should be very interesting."

Katie cleared her throat. "I was so nervous that it was going to be interrupted, I couldn't breathe! I can't believe you pulled it off."

"I didn't pull off anything . . . yet. I mean we *think* we covered our tracks, but you never know. It's hard to tell how people will react. You know we've kept so many secrets from the public for so long, it might take some time for them to wrap their brains around the fact that we've *never* been alone in the Universe. We've got an uphill road in front of us. We just dropped a bomb on the world." He combed his fingers through his hair. "And now I have to get to work. We've got a special edition to get out."

"We're really proud of you. Thank you so much for believing us." Katie said.

"It wasn't you I believed . . . it was Sadie," he said as he went to the door. "Ladies, you've got a job to do. I suggest you get your asses in gear!" He smiled as he said, "I'll see you at the office." and he closed the door behind him.

☯☯☯☯☯☯☯

Sounds of jubilation rang out from all who had participated in the project. Nate danced with his mom in the kitchen. Christopher watched the broadcast with his girlfriend, who thought he was a hero. Jessica whooped and whistled in the front yard of her house, causing the neighborhood dogs to bark. Dove and Sadie sat holding each other in the tiny crowded room with Sadie's family, and Michael . . . almost fell off his treadmill at the gym.

Teddy and Cristy were at the Inn. Mrs. Beal had made a nice lunch for them and was serving them on the porch. When they heard the warning tone coming from the kitchen, they all ran inside to watch the broadcast. "It took a lot of balls to do that. I don't know how they convinced their editor to take on the whole government and the industry giants, but he's got some brass ones. I'll give em' that." Teddy nodded his head toward the screen.

"It's almost worth losing my house to see those bastards squirm. I can't wait to see how they handle the speech tomorrow." Cristy was grinning ear to ear as she sipped her iced tea.

The Officers Club was crowded for happy hour and buzzing with talk about the broadcast. Bree was gliding behind the bar, refilling mugs and pouring drinks. Parker sat at the far end where she found an open stool. "Parker Poo Poo Butt! Hey Darlin`, what's up?"

"Have you seen my friend Heidi? She's supposed to meet me here." Parker said, looking around the crowd. "Never mind, I see her." Bree set down the beer. Parker thanked her and walked over to the pool tables.

"I owe you an apology, Heidi, I'm so sorry I ran out like that. And then afterward . . ." Parker said quietly.

CRACK! Heidi broke the rack. "No problem . . ." Heidi continued to shoot while Parker stood by silently. "Okay, I'm over it." Heidi put her arm around Parker's shoulder and whispered in her ear. "I was grabbing a sandwich at Murray's today when the whole restaurant got up and went to look at the TV in the bar, so I followed. Shit Park! You came so close . . . What happened at work?" A broad smile was plastered on her face.

Speaking in a low tone, trying to keep a straight face; "Well, you would have been proud of me. I was genuinely shocked, but it took every ounce of self-control to keep from laughing. Apparently there were a couple of players we didn't know about. Reporters, if you can believe that stroke of luck. We never knew about them and so they didn't sign the security agreement. We can't press charges, so there's really nothing they can do now except write a speech for the President. Truth be told, they could have made the President look a lot worse. They actually gave him a way out to save face, which was brilliant, if you think about it." Parker couldn't keep from smiling. "I'm so glad they're safe, and I'm really, really glad that we didn't storm the castle."

Heidi chalked her stick. "Me too . . . wanna play?"

☯☯☯☯☯☯☯

They didn't get to watch it live at the Montgomery farm, but it hit the internet at record speed. Tom had gotten a call from some friends and set up the laptop for Beth so she could lie on the chaise lounge, while others watched on a 24" monitor. After it was over, Tom looked back from his office chair. "So this is what you've been up to."

"You just may have saved the world, Clairee," Beth said in a hoarse whisper. "I'm so proud of you." She began to cough.

"Momma, are you okay?" Claire rushed over to her mother and lifted the water glass to her lips. David stood by silently.

Arlene stood in the corner of the small room, arms crossed. "It must have taken *some* convincing to get their editor to stick his neck out like this. He won't be anonymous for long. I bet the C.I.A. is working overtime to find out who leaked this story." Arlene looked toward Claire and her mother. She knew it wouldn't be long now.

Beth was coughing and finding it difficult to breath. Her eyes watered from the strain. "Daddy? I think it's time to call Sarah . . . and you should probably call Holly too."

~ - 327 - ~

Chapter 41

Holly had been a lifelong friend to Beth. She was a nurse and would be needed for more than moral support. Holly was also friend to Grandfather Yellow Moon who had been supplying Beth with natural remedies to help her breath easier, once the cancer had spread to her lungs.

Sarah was from the area hospice program. A stranger to them a few months ago, she had become one of the family. Beth loved her as a sister. "Let's move her to her room where she'll be more comfortable," Sarah suggested.

Tom bent down and easily lifted her frail body. "David, will you put the kettle on and make her some tea?" Claire shot a look at her father that said, *hey, that's my job.*

Tom saw the look on her face and said. "I'm sorry honey, David's been my right hand man ever since he arrived. Why don't you come with me and get your mother settled in." Claire shook off her momentary wound and followed her father down the hall.

"Hello . . . anybody home?" Holly came through the door. There was no need to knock. The dogs didn't even bark at her arrival. She sat down her medicine bag and headed for the kitchen.

Arlene and David were alone at the table. Tom and Claire had not emerged from her room yet. "I think they're giving her a bath," David said as he got up to get Holly a mug. He chose one Holly had made many years before when she worked her way through nursing school as a potter.

"How did you know?" she asked as she turned the empty mug up-side-down revealing her mark.

"Beth told me all about your college days. You two were pretty wild." David raised his eyebrows.

Holly smiled, and then sighed. "We were so young and full of ourselves. Make peace, not war . . . far out . . . man." Holly was making fun, but she held those memories of her hippie days in the treasure chest of her heart. "I never expected to be here . . . watching my best friend . . ." she trailed off.

The steam from the bath had eased Beth's breathing, but the effort wore her out. She slept propped up on a cascade of pillows, her golden hair fanned out to dry. "She looks like an angel Daddy," Claire said as she dimmed the light.

Back in the kitchen Tom asked David if he would help him finish up with the truck, which left the three women together to talk. He couldn't bear to fill Claire in on the details of the past four months. It had been difficult enough to live it once.

"What happened with the treatments Holly? I thought she was being *treated*." Claire wanted answers and wasn't beating around the bush.

"She's had at least one treatment every day in one form or another. I've done Reiki; Sarah put her on the Bio-mat. Grandfather's wife gave us herbs and vitamins; Grandfather himself, along with other Elders, performed ceremony after ceremony. When we discovered the cancer had spread to her brain and her lungs, your father even tried to get her to consider some form of traditional treatment, but she wouldn't hear of it." Holly began to cry. "We've tried everything we could think of Claire. She's . . . she's just going so fast."

Claire's face didn't change. She slammed her hand on the table, making the other women jump. "I don't accept that! I won't let her go! This can't be happening to her!"

Arlene had been silent, respectfully allowing them to talk through their grief. "Nothing is happening *to* her, Claire. Everything is happening *through* her. She is choosing to leave at this very time, in this very way, and to leave you with the knowledge that her love for you was her reason for coming in the first place." Arlene took her hand. "She wasn't hit by a bus, or bitten by a snake. She was given the gift of time. And she couldn't leave until she knew you were safe. She's finished what she came here for. You had a sacred contract with her and she's fulfilled her end. Remember what the Guardians told us. You two set this whole thing up."

Claire was silent for a moment. "Well, I want to renegotiate!" And then in a whisper she said; "I'll . . . *miss* . . . her." Claire's throat was closing up again. She left the kitchen to go sit with her mother.

There was a soft knock on the kitchen door. Sarah had returned. She had gone to get a new tank of oxygen from the pharmacy before it closed. Acknowledging the others, she said, "Tom told me she's having a pretty hard time of it."

"Elizabeth or Claire?" Holly got up and put fresh water in the tea kettle.

"He said *Elizabeth* is having trouble breathing." Then the light bulb went off. "The daughter is taking it badly I presume."

Holly nodded. "She's pissed."

Arlene sat forward. "Sarah, maybe you could talk to her. She's struggling with the thought that she is somehow responsible for what has happened to her mother. We've talked about how we manifest our dis-ease and about sacred contracts, but she thinks that because she's been an *unusual* child that somehow it's her fault."

"She thinks she's *that* powerful huh?" Sarah raised her eyebrows. "I'd be happy to talk with her, but she may not be ready. She's grieving and I suggest we let her." She went to the stove and made herself a cup of tea, then came back to the table and sat down. "Death feels like a mistake to most people. It's challenging to be in agreement with it . . . to be a friend to it. Death is not our enemy or a punishment. It's another beginning. Beth is the only one in this house who isn't afraid of it. I don't think she'd mind if I told you this . . . but she's been seeing her grandmother sitting with her in her room. She feels comforted that her grandmother has come to help her on her journey home. I for one do not believe that you die alone. I have been witness to many beautiful transitions, where the patient smiled all the way to their last breath."

At her mother's side, Claire brushed her hair. She hummed a song she remembered her mother singing to her when she was young. Then she started singing softly, "Hush little baby don't say a word, momma's gonna buy you a mocking bird. And if that mocking bird don't sing, momma's gonna buy you a diamond ring.

~ - 331 - ~

And if that diamond ring turns brass, momma's gonna buy you a looking glass. And if that looking glass get broke, momma's gonna buy you a billy goat. And if that billy goat runs away . . . momma's gonna buy you another someday." When she finished, she laid the brush aside and put her head next to her mother's.

"My sweet, sweet child." Beth whispered. "I never knew love, until I met you." She hesitated struggling to breathe. "I should be sad to leave you, but I'm not." She stopped again. "Because I'm not going very far." Claire raised her head. And her mother continued. "I will only be a thought away." She pointed to the water beside the bed. Claire quickly responded. After she took a sip she said. "Just call my name and I will come. Grandmother Bee has always come to me. In fact she hasn't left my room in two days. I think I'm getting close." She smiled.

"Don't say that! It's too soon." Claire pleaded.

"Everyone arrives right on time and everyone leaves . . . right on time." She took Claire's hand. "Your Guardians talk of a time of great change. They say that there will be a great exodus from this earth. Many will be needed to receive these souls and help them cross over. This body feels so heavy to me now. It doesn't even feel like it belongs to me anymore. I'm ready to fly! Claire . . . my spirit body wants to be free. Darlin', I cannot leave this world until you let me go."

"My heart is broken momma. It feels like all the joy is gone from the world." Claire cried.

"Why do you think David showed up on our doorstep?" She wheezed.

Claire was silent and thought about it. Joy was *not* gone from the world. Just the mention of his name made her stomach tingle and her heart jump. "You're right. He showed up right on time." She paused in thought and then said, "God, he's so handsome."

Her mother smiled. "He is a cutie-patootie."

There was a soft knock on the door. "I heard you coughing, can I come in?" Sarah had the oxygen tank in tow.

"Sure." Claire got up from her mother's bed and kissed her forehead. "I'll be back in a little while, get some rest."

Chapter 42

Three years later…

"Elizabeth! Your Papa is going to tan your hide! He picked all those strawberries for the picnic! Where *are* you child?" Claire was looking out the back screen door with a bowl of half eaten berries in her hands. "I swear . . . that child…" Before she could finish her thought, a pony drawn cart emerged from the barn. She smiled at her husband and stepped out the door. "Is this what you've been working on at all hours of the night?"

David was leading the pony gently, hoping that it wouldn't resist the new rigging. "I thought it would be a nice touch for the party." He clicked his tongue and gently led the pony around the yard. "I heard you yelling for Beth . . . she's with your dad."

"Well when you see him, tell him that his darling granddaughter took a bite out of every strawberry he picked yesterday." She couldn't hold back the grin. She covered her mouth and said to herself, "Momma would have thought *this* was funny." She untied her apron and came out to take a closer look at the beautiful cart.

They were expecting a crowd of people today. Claire was excited to see her dear friends. Holly, Sarah, Grandfather and many of the SETI crew, were all due arrive in a few hours.

It had been three years since the Guardian's message was brought to the world. Many of the people involved hadn't seen each other since they all left the cabin on Eagles Ridge. Sheriff Tom and Beverly were coming. Thomas wouldn't miss the chance to see Sadie Moon again, but Charlotte had a commitment for that weekend and couldn't make the trip.

Dove and Sadie were living in Dallas. She had followed in her father's footsteps and accepted a research position at NASA. Sadie was thriving there. Dove had enrolled her in a pilot school for the gifted. Soon, the concept of no classrooms would be available to everyone.

Christopher married his longtime girlfriend. They had one child and another on the way. Nathan had gotten a job as a mix-master in Nashville. He was still known as the 'Nateman' and was happy composing his own music and playing guitar with his friends in the clubs. Jessica went on to become a mission specialist for NASA. But with the end of the Space Shuttle program, she would have to wait to see the Eagle Nebula up close and personal.

Michael stayed with SETI through the restructuring. Cristy left the day of the broadcast and never went back. She rebuilt her house with all details she could remember, including the bath with the view.

Amanda returned to the Inn after she was fired from the paper. The axe had fallen across the board, sparing no one. She and Teddy had not yet set a date, but a wedding appeared to be eminent.

Katie was offered an anchor position by a local station in San Francisco. Garvin Miller was invited, but no one had seen or heard from him since he left for Aruba. Everyone assumed he was probably still sitting on a beach, with a cocktail, watching the bikini's go by.

Even Captain James was invited. She R.S.V.P'd, asking if she could bring a friend. Heidi had never gotten a chance to meet them, and truly wanted an opportunity to thank them in person.

Most importantly to Claire were the two good doctors who had made it all possible. Lesser women would have crumbled under the pressure. They demonstrated courage and the willingness to set things right. Because of them, the world was a different place today.

Epilogue

1-1-2012

Happy New Year!

I've wanted to journal for years, but never have found the time. David gave me this blank book for Christmas and asked that I consider writing my memoir. But I think it's too soon to tell this story. How would I end this beautiful tale?

So much is being speculated about what will occur at the end of the year. As we complete our 225-million-year lap around the Milky Way and align with our galactic center, the Mayan calendar and the I-Ching come to an end. People are making predictions and trapping themselves in fear. Dad and I have been studying our charts. If our calendars aren't too far off, the sun will rise in the center of the Milky Way on December 21st. It is very possible that we will have 3-4 days of darkness, or 3-4 days of light. It depends on whether the sun goes through the

Photon Belt first or we do. We could be years off. We are just guessing at this point. We have no records to show exactly what happened last time. We have also been following the electromagnetic field fluctuations. If this is leading to a pole reversal . . . this event we do have geologic records of. According to scientific experts, we are long overdue. If this does occur, we're in for quite a ride.

Already we have experienced massive power failures from the solar flares. This year marks the peak of the sun's 11 year cycle. Many communications satellites have been critically damaged. People have been unprepared for the interruption of services and lack of supplies. The Guardians warned us this would occur as our solar system moves in to position. The good news though, is that without H.A.A.R.P. and the low frequency microwaves, people are thinking more clearly for the first time in decades.

Being raised on the farm and living a simple life has been such a blessing. The change has not been so great for us since we are off the grid and depend only on sunlight and wind. But for those who rely on supermarkets, credit cards, pharmacies and power companies . . . well they are having a difficult time of it. And I pray for them each day.

As I sit here at my desk, I can see David and Elizabeth leading the pony through the snow, delivering their wagonload to our roadside stand. Each day we have taken fruits and vegetables that we canned in the fall, honey and eggs to the stand for anyone who may be in need. And surprisingly there is always something left over. People are only taking what they need and in spite of the fact that we've changed our sign to "help yourself" trinkets have been left in gratitude. David and I have both marveled that our cellar is still full, despite all that we take from it each day.

So many families are scattered across the globe, separated at a time when they need each other the most. I think this has caused the most worry.

Since the messages were published, there have been scores of workshops across the globe teaching "back to basics". At the same time, some are holding on to the idea that they are powerless without technology. I wish they could see that this is temporary. Our technology is not lost. We don't have to start all over again with sticks and stones. But it will take time to restructure and restore balance.

I wish I had a giant loud speaker so I could address the world. I would tell them to go to their grandparents or to nursing homes where the wise ones live and ask them to remember how they made butter and soap and jelly. Ask them how they entertained themselves before television and how they got to school without a bus.
If we could wake them up from their medicated stupor long enough, we might be able to find out how grand the

world once was. The world has gotten so small. We are used to having everything in an instant and served to us on a platter. The drive-thru life we created has not served us very well.

The Guardians came and showed us who we were and who we could become. One day at a time I think we are developing and growing into our potential. Grandfather Yellow Moon and others around the world have been holding ceremonies to bring in more light. We gather in large groups and raise the vibration of love. Maybe the great change will take a long time and not happen so suddenly. I don't know.

When the knowledge of the shadow government became public, corruption on a global scale became exposed. The heads of state of many countries were unseated by angry mobs. But many of the peacemakers who had been exiled from their homelands have returned to lead their people. Some of these men and women are very old. I have been told that they will hold this space for the young peacemakers who have finally come of age. I think they are talking about the Indigos and the Crystal children. However, there are still a few stubborn souls who will not give up. They scream warnings of breaking our addiction to oil, threatening us with world economic collapse. I don't think we will ever again allow some small faction of misguided souls to wield such power.

Now that we know better, I don't think we will ever again look at ourselves as separate from each other, allowing selfishness and greed to create poverty and despair.

Our beautiful Earth is rejoicing at our promise to clean up our mess. In spite of the unusual weather, the skies have been beautiful since the Chemtrails have disappeared.

The world is spinning so fast right now; it's hard to hold on. I look forward to the day when all the dust settles and we begin to live out the prophecies of peace. Every culture has told of it. And I think that time has finally come.

Even with my gift of foresight, I cannot see exactly how things will unfold. I hold in my mind's eye a vision of the New Earth. It is a beautiful sight to behold.

I'm so grateful that our lives were touched by the Guardians. I fear that without their message we may have been unprepared. It's wonderful to know we are never alone and that they watch over us with love.

The Guardians also brought us an unexpected gift. They showed us that there is only one race on this planet. The human race.

As I say my prayers each day, I wrap the world in rainbows. I thank Creator for the perfection all around me, and I call upon the seven sacred directions.

From the East I invite and invoke clear vision and new beginnings. From the South, I am invoking playfulness, action and humility. When I call to the West, I accept the gifts of strength and courage. And from the North . . . wisdom and discernment. I ask Father Sky to watch over us all and thank him for showing us that from this perspective, judgment is unnecessary. To Mother Earth I express my gratitude for her support and protection. And finally I call upon the Creator in my heart. That through my heart I may give back to the world, all that has been given so freely to me.

I realize how fortunate I am to be alive at this most auspicious time in history, to be witness to the transformation of our world into the Golden Age.

I believe I will write my memoir. I think I'll call it "We Heard You".

Claire

PART 2

The Report

Please note: The following message is a collection of transmissions received by SETI radio telescopes around the world. The first transmission was recorded in 1960 when SETI began its program and has continued to this day. Sound bites of information were recorded in a format not previously known to the human race. Thereby, the messages were not discovered until June 2008. Over the years, many of the statements were duplicated, sometimes thousands of times. To create a coherent message, the order in which they are presented is the work of the SETI discovery team. There is still much to learn about those who sent this message, as they say little about themselves. The Report is not yet complete. Many years of data are still being translated.

Hello, we are the Guardians.
We have come at your request.
We heard you. We heard you cry for help, and we are here.

We travel with the speed of thought, as we no longer require a physical body.

We are not so different from you; in fact we are all the same. In time you will know our full story.

You have been searching for intelligent life beyond your planet since you became aware of the stars. But your definition of life is so narrow that you've missed what you're looking straight at.

Intelligent life is all around you.

Creative intelligence resides in every particle of matter.

Every particle of matter is alive.

Every particle of matter vibrates with a frequency.

Rocks vibrate at a very slow rate. They appear not to change or to move, but they do every second of every day.

Angelic beings vibrate at a much higher rate so as to appear invisible, like the wings of a humming bird. Because of this you have long debated their existence.

Our hope is to broaden your definition of life, so that you may experience a fuller meaning of the word.

We have not come to criticize or to condemn you, but to hold up a mirror so that you can see yourselves more clearly. Our intention is to reflect back to you what you already know.

We have agreed not to artificially advance your planet. It would be detrimental to all life to do so. So in fact, this message to you is from you.

We are here to help you understand universal principals. These are natural laws that you are bound to whether you are aware of them or not. These laws apply to every part of creation. Knowing these laws will help you understand where you have been and where you are going.

We are here to aid you, to bring this information to all of you in a way that you may finally be able to hear.

We are stardust, you and I. We are the same.

We are the sun and the spider, the mountain and the molecule, the comet and the cucumber; we are all the same basic elements.

We began all at the same time. Every conscious being everywhere knows this. We call it the spark of life or the great exhale. Your science calls it the Big Bang and that is as good a description as any. Life began in an instant and from that point we all sprang. What you have long forgotten, is that we are still connected, all of us.

All life, and its cycles, is the in-breath and out-breath of the Creator.

Every being in existence feels your life energy. We are all connected to each other. No being is totally independent.

You have no idea what you are a part of. You have no idea how big your family really is.

You are connected to a family you don't remember. It is one of life's most precious gifts. When you came into this life body, you passed through what some call a veil of forgetfulness. Some call it the pool or the river. There are many names for it. Before you passed through, you made arrangements and agreements for certain people, places and events to occur so you could fulfill your purpose for this life. You have called them *sacred contracts*.

How many times have you met someone for the first time but thought they were familiar?
How many times have you traveled some place for the first time and thought '*I've been here before*'?

Do you really think this whole life experience is some kind of coincidence?

Do you really believe you are just sloshing around in some kind of cosmic soup?

You have a spirit family. You have traveled together for many lifetimes. You change roles and you change identity and you hope more than anything you will remember each other *this time*.

In the realm of the Absolute, are legions of Beings you call Angels. This is a most diverse realm, the likes of which are beyond your imaginations. This extension of your family is guiding you in your daily life, yet you discount their guidance because they don't always communicate in the physical. Your intuition is a communication. Some messages inspire you and others warn you of danger. These Beings have been captured in your photographs, where they appear as light or mist. Some can even be seen in their full winged brilliance, but those of you with still closed hearts cannot embrace them.

You have a cosmic family as well. You are ONE with every life form that has ever been created. Most of them have not yet been to Earth. Some of them you have already met. They live among you unnoticed because of your similar physical characteristics. Others, who choose to stay out of affairs of Man, still live in the shadows to avoid being hunted or exploited. You have not yet matured to the point where you can accept the qualities that make each species unique. Even within the human family you judge each other's differences. Your selfishness, hate and intolerance are demonstrated by poverty, violence and war. Imagine how these Beings would be treated if they were discovered!

You are not alone my Dear Ones. You have never been alone. The way is open, it has never been closed. Many of you already know this.

You see these things, but most of you ignore them because you can't explain them. Most tragically though, some of you discount them because someone told you that it wasn't true. You ignored your own experience and shrank smaller in size.

Every one of you is bigger than you think you are. You have a saying; "I'm only human". How sad that you believe this. Human is the least of what you are. Human is the fabric that you are wearing. Your body is a vehicle. You are not your body.

You are powerful beings, every one of you. If you don't feel powerful then you have given it away. No one can take it from you. It is not possible for anyone to steal it from you. It is your inheritance. You are an individual expression of the whole. Each part is equaled, no part is more important than any other and you may reclaim it whenever you like. You only loaned your power to another, they cannot keep it against your will.

Collectively your strength is unfathomable. Unified intention has great influence. This you are currently experiencing but most of you aren't aware of it.

Those of you who know this are directing your energy with intension and the result is that you are getting what you want out of life, getting where you want to go and enjoying the journey along the way.

Those of you who do not know this are wielding your energy in no particular direction and seem to be getting nowhere. You are frustrated, feeling like your prayers are going unanswered. You feel like nothing works out for you. You are left wondering why life is so hard and unfair.

Individually, you are capable of creating great beauty and sometimes horror. Your very thoughts about life create what you experience. Sometimes you create a life of joy and sometimes you create personal disasters.

Together, or what is called collective consciousness, you are creating your reality on a global scale.

Some of your creations are truly wondrous, but much of what you are creating is ugly and chaotic.

As within so without, singularly and collectively. Your outer world is an out picturing of your inner world.

Sometimes you like what you create and call it *good luck*.

Sometimes you don't like what you've created and call it *bad luck* or worse, you call it punishment from God.

You have imagined that The Most High is a male. Spirit has no gender. You have imagined that this Creator of all things could separate itself from itself. Think again. Worse, you have imagined that your Source of Life could love one part of itself more than another. Do you favor one hair over another hair on your body?

The Light of Love cares not HOW you conduct yourself.

Life is already perfect. Without fail the Laws of Life work for the good of all.

The laws that govern EVERYTHING were set in place for all alike and it is the Law that corrects and restores balance, not a God that says "yes" to some and "no" to others. As within, so without. What you sow, you will reap. Life is self-governing. No action goes unanswered. Everything you send out comes back.

Earth is not a contained unit. What you produce individually and collectively radiates out from the planet. AND WE ALL FEEL IT!

You are at a tipping point in your history. The imbalance you have created is chipping away at your collective state of mind. Your arrogance and your greed are changing the climate on your planet.

Climate change is natural, but not at the rate that you are accelerating it.

The Earth itself is a breathing life form and like all life forms, great care is required to help it stay healthy.

Must we point out that when you poison Her, you poison yourself?

Even the lower life forms on your planet will not foul the area where they sleep or eat.

You are just beginning to understand that you are causing serious damage to your atmosphere. If you do not address this critical issue, nothing else matters.

You were given dominion over your planet as all highest life forms are. With great gifts comes great responsibility.

You know that you are causing great distress to your planet and yet you would allow personal agendas to stand in the way of healing it.

Money will not give you much comfort against catastrophic storms and starvation. You cannot bribe the Earth to do your bidding.

Many of you on the planet already know what to do. You already have the information and the power to solve these problems, but some of you will not share it and others of you will not hear it.

Your home, your planet that supports your very life is crying out to you.

Your scientists are screaming at the top of their lungs to bring your attention to the crisis facing your planet.

Your very lives depend on saving the atmosphere. You have a delicate balance that keeps the Earth a hospitable place to live.

You will not like the consequences of your inaction. You cannot wait for future generations to deal with it. The crisis is upon you now.

You have already seen what she can do. She will survive you. She has been through many ice ages before.

Change is natural. The Earth is never at rest. She stretches and vents. She spins through space, interacting and playing her part in the cosmic ballet with grace. You are interfering with natural order. Remember, the Earth is a celestial body. Regardless of what you do, she must have balance. So do not curse her as she works to counteract your creations.

The climate change you are creating is the number one threat to your survival. Not weapons of war or pandemics.

You will be unable to fight your wars when sand storms, hurricanes, floods and droughts, earthquakes, cyclones and volcanoes keep you busy boarding up, digging out, or running for your lives.

There will be no time to worry about AIDS, cancer or pandemics when you are trying to draw a breath of clean air through the sand, smoke, ash or toxic clouds.

You are not the first advanced civilization that has made Earth its home.

They, like you, developed their technical knowledge far faster than their spiritual knowledge.

They, like you, got stuck at an age of time deemed *holy*, not willing to evolve the spirit, thinking they had found the *truth*. Meanwhile they advanced in their scientific endeavors by leaps and bounds. Leaving them too spiritually immature to deal with what they had created.

In the end they self-destructed and passed into memory.

You have no idea what you are a part of.
You have no idea how big your family really is.

Some of you know this.
Some of you know and live in harmony with what is.

Some of you are awake.

Those of you we speak of know something of Ultimate Reality.

Not the reality you have created.

Most of you are deeply asleep.

Many of you are so ravaged by war and famine, that you are barely alive.

Many of you are so twisted by perversion that you are barely human.

We say again: You have no idea what you are a part of.

You have no idea how big your family really is.

Reality is subjective. There is *Our* reality, *Your* personal reality and then there is *Ultimate* reality.

In *Our* reality, all things connect to one another. We see how the action of one affects the whole. It is this knowledge that prevents us from harming anything or anyone. We know that physical form is just one way to exist consciously. We know that death is an illusion. We know that we are unlimited. We know that we are co-creators with each other and *that* which is unseen. Still there are realms that are unknown to us and other Beings who need our assistance.

It is this which gives us purpose. However, we are still unified in our reality.

In *Your* reality you are victims of fate. You believe in coincidence. You don't feel responsible for what is happening around the world or beyond. You think you can act independently of others. In Your reality you believe that you actually have private thoughts and that what you think has no effect on the whole. You believe that you are human. In truth, your reality is a figment of your collective imaginations.

The truth of your reality is so unreal that many of you will be shattered by the knowledge of it. Most of you will be bitterly angry to find out that just a few misguided souls took control of all the knowledge and all the resources. Doling out or withholding the basic needs of life at their discretion.

They have been playing God on your planet for thousands of years. They could have ended poverty and hunger but that didn't fit into their plan. They could have ended all war, but that would not have served their purposes.

At the turn of the twentieth century, just when man evolved to the point that he could have made enormous strides in the fields of faith, medicine and energy, the wondrous technologies were hidden away. You were denied access to the secrets of the Great Masters. You were kept from the true miracles of medicine and stolen from you was the technology for free and clean energy.

The dark force was losing control, afraid of being dethroned.

And so it began in earnest . . . the race to see who could build the most powerful war machine, amass the most money. Control the most people. World wars erupted, the financial world collapsed and despair won out. While you stood in bread lines to feed your starving family, they gorged themselves and continued to live the life of Kings.

Your world is controlled by a savage few. A Shadow Government that crosses national lines and controls your whole world. It is a dark force, under no control. The mock Governments of your world do attend the daily affairs of their respective countries, but they are at the mercy of this rogue agency. It is a bloody mix of corporate, institutional, financial and religious entities. As this core group expands it breaks into smaller more fanatic sects, new agendas are formed and the chaos expands. One hand does not know what the other is doing, nor does it care.

It was the very people who you sought for protection and solace that discovered They could manipulate the course of the world. They had already amassed great wealth, but you gave Them more. They have held themselves up as the most high and told you that God wanted you to help Them fight evil. They told you that you were sinners and that only through Them could you be saved.

If you are one who could not be manipulated by fear, then They appealed to your lust . . . lust for more of everything. They created a great sense of need, so They could lull you to sleep with television, sex, material goods, drugs and artificial food.

With your bellies full and your senses numbed, your society is crumbling around you. The fabric of your world is unraveling right before your eyes, but you are either too comfortable, or too weakened by addictions to do anything about it. The water that you need for life is so heavily laden with chemicals and drugs, it's toxic.

They have kept your beloved spirits captive all these years. They have lied to you about everything. They have the technology to generate free energy, completely non-polluting, but They have decided to use the technology for Their own purposes. They could light every village in the world. They could end hunger tomorrow and wipe out diseases worldwide. They could have ended wars long ago, but that would mean that They would have to share . . . and that is not going to happen.

This dark force has been responsible for the rape of the Earth and her most beloved people.

They want you to believe that there is not enough. They want you to hate each other. They want you to be afraid of each other. They want you to think that you are small. They want you to think you are powerless. However, Their deeds have not gone unnoticed. In the last sixty years They have expanded their aggressions to include Earth's celestial neighbors.

When Man discovered the power of the atom, he unleashed a power that he did not have the wisdom to use. The demonstration of this power has caused other civilizations to become very concerned. Unleashing weapons of such magnitude beyond your planet is forbidden and will not be tolerated.

A division of this dark force is determined to bring about the fulfillment of a prophecy that it does not understand. They are using up all of Earth's resources, starting wars and terrorizing her people because they think that *time* is short. They are attempting to trumpet in an event of biblical proportions.

These dark times will give way to a time of peace, a very long time of peace from your perspective. What you are experiencing now, are the birth pangs of a new age. It is a painful process, one that many fear they will never survive. When the dawn of the new age emerges like the precious life of a child, all the pain and all the suffering will be worth all the trouble it took to get there.

The Shadow Government knows that its days are short. The dark force of your world is desperately trying to stay unnoticed behind the curtain, but They have been discovered.

The nest has been stirred, but do not despair, upheaval is inevitable. This beast will not go down without a fight. They will throw tempests and droughts to show you how powerful they are! But you will respond with your numbers all in harmony all in one thought and you will show your power. You will calm the skies and restore balance.

Until that day, the inhabitants of nearby planets will remained cloaked to your eyes and interstellar species that inhabit your Earth will remain in the shadows . . . unwilling to make themselves known. As a species, you have demonstrated your love of hostility and lack of compassion. You murder the peace makers. You are deeply asleep.

There are many who welcome Earth's visitors and to them, sightings are a daily occurrence. No hostilities are exchanged, only curiosity. Many have returned to South America, where they were welcomed in the past. The Ancient Cities still visible there and elsewhere are a testament to the efforts of interplanetary cooperation.

When you finally recognize your celestial family, you will once again remember that you are the Brotherhood of Man. There is only one race on your planet . . . the human race.

In *Ultimate* Reality there are no borders or limits, nor is there lack. There is nothing that separates you from anything else. You are already perfect. You need nothing. You have everything. You are an individual expression of the whole. Just as a drop of ocean water is still the ocean. You are co-creating every moment of every day. Every thought you have shapes the world you live in. You can and do choose the kind of life you would like to have. There are no victims and there no villains in Ultimate Reality.

Many of you already know this, but most of you haven't even tried to peek behind the veil of illusion.

Those of you, who know this, focus your attention on creating lives of wonder and joy not only for yourselves but for all. You are using your inheritance intentionally. You are using your gifts wisely. You are the Gods and Goddesses of your world.

You must wake up the others.

As humans you have inherited great power. All through your history, the truth of your power has been kept secret by those who would use it for themselves in order to keep others in their place. Your gift, it seems has been your biggest secret. You have forgotten who you are. It is time for you to know exactly what you have been given.

You were given dominion over all living things on your planet. You are the stewards of Earth. That is a title of caregiver.

There was a time when you honored your Earth and each other. Some of you still do.

Your greatest gift and power is co-creator.

Your sacred texts tell you that you were created in the likeness and image of your Creator.

Indecently, so are we. No, we are not human. Creator is not human. Most of you know this.

Being co-creator means that you are unlimited. It means you can create anything you like. You are creating all the time and don't realize it!

Your bodies were designed to live much longer than they do today. Your human body is an amazing machine. It regenerates itself and heals itself naturally. Your bodies were designed to live for centuries and when you achieved all that you wanted to in a life time you dropped your body and went home. The Ascended Masters took their bodies with them, so they could return at any time.

You have recorded in your history the accounts of humans living many centuries, but you think it's allegorical. It's not.

Death, as you call it, was looked upon as a well-deserved rest. Nothing ends. Every living thing has a cycle. You can change forms, but you cannot cease to be. There is nothing tragic about going *Home*.

You fear because you do not know. You do not remember your Home. You do not remember where you come from. You do not remember your Creator.

Your master Jesus put it in the most beautiful way when he called Creator, "Father". Of all the names in all the worlds, Father or Mother is the most commonly used. It is universally understood to be a parent-child relationship.

Being created in the likeness and image means that you have the same attributes as Creator.

You are love. You are life. You are spirit. You are soul. You are truth. You are intelligence and you are principal.

All of the attributes are self-defining except 'principle'. The divine principle means the same thing as universal or cosmic law.

You inherited a set of laws that govern your entire life, in fact all of life, and yet most of you have never heard of them.

You don't teach them because most of you don't know them. Those of you, who do know them and selfishly keep them secret, don't understand them.

Hear this if you can! The Heavens are at the ready and at your service. The Universe has only one answer to any request. Yes. It is that simple. The answer is always yes!

The universe is in constant agreement with you. It has always been this way. It is this way for us all . . . everywhere.

You cannot manipulate the Laws of Life. The Law treats everyone the same. It does not care who you are.

What you put your attention on expands. That is law.

What you resist persists. That is law.

What you look at disappears. That is law.

You attract what you fear. That is law.

What you put out comes back to you. That is law.

Like attracts like . . . always.

If you are going to survive, you must stop keeping secrets.

Your attachment to secrets comes from fear. Fear of not being superior.

You have a strong attachment to this.

If you could heal this fear, you could feed the world.

If you could heal this fear, you could stop killing each other.

If you could heal this fear, you could stop poisoning your Earth.

The Earth is never at rest. It is her nature. Volcanoes are not personal, they are vents. Earth quakes are not personal; it is her crust making needed adjustments. Without them, there would be no islands or mountains. Those of you who are in rhythm with the Earth, instinctively know when to leave an area or are provided a safe shelter from harm. Follow the animal kingdom.

Whether you face a wild fire or a hurricane, your collective reaction to it will determine its strength. Stand together and picture a solution. Bring to the fire a drenching rain. See

~ - 371 - ~

the winds calm and the hurricane dissolve. Join your brothers and sisters that already practice this way of life. They are not annoyed by the weather! They do not fear their Mother! They understand that perfection is all around them and what appears to be imperfect or catastrophic is merely a reflection of man's thoughts of imbalance.

Your world governments are in a race to control the weather, believing that He who controls the weather controls the food chain and therefore controls everything.

Mastery of the weather cannot be attained through the use of chemicals. The trails of toxic heavy metals being sprayed across your skies are already having adverse effects on the health of your population. Continued use of these lethal chemicals will result in a drastic reduction of the population. Not only do these chemical trails affect the heath of humans, but the heavy metals adversely affect animals, plants and the topsoil you need to grow your food.

Through your fear and greed you have discovered a way to genetically alter natural life forms, naively pursuing profits without regard for potential hazards. With biotechnology, roses are no longer crossed with just roses. They can be mated with pigs, tomatoes with oak trees, fish with asses, butterflies with worms, orchids with snakes.

The technology that you call biolistics is a gunshot-like violence that pierces the nuclear membrane of cells. This essentially violates the consciousness that forms and guides living nature. Some also compare it to the violent crossing of territorial borders of countries, subduing inhabitants against their will.

The experiments taking place in laboratories around the world are producing horrors beyond any science fiction your movies could portray. This is not creation, it is manipulation.

The new genetic science raises more troubling issues than any other technological revolution in your history. In reprogramming the genetic code of life, you risk a fatal interruption of millions of years of evolutionary development. The artificial creation of life could spell the end of the natural world.

Inside every seed is the memory of its parent.

You would do well to ask yourselves the question; will the creation, mass production, and wholesale release of thousands of genetically engineered life forms . . . cause irreversible damage to the biosphere, making genetic pollution an even greater threat to the planet than nuclear or petrochemical pollution?

You did not set out to create these horrors on your planet out of evil intention, but instead out of curiosity and genuine concern for your people. You strive to feed your hungry. You dream of a better world.

By forgetting your original instructions, you have forgotten that you can have perfect health, that you can enhance and protect your crops with prayer and affirmation. You have never needed poison to protect them from harm.

You have decided that it takes a set amount of *time* to grow your food, so you add toxins instead of focusing your minds to speed the growth. It is not the toxin, but the mind believing in the toxin that makes it work! It is not the pill, but the belief in the pill that makes you well!

The work that is being performed to alter life goes against all laws of nature and the results can be nothing but disastrous. Cloning animals, humans and other beings is a dangerous business, the consequences of which you truly do not want to experience.

This was the fate of a previous civilization. In their vain attempt to manipulate and control Nature, they perished very suddenly and passed into memory.

This does not have to be your fate.

You are energy. The Earth is energy. It was explained earlier how your thoughts shape the course of your life. Earth is delicately balanced. The weather is influenced by rifts of energy. Any thoughts, let alone deeds that are violent send a shudder through the balanced energy and create a rift. Multiply that by millions or billions at once and you can see how powerful the rift becomes.

Pumping megatons of pollution into your atmosphere is only one way to affect the global climate. Your hate, greed and perversion contribute to its demise as well.

Your collective attitudes affect the weather.

You behave as though you are at its mercy. You shake your fists at the skies, wondering why nature is so cruel.

Nature is not cruel. Nature is gentle when cared for.

You, dear Humans, have set yourselves up for catastrophe.

It goes against all logic to place millions of people at the foot of a volcano.

It goes against all logic to place billions of people on top of natural fault lines.

It goes against all logic to destroy natural coastal barriers so that millions can live by the sea, only to be drowned by it.

There are a few on your planet today who can conjure up a snow storm or make it rain on a spot of land. Not only can they produce it, they can remain dry in the midst of it.

There are those, too, who can walk on water or through fire unscathed.

They can travel great distances in a moment of *real time*, unseen to the human eye.

They are not magicians nor are they tricksters. They have a full understanding of their original instructions. They know that they themselves are the vessels which Spirit flows through. They create at will. They are Masters.

It could take millions of years to correct the damage you have done already, or it could take a moment. It all depends on you. How many of you are willing to put your attention on clean water and air? How many of you are willing to put your attention on peace? The more who do, the faster it will occur.

Wage no more wars . . . against anything! To do so only increases its strength.

Focus your mind on the outcome you wish to see and only that. Stop feeding what you do not wish to grow.

You do not create by wishing. You create by *stating* what is so.

What you think matters. What you think *becomes* matter. What you do matters. What you do *becomes* matter.

What you think, say and do creates a result. What you *meant* to think, say and do creates a completely different result.

The Universe does not operate in judgment. It does not care how it got this way, or whose fault it was. It only responds to thought. If you stop focusing on the problem the solution can emerge. Miracles are just the manifestation of a focused mind.

You have shrouded your inheritance in mystery and have called the demonstration of it miraculous.

No one person is better known for his miracles than your Jesus of Nazareth.

He was fully aware of his inheritance from birth. The original instructions were deeply entrenched in his way of living. Many called his demonstrations, miraculous. Most importantly he demonstrated the power of love.

But curiously, even the followers of Jesus have failed to recognize the meaning of His life.

It seems his words fall upon deaf ears.

"Behold, what I have done you can do and more."

"Ye are all gods."

He knew without a doubt where he came from. He knew without a doubt that in union with Creator he was limitless. He knew that his life would be sacrificed. He came to show you that death is an illusion. He knew that the human robe he wore was not his true identity.

Even those who lived and walked with this man did not fully understand the meaning of his life. They did go on to demonstrate great healing powers, and teach many truths but they failed to convey the potential and the divinity of *every* man.

Your religions and your governments have insured that Man stays in his place by controlling knowledge. Anyone daring to claim this right to divinity has been labeled heretic, blasphemer or worse, evil. Some have been killed in secret, but others have been publicly executed, in front of those who would replace them, making them afraid to proclaim their own rightful place in the Universe. This began long before Jesus and has not ended yet.

Each of your religions claims to have *the truth*. Each claims exclusive authority on the subject of God. More blood has been spilled for God than all other disagreements combined.

The human language does not possess words in *any* tongue, which could possibly describe what The Truth really is. You will understand this someday.

Truth is felt, not spoken.

Truth is what you live, not what you utter.

To follow the leader, means you are living someone else's Truth.

Every man, woman and child knows in his core that he is more than he appears to be.

Your potential haunts you. Always, it gnaws at you.

You will never feel satisfied until you realize your birthright and claim your inheritance.

You have the ability to solve all your problems.

You have the ability to make solid objects appear out of thin air.

You have the ability to travel through what you call *time.* Time does not actually exist. It is *your* creation, meant to bring order to your experience.

You have the ability to communicate with the unseen.

You have the ability to influence the weather, to purify your water, to feed your hungry, to heal yourselves and your planet. You have the ability to create a life second to none!

But someone told you that you were only human and the Heavens cried.

We love it that you call your Earth 'Mother'. Would it surprise you that most civilizations refer to their planet in the same way?

A mother nurtures and supports her children. She is gentle but she can only be pushed so far.

You have forgotten that she lives and breathes.

You have forgotten that *She* is your life support.

Just try to take a deep breath without her assistance.

Just try to fill your stomach without her bounty.

She will be just fine without you, but the reverse cannot be said.

You have decided that you *own* her. You have decided that dominion means domination.

You have decided as owners of the Earth that you can make any changes that you choose. You can create imaginary boundaries, separating her people.

You have decided that you can level mountains without consequence.

You have decided that you can stop rivers without consequence.

You have decided that She does not need her lubricating oil that took her millions of years to produce.

You have decided that you can strip the bowels of the earth of metal and stone and redistribute it across the surface without consequence.

You have decided that you can strip the surface of its oxygen producing trees without consequences too.

You have decided that you can dump your garbage anywhere you please.

You have decided that you can destroy billions of animals on land and at sea to the point of extinction without consequence.

You have decided that you have the right to decide what lives and what dies.

You have decided that you know better than your Mother AND your Father.

The fury of a mother bear is nothing compared to the fury you are about to bring upon yourselves.

And a good Father allows his children to learn from their own mistakes.

This, He will allow.

He will allow you to make your mistakes, as he did with previous civilizations. He will allow you to learn or not learn from your mistakes as well.

He has given you a free will and has no attachment to what you do with it.

He knows that ultimately you cannot fail. It is not possible.

He knows that you will return Home. Everyone does.

Your Home is your greatest inheritance yet. Very few on your planet can even begin to grasp the magnitude of it, the infinite choices; the variety of beings, the joy and the light. Again, there are no adequate words in any language to describe the Realm of the Absolute.

As humans you cannot imagine who would want to leave such a place, to come back to Earth lifetime after lifetime.

Life is expanded through conscious experience. Earth is the ultimate playground for experiencing anything and everything! You have it all here!

Let us just say for now; Imagine . . . you get to the end of your days as a human. You review your life and discover that the only reason you came *this time* was to experience yourself as forgiveness. And during your review you see yourself fighting with your family and cursing your boss and hating your enemy. You see at this point, that the big YOU set it all up, so that you could BE the attribute of forgiveness. You lived all of those years, given one opportunity after another, but could not find it in your heart to forgive. You thought people were just being unfair to you. You forgot that you made Sacred Contracts and that they all agreed to meet you on Earth and each play their part, out of their love for you. This is why so many of you want to go back and try again.

You have forgotten who you are, who you REALLY are! The whole life experience is designed for you to discover yourself while still in the physical form. This is what Jesus came to show you. It is the same thing that Buddha and Mohammad and all the rest came to show you.

Next to your climate, man's cruelty to man is the greatest threat to your happiness and well-being.

Anger is contagious. It spreads like a virus from person to person.

Violence has become like a tidal wave on your planet, destroying countless lives.

In the last decade your focus has turned to terrorism. You are feeding terrorism, giving it more life. What you place your attention on expands. That is law.

You have developed sophisticated weapons and technology capable of destroying every living creature on your planet and yet you claim to do this in hopes of peace. This does not sound logical even to a child! What you resist persists. That is law.

Peace cannot be achieved through violence. The two are not compatible. They are opposite energies. Like energy attracts like. This is law.

Like energies attract. Your science has proven this to you.

When you wage war you can attain land, resources and sovereignty but never peace. The fighting may end, but there is a difference between submission and peace.

You can beat a child into submission and the result may be a quieter child on the outside, but the inside of them will seethe with resentment. So in turn this child will at some point, inflict harm upon himself or upon another just to express this resentment and frustration of being powerless. And so the cycle of violence continues.

Developing your Spirit in this life will bring you the peace that you desire. It will not give you the lion's share but it will give you enough. It will not give you hoards of goods but it will provide you enough of anything you desire. Why do you need more than enough? Isn't enough, enough?

If you knew that *you* were enough, you would not have to have more than enough to make yourselves feel like enough.

In fact, if giving yourself enough was possible you would not need more. Do you see the cycle of this?

What you place your attention on expands. That is law.

If you think there is not enough, there appears not to be enough. This is an illusion that you are creating. It is a lie.

There is enough. There is enough of everything. Shortage is an illusion, but you have made it your reality.

The storehouse of Heaven is full to overflowing. There is always more.

You throw away more food than would be required to feed all the hungry in your world. You would rather see it rot than share it. Hunger could go away tomorrow.

How much wealth stays hidden in dark vaults not seeing the light of day? Hidden away out of circulation providing nothing but a false sense of security to someone who may never use it?

Governments create poverty. Poverty creates hunger. Hunger creates fear. Fear creates desperation. Desperation creates retaliation and then someone kills his neighbor, or worse, starts a war.

Your governments are the stewards of your societies, but power and control are placed above care giving. To empower a person is to make them an equal.

Knowledge is power. Share that and you share the wealth.

In your attempt to maintain order, you have formed governing systems. Of all the models of government, we found the idea of Democracy most liberating and natural to the human spirit. However, in the time that we have observed your planet, we cannot find a model for Democracy anywhere. We find that curious.

We believe we understand the concept of majority rule as well as the concept of social equality and respect. The idea that the common people are considered as the primary source of political power is a just way to live, but it is not practiced anywhere that we can see. You lay claims that you have achieved this, but you have not. Call it what you want Dear Ones, but first change your definition of the word.

We have observed that no matter what governing system you choose, selfishness and greed take priority over the people they have been entrusted to nurture and protect.

For thousands of years you have made it a sport to publicly torture and slay fellow humans.

As you have matured as a species most of you have awakened to realize that the very act of taking another's life robs the soul of peace.

It was during the reign of the man you call Hitler that we first heard your cries.

You pleaded for help because millions of people were dying at his hand.

Many of the people who helped him carry out this genocide did not share his ideals. They followed like sheep always in fear that the Shepard would soon turn on them.

The world stood by for far too long watching.

The world stands by today watching as it happens again. Over and over again the world stands by and decides who is valuable enough to save.

Violence is a demonstration of fear.

You are afraid you will not get what you want, whether it is oil or land or diamonds or gold. Most of all you want power, power over others so you can feel superior.

Every day you allow your precious children to be sold into slavery.

Every day you allow your women to be raped.

Every day you allow your young men and women to be slaughtered in war.

Every day you allow your cities to be overrun by thugs.

You tolerate and protect hate groups.

You tolerate the systematic elimination of entire tribes of peoples.

You turn your heads and close your eyes because it hurts too much or you think there is nothing you can do.

You can no longer say that you don't know. Your technologies have advanced you to the point that you can see it play out as it happens. You sit in your warm home while others freeze. You sleep in the safety of your town while others must hide in the jungles at night and you will allow the children of your earth to starve to death because they don't have oil to trade for food.

To do nothing, is to contribute to the harm being done.

It is within your power to stop this.

A peaceful world begins with you.

What you place your attention on expands.

As within, so without.

The peace in your mind begins by connecting to your Source.

The peace in your family begins when you decide to be happy instead of right.

The peace in your community begins when you reach out to those who do not know how to help themselves.

People would act better if they knew how and they would take better care of themselves and others if they knew there was only ONE. They don't remember who they are.

Teach them.

Teach them about the illusion of RIGHT.

There is no such thing. You made this up.

You have an obsession with RIGHT and WRONG.

You have made this up. This is a lie you have told yourselves.

It is an illusion, an illusion of your own creation.

Albert Einstein was correct in his discovery of relativity.

There is black and white, short and tall, here and there, high and low.

Without its opposite you could not know a thing.

How could you know tall if everything was the same height?

Celebrate the diversity of your world and know that it is this very thing that makes life so delicious!

Of all the worlds that we have traveled we have rarely come across a planet with so much diversity and so much to celebrate.

We beg you to reconsider its destruction.

The movement to restore your Earth to paradise has already begun.

The Divine Feminine is a powerful force and its vibration can be felt across the cosmos.

Though it is the women of your world who are tired of war and chaos, do not mistake feminine or masculine energy for human gender.

The people of your world are weary from the burden of war and all of its fallout. They are tired of their homes being bombed. They are tired of hiding in the jungles at night with their children.

They are tired of being hungry and heartbroken as their children waste away.

They don't want to send the world any more children to fight the wars of unreasonable men.

Long have they silently witnessed the murder and mayhem, but no more.

They want to feel safe. They want their children to grow up unafraid.

They have already begun to move. They are beginning to stir.

They were weary with grief, but now a light is growing inside of them that will outshine the dark force of violence.

They will not wage war on the world as it is. They will never wage war again.

They will not play the game anymore. They will remember who they are; they will wake each other up. They will teach each other the way. They will not be selfish with this discovery. They know fully know the power of information.

You will not see them shouting in the streets. They will not take up arms or threaten anyone. They are moving like the wind, undetected. The fresh air they carry with them will overtake the stench of war.

Oh beloved Women of the Earth, end the madness, end the rape of the world, and end the suffering. Show them how.

Rise up and take your place beside the Goddess. Put your crown upon your head and hold it high.

Hold in your mind a picture of peace. Hold in your mind the home of your dreams. See in your mind's eye, healthy and happy children. Hold in your mind the work you most enjoy. Imagine being in love and feeling safe and secure.

Do not take your attention from these ideas. Do not stray from these thoughts. Do not worry about anything. Allow the process to work. Do not be tempted to open the oven to check on the cake.

Your prayers have been heard!

Ask every day for the opportunities that will bring these things into your reality. Watch the red carpet unroll before you. You will be guided. You will not be able to miss the way.

Your world has been dominated by masculine energy for over four thousand years and the result has been nearly disastrous.

Masculine energy seeks power. Feminine energy seeks to empower.

Masculine energy dominates. Feminine energy nurtures.

As a model for you, there is a small kingdom in China. It is a matriarchal society, the last of its kind on your planet. There is no hunger there. There is no crime. Everyone has a job. The wealth and bounty of the kingdom is shared by all. In this kingdom, wealth is not measured by earthly treasures. In fact there is no palace. This arrangement has worked beautifully for thousands of years.

There are micro communities that model this idea, the idea of shared wealth, and the idea of shared responsibility. This is your future.

You are forming a global village, a world community. No longer will you watch the suffering of another without feeling the pain in your own body.

You must clear out the old energy. Start with your own self and move out from there. It will be tempting to point your finger and think that something over *there* needs to be fixed.

You will see the behavior of some as irritating or intolerable. In others you will see wonderful qualities. What you see is only a mirror. *You* are being reflected. I know this idea will be met with some resistance but it is true.

Everyone is a mirror to you. You can sometimes see yourself in others but you delude yourself with the thought that their behavior is better or much worse than yours. In truth, their behaviors (good or bad), are being magnified so you can't miss them.

Whatever you do, don't get discouraged by the state of affairs *anywhere*.

Some of you will claim that the job is too big or that it will take too long and despair.

Remember that *time* is a human invention. It is an illusion. It is another lie you have told yourselves. Ultimate Reality does not recognize it.

Some of you will say "it will take a miracle". Do not despair! Miracles are a natural occurrence. When miracles *don't* happen, something is out of balance.

"Ye are all Gods".

Hear this beloved people of Earth; you can have, do or be anything you want. Nothing is being withheld from you. You are truly the Masters of your own destiny.

You are standing precariously on the edge of your new world. You have agreed to be present at this time.

Those of you who choose to stay to witness the dawn of the fifth age will be the teachers of your tomorrow.

The technologies that have been secretly hidden will be used to save your planet. You will finally realize your connection to the One and you will take your bother by the hand and lead him to his destiny.

You will teach love instead of fear. War will no longer have a place among you.

There is a host of help available to you right now. Standing at the ready are the Angels you have forgotten. They await your invitation.

Out from the shadows of the wilderness and from under the seas will come the inter-dimensional beings that have lived on your planet for thousands of years. No longer afraid of being hunted, they will share their wisdom and help to guide you. For millions of years these benevolent beings have aided Man and stand at the ready to do so again. Although they have quietly lived out of sight, they are directly responsible for your survival thus far.

With the knowledge that you are not alone, you will finally see yourselves as one race, the human race. You will awaken to the fact that you need each other. Then the divisions will melt away.

A higher energy signature has made its way to the Earth. There are now millions of souls on your planet who have come to help. Many, who came before them as Scouts, prepared the way. The first wave born to you were the Warriors, sent to clear out the old and create a path for the higher vibration. These souls are restless and uncomfortable in your world. They are more evolved and extremely sensitive. Some of you have recognized them and nurtured them, but others have been confused or intolerant, unable to control them.

The next wave of souls is known as the Peace Makers. Their sweet dispositions have saved them from many of the troubles their predecessors experienced. They have come through the veil, but have not forgotten everything. They hold and vibrate a level of energy unparalleled in your modern times. They are still very young in age, but powerful as seers and healers. They have called for more help and have been answered.

The way for this new, even higher vibrating soul has been opened. They are the Transformers. They will teach the world an ancient way, a way that will transform your world. They come to heal your world, to comfort those who suffer. More importantly, they have come to teach. They will remind you of your divinity and your connection to all that is. Their works will appear miraculous and again there will be those who will fear them, but do not fall prey to their paranoia. They will not ask you to look to them for the truth. They will ask you to look within your selves.

". . . and the children will lead them." How beautiful is that?

Your little planet is seen as a jewel in your galaxy. You share it with many still unknown to you.

We have said before and we shall continue to say; YOU HAVE NO IDEA WHAT YOU ARE A PART OF AND YOU DO NOT UNDERSTAND HOW BIG YOUR FAMILY REALLY IS!

Life on your little planet is about to change. Change in a way that will frighten some of you in the beginning. The continents will shift, destroying your illusion of borders. While some will sink in to the sea, ancient lands will rise again to see the sun. The logical mind will shatter at the speed in which this will take place.

Many of you will not make this transition. For some the dense human body will become too cumbersome. You will long to free yourself from this bondage and offer your service with your "light" body. But others will not know how to raise their vibration to match the new world which will be essential to make the shift into the new age. You will either stay to help or you will leave. It is really that simple. The new age will not function in the old way. It will not recognize selfishness. It will not tolerate greed or disrespect in any form. If you cannot adjust, you may leave and when you are ready you may come back.

The Age of Peace has come. We heard you and we are here to help.

Dear beloved humans of Earth do not despair. There is help available to you. They have always been there, but along the way you lost your ability to see them. You still hear them, but you have forgotten the sound of their voices and call it your imagination.

Spirit Realm is accessible to you. It has always been this way. You have just lost sight of it. In order to regain access you must elevate your spirit self by increasing your vibration. This is accomplished by clearing density and removing obstacles.

Here is a short list of what adds to your density:

Processed foods
Intolerance
Pollution
Fear
Doubt
Pharmaceutical and recreational drugs
Lack of sunlight
Anger/Resentment

Lack of fresh air

Chemically treated garments

Judgment

Greed

Jealousy

Chemically treated water

Living in the past

To raise your vibration and regain your connection with unseen realms, consider adding these items to your everyday life:

Gratitude

Sunshine

Laughter

Fresh live foods

Love

Tolerance

Patience

Fresh air

Generosity

Compassion

Prayer/Meditation

Animals

Nature

Living in the Now

There are many kingdoms and realms designed to function for the benefit of all of its creation. The Angelic realm is the most familiar to you. They are a diverse group which range from Archangels to your individual Spirit Guides. They are at your service. They stand at the ready to help you.

Also at the ready are the Elementals. They are unique to the Earth and do not exist anywhere else. Each Element has its own purpose. The Sylphs are the Air and wind Spirits. Not only can they cool you on a hot summer day, they are helping to clear the skies of Chemtrails. Battles rage in your skies day after day, right over your heads, but most of you never look up. The graceful image of the Sylph appears each time a spray campaign is occurring. You can call upon them any time you need a breath of fresh air or you may ask them to gather the rain.

The Undines watch over the element of water. Your Dr. Emoto of Japan has discovered the link between healing and water. He has discovered that water is intelligent. His photographs of ice crystals, has revealed the ancient knowledge of blessings. What you bless becomes beautiful and healthy. What you curse becomes ugly and malformed. This wisdom could restore your oceans. It could clean up all of your waterways, not to mention your bodies.

The element of Earth is the Gnome. Call upon this helpful element to accelerate the growth of any plant. *Time* as you recall is a fiction of your collective imaginations. Call upon this element to show you the power of the stones. They only appear to be still. The history of your planet is stored in their memory.

Salamander is the element of fire. From your powerful sun to your quick tempers, this element is responsible for all warmth. Without it, there would be no passion, no light and no life.

The Elements have no ego or agenda. They are the ballast of your world. They assist the Earth and strive to bring balance to a world that is tipping over. When you see catastrophic natural events, you are witnessing Nature seeking to balance itself. Sometimes the energy becomes so toxic or static in a concentrated area that an epic event is the only way to clear the imbalance.

Being absent of ego, the Elements and the Angels neither require nor wish to be worshiped in any way. However, all of creation thrives on being acknowledged and loved by others. Working with the Elementals and calling upon the Angels is beneficial to all living things.

The planet you live upon is a living, breathing life form. You have forgotten this.

Previous civilizations used the wisdom of the elements as well the wisdom of the other realms. Today you surround this wisdom with foolishness. Your ancient texts and stories of lore contain more truth than you realize. Fairies and other mystical creatures have always shared the planet with man. Once you decide to open your spirit eyes, you will see them once again.

Not only are the unseen available to you, your cosmic family is willing to help as well, but first you must stop shooting at them! They are here to protect and guide you. Their vast knowledge is of great value and could propel you forward in a very positive way. Not only do they possess technical knowledge, but spiritual wisdom as well.

There is nothing to learn. There is only remembering. As you mature spiritually, your memory returns.

The time for awakening has come.

You are calling it forth.

Remember . . . You already know this. Give up your secrets and share your knowledge.

We have heard you.

We are here to help.

Be at peace Beloved Ones. The dawn is on the horizon.

WE ARE ONE
By Janie Torrence

The light was bright and golden . . . swirling all around me!
Captured in its glow yet a part of every ray of light. The surging,
pulsing light filled me, circled me . . . it was me! I am not alone. I
am never alone.

The light becomes a ball, spiraling down to earth. Golden, amber,
brilliant light; an energy all its own. I am not alone.

As the ball spirals to earth, there is a sense of joy and anticipation.
Going on to a new adventure! The next life! The next experience! I
am not alone.

I know the presence of others. The unity, joy, love and bliss. That
feeling of being part of something, yet everything. We are heading
to earth! Closer, closer. I am not alone.

The time has come to part. Our mutual existence temporarily
parted. Our new lives await. All that we have been together, takes
on a new form separately. We are born! I am not alone.

Mixed with the joy is the sorrow . . . missing a part of ourselves.
Totally disconnected, our memory is forgotten for now...still...the
distance is felt. We each have picked our adventure. To follow,
explore and evolve. To grow in ways never thought of. To someday
return to the stars. I am not alone.

Through this adventure each senses a loss, a part missing, all not
quite there. Always searching for some part, missing. Gradually,

through years of exploration, we find what we are looking for. Knowing that missing part of ourselves, with great love and joy. Coming together on earth, as we have so many times before. To love and cherish this life together; each apart of the other. I am not alone.

There are three of us, that is certain. It is comfortable, strong and safe. But . . . oh my! Are we sure? There seems to be one other face! And who may this fourth be in this life? Will we soon meet this missing link? I know we all came from the same place. Being one for so many eons. How long do we live without our "self" to be whole again once more. One day "he/she" will find us. We will know them for sure. But for now, we have each other. To grow, experience and explore. With love, bliss, joy and yes sadness. Till we are all one again, as before.

We are not alone.

A final note from the author:

Thank you for picking up this book. I hope you enjoyed the ride.

The first two hundred books have been sold and most of my mistakes have been corrected for this printing. If you found more . . . well . . . it's my first book. I hope it didn't distract you from the message.

As I stated in the introduction, this information came through me, not to me. I didn't believe a word of it at first. I thought it was just a story. But something told me to go look it up, so I researched each topic as it appeared in the story and discovered that it wasn't all fiction. I went through a great deal of strife as I processed new information. I became angry, sad and sometimes overwhelmed. This is why it took me six years to finish it.

I was going to make a bibliography at the end to share all of my resources, but I was "told" that each person was responsible for his/her truth.

I have to admit I was afraid to publish this book. I became afraid of what people would think. I worried about how to explain the manner in which I received the message. My experience didn't match what others describe as channeling. I really don't like that term anyway. I was never in a trance or spoke in a voice unlike my own. I just got up every morning between 3:09 and 3:11, and watched a movie. As it played in front of my mind's eye, I would write what I saw (or heard).

I've had many people contact me since they've read the book. A lot of people have questions. Some of them just want to discuss it, so I'm creating a Facebook page for it (search the title). Maybe we can all help each other navigate the winds of change. Maybe we can help each other get a new perspective on what is happening around our world.

I am no expert in any of these areas. But I finally know who I am. And I know who you are too. So let's go wake up the others.

My old buddy, Papa Fritz used to tell me; "You can't fix the world". He was right. I can't fix the world, but I can fix *my* part of the world.

Do the best you can, and then, do just a little more.

Today, I don't look at the world as a scary place. I see perfection all around me. The things that are passing away need to go. I welcome the changes that will lead us into the Golden Age.

Thank you again. I wish you happiness, joy and laughter all the days of your life.

Susan

p.s. I'm waking up in the 3:00 hour again. My next book will be called *The Magical Nature of Humans,* subtitled; *We are much more than we appear to be.* This one will not be a work of fiction.
In addition to the *We Heard You* facebook page, you can email me at theriverangel@hotmail.com.

Made in the USA
Columbia, SC
06 August 2020